“I did not come to bring peace, but a sword,”

Matthew Chapter 10 verse 34
New International Version

Also by Iain McLachlan

Moon Dancing Volume 1 (Silver Bow Publishing) 2019
Moon Dancing Volume II (Silver Bow Publishing) 2020

Moon Dancing

Volume III

Iain McLachlan

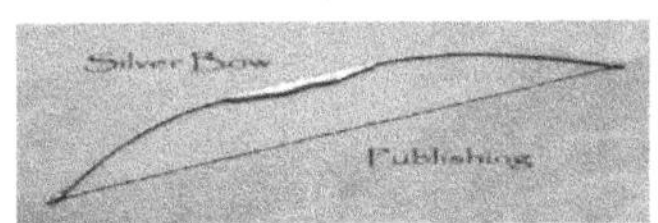

720 – Sixth Street, Box # 5
New Westminster, BC
V3C 3C5   CANADA

Title: Moon Dancing Volume III
Author: Iain McLachlan
Publisher: Silver Bow Publishing
Cover Design: Candice James

www.silverbowpublishing.com
2023 © silver bow publishing
9781774032831(print)

Library and Archives Canada Cataloguing in Publication

Title: Moon dancing / Iain McLachlan.
Names: McLachlan, Iain, 1969- author.
Description: Second edition. | Contents: Volume III [3].
Identifiers: Canadiana 20230561004 | ISBN 9781774032831 (v. 3 ; softcover)
Classification: LCC PR6113.C49 M66 2023 | DDC 823/.92—dc23

Foreword

They had their backs to a wall, those that should have helped, did not, but one did rise and stand against those that wished them harm and that filled them with inspiration. Now, they have to face a greater challenge!

Dedication

For Albert

Acknowledgements

Thank you to everyone who proofread chapters, gave advice and guidance on background occupations; you helped keep it real.

6

Chapter 1 – Murlough Nature Reserve 1st July 2010.

The car slowed as they approached the turning, his eyes glanced at the time display on the dashboard of the hire car, it was just after 4PM. He was smiling as he was happy, coming to Northern Ireland for a short holiday had been a great idea. He eyed the sign directing them to turn left from the main road. He looked up at the Mourne Mountains, the walk they had done yesterday had been brilliant, the views were breath-taking from the top of Slieve Donard. A local walker had pointed out different landmarks in the distance, including Samson and Goliath, the giant yellow cranes at the shipyard in Belfast. The road was clear, so he turned the car in through the entrance, this had been recommended to him by the couple who ran the guest house they were staying at. Warren Cummings looked around the nearly empty car park of the Nature Reserve. In the passenger seat, his wife Chloe was smiling as well, the whole trip had been a surprise for her birthday. The car slowed as they passed through the gates, the car park was empty except for one car that was parked over to the right, beside the single building. The tiny café was closing, there was someone who had a large jacket with a hood up that covered their features so he could not tell if it was a man or a woman. They were busy shutting down the café and seemed to be in a rush to get away. Warren reverse parked the car near the wooden fence and entrance to the reserve. The excited couple jumped out. They were met by a wind that swirled around them, even though it was July it was still windy, but they were beside the coast.

"I am so looking forward to this!" Chloe stated as she was zipping up her jacket, "it has been such a long time since we had a picnic!" her face had the same grin she had the very first time they had met eight years ago, and now they had been married six of those.

"Well, I do have good ideas, occasionally," Warren answered pulling his own jacket on.

"When was the last time we had a picnic?" she asked as he opened the boot of the car. He grabbed two small day sacks and threw one over his shoulder, he handed Chloe the other one.

"The time we went to Glastonbury Tor," he replied as the boot slammed shut.

"That was nearly two years ago!" She had a fire in her eyes, a fire her dark rimmed glasses could not hide and had never gone away the whole time he had known her. He stepped close to her and wrapped his arms around her shoulders, he kissed her forehead, she hugged him back, the car park could have been full of people, but the two of them would not have noticed, they had each other, they were complete.

"Well, we will have to make up for that then, won't we!" he said as he looked into the face of the woman he adored. She closed her eyes and snuggled into his embrace.

"Yes, we will," she whispered. Releasing the embrace, he stepped back, reaching out his right hand towards her. She almost skipped as she took his hand and the loving couple walked towards the wooden gate that broke the straight lines of the fence. They went through the small gate and onto the wooden walkway that led off through the dunes and towards the beach. Warren's eyes looked ahead, he picked out details of the shape of each rise, the grassland was well kept. His arm tugged, Chloe had stopped and was reading the large information panel that was on the side. "Oh, there are wild pony's here!" she exclaimed. Warren looked over his left shoulder, she was engrossed. The metal panel, mounted on a stand, was tilted at an angle to make reading it easier. It had information about the local wildlife that could be seen.

"Ponies?" he asked, her dark hair hung over the side of her head, she flicked her head up and the beaming smile filled her face.

"Yes, isn't it great? Hopefully we may see them!" she stepped away from the panel and started to lead him down the walkway. They saw the dog coming over the small rise, it was a large husky type dog and it stopped when it saw the couple. It stared at them. Following behind was a young woman with bleached white hair, a bright red jacket, and jeans, she was at the other end of the rope lead that was attached to the dog. She was not expecting to see anyone, never mind a couple holding hands. Her eyes looked at the man first, he was tall, thin, he kept his light-coloured hair very short so at a distance he looked bald, the small, rimmed glasses looked like a throwback to the 1960's, the girl with him was shorter and she had shoulder length brown hair, they both shared an excited smile. Her right hand tightened on the lead. The dog looked at her, she motioned with her head to carry on. The dog walked at the same pace as her, she stepped to the left side of the boardwalk to allow the smiling couple to pass. The guy stopped and held out his right hand to pat the dog.

"Hi, is it ok to say hello to your dog?" his accent was English, Southern English and it really stood out compared with her own,

"Aye, that's no problems," she relaxed the lead and the couple descended on a barrage of pats and cuddles. To the dogs' credit, he just stood there and took it on.

"What is his name?" the woman asked, she was English as well.

"Hod,"

"Hod?" the man asked, "Bit of a strange name for a dog?" She tightened her grip on the lead before she replied.

"Hod was one of the original Norse gods," she paused and looked at the couple who were still making a fuss of Hod. "Are you on holiday?" the man stood up and held out his hand.

"Yes and 'Hi', I am Warren," he had a firm grip, she looked into the blue/grey of his eyes,

"Hi, I'm Amy,"

"And this is my wife, Chloe," more smiles and handshakes were exchanged.

"Nice to meet you,"

"Nice to meet you as well .... Have you been over here long?" Amy asked as Warren and Chloe locked hands again. The two were obviously very close.

"Just over for a couple of days," Warren smiled, he looked at his wife, "brought this one over as we have a milestone to celebrate!" The two locked eyes smiled and shared a giggle, it was making Amy cringe as she could not imagine being so 'lovey-dovey' with anyone. Romance was for poets and films. Chloe looked at Amy.

"Do you live nearby?"

"Yes, just over there!" Amy liked the change in conversation, she pointed with her left hand towards the town of Dundrum.

"Oh wow, it must be amazing to live right next to such a beautiful place, do you come here every day?" Chloe asked. 'How many times had tourists said that to her,' it made her cringe again.

"Not every day, but I bring him here when I can," Amy was already wanting to carry on, she should have walked straight passed them.

"He is not a wolf, is he?" Warren asked. Amy had to hold in the laugh, he looked nothing like a wolf.

"No, he is a Siberian Huskey, he is a lot bigger than a wolf, plus, there are no wolves in Ireland," her eyes looked around, the couple's attention had returned to Hod.

"Wow, he is beautiful," Chloe stated as she was patting down the back of his neck.

"Yeah, he kinda is," she agreed.

"Didn't that 'Monster of Mourne' thing last year turn out to be a Husky or something?" Warren asked, he recoiled from a gentle punch into his side and a wide-eyed look from his wife. Amy smiled; her own eyes looked around then back at them.

"Aye, but it was diseased with something in its bones, but who ever owned it, should not have had it in the first place, there is a lot of work that goes into keeping a husky, they need a lot of daily exercise for starters!" The couple agreed, Amy's eyes looked up, then at them, "Say, bit late to go for a walk on the beach?" she asked.

"Oh, we are going to have a picnic and watch the sunset!" Warren beamed as Chloe snuggled into him again,

"Oh, ok," Amy took a step past them "Well, I will let you get to it then!" she gently jerked the lead and the dog moved off.

"Nice to meet you," Chloe stated,

"And you, enjoy your picnic!" Amy replied as she walked away. Warren turned and started to lead Chloe towards the rise.

"That was a lovely dog!" he was smiling as he spoke.

"You should not have asked about that Monster thing," Chloe injected.

"Why not?" he protested.

"Because it turned out to be a Husky, she has a Husky ...... just, not good," The two walked over the rise and followed the boardwalk through the green covered dunes and down onto the beach. They turned left and slowly walked hand in hand along the shore enjoying the views around them as well as each other. Warren looked at a natural gap in the dunes that were now on their left, there was a large hill, and the gap was near the foot of it.

"Let's look in there!" he pointed. The two walked over and up the small rise. The space behind the dunes opened up into a natural bowl at the foot of the hill. Just as they came over the rise there was a small leafless tree on their left, the branches reached out and formed a natural covering, the space underneath was large enough and perfect enough for them to spread out the blanket and enjoy their picnic. The two sat there, under the small tree with the Mourne mountains standing along their horizon. The tea and most of the food was quickly consumed.

"Oh, wait," Chloe stated as she turned and looked into the unzipped day sack.

"What?" Warren asked. Both her hands reappeared, and her torso turned and presented herself to him. In one hand were two clear plastic wine glasses and in the other a small bottle of white wine, and right in the middle was her beaming smile. "A proper Essex Bird!" he exclaimed; she laughed out loud.

"Well, it is nearly sunset after all!" she explained.

Warren looked at his watch, it was nearly 7PM, it had been dark for over an hour and had become cold so quickly. His boots still had his socks inside them, they were sitting as a pair beside his day sack, his jeans were still open, and he was still topless, Chloe was standing in front of him, she had just finished wrestling with her top and was now doing up her own jeans. He had fallen asleep after they made love, they had toasted the sunset with the wine and passionately kissed, that had started it. He sat upright.

"Glad there wasn't anyone around!" he stated, she looked at him quizzically.

"Why?" she asked.

"Well, with the volume of noise you were making I am surprised the wild ponies did not make an appearance!" her playful punch landed on his side.

"Well, I wasn't the only one, Mr 'oh darling ... oh darling .... Oh darling!" his shove was as playful as her punch. The two then stepped towards each other and embraced.

"It's getting cold, time we should pack this up!" they broke off and as he was pulling on his top that had been cast aside, she sat down and laced up her boots. Warren picked up his day sack and started to lift the empty packaging on his side of the blanket, Chloe's side was already packed as she stepped off the blanket and picked up the edge. She tugged at it.

"Well, come on then, slow coach!" he smiled as he jumped off it. The blanket flew into the air, and in seconds was controlled and folded in her arms. She winked at him as she bent forward and packed it away. Warren gathered up the few items left and shoved them it to his own day sack. "Hey," she whispered, "who is that?" Warren first looked at Chloe then back over behind him at the four dark figures that had appeared over the far side of the bowl. The momentum of the slope dropped them into the centre of the bowl. The four shapes slowed as they came together, then they started to spread out a little as they came towards them. Warren stood up to his full height, Chloe stepped closer to him, the atmosphere was now one of concern. The four shapes were young men, and they seemed excited.

"Well, well, well, what have we here!" it was a local accent, the four figures slowed to a walk, the one who spoke stepped towards them, the others fanned out in a closing circle.

"You take the two on the right, I will take the two on the left," Warren whispered, Chloe nodded as she took off her glasses, both their bodies tensed for the anticipated fight that may be about to happen. "What's it to you?" Warren stated, his voice seemed to echo in the night. Both of their heads shot up to the right as a fifth person appeared through the gap they had first come through when they had found the bowl behind the first row of dunes, like the others he was young, mid-twenties and he was excited.

"Just them, no one else around for miles!" all five looked at each other.

"Looks like it is time for some fun then!" it was the first one who had spoken, a ghoulish laugh followed as he stepped towards Warren.

"I don't think so!" Warren nearly shouted as his bare right foot slammed into the middle of the chest of his attacker sending him flying rearwards. The fifth one jumped at Chloe who reached out with her right hand, grabbed the centre of his chest, and pulled him towards her; he was off balance and had not expected that, he certainly wasn't expecting the force of the left hook punch that hit him like a sledgehammer into the right side of his face. He squealed as both his hands came up, his head spun, and the momentum sent him to the ground. It took a few seconds for him to recover, he raised himself up with his arms, the couple they had watched having sex on the blanket were now standing almost back-to-back, his four friends were being fought off and fought off well, the blood was flying but it was all theirs, not the couple. He paused a second, he was unsure of what to do, one of his friends was held in an arm lock, he was screaming for it to stop, the guy with the short hair was punching him as well as kicking out towards the first one who spoke, the girl had a fighting stance up and was stopping the other two getting close, her attention was on those two. Chloe spotted the movement of the leap that cannoned into Warren, they clattered over onto the ground in a mess, the two in front for her jumped at her again, the first one was met with a rapid kick to the groin, then to the left knee and as he fell, a kick to the head. The second started throwing punches that missed completely, a trip let his forward motion carry him onwards and he toppled over, she spun on her axis, all of her attackers were in front of her, her two attackers were on the ground and one of them would not be getting up imminently, she glanced at the three around Warren, her confidence turned to shock as she saw one of them open their mouth, their incisor teeth seemed longer than usual and, like an animal sank them into his neck, she screamed and jumped at them, trying to pull them off of him. She lost sight of the whole scene and as she dug at the back of the body that was at Warrens neck. One of the others jumped on her. Her body slammed into the ground and her breath left her, the body that was scrambling at her pinned her arms into her chest and she looked at the face above her. The face had a frenzied look on it, his teeth were the same and he was squealing with delight as he pounced on the left-hand side of her neck. He bit, and he bit hard. A hand grabbed her hair and yanked her head to one side, opening up her neck for her attacker. She fought and fought but a dizziness started to come over her, she could feel a weakness she had never known before covering her, her strength was leaving her at a pace she had never felt before. She was losing. She heard the high-pitched squeal but did not register it. It was not her, or her attacker. Another followed in close succession. Her attacked looked up and released the grip on her neck. Her eyes looked at the blood that was all over his face, she knew it was her own. She could feel the pulsating that was coming from her own neck. Her attacker jumped up.

"Oh shit, guys, guys!" he suddenly shouted before he jumped out of her view. There was a lot of movement and screaming around her but all she could do was stare up at the stars in the cloudless sky. There was commotion, another fight had started, she recognised the sound of breaking bones, the squeal of confirmation, followed by the sobbing. She felt herself smile. Warren was winning, he would make them pay for what they had done to her.

"I'm gonna tear you apart!" she heard one of the attackers' shouts. Commotion. Another fight, then a noise, a squeal, then silence. The pulsating in her neck was slowing, she felt exhausted. She had no strength left in her arms or her legs, she felt a single tear roll down the side of her face, she tried to whisper his name, but no sound came out. She gulped. Her eyes bounced from star to star. She wanted to see his face, feel the warmth of his arms around her, but all she could feel was the coldness of the night creeping over her. Her world was silent. Her eyes focused in on the face that appeared and slowly came into view. He was standing beside her and was looking at her. He had a dark ginger beard, and hair tied back into what could have been a small ponytail. His face was emotionless. Her mouth moved, he knelt down beside her cradling the long crossbow in his left arm, his right hand reached out and took her hand.

"Wa-wa-wa-warren," the sound was quiet, he only just heard it. He looked over at the person he was guessing was Warren. He looked back into the greying face of the dying woman.

"He is gone," the tears rolled from her eyes, he bit his lips, his face contorted in anger. "I am sorry I did not get here sooner to stop the vampires!" her eyes widened, she gasped for breath. He nodded, "Yes, they were vampires." Her grip slackened; her eyes darted around as Jason stood up. "Don't worry," he comforted. Chloe looked at the crossbow, she had never seen one like that before, it looked like there were in fact two bows and they had two black wheels at either end and the string went back and forth, she had never seen a compound bow before, but she knew what the black scope across the top was. He lifted the weapon into his shoulder and took aim at her. "don't worry," he repeated, "I will not let you become one of them," Chloe Cummings did not feel what happened next.

Chapter 2

The sound of the phone buzzing on the bedside table woke Mike Dear. The bedroom was still in darkness, the phone was on silent, but the vibrating still made noise. His wife angrily turned over, taking a large portion of the duvet with her. Mike reached out and lifted the phone. The light of the display lit up his face, it was just after six thirty, his alarm would be going off in another fifteen minutes. He opened the text message from Darren. 'AT LEAST TWO DEAD AT MURLOUGH NATURE RESERVE – NOT ALL THE BAD PEOPLE HAVE GONE AWAY' Mike was confused for a second, he initially did not know what he was making reference to. An angry elbow to his side was the message he needed to propel himself up at out of bed, he slid his dressing gown on and headed for the bathroom. He would still be in the shower when the alarm did go off, this was not the start to the day his wife had wanted. It would be another hour and a half before Mike was approaching the car park of the reserve. The entrance was partially blocked by a marked police car, two uniformed officers stood blocking the rest. Mike slowed before turning the front of the car towards the entrance. One of the officers was walking towards the drivers' window with their right hand out, their palm was down, and it was moving in a patting motion, wanting him to stop. Mike kept his foot on the brake and held up his police ID up at the open window as the officer approached.

"Good morning," Mike opened the conversation. The officer studied the ID, then looked at him, the sullen face gave nothing away.

"Good morning," the constable replied.

"Has Detective Superintendent Forester arrived yet?" Mike glanced at the face, there was a pause.

"Err, I am sorry Sargeant, I don't know" the officer stood up and pointed at the row of parked transit vans, "But you could try over there. Inspector Wells was there a minute ago." The officer stepped back as the other moved out of the way.

"Ok, thanks," Mike was looking ahead as he released the brake, the second officer waved, Mike replied by raising the fingers of his right hand as he gripped the steering wheel. The car moved forward slowly as he looked around. There was the usual collection of blue and white transit vans, marked police cars and unmarked cars in the car park. Several uniformed officers were walking around, he spotted a space off to his left where three unoccupied cars were all reverse parked. Mike reverse parked at the end of the line and got out of his car. He was not dressed like he used to when he was in M.I.T. with Sean, in fact he had been told not to, *'Oh My God, would you stop dressing up like a police officer!'* Darren kept telling him. He had trainers on his feet, clean jeans, and a dark blue hooded sweat top. He had been told only to wear tops that did not have any emblem on them when he had done the surveillance part of his training at the fort. The next problem was finding tops that did not have a logo on them. Mike pushed the phone into his pocket, there was no new message after the 'meet you there' text Darren had sent him when he was still eating his breakfast. He headed towards the nearest van as a figure in a white disposable suit, with a face mask walked towards the open rear doors, Mike recognised the evidence bags they were carrying. Mike stopped as he got there, the figure had not seen him approach, they were busy organising the bags in the rear of the van. Mike knocked the rear door.

"AAAHHH!" the figure jumped in surprise; several heads all turned to the squeal. The white figure dropped down onto the rear of the van with one hand in the centre of their chest. *"DON'T DO THAT!"* she shouted.

"Sorry, I ...." Mike started, the woman jumped up and started berating him.

"Just what do you think you are doing sneaking up on people like that!" She looked him up and down, he was not a senior officer. "Who the hell do you think you are anyway?" she demanded. Mike held up his ID, which she studied.

"Detective Sergeant, Special Branch ...." Mike paused, he did not say his name, it was on the ID, he looked sternly at the officer, "Where is your Inspector?" he demanded. The young woman paused then relaxed.

"Sorry Sergeant," she looked around and now avoided eye contact. She raised her right hand and pointed over towards the entrance to the reserve, "She is over there," Mike turned around and looked in the direction she was pointing, there were four people all in white suits and masks all talking to a uniformed Inspector.

"Ok, thank you," Mike walked away and did not acknowledge her further. He walked along the tarmac of the car park until he got to the wooden fence line. The uniformed inspector noticed him approach, all four white figures turned to face Mike when the inspector spoke.

"Watch out, Special Branch are here!" the uniformed Inspector smiled at his own joke. Mike stopped at the opposite side of the fence to them.

"Who is in charge here?" Mike asked.

"I am," replied one of the white suits, "and who are you?" she asked as she pulled back the hood and pulled down the face mask to reveal her dark blonde hair that was tied back into a ponytail, the young face sternly looked at him. Mike held up his ID for her to look at.

"Detective Sergeant Dear, Special Branch," Mike lowered his arm, he looked up the boardwalk at the two white suited figures who appeared carrying evidence bags. "So," Mike continued, "what is happening here then?"

"What the hell has it got to do with you?" the inspector snapped. Mike's head spun round to look at her, her face was twisted in anger. "You don't work for M.I.T. anymore and you certainly don't work for me!" the uniformed Inspector looked embarrassed as one of the white figures turned and walked away. "So, to answer your question, 'what is happening here?' is nothing to do with you, if you want to find out you can wait, like everyone else for the press briefing later!" She stared at Mike; Mike stared back. There was a silence for a few moments before Mike spoke.

"Ma'am .... My boss, Superintendent Forester tasked me with coming down here to find out what happened here,"

"What is happening here, is nothing to do with Superintendent Forester, this is an active criminal investigation therefore nothing to do with Special Branch!" she snapped again. The uniformed Inspector looked at him.

"You work for Grey Fox?" he had lowered his voice, Mike looked at him and nodded.

"Yes, I do," Mike replied.

"So, if the Superintendent wants to know anything he will have to ask as I don't answer to Sergeants!" the female inspector turned to walk away, the other white suits turned with her.

"INSPECTOR WELLS!" The stern shout from behind Mike made everyone look around, it was Darren and he looked furious. He was stomping towards where Mike was standing. "INSPECTOR!" he repeated. The Inspector stopped and turned towards him, the uniformed inspector, looked towards the ground.

"Superintendent Forester," she had lowered her voice, but her look was very condescending. Darren stopped beside Mike. He was glaring at her.

"I tasked my Detective Sergeant to act on my behalf," he stated. The Inspector turned towards him and as she stood a short step towards him, she replied.

"Superintendent, this is an active '*criminal*' investigation, and it has happened in my operational area, which means, I am in charge, so that means I decide who is allowed access to all evidence we gather, and as I was explaining to your very rude officer here" She looked down as she turned her hand uppermost and pointed with her forefinger, Mike's eyebrows raised at the insult, "that if you want anything it will be released at the press conference later, ok!"

"What!" Darren shouted. The inspector titled her head before she spoke again.

"Yes, this is a *'criminal'* investigation and not a special branch matter, so your 'tea-boy' here …. would be out of his depth in a real investigation!"

"HOW DARE YOU!" Darren had stepped forward and pointed directly at her, her eyes widened in surprise, "WE ARE CURRENTLY TRYING TO CURTAIL THE ACTIVITIES OF VERY VIOLENT EASTERN EUROPEAN ORGANISED CRIME GANGS FROM COMPLETELY TAKING OVER HERE!!!" Darren lowered his arm, but stared at the shocked inspector, he carried on, "now tell me, has 'at least one' of the victims here got very aggressive trauma wounds to their neck?" Darren did not give the inspector time to reply, "like what happened up at Portstewart and around Coleraine nearly two years ago!" he paused, staring at her, "Well? Do they?"

"Two," all heads turned to the other officer that was in a white disposable suit, their face was still covered by the mask, only their eyes were visible.

"What?" Darren demanded.

"Two," they repeated, "there are two with severe neck injuries," they had only just been louder than a whisper, but everyone had heard what they had said. Darren placed both his hands on the wooden fence and leaned forward.

"Inspector, I am not asking for your co-operation, *I am demanding it!*" he hissed. The Inspector was flushed, she was not used to someone speaking to her like that.

"Well, that is for me to …." She started.

"NOTHING!" Darren cut her off, "My operational area is the whole country, and if I do not start seeing some co-operation, I fully intend of going straight to the Chief Constable," Darren straightened up, "and believe me when I say, I will not stop until you are replaced, do you understand?" Darren was staring directly at her, her cheeks flushed with anger at the threat. The group fell silent as everyone waited for her response. She was furious, that was clear.

"Fine," she turned to walk away, "your boy better keep up and not get in the way!"

"INSPECTOR!" Darren raised his voice again, she stopped and glared at him.

"Super?" she had lowered her voice.

"How many commendations have you got for securing terrorist convictions in the court room?" he asked, Mike tried not to smile.

"What?" she spat.

"How many commendations have you got for securing terrorist convictions in the court room?" Darren repeated the question, her face flushed again. "Well, Detective Sergeant Dear has got two," all eyes turned on Mike, Darren carried on, "that is two full commendations and he will not be happy with me telling you all that he turned down a Police Commendation Medal for his actions several years ago," Mike's eyes shot over at Darren, Mike had a quizzical look on his face, 'how the hell did he know that?' he thought, Darren carried on, "and you may remember the incident at Mussenden Temple two years ago where we interrupted a major feud between two very violent gangs!" Darren smirked, Mike looked at him, that was not what had happened, but Mike could not say what had really happened, Darren poked the thumb of his right hand towards Mike, "that was this guy, almost on his own, he also had to carry on with an investigation that included the murder of another Sergeant from the same team …." Mike looked back at the silent Inspector who was now glaring at him. "So," Darren carried on, "I think it may be a case of him helping with his extensive investigative experience compared with your …… wait, how long have you overseen this M.I.T." she muttered something that Mike did not hear. "I am sorry Inspector, I did not hear you, how long?"

"Four months,"

"And how many of your team have commendations ... for anything?" Darren was staring at her again, the uniformed inspector, looked embarrassed, she still looked enraged, the answer was obvious. She glared at Mike.

"Well, suit up, one of the others will bring you up to speed!" she turned and stomped off, she was followed by the other white suits.

"Well, I have things to do as well," the uniformed inspector stated.

"Have you briefed your officers on dealing with the press?" Darren asked, the inspector stopped and looked initially confused.

"Well, yes, they ...."

"When I was coming in the two at the entrance very nearly let a local journalist in, think they need to be reminded of their duties!" Darren was looking past him. He nodded.

"Yes, of course, I will deal with that, right away," The inspector was looking for a way of getting away from this situation as quickly as possible. He turned and headed over towards the small gate. Darren looked at Mike, he was almost giggling.

"She is not going to help me in any way at all!" Mike stated, Darren nudged him with his shoulder.

"Don't worry, it's just power politics, she wants to stop Chief Anderson stepping in and directly taking over," Darren looked at Mike as he continued, "if he takes over, he gets all the credit." Mike went to say something, but Darren cut him off, "What I want you to do is, have a good look as see if it was 'our friends'," Darren breathed out loudly, "or even if it was our friends of our friends!" the two shared a glance, he did not want to openly use the word 'werewolf' or 'vampire' but that is what he was talking about.

"Yeah, sure, now I know what to look for!" Mike relaxed.

"Yeah," Darren straightened up. Mike glanced back towards the parked vans.

"Well, I better suit up and get to it," Mike folded his arms, a look of deep thought came over his face. Darren stared at him.

"Mike," he said quietly, Mike did not respond. "Mike," Darren repeated, this time slightly louder.

"Mmmm?" Mike's head turned and looked at him.

"Sean is gone, and nothing you can do can bring him back," Darren reached up and placed his hand on Mike's left shoulder. Mike looked down then back up at him.

"Yeah, I know," Darren withdrew his hand, Mike seemed uncomfortable, "You know," Mike started, he shifted where he was standing, "this will be the first active crime scene I have been on where I wasn't working with him!"

"Go to it, big guy," Darren said. Mike nodded, looked around then turned to walk away, "and don't worry about her, she knows exactly who you are, she is intimidated by you," Mike looked up at him.

"That does not change things, I am not expecting her to be 'overly helpful with this!"

"Did you know she put a request in to have you transferred to her team?"

"What?" Mike was surprised. "No, no I didn't." Mike breathed out and headed back toward the first of the open vans, there were three people dressed in the white disposable suits.

"Hi, I am Mike Dear, the Inspector wants me to suit up then head over to the incident site." The masked people all turned and looked at him, no one spoke as one of them turned and reached into the van, Mike was handed a packet with a suit, gloves, and mask in them. As Mike started to get changed the three people all looked at each other, then one finally spoke.

"Excuse me Detective, but is true that you still work for 'The werewolf squad'?"

ꝏꝏꝏ

"I haven't seen Tony in a while, have you heard from him?" she asked. Paul had his phone in his hand, he nodded.

"Yeah, yesterday in fact." Paul looked away and carried on walking, talking as he did so. "Since the birth of his child he hardly ever leaves his house now,"

"Yeah, I know what that is like!" they shared a glance and a smile, her own child was taking up a lot of her time now.

"Well, Becky and Fiona still go there once a week and the security team are linked in with his cameras, he seems to be ok," Paul explained. Tyler smiled at the thought.

"I will have to pop out someday," she muttered out loud. They walked on. The single road dipped and rose with the land, red and white poles stood either side. The foot path went over a small culvert, the large rocks formed a tunnel to allow the flow of water to come from the field down into the small pool that separated the road from the path.

The café up ahead was inside the single-story stone building, the slabs of the path led from the road down to the corner of the building, there were no windows on this side of the building. There was a wooden structure at the end that had a corrugated metal roof, they walked along the side of the building to the single door that broke up the side of what had once been a farmhouse. The metal outer door was open, but the inner door was shut, there was a handwritten note on the glass with 'back in 15 minutes' written on it.

"So much for getting a coffee then!" Paul stated. He pressed his face up to the glass to look inside. The room was small, there was a window on the far side of the room with two small round tables each with three metal framed chairs around each one. There was a poster about the reserve on a large hearth that had once held open fires.

"We can get one on the way back," Tyler stated, Paul looked at her and nodded. As she turned and headed back towards the road, she looked back down the way they had come. The single figure of the security detail was about one hundred metres away, if anyone was looking, they were just another visitor to the site. Tyler made the point of not making a fuss and walked over the grass and back on to the tarmac. She walked on as Paul spoke; she did not look at him as he was not speaking to her.

"Roger, just passing location one, heading back onto red one," Paul was telling the rest of the security team and the communications building back at the farm what they were doing. Paul cast a glance past her and over at the hill off to their left. He nodded. Tyler felt her eyes move that direction as well, the overwatch was in place, but she did not know exactly where they were. Her eyes moved over the landscape, but she could not see them, which confirmed how good they were.

"Did he say exactly where to meet him?" she asked.

"No, Paul replied. Tyler was walking on the right-hand side of the road, to her right was a small wooden bridge that went over the waterway. The bridge was not more than four feet wide, it looked quite new and led over the marsh land to a more open piece of grassland. There were no sides to the bridge, Tyler's eyes followed the natural lay of the land. In the middle of the grassed area was a small stone wall.

"Let's wait here," she said, she glanced over at Paul who nodded. Paul spoke, but not to her, he told the overwatch and the security that they were stopping here. Tyler walked over the bridge and headed for the stone wall. It was only part of something that had once been a wall, it was nearly two feet thick, three feet high and she would guess about ten feet in length. Whatever it was a part of, the rest was long gone. Tyler walked over, turned and sat down on the wall. Paul followed but stopped in front of her. He was looking around.

"As good a place as any," he muttered. Tyler looked at him, then back up the way they had come, the security had stopped at the gate, they had line of sight to them and were in touch with the rest of the team. Paul was looking around where they were, "we will see him coming no problems," Paul touched his ear, then looked at Tyler, "roger, we will stay here until the meet up,"

Tyler pulled back her sleeve to look at her watch. "Hope he hurries up, don't want to be here too long,"

Paul looked over at the gate and nodded, the security team member turned and looked back down the road, before looking back and nodding.

"Roger," Paul looked back at her.

"What?" she asked.

"One of the other cars in the car park has just left, young couple, heading away towards Belfast," Tyler looked away, her eyes followed the shape of the horizon, Paul took out his phone again, he looked at the screen. "Have you got signal on your phone?" he asked without looking up.

"No idea, it's in the car," Paul let out a short laugh then replaced the phone back into his pocket.

"Do we know what he looks like?" Tyler asked.

Paul looked over at the security at the gate. "No, he should I.D. himself to us, but we will have notice before he gets here," Paul replied.

"Hope that is not too long," she repeated.

"Sorry, didn't mean to keep you," The male voice from behind made her jump up and spin around, Paul jumped so he was in front of her. Standing still, less than ten feet away from the rear of the small wall was a young man. He was less than six feet, his hair was pulled back in a tight ponytail, his full beard was a light ginger. He was wearing a dark green outdoor jacket that was open, underneath was a tee shirt with an emblem on it that Tyler could not make out. Wrapped loosely around his neck was a large grey scarf, his hands were in the pockets of his jacket, his jeans were clean, but his brown boots were covered in mud. Paul was not totally blocking her as she could still see him, Paul's left hand was extended, shielding her, by the way he was standing she knew his right hand was on his pistol that was on his belt.

"HANDS OUT OF YOUR POCKETS .... NOW!" Paul shouted at him.

"I mean you no harm," the figure stated, he slowly took his hands out and held them up, showing Paul the palms, "I am not armed," Paul relaxed slightly, Tyler moved around Paul so she could fully see the figure. The accent was local, but there was a hint of something else. Paul looked over to his right, his right hand shot out and he held his hand up to stop the security member that was running down the road. Paul looked back at the figure. Tyler stared at him, she breathed in through her nose, he had practically no scent.

"Sapien," she whispered, Paul nodded once, Tyler smelt again, "you use shower gel and body spray, and you smoke," she lifted her head sniffed again, making it obvious what she was doing. Paul stared at him; his face was emotionless.

"I mean you no harm," he repeated.

"You will keep your distance, if you make any sudden moves, I will react with force," Paul stated aggressively.

"Again, I mean you no harm," he looked at Paul then at Tyler, "but if I did, I would have already dealt with your two with the hunting rifles on the hill and your people down at the car park would not hear me coming!" The figure slowly lowered his hands.

"Who are you?" Paul demanded. The figure replaced his hands back in his pockets.

"My name is Jason, and I believe we share a common enemy,"

Tyler stared at the single figure in front of them. She could pass him in the street and not notice. "I can see plainly, what you are, but may I ask, who you are?" the figure enquired. Paul still stared at him, his eyebrows were lowered, and his right hand was back on his weapon. Tyler placed her right hand on his left shoulder, they exchanged a glance, she stepped over to the left, if Jason did anything Paul still had a clear line of fire. If he got past Paul, she would take him down. She stared at his expressionless face.

"My name is Tyler,"

"My name is not important," Paul injected without taking his eyes from Jason.

"My name is Jason," he repeated, "and I will say again, I mean your kind no harm!" this time, Jason looked down before looking up again. Tyler spotted it.

"Our kind?" Paul stated, Jason looked at him.

"Yes, you both are werewolves," he let out a short chuckle, it was the first time his expression changed. "I did not believe it at first, but then, I found out the hard way that the vampires are real, so,"

"How?" Paul asked sternly.

"What?"

"How did you find out they are real?" Tyler watched as Jason twitched slightly, whatever was coming was uncomfortable for him. He looked down again before he spoke.

"Well, you may as well know," he paused, he lifted his head, but he was not directly looking at them, "we were on a family holiday," Tyler took a step forward, she looked at his reddening eyes, "I had booked a country cottage, Antrim coast, just for us, no one around,"

"Who is 'US'?" she asked. Jason looked up, then looked away.

"My wife, Rachel, and both my boys," Jason looked directly at her, "we were sleeping," Tyler watched as Jason's face twisted, "they came ...." Jason stopped talking, the only sound for a few seconds was the sound of the passing wind until he continued, "one had my arms behind my back while the other was biting at my neck," he looked up, anger flared in his eyes, "they had dragged Rachel into the living room, I could hear her, screaming, then I heard my boys," he looked away again, there was another pause before he looked up again. "I woke up in a hospital two days later," the anger was back in his eyes, "do you know what it is like to be told everything you loved is gone?"

"Yes," Tyler spoke., She looked directly at Jason, "Yes, I do, five of them came to my house while I was out, they took my husband and ...." her voice faded.

"How did you survive?" Paul asked, looking at Jason, Jason looked straight at Tyler.

"I don't know, the doctors told me I should be dead, they severed my artery in my neck, a 'non-survivable wound' they said," he looked down, "they were wrong."

"What about your family?" Tyler asked, Jason shrugged.

"They said that they raped Rachel before they slashed her neck open," he looked up again, "that's what they kept saying, I had not been bitten, but that I was attacked with a knife, I know what they did, and it was no knife," Paul and Tyler shared a glance.

"That sounds familiar," Paul stated as he relaxed slightly.

"What about your sons?" Tyler asked. Jason stared at her; he did not have to answer. Tyler nodded before she spoke. "When I got back to my house, they had set fire to it and my husband was staked out in the garden," Jason blinked and looked away. "They had cut his heart out," Tyler stated, Jason turned and took a step to the side.

"Yeah, some of them like doing that!" he spoke quieter than before, but both of them heard him.

"When was that?" Paul asked, Jason turned his head.

"What?" he asked.

"Your family? When was that?" Paul repeated the question, he had not taken his eyes off Jason the whole time. Jason nodded his head and shuffled where he was standing, he turned so his left side faced them.

"Five years ago,"

"What about the police? What happened with them?" Paul's posture had changed, he relaxed more.

"The police? Ha!" Jason started a slow walk, he looked away, "they were not much help." Jason stopped, pushing his hands deeper into his pockets as he looked over the horizon.

"So, what have you been doing since?" Tyler asked. Jason did not move, he kept looking into the distance.

"Once I knew exactly what they were, and what they did, I swore that I would spend the rest of my time hunting them down," Jason's face tightened, "every single one of them."

"Me to," Tyler spoke quietly. Jason turned his head and looked at her, he lowered his view and nodded his head gently, before looking away again.

"So how did you find out about us?" Paul asked, Jason smirked.

"Nearly two years ago." Jason turned and looked towards the sun; it was starting to set in the distance behind the Mourne mountains. "You know, I have only been here once before, it was a long time ago,"

"Yeah, I am going to need some more detail than that!" Paul stated. Jason glanced over at him and smiled; he looked back at the sunset as he spoke.

"I was up in Coleraine, I was following a vampire from England," he looked back at them, "What is it you call them? Knock's?"

"Noctrailis," Tyler corrected.

"Why that?" he asked.

"That is what they are, Noctrailis Vampiri,"

"And what language is that from? It isn't Latin."

"No," Tyler explained, "it is a dialect of an ancient Russian,"

"Oh," Jason looked away, Tyler walked towards him, so Paul walked off to the side so he could still fully see Jason.

"So," Paul injected, "this vampire from England?" Jason smiled again.

"Yeah, she was some sort of princess or something but two of yours found her and handed her over to one of their elders in a car park in Portrush!" Tyler and Paul shared a glance.

"May I ask how you know that?" Paul asked, he was concerned now.

"Simple really," he started, "I had made a deal with these two Bulgarians to grab her," Jason looked over and shrugged, "they really messed up, I was watching," he looked away again, "I had not been that close to one of your kind before, heard rumours, but didn't believe it of course," Paul watched as Jason breathed in before he continued, "that was the last time I used someone else, only done it myself since then," Jason seemed to bask in the sunlight, he closed his eyes briefly. "Pity she got away, never found out her name."

"Dani," Tyler answered. Jason opened his eyes and looked at her.

"Pardon?"

"Her name was Dani," Paul stated, Jason looked at him.

"Was? As in past tense?" Jason asked.

"Yes, we took her down as well as over thirty of them a year and a half ago!" Tyler replied. Jason nodded and looked away again, "yes, I know, I saw what you did with them at White Park Bay," he glanced over, "very impressive I must say,"

"Thanks," Paul muttered.

"So, you have a history with them then?" Jason asked.

"You could say that?" Paul replied. Jason smiled and turned back towards him.

"Tell me more." Tyler glanced up at Paul, he would never give any details to someone who was not pack, so she decided to.

"Our two kinds fought a war that lasted nearly three hundred years," she explained, Jason's eyes widened, he clearly did not know that.

"Really?"

"Yes, really, our high council has a truce in place with their top level, it has held worldwide for over one hundred years," Tyler replied, she let a small smile spread over her face. Jason reacted, his face was shocked, and his body twitched, both of them noticed it, Paul would remark later that he would never have made a poker player.

"Worldwide? You mean there are more of you?"

"Yes," Tyler was being more friendly with him, Paul looked sternly at her, but she was alpha, and he would never disagree with her, especially in front of a sapien, Tyler continued. "There are over twenty main packs, worldwide,"

"What about them? What about the vamps? How many are there?" Jason asked.

"There are also covens all over the world," Paul answered.

"What about here? What about Ireland?" Jason asked, Tyler noticed that he just used 'Ireland', and not Northern Ireland or 'the Republic of Ireland.

"Well, we have certainly thinned them out, as far as we know there is less than ten left over the whole island!" she smiled as she spoke. "When was the last time you took one down?" she asked.

"Five,"

"What?"

"I took down five yesterday!" he stated, both Tyler and Paul reacted.

"What the hell!" Paul shouted as he moved towards him, Jason stepped back, Tyler's right hand shot out and stopped Paul, "you need to get our permission first before you try anything like that!" Paul was annoyed, Jason twisted his face.

"I don't have to do anything of the sort, I don't need your permission at all!" Jason stated, he looked disgusted. "You don't control me!" he spat back at Paul. Tyler felt the anger in Paul rise, she knew Paul wanted to grab him and throw him to the ground, he wanted to dominate him and make him do what he wanted, the alpha wolf in Paul wanted to come forward. Tyler stopped him by grabbing the centre of his top, this made Paul look at her, she stared at Paul. She would deal with this, she felt Paul's wolf retreat. Paul took a single step backwards as she released her grip. Tyler stepped in front of Paul and looked at Jason.

"Yes, yes, you are right, you don't have to do anything, but I do want to know where this happened?" Tyler was being direct. Jason's eyes bounced between her and Paul, he certainly was not afraid of either of them, that much was clear.

"Why?" it was more of a statement than a question. Tyler relaxed her stance before she replied.

"Well, we have a very delicate balance to observe," she explained.

"I don't," he twisted his face again, "and frankly I don't care about any 'truce' you have with them, I certainly don't!"

"What is your intention?" asked Paul with a raised voice. Jason looked past her and looked directly at him.

"Every one of them I find, I kill." The blank look had returned to his face.

"Where and why did you kill five of them?" Tyler asked. There was a pause, he looked at her, then relaxed slightly.

"They went for a couple of tourists down at Murlough Nature reserve, you know, down near the mournes?" he said. Tyler nodded, he continued. "I had been tracking them for a while, I was not sure where they were sleeping, there were no people guarding them during the day, so it was harder to spot." Both Tyler and Paul knew what he meant, Tyler did not interrupt and let him carry on. "The tourists were as it turns out, over from England and were on a holiday, they went for a picnic and just as they finished shagging, the five vamps went for them." Jason tilted his head and his face widened as he recounted what happened, "they were initially fighting them off, but by the time I got there and took the vamps down, the guy was already dead, the girl was still alive but they both had been bitten." The sternness returned to his eyes, "I could not let her suffer that, so I finished her with a bolt through the heart," Tyler listened and pictured what he was describing, he carried on, "I stacked the five of them and burnt them, I knew that daylight would finish off what was left," he shrugged, "just made sure the two tourists didn't end up like them, have you ever seen what sunlight does to the vamps?"

"Nocs," Tyler answered, "and yes, I have, several times." Jason let a small smile spread over his face.

"Well then," he smirked, "you know then!"

"What makes you think you can kill sapiens without permission!" Paul demanded; Tyler glanced at Paul before looking back at Jason.

"Kill what?"

"Sapiens," Tyler explained, "it is our word for normal humans,"

"Oh," Jason shrugged, "well, after they were bitten, they were not human anymore."

"You still can't go around killing what you want, there are rules!" Paul was getting angry again.

"Maybe for you!" Jason reacted, "I fully intend to kill every single vamp ... or ... what is it you call them again?"

"Nocs" Tyler replied.

"Yes, well I will kill every knock I can find on this island of ours," there was a silence again, Paul was angry, Jason was annoyed, but Tyler wanted to know more.

"You said you used a bolt to kill them?" she asked.

"Yes, from my crossbow, turns out, you don't need 'holy water' or anything like that crap you see in films!" he snorted.

"Yeah, Hollywood has a lot of misinformation to answer for." Tyler tried to lighten the conversation.

"Why do they do that?" Jason asked.

"Do what?" asked Paul.

"Say so much stuff that isn't true, why don't they give people information that they can use against them!"

"Because they control it," Paul stated. Jason looked at him, then at Tyler who nodded.

"Yes, it's true, in the USA they dominate most of the bigger cities, where we are slowly building a strong holding in the mid-west." Tyler explained.

"So, they are everywhere," Jason looked at the ground, there was sadness in his face.

"Look we can help each other; they are our enemies as well!" Tyler took a single step towards him as she spoke. Jason stepped back, looked her up and down and contorted his face.

"Look, I'm not interested in 'your little lot' and as far as I am concerned, you lot can do whatever you want, as long as you don't get in my way!" Jason had a disgusted look on his face, "and I fully intend to take down every single one of them I find!"

"You reached out to us," Tyler replied, she reached out with her right hand for a handshake, Jason kept his hands in his pockets, "we can help each other!" she looked straight at him. Jason stepped back and half turned away from them, Tyler dropped her hand.

"Yeah, I got in touch, took me long enough to find you,"

"Why?" Tyler asked.

"Why what?" Jason asked.

"Why get in touch?"

"I wanted to find out if you were on their side or not, now I know." Jason turned and started to walk away from them.

"What are you going to do?" Tyler asked.

Jason stopped and looked back over his right shoulder. "What do you know of him?"

"Who?" Tyler replied.

"The American," Jason spoke quietly. Tyler and Paul shared another glance.

"Don't know much about him, but we cut his plans here to shreds and year and a half ago," Tyler answered. "What do you know about him?" she asked, Jason looked away.

"I know he is from Arkansas, hates your kind, in fact," Jason looked back at her, "did you know he swore to kill all the werewolves here in Ireland?"

"Yes, we did," she replied.

"And he tried," Paul injected.

"Did he?" Jason remarked.

"We took them all down," Paul was defiant, Jason looked away again.

"Not all of them, don't suppose you know where he is presently?"

"If we did, we would take him down for what he tried doing to us!" Tyler said. Jason shrugged and looked back at the mountains in the distance. "Look, Jason, we can deal with them, we know how to, probably best if you leave it all to us."

Jason spun around at what she had said. "They took everything that was precious from me, they slaughtered my children, raped then killed my wife and nearly killed me," Tyler looked into his grey eyes, she could see the pure hatred there, he carried on. "I have no quarrel with your kind, as long as you don't give me one!"

"They took my family as well," Tyler explained. Everyone stood still, the wind picked up again. Jason nodded then looked past them.

"I think your over watch people are having problems!" Both Tyler and Paul spun around and looked in the direction of the over watch.

"November, Kilo, over," Paul nearly shouted into the communicator, Tyler looked back at the empty space where Jason had been standing, "Roger, any problems at your location over?" Paul asked. He turned back, looked at Tyler and shook his head, they both walked forward to where he had been standing. Paul knelt down and reached out with his hand, placing it on the ground. "There is no scent!" he stated.

"I know," Tyler replied as Paul stood up, he was studying the ground.

"He isn't a Noc," Paul's eyes were looking for and sign on the ground, "I could track him," he suggested.

"He isn't fully sapien anymore either!" stated Tyler. She looked around, then at Paul. "No, don't track him," she turned away and started to walk towards the wooden bridge. "But we will have to keep an eye on him," she looked back at Paul. "What happens to sapiens who survive a Noc bite but don't turn?" She had a quizzical look on her face. Paul shrugged.

"I don't know, I have never heard of that before."

She nodded and walked over the small bridge and back onto the road.

"We could get the police to find out more about his family!" Paul stated as he caught up with her. The two were walking quickly along the road back towards the gate.

"Good idea, I will ask the council about him, see what we can find out!" Paul looked at her, he knew Carl would not do that, also she did not mention Connor or the Southern Pack.

"Sure, we can start that when we get back to the farm." Paul stated as he nodded towards the security team member that was by the gate, she replied with a nod. They turned and headed away from them along the road.

"I think we should check out that little café and see what their coffee is like!" it was more of a statement that a question from Tyler.

"Yeah, sure," replied Paul.

"In fact, call in the security team, it is my treat."

Chapter 4

Becky was driving slower than usual. The old car was not what they would have chosen, but it is what they were given. She looked over at the intense look on Fiona's face. Becky glanced down at the G36 rifle that was lying across Fiona's legs, then at the large briefcase that was under her own. Becky looked around before they turned into the yard at the rear of the old farmhouse. She looked in the rear-view mirror and looked at her face. Her hair was tied back and although it was sunny outside, she still had her outdoor jacket on.

"Ready?" Becky whispered.

"Hell yeah," Fiona whispered back, Fiona moved and reached inside her jacket.

"Can you see them yet?" Becky asked as the car drove across the yard towards the open gate. The wooden fence ran along the edge of the field, the hedge stood on top of the purposely built earth mound that was the opposite side of the fence and ran all the way along the edge of the field.

"No, I will let you know when I do," Fiona pulled her Sig pistol out and gripped it in her right hand, she was concentrating on looking around as much as she could. The field was exactly one hundred metres square, and the earth mound ran all the way around, the burnt-out wreck of a car was at an angle, Becky drove the car around it and through the middle of the wooden frame's sack cloth faster than she had driven into the field, both of them were anxious. There was a series of loud bangs outside the car.

"TARGETS!" screamed Becky as she slammed the breaks on, Fiona raised the pistol and keeping it in a double handed grip started firing through the windscreen, she was firing two rounds in quick succession at the two targets. Becky's left hand slapped the seatbelt release as her right hand pushed the driver's door open. Becky jumped out at speed, as she got down on one knee behind the open door, she gripped the handle of the briefcase, as she pulled it out of the car, the sides flew off to reveal the G36 rifle. Her right hand unfolded the butt and as she stood up, she brought the butt of the weapon firmly into her right shoulder, her left hand gripped the front stock, and her right was on the pistol grip. She was already firing two bullets at a time into each target through the window of the driver's door.

"Moving!" screamed Fiona who had flung her door open, the pistol was back in her belt, and she had her rifle in her hands. Fiona sprinted over to the first cover she could find. Fiona went down onto her right knee, as she was raising her rifle, she looked at what Becky was firing at. She raised the rifle and started firing as well, two bullets at a time, in very quick succession. As soon as she did so Becky turned the rifle vertically in front of her as she ran.

"Moving!" She screamed as Fiona kept firing. Becky stopped a few metres and positioned herself so she could engage the targets. She concentrated then raised the rifle. As Becky started firing Fiona turned and ran a few metres keeping her rifle vertically as she ran.

"Moving!" she heard Becky shout. Fiona kept the rate of fire up, she saw Becky move to her right, as soon as Becky started firing again, she turned and ran back again, this time she ran around the burnt-out car and took up a position.

"Magazine!" Becky shouted, so Fiona opened fire, again Becky was running backwards. Fiona kept firing until she heard Becky shouting again. "On me, on me," Fiona paused and looked over at Becky. She was firing around the side of one of the wooden frames, she had found a way out, that is why she was shouting for her to go there. Fiona's thumb moved up and clicked on the safety catch before she jumped up and sprinted as fast as she could over to where Becky was. Fiona ran behind her and came to the far edge of the frame. She knelt down and looked at what they were firing at. Fiona again started firing at the targets.

"STOP!" the male voice behind then shouted. Both the safety catches of the weapons clicked on, then slowly they both stood up. They kept the rifles pointing down past the car in the direction they had been shooting. Dermott walked up and as he was removing the safety headphone from his ears, Steve Minister and Chris Abbey followed him. "Right," Dermott started, "keeping the weapons in a safe direction and ... 'unload'," he commanded. The two sisters stood beside each other, the rifles pointed down the range as they both removed the magazines and cleared their weapons, they then had to do the same with the pistols. Once that was done the two smiling sisters looked at each other as they removed the small ear plugs, they were wearing, then back at Dermott for a debriefing on the training they had just done. The pistols were back on their belts and the rifles cradled in their arms. Dermott walked past them and stood looking down the range, Becky and Fiona walked around so they were at either side of him. "Right then, good entrance, good commands and good movement," Dermott talked through each part of what they did, "So, only minor points, but on the whole, very good," Dermott turned to the two soldiers and extended his right hand. "Any points?" he asked. Steve and Chris looked at each other, Chris stepped forward, then looked at the two women.

"Well, first of all, that was very good, I may say that we train a lot of different people and ...." He glanced over at Steve, who nodded once, Chris carried on, "that, was first class, I can tell you there are a lot of serving SF that would not have done as well!" Becky and Fiona looked at each other and grinned. Steve stepped forward.

"Yes, I must agree, that was very impressive!" Steve had a small smile on his face.

"Right then," Dermott stated, "Any points from you?" he asked the two women.

"That was brilliant fun!" Fiona beamed,

"Yeah, loved it," added Becky.

"Ok then, get down there and patch up the targets, pick up the empty cases and clean out the car, we have several more to go through this today." Dermott commented.

"Thanks," Becky smiled and turned and headed off towards the car she had driven onto the range. Fiona grinned and let out a short giggle before turning and walking after her sister. Dermott watched them go before turning towards the two men who stepped in closer.

"So, you see, we do train to a high standard," Dermott started.

"That is very obvious!" Steve replied.

"Yeah, I must say, that was very good," Chris looked at Steve.

"Well," Dermott continued, "any help you guys can bring we are all ears,"

"Sure," Chris smiled, "in fact, can we go through it ourselves?" Dermott laughed.

"Only if you can get us a few more cars we can use for training!" Dermott stepped around Chris and started to walk away, again the two soldiers looked at each other.

"Yeah, that should not be a problem," Steve said, Dermott glanced back at him, smiled, and nodded before he walked towards the small group of people who were all standing in the far corner of the field. As Dermott walked on Chris spoke to Steve.

"Damn, that was really good!"

"Yeah," Steve lowered his voice, "that was top notch."

"Have you been to their four hundred metre range yet?" Chris asked.

"No," Steve answered.

"I want to have a go on that as well," Chris paused, "but are we really going to teach them CT?" Steve looked around then back at him.

"Well, I have seen the disused farmhouse they are going to convert into a training site to learn Counter Terrorism, but we will keep it at a low level to begin with."

"Did you get the email from Rupert?" Chris asked, Steve looked at him, then turned and looked at the two women who were counting holes in the targets.

"About his 'fire force' idea? Yeah, I did,"

"Dave Priest has already put his papers in, he is going to leave and go for it,"

"Well," Steve replied, "I would be lying if I said I had not thought about it!"

"How is your missus with the baby?" Chris asked, Steve smiled before he answered.

"Well, she certainly would be happy if I was not away so much." The sound of Dermott's voice in the corner made them both look over, two more were walking towards them, they also had pistols and folding stock G36 rifles. It was their turn next; the young man was smiling, and the girl had long hair and glasses, Steve spoke to her as they walked past. "Hey, are you supposed to be here?" the teenager glared back at him.

"Yes, are you?" she spat back.

"Yes," Steve replied, the teenager glared at him again then carried on walking towards the car. "What is your name?" Steve asked. The teenager looked back at him.

"Rhydian," she looked him up and down, "don't need to ask who you are!" she turned and carried on walking towards the car Becky had driven. Steve's body tensed up; he was about to verbally jump at her when Dermott stopped him.

"Let it go," he said, Steve looked at him, then back at the two people that were now walking around the waiting car.

"Isn't she a little young?" Steve asked as he watched her climb into the passenger seat of the car.

"When she was ten years old, she used a hot poker to fight off a Noc that had just killed her parents then a few years ago, she killed one with a sword and held off another four before Tyler dealt with them!" Both Steve and Chris looked at Dermott, who looked both of them in the eye. "She can certainly use a straight sword, and she has excelled on the static range with both pistol and rifle," Chris took a deep breath in as Dermott carried on, "so, I want to see what she can do here."

"She has never done this before, that could be dangerous live firing?" Chris asked. Dermott stared at the car as the driver's door slammed shut and the engine roared into life. The other side of the car Becky and Fiona were chatting as they picked up empty bullet cases.

"Rhydian has done the dry walk throughs, so this was the next step anyway," he said as he placed the safety headphones on his head. The car reversed and suddenly spun around in an aggressive J-turn, before racing back out of the entrance.

"Right then, let's see what these two can do then!" Chris stated and he and Steve turned and started to walk back to where they had been standing.

"Come on you two!" Dermott shouted at Becky and Fiona. He then looked at Steve and Chris, "Oh, if you are interested, we are having a pistol shoot on the forty metre later if you want to join in." Steve and Chris glanced back at him, then looked at each other.

"Sure, I can," Chris replied.

"Sorry, can't" stated Steve.

"Yeah, I suppose getting beaten by a group of youngsters would be embarrassing for the SAS!" they both looked at Dermott again, he was baiting them, and they knew it. "Oh, Tony will be there as well, he is an Ex-para after all!" The baiting would continue for some.

∞∞∞∞

Tony slowed the car down as he approached the entrance to the lane that led up to the farm, he looked around the familiar countryside, there would be at least one pair of eyes watching him turn up the lane. He smiled, he always felt comfortable coming back to the farm. The car made the short journey up the lane, and as he reached the top there were two Land Rovers from the farm reverse parked by the entrance to the barn and another in front of the farmhouse. Behind the Land Rovers by the farmhouse was a car he did not recognise, the farm had visitors. Tony waved at a small group of farm hands heading into the barn, two of them waved back. Tony reverse parked the car beside the two Land Rovers, turned the key and the engine of his car went quiet. The cold from outside blew in as he opened the car door and jumped out. Another farm hand was walking past heading out of the barn.

"Hey, where is everyone?" he asked, the farm hand looked over.

"Half are at the drive-in range and the others at the forty metre, they are going to have a pistol shoot with the SAS guys," the farm hand walked on. Tony nodded, the farm hand stopped and looked back at him. "Did you bring your pistol?" Tony grinned, and lifted his top to show where his weapon was, the farm hand smiled turned and carried on walking.

"That is why I am here!" Tony whispered as the farm hand walked around the side of the building. Tony shut the door of his car and walked over towards the farmhouse. He stopped, looked around and walked back to the car. Tony walked around to the passenger side door and once he opened it, he reached in and grabbed the jacket on the seat.

"Tony!" Tony looked up and spotted Paul coming out of the farmhouse, Tony raised his hand and as he pulled the jacket on, he started over towards Paul.

"Hiya," Tony greeted as he approached.

"Hi mucker, how are things?" Paul was smiling as he took Tony's hand.

"Yeah, pretty good," they released the handshake.

"So, how is life as a new dad?" Paul asked with a smile. Tony let out a shout laugh.

"Well, I could say I am loving the sleepless nights!" the two men shared an understanding laugh.

"Yeah, I remember them!" Paul acknowledged, "So, are you heading to the forty metre?"

"Yeah, I heard there's to be a pistol shoot off with the regiment guys?" Tony asked.

"There is, should be good," Paul confirmed, "I am heading there now, fancy a lift?" Paul pointed with the thumb of his right hand over his shoulder and motioned towards the parked Land Rover.

"Sure, saves me walking." Tony replied, Paul nodded walking around the Land Rover.

"Get in." As Tony landed in the passenger seat Paul was already doing up his seat belt, the engine of the 4 x 4 roared to life. Tony clicked the seat belt in place as the Land Rover started off towards the forty-metre range.

"So, what has been happening here?" Tony enquired.

"When was the last time you were here?" Paul asked, Tony paused.

"Err, the Moon Dance two months ago," he replied.

"Well," Paul was looking ahead, the Land Rover speeded up. "We got the last of the order for Scotland sorted," Paul glanced over, "they were very happy with that,"

"I bet they were,"

"Oh, Matthew Cairns finished the first part of his Close Protection Course in Kent,"

"Nice one, how has Tyler been with her son?"

"She is good, that one Rhydian lives in the farmhouse with her,"

"Don't really know that one," Tony stated, "she doesn't really talk to me,"

"She doesn't really talk to anyone," Paul let out a short laugh, Tony spotted it.

"What?" he asked, Paul was grinning as he explained.

"Well, after the last dance there was two of the younger ones, one of which had taken a bit of a 'shine' to her and decided she should be with him," Paul glanced over again as they drove through the open gate, a farm hand waved at them then closed the gate behind them. Tony started grinning as well.

"So, what happened?"

"One minor head injury, one upper arm injury and two very damaged egos!" Tony laughed out loud.

"She put them down then?" he asked.

"Hell yeah," Paul explained, "that girl is fast!"

"So, do we know what happened down at Murlough reserve the other day?"

"You didn't hear?" Paul glanced over at him as they followed the path along the side of the field.

"No," he replied, "was it the Nocs?"

"Yeah," Paul started, "a couple of sapiens on holiday over from England, went for a late-night picnic and got jumped by between three and four Nocs."

"I saw something on the news about burnt corpses or something, but they did not go into details, what happened there?" Tony sat upright in the seat as he asked the question.

"Well, we are not 100% sure but we think it was that fella Apollyon who did that."

"Who?" Tony asked, Paul looked over at him.

"Where have you been?"

"What?" Tony asked.

"Where the hell have you been? This guy came up on our radar a couple of months ago," Tony looked over at Paul.

"I have been with my family and my baby, kinda had my hands full the last wee while!" Tony protested. Paul glanced over at him, then looked at the road.

"Ok, his name is Jason Apollyon, and five years ago the Nocs attacked his home, raped and tortured the wife, before killing her and the kids," Tony's eyes looked over the countryside that was passing by them.

"Yeah, I think I remember that" he muttered, "didn't know the Nocs did it though!"

"Neither did we, it seems we missed one!"

"If they killed his family, why leave him alive? That is not like them!" Tony stated.

"They didn't, he was bitten, half drained him as well." Paul continued; Tony looked over at him.

"So how is he still alive? I thought that was impossible!"

"No idea, Tyler has raised that very question with the council."

"And what did they say?" Tony asked.

"Nothing yet, I only sent the email this morning!"

"So why are we interested in a survivor?"

"Turns out, he is a lot more than a survivor," Paul stated, Tony glanced over at him.

"More than?"

"Yes, he started his own little war, and by all accounts he is quite good," Paul glanced at him, "he said he was about to grab that Noc, Dani, in Portrush but you interrupted it."

"That was Bulgarians!" Tony protested.

"According to him, he had hired them to lift her, but .... met you instead."

"How do you know this?" Tony asked, "what do you mean, 'he said!'"

"Tyler and I had a face to face with him yesterday,"

"What?" Tony reacted.

"Yeah, we went to Divis and Black Mountain, had a face to face with him. He claims he took four down at Murlough after they had killed the two sapiens," Paul was totally relaxed.

"And .... you believe him?"

"Well," Paul started, "We don't dis-believe him, so we are investigating as much as we can." Paul turned into the small car park at the bottom of the forty-metre range. There were several cars parked with different groups of people standing around, some acknowledged them with waves. Paul parked the car and waved at the two soldiers who were walking towards them.

"Oh, we have passed it all over to them and the police, so we should get loads of info back from them," Paul, looked at Tony, "Oh, by the way, I have a bet on you beating that fella, Chris!" Paul grinned at Tony then opened the door and jumped out. Tony sat for a moment, as he was getting out the three of them were exchanging greetings. Paul turned and motioned to Tony, "and I don't know if you guys have ever met," Tony closed the door of the Land Rover and walked the few steps towards the small group. "This is Tony Fallon, Tony," Paul turned to the two soldiers, "this is Steve and Chris," as the three exchanged handshakes, Paul started to walk away, "Ok, I will leave you guys to it!"

"Hi," Chris started, "we met briefly last year, you live outside Portrush if I remember?"

"Yes, yes I do,"

"Was it your place that ... 'they' went for just over a year ago?" Steve asked.

"Yes, it was," Tony responded, it was obvious the current direction of the conversation was uncomfortable for him.

"I hear you are an ex-para?" Chris asked.

"Yeah," Tony nodded, "I was in One Para for six years," Tony spotted the both of them relax a bit, "what were you before you joined the regiment?"

"Royal Green Jackets," Chris replied, Tony nodded.

"I was Three Para," Steve injected, Tony's face lit up with a smile,

"Really?"

"Yes, really," Steve smiled back, "been here sixteen years so a bit before your time!" All three looked over to where Paul was waving at them to join him, the three of them slowly turned and headed that way.

"Three Para, say, by any chance do you know ......"

Chapter 5

Cara-Marie looked up through the trees at the clear night sky. The snow covered the ground, there was a chill in the air, but she did not notice it. She looked around where she was standing, there was a natural path through the trees, she had been here before. She slowly walked forward. Her jacket was open, it swayed in the mild breeze. She listened to the snow crunch under her boots as she took each step. Something moved over to her left, her eyes darted over, searching for the source of the movement. Her head turned slowly, then she saw him. The large wolf walked slowly through the trees. He looked over at her, then nodded his head. The wolf turned and trotted off through the trees and into the darkness of the night, his interest was elsewhere. Cara-Marie looked around herself again, nothing else moved. She carried on along the path as it weaved through the small forest, everything seemed calm, then the feeling started to grow, she was not alone, and it was not the wolf who had been by her side moments ago. In the distance, a wolf howled, her head turned to her left, the wolf was some distance away. The sound calmed her, she turned and walked on, but the unsettled feeling came back again. Cara-Marie walked into a small clearing and stopped in the middle of it. She did not feel afraid, but there was someone up ahead. She walked over to the edge of the clearing and stopped. She felt herself staring at the shape that was standing among the trees. It was the figure of a human. She could not make out any details, all she could see was the shape, standing there, facing her, then it opened its eyes.

Cara-Marie took a sharp intake of breath, she had started to hyperventilate, her right hand came up to her chest as she sat up in her bed. Her bedroom gradually came into focus as her breathing started to slow down. She took a few moments to calm herself from her dream before she flung the duvet to one side and swung her legs from underneath it to sit on the side of the bed. She looked at the small clock on the bedside table, it was just before 6AM. She pushed her hair back, then stood up. Her dressing gown was hanging on the back of the door. She slipped it on. As she walked through her flat, she felt the early morning cold, the coldness of the kitchen floor through her feet, this was when she realised she should have put her slippers on. The kettle clicked off and she filled the mug with the teabag in it. Once it was ready, she held the mug in both hands and walked back to her living room. She pulled the curtains back and looked over the quiet area around the flats. She sipped at the hot liquid and stared. She did not stare at anything, she just stared. She would not get back to sleep tonight.

∞∞∞∞

Cara-Marie walked through the rear door of the office, the lights were on, but the only person in was one of the reception staff busy with something down at the front desk.

"Morning!" Cara-Marie shouted down, a head turned, and a hand was raised in reply, without speaking. She took off her jacket and hung it over the back of her chair, she dropped her shoulder bag on the floor as she landed on the chair. She was tired, and she felt it. She tapped at the keyboard and the screen burst into life. She placed her right hand on the mouse and clicked on her email inbox. Her eyes looked at the number in the corner. Six hundred and two. She smirked; she could spend all day just going through each one. She started scrolling, she was just glancing over each title, the first one that caught her eye was from Kevin, the newspaper editor. It only had two words, it said 'JOB OFFER'. She clicked on the email to open it and read the short contents. 'HI, WHEN YOU GET IN COME FOR A CHAT, THERE IS A POSITION IN BELFAST THAT HAS COME UP. K.' That was it, no details. She glanced up at the clock, she was twenty minutes early, it was going to be a long twenty minutes. She looked around at the empty office, she could get a coffee first. Cara-Marie closed her desktop then reached for her shoulder bag, there was a new coffee shop that had just opened a short distance down the street that she had yet to try. She would be out and back again before more of the staff arrived. It was only when she returned with a coffee in one hand and a cream filled doughnut in the other that she remembered the reception staff at the far end of the office, and she had not offered them a coffee. They exchanged glances and polite acknowledgements when she came back through the rear door. It would not be long before she was back in front of her desktop and starting on her email list. She was still getting lots of emails about werewolves, and different people, mostly fantasists from around the world asking about different werewolf stories; they got deleted without being answered. Sometimes she recognised the names as journalists from different newspapers, with the odd thriller writer looking for inspiration for their latest book. She glanced at the 'delete' button on her keyboard, it was being used a lot. She lifted the coffee to her lips and took a small sip. She was not sure if she liked this one or not, but the shop was close and it was better than anything she could make with the instant stuff in the jar they had in the small kitchen upstairs.

"Morning!" She looked up as the back door swung open and Mark walked in, he was holding a mug with the same design as the one she had.

"Morning," she replied, she noticed he did not have any of his camera bags with him.

"So, you got a coffee from that new place as well then I see," he put his cup down.

"Yeah, I was passing so I thought that I would give it a try,"

"Verdict?" he asked as he relaxed back into his chair.

"Yeah, not bad I suppose," she glanced at her screen, then over at him. "Say, did you get an email from Kevin about a job offer?" she asked, Mark sat up in his seat.

"No.,"

"I got the email this morning," she replied. Mark sat forward and took control of the mouse with one hand and tapped at the keyboard with the other. He moved closer to his screen. He was studying whatever was on it. She smirked at the look of concentration on his face.

"Mmmm, no, nothing here," he stated as he looked up, "what job offer did you get?" he asked. Cara-Marie scrolled down to Kevin's email and opened it again.

"Well, all it says is," as she was reading the contents Mark jumped up and almost ran around to her screen, he placed his left hand on the back of her chair and the right on the desk and leaned over her shoulder.

"Hi, when you get in come for a chat, there is a position in Belfast that has come up. K," Mark straightened up, "What job? What the hell is he on about?" Mark looked annoyed, "and since when did he sign off emails with 'K'?" Cara-Marie glanced up at him.

"I have no idea," she shrugged, "I guess we'll have to wait and see when he gets in,"

"Hey, a doughnut!" Mark grabbed the doughnut and took a bite out of it.

"Hey, that's mine!" she protested, but by the time she said it, most of it was already gone. "You owe me a doughnut!" she demanded. The contents of his mouth muffled his voice.

"Oh, I'm sorry," he opened his mouth to show off the contents, "want it back?" The half-eaten doughnut in one hand and the disposable coffee mug in the other could not defend his face from the notebook that hit him. The reception staff would later agree he deserved it.

"So," how is life as a daddy these days?" Cara-Marie shifted her chair closer to her desk, Mark threw the notebook back, but he missed completely as it hit the wall behind her. She looked at another email, it was from Rupert Baskerville. She double clicked on it.

"Well, things have been better," Mark started, she was listening, but she was also reading the very long email.

"Why? What's up this time?" she asked, her eyes started to scan the first paragraph, it was all very polite and courteous, but there was nothing hinting to what he wanted.

"Her mother has convinced her to prevent me from having any access at all!"

Cara-Marie's eyebrows rose. "She can't do that!" she stated.

"Well, they managed to convince a judge that I only get minimum access,"

"That's better than nothing, she can't stop you completely!" she informed him, she started on the next paragraph, he was using 'them' and 'they' a lot, she did not have to guess who Baskerville was talking about.

"Yeah, yet on the days I'm supposed to have him, *something* always comes up, or they have *something else planned,* and I have to come back the following month." He was looking at the screen of his desktop, but he was sullen.

"How long has that been happening?" she asked, he did not look up from his screen.

"Well, her mum forced us to have 'supervised' visits ..." his eyes did not move, whatever was on the screen, he was not reading it, she did not interrupt him. "Do you have any idea what it is like, having a complete stranger, standing there, saying that I am not allow to hold my own child?" Cara-Marie shook her head, she could sympathize but that had never happened to her, "I mean, her mum made it clear, that after social services could find 'no evidence' of my absence, negligent or mistreatment, the supervised visits stopped, that was something I suppose,"

"Is it all her or her mum?" Cara-Marie asked.

"Her mum," he sighed.

"What does your ex say?"

"Whatever her mum says, she does!" Cara-Marie looked at him, he was staring at the screen of the monitor, but he was still not reading whatever was on it.

"Hey!" she raised her voice slightly; he looked up at her. He raised his eyebrows as if to say 'what?' "They can't do that!" she stated.

"They are!" he injected.

"THEY CAN'T!" Cara-Marie raised her voice back at him.

"Well, what can I do about it?" he raised his hands with the palms uppermost.

"What did your legal rep say?" Cara-Marie looked annoyed as he looked away, "you have spoken with them .... Haven't you!"

"I wish I had never got together with her ...." He muttered, Cara-Marie looked at the clock on the wall, this was going to take a long time.

"Look, let's discuss this over lunch shall we ...." Her eyes turned towards the front door of the office. Kevin had just come in and he was happy about something. Mark was muttering something, but she was no longer listening. Kevin was chatting to the reception staff, and he kept looking up at her, he moved around them and started moving up to the office. He was speaking to everyone in turn and like a slow wave crashing on a beach they all stopped what they were doing, rose from their desks and followed him. He leapt up the three steps that divided where her desk was with the lower office.

"Cara!" it was more of an exclamation than a greeting, she went to answer but he was already bouncing towards his office with the rest of the staff in tow. There were smiles all around, Mark turned to look at him. Kevin headed towards his office and beckoned with his right hand. "Come," the rest of the staff slowly gathered around the door of his office.

"What is this about?" Mark looked back at Cara and whispered.

"I've no idea," she responded as she rose from her seat. The small crowd gathered, and Cara-Marie walked into the middle of them, Mark followed. Kevin re-appeared at the door of the office with a single sheet of paper in his hand.

"Well," he started, he looked up at her, "Cara, come here!" he was grinning, Cara-Marie was suspicious, she guessed he was up to something, she stepped forward, he turned her to face the staff of the newspaper. "Right, now everyone is here," he paused, she looked at the faces in front of her, everyone seemed happy, everyone except her. What was the job offer he had emailed her about? And is this how he is going to tell everyone? He looked at the printed paper in his hand, she spotted the newspaper group header across the top. "I got the message last night, but I wanted to tell everyone at the same time," he turned and looked at her, "Our Cara has been recognised by the IPR Awards," there was an instant reaction from the others, smiles and a chorus of 'well done' and 'brilliant'. Cara-Marie smiled politely, she shook hands and accepted the accolades, she raised her voice as she turned towards Kevin.

"And what has the Institute of Public Relations recognised me for?" she asked, Kevin extended his arms, as if to raise her up in praise.

"The story series you did on the men from Coleraine from 6 Air Defence battery during World War two, it is to be made into a documentary for TV!" Kevin was beaming, "and the production company wants to use you as a reference for it!" the rest of the staff reacted, yes, she would later agree, this was good for the newspaper. The crowd soon dispersed back to their desks and Kevin retreated back into his office. Cara-Marie followed him in and quietly closed the door behind her. As he re-took his seat he was still smiling. "Well done again, the group editor phoned me about its last night," he reached out and moved the mouse of his desktop, he was no longer looking at her.

"Thanks, but that is not what I want to talk to you about," she stopped in front of his desk, he was still not looking at her. "The email you sent me about a job in Belfast, I just read it this morning." Kevin was engrossed in whatever was on his screen, he glanced over his desk.

"Oh, that," he reached out with his left hand and lifted a printout which he then handed to her. "The newspaper group think you will be better suited at the daily and have offered you a position down in Belfast!" Cara-Marie took the printout and started reading what was on it. The name at the bottom was the news groups main editor.

"I take it I have a say in all this!" It was a statement, not a question, she stared at him. He stopped what he was doing and looked up at her.

"Of course, take that, have a read and let me know what you want to do." Kevin smiled at her then went back to doing whatever was on his desktop computer, she was being dismissed. She turned and left; she deliberately left the door of the office open. When she got back to her desk, she spotted the screen of her smart phone was lit up by the arrival of a message.

"Are we still doing lunch?" Mark asked as she sat back down, she was engrossed with what Kevin had given her.

"Mmm, yes," she replied without looking up, the phone buzzed again. The landline on Mark's desk started ringing, he reached forward and lifted it to his ear.

"Herald!" he said as he spoke into the handset. Cara-Marie looked up, he was engrossed in the call, her eyes looked over to her own phone, the screen had *'message received'* across it. She opened the message, to her surprise it was from Tony, she read the short message:

'HIYA, I'LL BE IN COLERAINE THIS AFTERNOON IF YOU FANCY MEETING FOR LUNCH,'

Cara-Marie placed the phone down on her desk, re-read the printout Kevin had given her and paused. She looked around the office taking time to look at each face, Mark was on the phone, Kevin had walked over and shut his office door, the other staff were busy with their own things, there was a level of chat around the lower office. She looked back at her monitor. She would answer Kevin's email later. She closed down her inbox and opened up her blog. She paused, she knew everything she was doing was being watched, she thought about what she would up post, a small smile opened her lips as she began to type. *'We may have to accept that there are things we still do not know everything about and our preconceptions may have to be challenged.'* She clicked the button and posted her update. Her eyes looked at the number of followers, it had gone up. She picked up her phone and replied to Tony's message. Mark would be having lunch alone today as she was possibly about to get some information that she could use to prove what she knew to be true.

Chapter 6

Mike Dear was sitting in the portacabin at the hangar with photographs and files laid out on the small table in front of him. He looked over at the windows at the sound of a revving car engine being driven off at speed. He tutted to himself then went back to what he was reading. The door opened and Darren walked in. Mike nodded to him as he approached, glancing at his watch at the same time, it was just after 1PM. Another car engine revved, there was the sound of voices cheering as the car took off after the first one.

"So, what do you think of this lot?" Darren asked as he stopped near him, he was looked out the window, Mike could not see what he could see.

"Well, they changed over while I was away," Mike went back to what he was reading.

"So?" Darren asked as he turned around.

"So .... What?" Mike asked as he looked up. Darren shook his head and walked over to the uncomfortable chairs opposite him.

"They are certainly different from Alan Dukesby's crowd," Darren sat down.

"Steve and Chris came back!" Mike replied. Darren nodded.

"Yes, but just as a point of contact for ...." Mike looked up from what he was reading, Darren did not finish his sentence. He did not have to.

"Well, after the gun fight just before Christmas when Alan's boys took down that lot in the woods near Portrush, I was not surprised when I heard they had all changed over." Darren did not say anything, Mike glanced up and looked directly at him. "So," he continued, "apart from Steve and Chris, we do not discuss our 'friends at the farm' with them at all?"

"That is what was agreed," Darren confirmed, Mike nodded. "So, what have we got at the moment?" Darren changed the conversation.

"First of all, Inspector Wells is treating the Murlough murders as robbery that went wrong," Mike sat forward, "two tourists from England on a romantic getaway, get jumped by 'persons unknown' but ..." Darren looked up as Mike continued, "they were not expecting a husband and wife both to be former cage fighters,"

"Really?" Darren chuckled, "I guess that would surprise most assailants!"

"Yeah, what is different about this one, compared to any other is," Mike picked up a scene of crime folder and opened it. He shuffled then turned it to show Darren. It was a picture of the scene. Darren took the folder and looked at the main picture, Mike explained what they had found, "the two tourists were here .... and here." Mike pointed with his finger, "there were at least two bodies here .... That had been completely incinerated ...." Darren looked up, Mike was looking at the folder, his finger moved over the different parts of the picture, "they found at least four different sets of footprints, but most had been disrupted by the time CSI started doing their thing!" Darren looked back at the picture.

"At least two bodies incinerated?"

"Yes," Mike sat back, "at least two as they are not sure, they were mostly dust by the time we all got there,"

"Why are they thinking at least two?"

"Burnt footwear, different clothing etc," Mike took a breath in, "someone 'really' wanted to make it difficult for us to ID what was left."

"What makes you say that?"

"Because ... the temperature that would have been needed to incinerate them that much would have to be very high!"

"So, what are Inspector Wells' thoughts?" Darren started to flick through the rest of the folder.

"No, idea, she was certainly keeping that one to herself."

"What about the two tourists? What killed them?"

"The guy," Mike sat forward again and re-took the folder, he flicked through to a typed sheet of paper in the folder then handed the open folder back to him. "According to the preliminary post-mortem, Warren, the guy, died of severe lacerations to the neck, causing a traumatic bleed that was fatal," Mike quoted from memory.

"And the girl?"

"The girl also had severe lacerations to the neck but also had a penetrating injury to the chest that ruptured the integrity of her heart, causing a major bleed that led to her death." Darren looked down at the information in front of him.

"Was it a knife?"

"No, wrong shape," Mike sat back again, "possibly a screwdriver or something similar." Darren kept reading what he was holding in his hands.

"And what do they think caused the neck injuries?"

"They are putting it down to a knife ... but it wasn't."

Darren paused and looked over the folder at him. "What do you think?"

"What do I think?" Mike repeated the question.

"Yes, what do you think happened here?" Darren partially raised the folder as if it was a small offering, then he relaxed back in the chair.

"I think ..." he paused, "a group of 'them' went for two people and whatever happened it all went wrong," Darren looked down at the folder then back up at him, he let him continue, "someone or some*thing* disrupted what was happening and whoever it was ... they did a pretty good job a covering their tracks!"

"Do you think it was the farm?" Darren asked quietly, Mike shook his head.

"No, why would they leave two civilians out for people to find, didn't they say they have been trying to hide for centuries?"

"Yeah, they did," Darren agreed. "I think we should give them a call and see if they know any more about this?" Darren stated.

"Yeah, I can do that today," Mike answered.

"Have you been in touch with them recently?"

"I think Chris and Steve were heading there either yesterday or today for some shooting thing or something,"

"Oh," Darren replied, "he did say something about that, yes," The door of the portacabin opened and both heads turned to the two figures that just walked in, the man walked straight towards them, and the woman closed the door behind her. Darren closed the folder and dropped it on the table then stood up as they approached. Darren extended his right hand as if to point towards them, but Mike could see the look on his face, whoever they were, Darren did not like them. As Darren started to speak Mike stood up and turned towards them as he was introduced. "Mike, this is Sam from MI6, and Lucy from MI5 .... They are taking over the situation with the farm and our 'friends.'"

∞∞∞∞

Cara-Marie looked at her watch again, it was just gone 3PM, Tony was late. She had not seen or heard from him in some time, past requests to meet up had been politely refused, 'looking after the baby' had been used a lot. She had seen him at Kyle's funeral, but she did not get a chance to talk to him, then she had met the two from the intelligence service after everyone had left. She did not believe his name was 'Sam' at all. They had met only twice since, they seemed to be interested in her research, even though they claimed to already have copies. Every time she stated *there is something going on at that farm!* They seemed to pass it off like it was nothing. Sam infuriated her, he came across as arrogant and both times he had said they would help her and give her information, but she was yet to see anything from them she did not already know. She thought about telling Mark about them, but he had enough on his plate presently, so she didn't. She looked around the upstairs of the coffee shop at the end of Long Commons in Coleraine. There was a dark-haired woman who was tapping away at a small laptop. She spoke with a north American accent and told the staff member who brought her meal she was Canadian and not American. She was wearing a light blue sweatshirt that advertised an attraction in Belfast and seemed happy about something. The man in the jeans and the fleece had just left and the background music was not loud enough to cover anything she would be saying to Tony, and because it was public, there was no way he would confirm anything about the farm.

She looked at her watch again, his time keeping was infuriating her. She looked outside. There was a middle-aged couple walking down the far side of the street. She could not hear them but there was an argument going on between them, she smiled, the woman seemed to be winning. There was raised arms and raised voices, pointing and finally the woman turned and stormed off at a very brisk pace, leaving the man standing there. He stood and watched her go, looked down, then turned and walked away in the opposite direction. She watched him slowly walk back up long commons. Her eyes looked at the woman with jet black hair who had just walked past him. Her hair was straight, and she had a stern look on her face, Cara-Maire recognised her as a local physiotherapist who ran her own business at the top of long commons, she would have to email her later about doing a story on a local business. That had been one of Kevin's directives, local stories of a local newspaper, he had kept repeating it. Her phone was sitting on the table, the screen lit up as it started to ring. She lifted it and looked at the number, it was a Northern Ireland number, but she did not recognise it, it could be anyone, but then, this number was almost public knowledge these days. She tapped and lifted the phone to her ear.

"Hello,"

"Hi, may I speak to Cara-Marie McKenna please?" the male voice was polite, the accent was from Northern Ireland, but she could not immediately tell from were.

"Speaking," before she could say another word the voice launched into an introduction, she missed his name and the full name of the production company he said he worked for.

"Brilliant, what it is, we are doing is a documentary to be shown on tv once our investigation is complete and we very much would like to chat to you about your own investigations, we can meet tomorrow, say midday here in Belfast?" Cara-Marie crunched her face, she was annoyed again.

"Hang on, what did you say your name was?"

"Martin, can we confirm for tomorrow, we are keen to get you involved with this!"

"Right Martin, just slow down a minute, who did you say you worked for?

"It's a production company, but it's all about tomorrow ...." She noticed he had not said his surname of the name of the company, he rattled on, "and it is a really exciting venture," she stopped listening as he continued. She held the phone away from her ear and looked around again. The Canadian woman was just packing up her stuff to leave and the street outside was empty. The voice on the phone had stopped and was now trying to get a response, "hello .... hello .... Cara-Maire .... Are you there?" the phone returned to her ear.

"Right, I don't know what you are talking about, but do you know my email?"

"Err, yes," he responded.

"Right, then email what it is you are on about and I will have a look at it, but I cannot chat now as I am with someone,"

"Oh, ok," she looked up as Tony came to the top of the stairs, she smiled as the two of them met eye to eye, he smiled as well,

"Right, got to go," she said as she ended the call. The phone was dropped on the table, she stood up as Tony walked towards her, she stepped away from the table.

"Hi," he greeted as the two came close.

"Hiya," they greeted each other with a gentle hug. Tony looked at the table. "May I get you a coffee? Going to get one for myself."

"Sure," she replied.

"Usual?" he asked as he stepped back.

"Yeah, sure," Tony turned and headed back downstairs. Cara-Maire sat back down and picked up her phone. She had found out that the smart phone made better recordings than her old dictaphone, so she would use it from now on. She placed it in her handbag so the small hole that was the microphone was exposed and able to get a clear recording of the conversation. She sat back, she had many things to try and get from him, but she would have to be careful. If she just went for it, he would close up, she knew better than that. She would start the conversation and get him talking about Karen and the baby, once he was flowing, she would let him talk, then slowly try and find out more about what was happening at the farm. She did not believe the story of how Kyle died and the fire at the hostel was a good way to cover losing lives in a gun battle with a group of vampires near Portrush. This would take time.

∞∞∞∞

Cara-Marie was walking towards her car in the car park. She looked at her watch, it had just gone 6PM. As she looked up, the doors of a car a short distance away opened and Sam and Lucy got out. Lucy was well dressed in a pressed suit and looked like a professional businesswoman, Sam looked scruffy with his trainers, jeans and a sweat top that was too big for him. They did not look like two people that would be in the same car. Cara-Marie felt her pace slow as she approached them. Lucy smiled and extended her hand, Cara-Marie took it.

"Hi," Lucy greeted,

"Hi," Cara-Marie returned the greeting, Sam didn't offer his hand.

"So, how did coffee go with the ex-police officer?" Sam went straight for what he wanted. Cara-Marie was standing in front of her car with the two intelligence officers in front of her. She folded her arms.

"Nothing,"

"What?"

"I got nothing that I did not already know!" Cara-Marie sighed, "the only thing he wanted to talk about was life with his new baby," Cara-Marie looked at Lucy, "it seems life as a new dad is suiting him!"

"Did he say anything about the vampires?" Sam butted in.

"No, the only reaction I got was when I asked about Foster."

"Did you record it?" Lucy asked.

"Yes, got it on my phone,"

"Can you send it to me?" Sam butted in again.

"Yes of course," Cara-Marie answered, "but I do not believe their story about Kyle getting killed in a Land Rover on fire!"

"Well, we have nothing to suggest otherwise." Sam stated, Cara-Marie looked at Lucy, her eyes looked away and for a moment her face tensed before she looked back at her, she was obviously not a poker player.

"I can get you a copy of the Health and Safety report if you want," Lucy offered.

"No thanks, I already have it,"

"Do you?" Sam asked, "where did you get that?"

38

"I got copies of that and the police report when I was at the coroner's inquest."

"Aah," Sam responded. There was a small smile on Lucy's face.

"What do you think about the documentary?" Cara-Marie asked. Both Lucy and Sam looked at each other, then at her.

"What documentary?" asked Sam. Cara-Marie turned and started to look in her handbag, she produced two printed sheets of paper.

"There is a production company in Belfast, they emailed me this," she handed it to Lucy, Sam stepped in, both studied what she had just given them. "They have two investigative journalists that are looking at some of the murders that have been happening around here, they are speaking to other survivors and witnesses, and they want to speak to me on camera." Cara-Marie relaxed; this was something they obviously knew nothing about.

"When?" Sam asked as Lucy let him have the printouts.

"They wanted to interview me tomorrow, but I already have stuff on, so I got them to put it off until next week."

"Did they say what it is about?" Lucy asked quietly.

"Well, going off what it says there, they are investigating the Castleroe murders, the Limavady murders and what happened at Mussenden temple, they said they were interested in some of my blog posts." Lucy and Sam exchanged glances before Lucy looked at Cara-Marie.

"No problem, we will have a look at this and get back to you,"

"One thing," Cara-Marie stated as Sam started to turn away, still reading the email.

"What? Lucy asked. Cara-Marie looked at both of them.

"Next time you want to chat, just drop me a message and we can actually have a meeting instead of 'just bumping into each other in a car park." Cara-Marie was still annoyed from earlier. Lucy pursed her lips before she answered.

"Yes, of course, that should not be a problem," she said, Sam nodded and started to walk away and headed back towards the passenger side of their car "I will be in touch then," Lucy smiled as she held out her hand. Cara-Marie took the offered handshake, this meeting was over. Cara-Marie turned and walked past her own car and headed into Tesco's, she might as well get some bits for her flat before heading home.

At the other side of the car park Becky was sitting in the driver's seat of the car. The seat was lowered so her head was not visible to the casual glance of someone passing by. Her laptop was on her knees and the communicator was in her right ear. A cable was plugged into one of the USB ports and it was connected to a black plastic box that was on the passenger seat. A smaller cable went out the far side of the box and around the seat across the footwell and up the side of the backseat. Sitting underneath the left-hand head rest was a box of cigars. The open end of the box let six of the cigars point out the rear window of the car. You had to look very closely to notice that the end of one of the cigars was a camera lens, and it was pointing directly towards where Cara-Marie had been standing. Becky watched on the screen as Cara-Marie headed off towards the entrance to Tesco's and the car with the two people in it slowly started up then headed towards the exit. Becky started to close down the feed to her laptop.

"Foxtrot, Bravo, over," she whispered.

"Foxtrot," Fiona answered.

"Roger, all complete here, did you get audio over?" there was a couple of seconds before Fiona replied.

"Roger, yes, full audio coverage from her entrance to the car park," Becky smiled at her sister's response, they had completed what they came here to do.

"Excellent, I will be mobile in two mikes, and I will be at the RV shortly." Becky placed the laptop onto the passenger seat and reached into the footwell where the open daysack was. She unplugged the laptop, and the box then placed them both into the daysack.

"Roger, see you soon," Becky could tell by her sister's voice that she was smiling. As she sat up, she looked around and re-adjusted the seat then clicked the seat belt into place. She looked around then spoke again.

"Foxtrot, Bravo, I will commence routine A – S before making my way there, over." Becky was telling her sister that she would be carrying out anti-surveillance techniques and would not head directly to the pick-up point.

"Bravo, Foxtrot, roger, I will as well. Out." Becky moved the car forward, it would take her longer than two minutes to get there now, but it had to be done.

Chapter 7 – Salisbury, England.

He looked at his watch then out the window of the house, it was 11PM, nearly everyone was there, except one and he was late. From the outside it was just a house near a hill in the rolling countryside. He did not know why it was called 'Salisbury Plain' as a plain was devoid of hills, and this place was covered in them. The car headlights cut through the night as they slowed, then turned into the lane. The light turned off. He looked to his left as another man walked up and looked out the window.

"Finally," he muttered. The single car came up to the front of the house and turned so the rear passenger door was close to the front door of the house. He watched as one of the security team jumped out from the passenger seat and the rear door that was at the opposite side of the car opened and another bodyguard got out. He watched them; he had trained them well. He walked away from the window and over to the front door of the house and looked out of the security view lens in the door. He waited for the car door to open and the short man to get out and start to walk towards the door. As they did so he opened the door and allowed them in. The short man nodded as he walked past, as did the two security personnel. The door was closed behind them. They had all been a part of the security of the short man when they had met the two wolves in Portrush nearly two years ago and they had got Dani back from them. The wolves had backed off straight away, which was a good thing, if they had not, they would have had to take them down so they could recover their prize. He followed them as they marched through the house and headed towards the kitchen.

Out the back of the kitchen was a door. The door opened to a stone spiral staircase that went down to a normal looking cellar. The cellar had a table and several metal framed chairs, sitting on which was another part of the security team who all stood up when the short man walked past them. He did not acknowledge them. Items for the house were stacked on one side but you had to look very closely to see that the stack of wooden logs for the fire did not cover all of the far wall. It was only when he saw it move for the first time that he fully realised it was a door, a door that led to the rest of the underground rooms, it was a small hotel, just all underground. The corridor went past several doors and there was lighting fitted into the concrete walls, the corridor went around to the left where the closed double doors were, there were always at least two protectors here, but tonight there were four, that was just because of everyone who was attending. The doors opened to reveal 'The Grand Room', the short man walked forward then the doors closed behind him, the security team could go no further.

The first part of Grand Room looked like the inside of a theatre but there was no gallery or viewing boxes. The stage was built to look like a throne room on a raised platform that had two levels separating it from the rest of the Grand Room. Some of the seats in the Grand Room were already taken, but most of those gathered stood around the sides of the room in small groups. The short man walked straight down the aisle separating the wooden seats that were curved in a semi-circle, they all faced towards the raised platform. On the stage the two large wooden chairs looked like dark, ornate thrones, with three smaller wooden thrones, on each side of them. Each chair had different carvings over the arms and the crown, each decorated to show the position in the coven of the person who sat there. The larger of the two thrones was empty, it had been for some time as there had not been a 'Coven King' in living memory. She sat in the smaller one, but she could, she was the Queen of the Black Witches after all. She was mid to late fifties, everything she wore was black, black jeans, black shirt, and black leather boots. She did not wear any visible jewellery. Her black hair hung down the side of her face. Walking down any street, she still could turn heads and she certainly did not have a problem attracting partners, unfortunately for most of them, their bodies would never be found. She stared at him, in his dark suit. His eyes looked at the other council members, the three women sat of the left of the throne and the three men always sat on her right, the only empty chair on the right was his and it was farthest away from her throne. The two men wore similar black suits and the woman a mixture of black dresses or formal business suits. All conversation between them stopped. He stopped at the bottom of the steps. It had been six months since the last Vampiri Council meeting and there was not supposed to be one due for some time and the Queen had called this one herself, obviously something was on her mind.

"Lord Protector!" her voice echoed throughout the Grand Room, all conversations in the room stopped. There was a shuffling and everyone who was there started to take their seats. His eyes looked at her boots, he would not look directly at her when she was sat on the throne.

"Ma'am,"

"You are late!" she stated.

"My apologies," he looked up, "things to attend to." The stern look did not leave her face, she nodded once. He bowed his head then walked up the steps and took his seat on the council. The packed room fell silent. It never failed to impress him that she, the Queen, was a sapien and still controlled all of them, it had never been done before in all of their history.

"Lord Inquisitor, report," As soon as the Queen stopped speaking the woman in the far chair stood. She had a black lace dress showing the whiteness of her skin. Her short blonde hair did not move as she first bowed her head towards the Queen then looked over the room.

"Ma'am, fellow council members, Vampiri," she breathed in, "since the last council meeting there have been no internal matters requiring attention or investigation by the Inquisitor Branch," she turned her head back towards the Queen, "the problem from last year was identified and both of them were dealt with in front of the whole coven!" the Lord Inquisitor seemed pleased with herself, yes they had identified the two sapien members of the coven who had spoken with the journalist from London, their contacts in London had made sure the story was rubbished and ridiculed so it was never published.

His mind pictured what they had did with them, it had been a long time since he had heard two people scream as much as they had when they died.

"Thank you, Lord Inquisitor," The Queen nodded before the Inquisitor retook her seat. He shifted; it would be his turn next. The Queen looked at the next woman off to her left.

"Lord Advocate, report," The tall woman with straight black hair in the black business suit stood up.

He looked around, normally it would go from one side to the other and it had not. His eyes looked around, no one else moved, they must have already known the Queen was going to do that. Now he felt different, now he felt annoyed that he did not know what was happening, was this going to be something against him? Yes, there were plenty who would love to see him fall, there were several that would and could take his place, now he was defensive about what was going to happen.

"Ma'am, fellow council members, Vampiri," compared to the Lord Inquisitor, the Lord Advocate looked in good health, she was slim, but not skinny and she had been turned longer than the previous speaker.

He watched as she lifted a small hardbacked notebook, which she started to read from. "the deeds for the properties we purchased in the last six months have now all gone through," she looked up and smiled at the seated crowd, "so, I can confirm we have now doubled the amount of safe houses around the country for members to sleep in, from Clevedon in the west, to Margate in the East and all the way up to Aberdeen in Scotland," she looked over at the Queen, "so that means members will never be more than fifty miles away from a safe house in all major cities here in the United Kingdom." There was a reaction from the rest of the room, members leaned in, whispers were passed between each other, there was a good response from them all.

"Thank you, Lord Advocate," the Queen was smiling as she gave a single nod, "that is excellent news," The Queen turned to face the centre of the audience. "I know you and your team have worked hard on this project and I thank you," The Lord Advocate sat down grinning as she did so. The Queen cast a glance at the older woman who was sitting closest to her. "Lord Governor, report." The Queen glanced over her right shoulder at the three men who were all looking at her, she looked back towards those sitting in front of her. The Lord Governor stood up. She was also holding a hard-backed notebook. The Lord Governor looked to be in her sixties, her white hair was tightly tied back behind her head, her black clothes looked like they were from the last century, but then, so did she. She always had a stern look on her face and in all the time he had known her he had never seen her smile.

"Ma'am, fellow council members, Vampiri," she opened the notebook and started to read. "since the last council meeting we have had one function with guests from our associate coven in France," she looked up, "and that went very well," she looked towards the Queen, "we settled the problem that concerned them and they are happy with our actions," she looked back towards the crowd, "we have maintained the supply of food to all those gathered and have done so in accordance with our laws and have not attracted any attention to ourselves during this time," that was not like her, the Lord Inquisitor glanced at him, he was now certain, something was definitely going on, "I can confirm the coven is well stocked for the foreseeable future and we have met all the financial needs of the other council members" she turned and nodded towards the Lord Advocate who smiled a polite smile. The Lord Governor looked at the Queen who turned her head and nodded once at her.

"Thank you, Lord Governor," As the Lord Governor sat down the Queen looked at the first man on her right. "Lord Councillor, report!" The Lord Councillor looked like he was the same age as the Lord Governor, his black suit also looked like it was from the last century. He stood but kept his hands behind his back.

"Ma'am, fellow council members, Vampiri," he straightened up to his full height. "Since the last council meeting there has been a small increase in the membership of the main coven," he turned towards the Queen, "and we are currently expanding into several markets and businesses we feel will be of use to us in the long term!" he looked around before lowering his voice, "but I have to report that two Vampiri have passed over since the last meeting," he looked up, "their names have been added to 'The Great Book' and they will be missed." He looked at The Queen, The Queen again nodded once. The Lord Councillor bowed slightly before retaking his seat. The Queen looked at the middle of the three chairs.

"Lord Mason, report," The youngest member of the council stood up. He was well groomed; his hair was neatly brushed back, and he was wearing a tailored suit, he stood taller than most, he had a natural charm about him that hid a much darker side. He had no problem attracting sapien women to his bed, very few ever went back. The Lord Mason liked to boast that he kept one screaming for nearly 72 hours before she finally died. He owned a construction company before he was turned, that was why he was now Lord Mason. He had his hardbacked notebook in his right hand and he opened it before he started speaking.

"Ma'am, fellow council members, Vampiri," he looked at the notebook but looked up before he started speaking, "the problems with the showers in the private quarters have been resolved as has the issues with the drains and the rest of the sewer system," he glanced down, then raised his head again before he spoke, "these were all finished before the requested time and we have updated the newly constructed visitors quarters," he looked at the Queen, "for the next solstice we can now accommodate nearly twice the number of guests," he smiled towards the Queen, who nodded once, so he sat back down. As he did so the Lord Mason glared at him, although construction was what he did, the Lord Mason had not hidden his desire for his own position. The Queen looked directly at him.

"Lord Protector, report." He stood up and bowed slightly towards the Queen, his eyes looked over the other council members, each one glared at him, something was about to happen.

"Ma'am, fellow council members," he turned towards the main audience, "Vampiri," he did not have a notebook, he did not need one, everything he had planned to say he knew the details of without having to reference them. "Since the last council meeting the Security and Protection Group have been very busy," his eyes moved over the crowd, most were emotionless, "we have continued with our mandate to supply protection teams for members while they sleep and move between locations both here in the UK and around the world ...." His eyes glanced over at the other council members, he was being glared at, he now knew something was coming but he carried on, "we also have dealt with the threats to our members in Northampton, Bournemouth and on the Isle of Sheppey in the Thames estuary, threats that were identified to us by Investigations branch, " he looked over at the three women who were on the far side of the Queen, "and with all the new properties that have been obtained for the use by our members by the Lord Advocate, and in conjunction with the Lord Advocate's team, I can confirm that all have been fitted with electronic surveillance and a subterranean strong room that is equipped with a panic button that will locate and activate the nearest protection team that will move at once to that location!" he tried to suppress a smile, it had taken quite a while but they had got it all done.

"What exactly were the threats that you have dealt with?" The Queen asked, he bowed his head slightly, he was looking at her knees.

"Ma'am, in Northampton there was a problem with a local gang that had been moving large quantities of narcotics," he looked out of the crowd, "and as the law states, involvement with such activities only increases our chances of exposure," he looked back towards the throne, "that threat was identified, and dealt with!"

"And what of the police there?" It was the Lord Councillor who asked the question, he looked straight at him.

"The four sapiens involved who had declared their interest in some of our members were correctly identified and left with a large sum of money and narcotics at the scene, which, we have confirmed the local police were looking at an inter-city drugs feud!" he looked back at the crowd, "there was no exposure to us at all!"

"And Bournemouth?" The Queen asked, he looked back at her knees again.

"Yes, Ma'am, an investigative journalist who had, incorrectly I may add, stated in a blog that he had found one of our safe houses," he looked up, "he had not, two local petty criminals were used through intermediaries, he died, the criminals tried using a car they had stolen from a small vehicle repair shop ..." he paused, "apparently the repair shop had not completed all the work on the car and it only had working brakes on two of the wheels ... they drove past armed police at speed who gave chase ...." He looked back over the crowd, "the chase ended after their car rolled into a field. again, none survived and there was no exposure to us." He looked back at the Queen, "and the Isle of Sheppey incident was when one of our newly turned members went after a family member .... Their attack failed, but" she was staring at him, he carried on, "once it was known that there had been a compromise, the member and the family where all permanently dealt with."

"And what of Ireland?" the Lord Councillor's question was asked with venom, there was an agenda.

"Ireland?" he responded.

"Yes, what about our members over there? we have been informed that members were lost recently." It was more of a statement than a question. He paused, he thought for a second before he answered.

"I am currently waiting for a copy of the police file into the incident you are referring to," he glared back at him, "it was not the wolves, if that was want you wanted to know!"

"Are you saying a sapien took down four, possibly five of ours?" The Lord Governor butted in, knowing every eye in the room was looking at him.

"I am saying I am waiting for the report before any rash decision are made!" He was making his point.

"But what of the wolves?"

"But what of them?" he replied.

"This could be them striking at us *AGAIN!*" she had raised her voice, there was a murmur from the crowd, they agreed.

"There is nothing, presently to suggest it was them," he looked around, "and if it was, we will know soon enough,"

"We lost nearly one hundred in Ireland last year and there was practically no response from us!" the Lord Governor slapped the armrest of her chair.

"I thought the wolves were unusually restrained in their response to what happened!"

"RESTRAINED! We lost nearly a hundred members!" she leaned forward but stopped short of standing up.

"Yes, restrained," he looked around at the council members and then the Queen as he spoke, "we received information that Vampiri were gathering from around the UK and Western Europe in Ireland ... and we did nothing," he extended his hand to help make his point, "one of our senior members ran away in 2008 and started uncontrolled feeding, which, I may add, the wolves not only stopped but they handed her back to me personally,"

"She was punished for what she did!" The Lord Governor remarked.

"At that time, yes, she was," he looked out over the room, "we thought the same person left here to go to France then Italy, but!" he pointed to the roof with the finger of his right hand, "we learnt from the wolves she was, in fact, in Ireland and had joined up with others and they went out of their way to force the wolves into a reaction that could have started another war between our kinds!"

"She paid for her mistake with her life!" The Lord Advocate stated, he turned back towards them.

"Yes, killed the new alpha of the An Rua's northern den but not before kidnapping his mate and chopping her hands off!" he paused as she looked away, "then she let her little coven carry out uncontrolled feeding that brought the attention of the sapien police to our kind and, from what we hear from a survivor, left a trail of destruction behind her that any journalist could follow! They then tried to assault the home of one of their senior members which was near to sapien farms with assault rifles and shotguns!" he turned away again, "she did not just 'poke' the wolves, she gave them every reason to wipe us out for what she did."

"And Reynolds has been found has she not?" the Lord Councillor asked. He had a quizzical look on his face.

"She has," the room reacted, there was shuffling, whispering. a movement of heads.

"And what have we done to deal with her finally?" the Lord Councillor asked.

"She was found on the Isle of Skye, but the American sent a group of teenagers against her," he looked back at the Lord Councillor, "not only did they fail, they alerted her to the fact that we had found out where she was," he looked back out over the room, "I can confirm she has moved into the den of the Northern pack and has assumed the position of Alpha after their new alpha was killed by Dani and the American," he paused again, "and .... we already know a direct attack against the farm would be pointless as we would not be able to ensure we would get them all as several members live off site, and if we leave even one alive ...."

"That would be all they needed to restart the war between us!" the Lord Mason injected.

"Indeed," the Lord Protector acknowledged.

"What of the Southern Pack? What was their response?" The Lord Advocate asked.

"As far as we can tell, they only took direct action against the members who took part in the assault and the truce still stands between us, but" he paused, "but we are keeping them under observation in case there is any indication they may be mobilizing against us!"

"What the hell were they doing!" the Lord Governor spat, "they nearly started the war again!"

"How many wolves are there, that we know about?" the Lord Councillor asked.

"Over all of the British Isles, and Ireland, just over 1,500," he looked away, "The main packs are the Iceni who have a main den somewhere in Norfolk, but they have smaller dens around the country and the An Rua who cover all of Ireland and Scotland," he looked at the Queen, "We on the other hand, only have 189 full Noctrailis Vampiri here and as few dotted around the country, in smaller covens."

"What if we hit them first? Take down their leaders in a pre-emptive strike!" the Lord Mason injected.

"And their response would be to wipe us out ... we do not have the resources or personnel, currently to carry out such an operation."

"What about the wolves near Dartmoor? Are they not a threat?" the Lord Councillor stressed.

"They are separate from the main clan system as they descend from a tribe of Romani travellers and have not or will not be associated with the packs currently in the UK!"

"What of the American?" he spun around; it was the Queen who had spoken and changed the direction of the questioning.

"Ma'am?" he asked, he had been publicly ridiculing one of her daughters and she looked furious, he did not know what she was going to say next.

"We all know what she did, but what of the American? We know he was responsible for organising a lot of it for her!" he lowered his gaze.

"I am sorry Ma'am; all we know is that he is currently somewhere in the North of Ireland but alas we do not know where."

"Do the wolves know about him?" she asked.

"Yes, but they have made it clear, unlike with Dani, they would not capture him, if they find him, they will kill him."

"I wish they would, it would save us from doing it!" it was the Lord Inquisitor who spoke. All the rest of the council looked at her. They were thinking it, she had said it.

"Indeed," he tried not to laugh at her response.

"So, how do we find him before the wolves?" The Queen demanded.

"We have alerted all our surviving members to inform us of any contact with him."

"We send a hunter after him!" The Lord Inquisitor cut in, everyone again looked at her. She slowly looked around then looked towards the Queen.

"Ma'am: we could send a hunter with the sole task to find him." The Lord Protector stated. The Queen nodded and looked back at him.

"Yes, Lord Protector ... how soon can that be put into action and who will you send?" he turned and looked back into the room.

"I will send our master hunter," there was a positive reaction in the room. "MASTER HUNTER, COME FORTH!" he shouted. Heads turned towards the rear of the room as a single figure stood up. He shuffled past the last few seats in the row and walked towards the front of the Grand Room. The Lord Protector smiled as the well-groomed man in a dark suit walked stopped short of the steps and then knelt on one knee.

"Arise, Master Hunter, I command you go to the Green land, find the American and end him!" The Queen spoke. The Master hunter bowed his head acknowledging the command.

"What will you need to carry out this command?" the Lord Advocate asked. The Master hunter raised his head and looked at the feet of the Queen.

"Ma'am, I will need access to safe houses across Ireland and all assets to be made available to me,"

"You have it," the Queen answered,

"I will also need a protection team with vehicles ready to move at a moment's notice,"

"You will have it," the Queen replied.

"Ma'am, I may also need ..." he was cut short. The Queen stood up, the room went silent, the council also stood. The Queen placed her right hand on his shoulder.

"Martin," she said, he looked up at her.

"Yes, Ma'am?"

"The council is commanded to give you every resource you need," The Queen looked over the room and raised her voice so everyone could hear. "I want him to pay for what happened to my daughter, also ..." she looked back at him, "if you get a chance to get Reynolds, take it; but for now, the main coven sapiens have a party planned for tonight do they not?"

"They do, they are all at the old ruins waiting for us," The Lord Governor replied.

"Great!" the Queen shouted, "Then let us see what they have brought us!" The room stood, members started to shuffle out of the seats and into the isle. The council members closed in around the Queen, she turned to them and spoke quietly, "I want him found and I want him killed, I want all of our kind to know what happens if you come here and break our rules," she was answered by a chorus of nodding heads. "Lord Protector!"

"Ma'am,"

"Lord Protector, I want you to take the lead on this," she turned to her hunter, "Martin, the Lord Protector will be your point of contact for this operation, how you do it will be totally up to you, but I want this done!"

"Ma'am, it will be," he was smiling as he answered.

"And if you want to fuck up any of those who helped him in the process, that will be ok too!" he was being released to do whatever he wanted. "Only one thing!"

"Ma'am?"

"Don't .... and I mean don't .... start a war with the wolves!" He lowered his head. The Queen looked around then walked past him. The council members all followed her except for the Lord Protector who stood in front of him.

"Well Mr Hanna ...." The Lord Protector was grinning, "we have work to do!"

Chapter 8

Mike looked across at the utter concentration on Darren's face. He was hunched over a book of crossword puzzles, tapping one of his teeth with the disposable pen in his hand.

"Stuck again?" Mike asked, Darren did not look up.

"Mmmm .... Err ... not really ...." Which was Darren speak for yes, he was stuck. Mike grinned and flicked through the scene of crimes folder on his lap.

"So, what do MI5 and MI6 want with us this time?" Mike asked. Darren stared at the book and spoke without looking up.

"Since we last spoke in this very room two days ago .... I have no idea,"

"Not helpful," a car engine outside the portacabin burst into life and was joined by shouting voices, there was a lot of activity outside. Mike placed the folder on the table and walked over to the window. "What has got them all excited?" he asked.

"Weapons find," Darren replied, again without looking up, Mike looked back at him.

"Really? Where?"

"Homemade mortar plus explosives found down near Keady, they received a load of surveillance taskings on a bunch of bad boys in that area.!"

"I thought we were all friends now." Mike muttered; Darren looked up at him.

"Ha! Where else in the world would you have a politician, who has previous convictions for the murder of police officers be on the policing board and have a say on the day to day running of the police service!" Mike looked back at him, then glanced out the window.

"Only in 'Norn Iron'," Mike spoke with a local dialect. He folded his arms as he watched the goings on outside. Two cars took off at speed. He watched as Chris Abbey exchanged greetings with a group of undercover soldiers. Mike could not hear what was being said but their mood was lite. Chris turned and headed to the portacabin and walked in.

"Hi,"

"Hi," Mike replied, Darren didn't look up, instead he crunched up his face in concentration. Chris paused by the door, he looked over to the table near the fire exit that had a white plastic kettle, some disposable cups, a small bag of sugar, a packet of tea bags and a cheap jar of coffee on it. Underneath the table was a small white fridge, it was designed for a caravan, but suited its use here.

"Fancy a brew?" Chris asked as he headed towards the table.

"Aye, tea please," Mike replied, Darren made a grunting noise that Chris took as a no. Mike returned to looking at the events outside. It seemed only seconds before Chris was standing beside him, one cup in his right hand and extending the cup in his left towards him.

"Milk one sugar, right?" Chris asked, Mike subconsciously smiled.

"Yeah, thanks," he replied as he took the offered drink. Chris stood beside him, and they both watched the mixture of faces separating and getting into different cars and a van. Chris let out a short noise through his nose. Mike spotted it and looked at him. He did not say anything, he did not have to.

"Most of them only completed their selection course and continuation training inside the last eighteen months." Chris signed at his own comment.

"Everyone has to start somewhere." Mike replied as he lifted the drink to his lips.

"Yeah, that they do," Chris glanced at him and smiled.

Darren looked up, then back at what he was doing "A Dutch match, a devil, seven letters," Chris and Mike looked at each other then turned and started to head towards where he was sitting. Darren looked up again, "it is a crossword clue!" he stated.

Mike sat down opposite him, and Chris landed on the nearest chair, he now had his back to the window they had just been looking out of. "What is it again?" Chris asked.

"A Dutch match, a devil, seven letters," Darren repeated.

"Lucifer," Chris replied.

"What?" Darren looked up; Chris sat back into the chair before he answered.

"I lived in South Africa for a bit, my ex-wife is from there and Afrikaans is the same as Dutch, and matches, in Dutch are lucifer's'" Chris drank from his cup as

Darren studied his puzzle. "Five ... six ... seven, yup, it fits!" he exclaimed with a smile. As Darren scribbled the answer down the door opened and all three turned to see Sam and Lucy walk in. Again, Sam was scruffy, but Lucy looked like a businesswoman. As Lucy closed the door, Sam headed straight for them. All three stood and greeting were exchanged.

"Would you like a tea of a coffee?" Chris offered, "the kettle has just boiled."

"Tea, thank you," Lucy replied with a smile.

"I'll have an espresso, thanks," Sam did not look at him as he was sitting down.

Chris carried on without stopping. "Only got instant," he shouted back at him as everyone sat down. Mike spotted the glare that Sam directed towards Chris's back. There certainly was no love there. Lucy was sitting forward and had a polite smile; she placed a leather backed folder on the small table. Darren sat back down where he had been, folding up the crossword book as he did so. Sam had walked around so he was at the opposite end of the table from Lucy, Mike was still opposite Darren. Mike looked over as Chris returned with the two disposable cups. He handed one to Sam who just nodded once without looking up at him. Lucy smiled as she reached for the offered drink.

"Thank you,"

"You are welcome," Chris had stepped in front of Mike to pass her the drink, he then sat down beside Mike between him and Lucy.

"Right then," Sam started, he was keen to get on with whatever he wanted to discuss. "This deer farm of theirs' I want to go there and see for myself," everyone looked at him, he had a stern look on his face, "we can go up there this afternoon!" he stated. Lucy did not move, but there was a reaction from the other three.

"Whoa, whoa, whoa!" Darren started as he held up his hands, "you just cannot knock the door and say 'Hi, we are here!'" Darren looked at Chris who sat forward, wanting to speak.

"Yeah," Chris pointed towards Darren, "he is right, if you try that you will get a door slammed in your face and they will cut all ties with us ...." Chris looked at Mike as he continued, "they have been fighting a war for centuries and they have done a very good job at keeping themselves hidden during all of that!"

"Well, they are not the ones in charge, we are!" stated Sam.

"No, you are not!" Stated Chris as he sat back in the chair lifting his cup to his lips. Darren and Mike shared a look then they looked towards Sam.

"Well, they need to be reminded we are, if they don't co-operate then I can make sure that every legal avenue will come down on them and shut them down!" Sam was annoyed, he was used to getting his own way.

"You can try," muttered Chris.

"Look, this is something we don't know anything about, and we just want to learn more about them!" Lucy injected.

"Everything they do is legal," Mike stated, he looked at Lucy then at Sam, "Their whole business is a legitimate business, they have a legal team, business managers, a board and they file all their returns legally!" Mike looked back at Darren, "we already looked at that, there is nothing illegal going on."

"What about their weapons! Rifles and pistols" Sam stated, "they are all illegal,"

"In the rest of the UK, yes, but not here in Northern Ireland, after incidents in England and Scotland all pistols and those type of rifles were made illegal but not here," Darren replied, "if fact they do have an armoury that holds all their Firearms certificates and weapons and ..." he paused, "it gets an official inspection from the police every twelve months!"

"All in all, everything is legal there," Mike added.

"In fact, until a year ago they only had magazines with five rounds, and we pointed out to them that because of the nature of their business and the danger from livestock they could have magazines up to 25 rounds," Chris injected, "in fact, they were quite pleased with that."

"Right, ok," Lucy said as she placed the small cup on the table, her movement made Chris, Darren and Mike all look at her. "What we would like to do is have a formal introduction," Lucy looked at each one of them in turn, "you must realise that we, as an organisation need to evaluate any possible threat to the nation,"

"There is no threat," Chris injected.

"We think there might be!" Sam butted in.

"How?" Chris demanded.

"Well, first of all, we have an un-regulated armed militia running around which has no oversight," Sam crunched his face, "I mean, what about political? What is their political view and standpoint? We have to know!"

"First of all, they don't care about politics, and as for an un-regulated militia running around, at one point in the troubles we had near 20,000 troops serving here and over that thirty years there was not one mention, not one patrol or intelligence report that they even existed!" Chris sat forward, "they have done an excellent job of staying hidden from view for centuries, we have only recently become aware of them," Chris was getting annoyed.

"They have been a help to us in our investigations!" Mike added.

Darren sat forward "Yes, they have certainly been a great asset to us, and they have been quite open with us about their worldwide connections with other wolfpacks." Darren looked at Sam, then cast a glance at Mike and Chris.

"Yes, about that..." Lucy reached forward and opened the leather folder, she lifted it onto her lap and started to read, "we are certainly interested in the two Russian businessmen that have come up a couple of times in the reports an ..." her eyes searched what was in front of her, "... Edward Grishin and a Viktor Tatamovich!" she looked up, her eyes moved between the men in front of her. "We would certainly like more information on them."

"Why?" Darren asked.

"Why?" Sam repeated.

"Yes, why? Why them? Apart from a minor assault on an off-duty police officer in Belfast a few years ago they have not come up on our radar since," Darren replied.

"Yes," Mike added, "I remember them, Simon was out on a date, and he broke up a fight outside a pub if I remember exactly,"

"Who is Simon?" Sam asked.

"Detective Sergeant Simon McAllister of Belfast M.I.T." Lucy injected, all eyes turned towards her as she continued, she looked straight at Mike, "murdered at the scene of a pervious multiple killing that you were investigating at the time," Mike felt himself react. He looked into her eyes as she finished speaking, "I am sorry for the loss of your friend."

"Thank you," he whispered.

"They did not have anything to do with that?" Darren stated.

"No," Sam replied, "but two former Colonels for the Russian Special Forces and the GRU," Sam turned towards Mike, "the GRU are the Russian Military intelligence, they are huge and very powerful!" he explained. Mike looked straight at him.

"I know who the GRU are!" he stated, his bitterness evident in his voice.

"Ok, gents," Lucy held one of her hands up, "we are all on the same side here, all we are after is more information on them and what is their connection to the farm?" she had lowered her voice. Mike gently smiled; she was being a diplomat between them all.

"That's easy," Chris stated, "I heard them talking about them, they are part of their worldwide council," Chris looked around, "they are like a board of governors' for all the worldwide packs!" There was an obvious reaction from both Lucy and Sam.

"How many packs around the world are there?" she asked, Chris shrugged.

"I think, and it is only an 'I think' there is about twenty of them."

"And who is on this council and where do they meet?" Sam butted in again, Lucy looked sternly at him, "we need to know about that!" he explained, he looked at Chris, "Well? Who are they and where are they?"

"Fuck knows," replied Chris as he reached for his drink.

"What do you mean, 'fuck knows!'" Sam demanded. Chris drank from the cup then looked at him directly.

"It means, I have no idea." Sam was not happy, he looked at Lucy then at Darren.

"I think it is best if we go to the farm this afternoon so we can meet them!" it was obvious that he was not asking. Chris shook his head.

"It doesn't work like that," he sat back in the chair.

"What do you mean?" Lucy asked.

"You just can't turn up, we need to let them know we want to go to the farm and they will want to know exactly who is coming with us," Chris looked at Lucy, "if we were to arrive with you, for example, unannounced, you would be kept near the entrance and not allowed in," he looked over at Darren, "and doing things like that would end all trust between us!"

"And stop all flow of information from them as well," Darren agreed, Darren looked at Sam. "We know how to approach them, so we will,"

"When!" Sam cut in again. Darren stopped. His body tensed up as he stared at Sam. The atmosphere changed; everyone knew a line had just been crossed. Darren spoke quietly.

"Listen ... very carefully ...." Sam went to speak but Lucy raised her right forefinger to stop him, Darren continued, "I don't know who you are used to talking to but let me be clear," Darren raised his right finger and pointed directly at Sam. "You will never speak to me like that again, is that clear!" Darren was staring at him, Sam visibly moved the way he was sitting, Darren was certainly making him uncomfortable.

"I just ..."

"*IS THAT CLEAR!*" Darren raised his voice. Mike tried not to smile; the Grey Fox was in action once again.

"It is just this is all so new, and our bosses want as much information as we can get, that is all!" Lucy explained. The room relaxed. Sam looked at Lucy who gently shook her head, he was not to say whatever was in his head.

"Ok," Darren sat back, "we will get in touch with them and see what we can organise for you,"

"We would like to see one of them ..." Sam muttered.

"What?" asked Darren.

"We would like to see one of them, you know, a were ...." He stopped himself. Suddenly it became clear to Mike that this guy had not believed a word of anything that he had seen so far. It was all fiction, fantasy, until proved otherwise.

"Well, we can ask, but expect them to say no to that one!" Chris injected.

"How so?" Sam replied. Chris looked at him.

"Because they are not circus animals that can be brought out to perform a show, so, like I said, expect a 'no' to that one!" Chris lifted his drink again.

"Ok, that is no problem," replied Lucy who reached for her folder and stood up. "You have my number, so let me know when everything is sorted," she spoke directly to Chris.

"I will," Chris replied. Everyone else stood at the same time, this meeting was over. She shook each of them by the hand and thanked them, Sam just nodded but didn't take the offered handshakes. Sam darted for the exit with Lucy fast behind him.

"What a prick!" Chris stated as the door slammed behind them. Mike nodded and murmured at the same time. Darren slowly walked over to the window and watched them leave.

"Yeah, seen his type plenty of times before," Darren was still looking out the window when Chris started fumbling in the pocket of his jeans.

"Oh, I nearly forgot," he produced a USB drive out of his pocket which he handed to Mike, "got this from the farm, this is a fella that has come up on their radar, asked if you could do your thing with it," Mike took the USB drive.

"Ok, who is it?" he asked.

"Oh, some bloke that is running around and killing vampires for them," Darren turned from looking out the window.

"Really?" he stated.

"Yeah, apparently this is the guy who took down those knock thingies at Murlough the other day, they say his name is Jason Apollyon."

"Well, since the brew here is crap, I am going to head over to the far side of camp for a decent cuppa, fancy coming?"

"Yeah sure," said Mike. Chris turned and headed towards the door.

"Great, I'll grab my jacket, see you by the car in two mins," Chris seemed happier now. Mike walked over towards Darren and held up the pen drive.

"Our way back into the farm!" he stated.

"Yes," Darren agreed. Daren reached out and took the pen drive, "I will get started on this, and when you two are chatting see if you can find any more out about that Lord What's 'his name' in England and that Fire force thing he is putting together,"

"Lord Baskerville," Mike smiled.

"Yeah, him," Darren confirmed, "the very chap!"

Chapter 9

Martin Hanna walked into the Grand Room; unlike last night, it was now empty. Security closed the doors behind him. He walked towards where the Lord Protector was sitting on the steps in front of the thrones. The Lord Protector looked up as he approached.

"Master Hunter!"

"Lord Protector," Martin replied. The Lord Protector stood up they exchanged a handshake and a smile; they both liked each other. The Lord Protector sat down on the carpeted steps. Martin looked around the empty room. "So, they want me to take down The American,"

"They do."

"And how I do it is up to me then?"

"It is."

"But what of the wolves? They control Ireland, will they to be told I'm coming over?"

"No,"

"And if I have to deal with them?"

"Then deal with them," the Lord Protector stated. Martin walked over and sat down beside the Lord Protector and looked over the empty room.

"It felt like last night was a stick up."

"It was."

"Why?" Martin asked, "What have you done?" The Lord Protector laughed.

"Just politics, our Mason friend has made no secret of how much he wants my job!"

"Yeah, he is not good at keeping quiet about what he wants,"

"No, he isn't" the Lord Protector added.

"That sapien girl he had over the altar at the ruins last night," Martin looked at the Lord Protector, "I actually thought he was going to kill her!"

"Yeah, he is not good at restraint. He has to remember most of the sapiens in the coven don't know our kind even exists!"

"So, what has really been going on in Ireland? I've heard rumours of course, but I need to know what I may be facing there!" The Lord Protector looked at him and nodded once.

"Yes, a fair question, it is simple really, he got members to join with him there,"

"Unsanctioned of course," Martin added.

"Unsanctioned isn't the word, if he had even suggested it, he would have been under lock and key!"

"So, what was he trying to do then?" Martin queried.

"Well, from what we have learned from a couple of the survivors, he gathered mostly youngsters in and around Belfast, gave them weapons then let a newly turned run amok."

"So, where did Dani fit in with all this?" Martin asked.

"The Lord Mason is not the only one who is not good at keeping their intensions to themselves!" Martin's head shot up, anger flared in his eyes, then subdued as quickly as it had appeared. "I know you had plans for Dani and yourself, but she wanted action taken against the wolves who handed her back to me in Ireland and we refused, unfortunately we did not know Dani and The American were in touch, or we would have kept a closer eye on her."

"Do we know who killed her?" There was obvious resentment in Martin's voice.

"Yes, the newly promoted alpha of the Northern Den, Kyle Foster."

"I'll take him down too," it was more of a whisper.

"You don't have too," The Lord Protector stated, "she took him down already,"

A smile broke over Martin's face, "that's my girl,"

"If you do have to go up against the wolves make sure there is no trace back to us. We have learnt that the police over there may already be looking at us! Make sure you correctly identify a wolf first before taking it down, then only if you have to!"

"Yeah, I will wait for them to go from lamp post to lamp post checking their 'pee-mail'" The Lord Protector let out a short laugh at Martin's joke.

"Yeah, but you do need to be careful, the wolves have been very restrained with us, they could have launched against us for what he did over there." Martin nodded.

"Do we know how many there are in Ireland," Martin looked at him, "I mean, total strength? What kind of force are we looking at?" he asked.

"We think, there is less than one hundred in the Northern Den, but there is at least three hundred in the southern den, but, and I do mean, *'but'* any action against them will give the other packs not just across Europe just cause to rise up against us!".

Martin nodded. "So, the truce is still in place then?"

"At the moment, yes,"

"What if we moved first?"

"What do you mean?" The Lord Protector asked.

"What if we organised ourselves and moved against them? Do it all in one strike?" Martin suggested.

The Lord Protector laughed, "Don't think we have not thought about that."

"But why don't we? It would take some serious planning, but it could be done, could it not? There are over eight hundred in the main coven, why not use them?"

"Firstly, we do not have the trained personnel to do it, the sapien protection teams are exactly that, protection, not assault teams, yes, we do have sapien numbers, but look at most of them, we could not use them in a fight and expect a good result! They need to be trained." The Lord Protector stopped and looked at him. "What are you thinking?"

Martin looked around and lowered his voice. "Ok, let's start with identifying sapiens in the coven that we could use and train," The Lord Protector looked at him and listened, Martin continued. "We can use them as protection and assault teams, when necessary, we track and find all the wolves, then in one night," Martin used his hand in a chopping motion, "crash, bang, we wipe them out!"

The Lord Protector smiled. "I like it. Only a couple of problems with that." he continued, "firstly, to organise all that will take at least a decade, and," he panned his hand over the empty room as if to reveal everyone who had been sitting there the previous night, "also, look at most of the members here, they may not live that long, we need to increase our numbers, not lose most of them in a fight we could not currently win!"

"But we have made advances over the world have we not?" Martin asked.

"Yes," the Lord Protector replied, "we control both the Eastern and Western seaboards of the United States, most of South America, we have made great strides in the Far East, we dominate nearly all of the continent of Africa and apart from the pack that covers Israel and Jordan most of the near east as well."

"And we have a growing presence over Europe do we not?" Martin stated.

"Yes, in every major city over Europe," The Lord Protector confirmed.

"So, if we get all of them to act together, we could do it!" Martin suggested.

The Lord Protector laughed. "Get every single coven to work together! Ha, it is hard enough getting them to agree on the time of day, never mind anything else."

"But it could be done,"

"No, it could not," The Lord Protector placed a hand on his shoulder, "You forget the Wolves control nearly all of Russia, China, Australia and the Pacific region and they control large parts of Canada, and ..." he paused, "they have a growing presence in the US, if we tried to organise something like that it would not take the wolves long to find out about it, plus we have to think of the sapiens!"

"Why?" Martin asked.

"Why what?" the Lord Protector asked.

"Why think of the sapiens? What has it got to do with them?"

"Because" the Lord Protector started to explain, "every time throughout our history, the sapiens have found out about us, we have been hunted to the point of extinction. We learnt from the mistakes of the past, so no, we cannot do something that would reveal our kind to the modern world." Martin nodded.

"Ok," Martin straightened up. "We could use sapiens against the wolves, therefore there would be no comeback to us!" he stated. The Lord Protector looked at him quizzically.

"What do you mean?" he asked.

"Simple," Martin started, "we do not have the trained personnel for something like this, so we hire it!"

"Hire it?"

"Yes, use front companies, and hire ex-military from different parts of the world and use them, without them knowing what the final goal is or who they are actually working for!"

"But what if the sapien police start to investigate them?" the Lord Protector asked.

"Easy, we close down, whatever the company was, disappear 'into the night' as they say, and leave the ex-military to answer for themselves." The Lord Protector was thinking.

"How would we recruit them? What would they be called, correct me if I am wrong, but mercenaries are illegal are they not?" he asked.

"Yes, calling them mercenaries are, close protection teams and security consultants are not, we set up security companies, through them we acquire land and sites to train and equip them and have them ready in different parts of the county when we need them." The Lord Protector thought about this; there was a silence between them for a few moments.

"That is certainly something we can look at," The Lord Protector was having ideas of his own with what Martin just said. "But first, we have to concentrate on your current task,"

"Yes, that comes first obviously," Martin agreed.

"What are your plans so far?" the Lord Protector asked.

"The protection team I've been given is outside; I'm going to chat with them a bit."

"I will not keep you anymore then," the Lord Protector stated. Martin started to walk away. "Oh, I forgot to ask," the Lord Protector's statement made Martin stop and look back.

"What?" he asked.

"Since Dani is no more, what prize will you want for all this, the Queen did not give you any parameters for that, did she?"

"No, she did not," Martin confirmed.

"Have you any ideas of what you will ask for?" the Lord Protector asked. Martin smiled in a way the Lord Protector had not seem him smile before.

"Since I cannot have the daughter, I may as well have the mother!"

The Lord Protectors stared. It was the Queen's choice, not the other way around.

"That will be some request," the Lord Protector warned, "it could have consequences and it will take not just the head of the American, but Reynolds as well!" Martin looked at him, then looked at the empty Kings throne behind him.

"Well, if it gets me closer to what I want," he paused, "What if I brought him back here alive?" Martin stopped talking and turned and walked away. The Lord Protector smiled, like the Lord Mason, the Master hunter was not good at hiding what he really wanted.

Martin walked through the empty kitchen of the farmhouse and on into the living room; the bodyguard was standing by the front door; he was waiting for him. He was dressed in a dark suit and was much taller than Martin. For such a large man he could certainly move when he wanted to. Martin nodded to him as he entered the room. The bodyguard reached for the handle and opened the front door. Martin walked past him and out into the night. The car was parked facing down towards the lane and the rear passenger door was already open. The driver was holding the door, looking round, taking in positions of any possible threats, it was a well-rehearsed drill. Martin climbed into the back of the car. He shuffled over so he was behind the passenger seat, seconds later the driver and the bodyguard climbed into the front.

"Before we go to Bournemouth this evening there are some things we need to sort out," Martin stated. Both of them turned around to face him. "Right, I have more details of this job we have been given," the driver relaxed, this was not for her, the bodyguard looked at him without flinching. "We have to go to Ireland, and we need a full team. "We will have access to safe houses, but we will need vehicles and weapons waiting there when we arrive."

"When do we go?" the bodyguard asked.

"Within a week, or as soon as we are ready, whichever is first," Martin explained. The bodyguard had a look of concentration on his face. "Which part of Ireland?"

"Mostly in Northern Ireland, but do not rule out having to travel via the republic," Martin paused, the bodyguard was already doing what he kept referring to as a 'dynamic risk assessment'. Things would change and would change very fast, but he had proven he could think fast. The bodyguard nodded, then sat back in his seat, facing out the front of the car.

"No problem," he muttered.

"Oh, the council has been instructed to give us every possible assistance they can."

"How credible is the threat?" the bodyguard asked.

"High, I can give you more detail when we get back here later, if they find out we are there, there will be fireworks, I will prefer discretion to be the key this time. The person we are going to find is somewhere around the north coast, and probably knows we are coming," Martin relaxed back where he was sitting.

"We will need two teams, at least three if not four, 4x4/SUV type vehicles," the bodyguard looked back over his shoulder as he continued, "with run flat tyres, powerful, upgraded engines, built in armour and a communications suite from the safe house that can cover all of Ireland then!" he stated.

"Submit your requests, like I said, the council has been instructed to give us every assistance!" Martin was grinning, this was exactly the kind of task that would get him what he wanted. The bodyguard nodded to the driver and the car took off down the lane.

"No problem," the bodyguard stated, "no problem at all,"

ooooo

Grishin and Tatamovich walked side by side along the corridor with other passengers who had got off the same flight they were on. On the left was panelled windows, you could see other parked aircraft looking directly into the terminal building, but behind them the airport expanded out and there was a view of a dark night over Belfast. To their right were advertisements for various visitor attractions around Northern Ireland. Grishin and Tatamovich, were wearing suits and light brown raincoats, their previous trip had taught them how much it rains here, a fact Tatamovich still continued to comment on. They passed through the automated doors and into the brightly lit baggage reclaim. They stood as others gathered, impatient to collect their luggage. Grishin reached into his pocket and produced his new phone. He tapped the screen and read a message that was waiting for him. He looked at Tatamovich.

"They are waiting for us," he stated.

"They should be!" Tatamovich responded. Grishin smiled and let out a short laugh. The first of the bags started to fall down the metal slide and onto the moving conveyor belt. Some people moved closer but the two of them stayed where they were. It was something they still did, was anyone paying them attention, was anyone watching what they were doing. They had lived lives doing counter-surveillance so much that they did it without thinking.

"So, what about this 'Jason' then?" Tatamovich asked. Grishin glanced at him.

"Well, 'if' such a person does actually exist, we need to find out more about him,"

"We have never had a survivor that did not turn before?"

"Not as far as anyone knows of, no," Grishin replied.

"And what of Connor?"

"He did break the law," Grishin explained, "but we will listen to both sides before making any decision."

"Hopefully this trip will not be as long as the last one!" Tatamovich commented. Grishin looked at him and chuckled.

"Has it really been two years since we were last here?" Grishin asked.

Tatamovich was looking around, "I have not missed this place."

"Me neither," Grishin replied. He nudged Tatamovich as the two black cases came sliding down and hit the bottom with a thud. They picked them up without speaking. They both extended the handles and pulled the cases behind them as they headed for the last part of security then to the arrivals lounge. They spotted Paul Hawkins standing at the side with two others either side of him. They walked forward and stopped in front of the two men. Paul only slightly bowed his head, anything else would have been too obvious and would be noticed.

"Welcome back, ..." he was cut short in his welcome by Grishin stepping forward and offering a firm handshake.

"Mr Hawkins, it is good to see you again," Grishin was smiling at the exchange. Paul smiled back; he understood what this senior council member was doing. Paul released the handshake and stepped back.

"If you would like to follow me, we will escort you to your hotel," Paul turned and started to walk away. The two either side of Paul stepped forward and took the luggage. Grishin smiled and nodded as he released the handle of his bag then started off after Paul, Tatamovich did the same without speaking. The two cars were waiting outside, and it was not long before they were on their way to where they were staying. They would enjoy a night out in Belfast before they started their official visit to the green land, but as far as the An Rua was concerned, nothing more would happen tonight.

Chapter 10

Mike turned into the layby at the side of the country road, Chris Abbey released the seat belt and opened the passenger door as the car came to a stop.

"Finally!" Chris announced. He left the door open as he ran towards the bushes at the side of the road. Mike chuckled as the soldier started to relieve himself at the side of one of the bushes. Mike released his own seat belt and got out of the car. He stood beside the car and stretched, he turned and looked over the car as Chris was walking back towards it doing up his zip. Mike smirked at him as he came to stop by the open door of the car. "

What?" he asked with a shrug of his shoulders.

"Nothing," Mike said as he turned and looked up the empty road.

"It is not like Dermott to be late!" Chris stated, Mike looked over at him and nodded.

"Yeah, and they keen for us not to go near the farm at the moment!" Mike replied.

"I am sure we will find out why soon enough," Chris remarked. Mike glanced over at him as he ducked back into the car. He reappeared with a small sandwich in his mouth. Mike tried not to laugh as it reminded him of a grizzly bear fishing. Chris mumbled something through his mouthful of food that Mike did not hear.

"Remind me again why I have never introduced you to my family?"

Mike was smiling as he spoke. Chris reached down into the car again and reappeared with a plastic bottle soft drink. "You have never introduced me to your wife because if she met someone as good looking as I am, she would leave you on the spot!" Chris smiled at his comment and Mike crunched up his face.

"The way she is at the moment that may happen anyway!" Mike replied, he glanced at Chris who had not picked up on his reply.

"Oh, I heard from David Priest last night, said to say 'hi' next time I saw you," Chris's comment made Mike smile again.

"Great, hi back, where in the world is he these days?"

"He did not say," Mike bite his lip, what was he thinking, that is a question you do not ask people like this. It was not that they will deliberately lie to you, but Mike knew they had to. They would never confirm exactly where in the world they were presently sending Special Forces troops.

"One thing David and I were discussing," Chris injected.

"What was that?" Mike asked, glad of the subject change.

"Wonder Woman or Batgirl?"

"What?" Mike replied.

"Wonder Woman or Batgirl?" Chris repeated, "which one would you like to date and why?" Chris was smiling as he took another bite of what was left of the sandwich.

"Can't say I really thought about it much," Mike replied, "but what about you? What is your preference?" he asked, deliberately turning the question back at him.

"Batgirl," came the instant response.

"And why?" Mike kept him talking,

"Well, there is the outfit for starters .... Then the bike she rides ..." Chris was about to continue when a Land Rover appeared on the road from the direction they had arrived. Mike smiled and waved as Dermott slowed and pulled in behind them in the layby. The layby was covered by trees and the fields rolled over the countryside in all directions, there was no one visible for quite some distance.

"Do you think they are watching?" Mike asked as Dermott tuned off the engine. Mike turned and started to walk towards the Land Rover with Dermott in it.

"Every time we met them when all this started, they had surveillance out," Mike looked over at Chris as Chris continued, "they were very good, so I would say, yes, they have people out there." Dermott climbed out of the Land Rover. His clothes were clean but did look like he had just walked off a working farm, he was not a stylist at all.

"Bout ye," he greeted. His accent even more prominent compared to Chris'. 'Bout ye' was the local way of asking how you are.

"Hi Dermott, how are you getting on?" Dermott shut the door of the Land Rover and stepped forward to take the offered handshake.

"Aye, none so bad," Chris walked up and joined the greeting.

"Hey Dermott, good to see you," said Chris, Dermott politely smiled.

"Aye, and you, and you,"

"So," Mike started, "busy at the farm?" Mike went straight for it. Dermott looked past him as he answered.

"Aye, a wee bit, got visitors today, they arrived the day before yesterday, but they are heading off later," he explained.

"Oh, anyone we know?" Mike asked, Dermott shook his head.

"Nah, farm stuff, Paul and Tyler felt best not to have you guys showing up where they are being given a tour of the place," Mike glanced at Chris, it was an obvious lie, but Mike chose not to push it, Dermott made eye contact with Mike. "You have stuff for us?" he stated.

"Yes, we do, Chris grab the jiffy bag in the front for us please?" Mike asked.

"Sure, no problem," Chris turned and headed back to the car.

"Something I didn't want to raise over the phone," Mike started.

"What's that?" Dermott asked.

"Well, we have new bosses .... And ...."

"And what?" Dermott pushed.

"Well, short version, they want to visit, you know, kinda do a 'see for themselves' sort of thing!" Mike waited for his response. Dermott watched as Chris rose out of the passenger door with the brown padded jiffy postal bag.

"Who are they?" Dermott asked.

"One is MI5 and the other is MI6, a man and a woman," Mike explained as Chris re-joined them, offering the padded envelope to Dermott.

"Thanks," Dermott said as he took the envelope. It was not sealed. He opened it and looked inside. He pulled out the contents and looked at the photographs of Jason Apollyon with Tyler and Paul at Divis and Black Mountain nature reserve.

"Everything about him is printed out is on the USB drive too." Mike explained.

"Thanks," Dermott repeated as he started reading one of the printouts, he looked up at Mike, "I will pass that on and see what the response is," he explained. "Oh, one thing for you," Dermott reached into the pocket of his jacket and pulled out a folded photograph and handed it to Mike. "These two have had several meetings with the journalist in Coleraine, who we think are something to do with the government." Chris stepped closer they both reacted at the picture. "This was taken by two of ours that were keeping an eye on her in Tesco's car park in Coleraine," Mike breathed in at the picture of Cara-Marie with Lucy and Sam. Mike and Chris exchanged a glance. "And judging by that reaction you do know them!" Dermott stated.

"Yes, yes we do," Mike pointed to each. "This is Lucy-MI5, and this is Sam-MI6, they are the ones who want to visit the farm," Dermott looked up at him as he continued, "they are our 'bosses' currently." Dermott did not say anything as he looked back at the picture.

"Unfortunately, we don't get to pick who the government puts in charge of us," Chris added, Mike agreed.

"Ok, I will pass this on,"

"Oh," Mike pointed at the contents of the jiffy bag, "I found details from the inquest into the deaths of his family, seems he was adamant; they were killed by vampires!"

Dermott's face reacted, "Really?"

"Yes," Mike continued, "it is all in there,"

"He certainly has quite a backstory, that one," Chris added, "how come you guys are so interested in him?"

"When Tyler met him, he claimed to have taken down the four Nocs at Murlough." Dermott started looking through what he had been given, "he claims he was too late to help the two sapiens but took them down all by himself."

"Ok, no problems," Mike added.

"Yeah, it seems he turned into a vigilante in Canada a few years back," Chris stated.

Dermott raised the jiffy bag, "Thanks for this, and we will let you know about them," he pointed to the picture in Mike's hand, Mike offered the picture back, Dermott shook his head. "No ta, keep it." Dermott turned and headed back to the Land Rover.

"Ok, bye for now," Mike said as Dermott shut the driver's door. The engine roared into life and both Mike and Chris raised a hand in farewell as Dermott headed out.

"Well, that seems to be that then." Chris stated.

"Yeah," said Mike as they walked back to the unmarked police car. The passenger door was still open, Chris went round the side of the car, he looked over the top towards Mike.

"I wonder who the visitors were that they did not want us there,"

"Yeah, I was thinking that myself," Mike replied as he opened the driver's door. "I wonder who could be that important that he would not want to say anything."

"What do you mean?" Chris asked.

"Listen to what he didn't say! He said they had visitors it was best we do not meet. If it had been something to do with the business, like, a visit from the tourist board or the health and safety etc, he would have said it. The fact that he didn't but changed the conversation straight away means he was protecting that information from us."

"You really have done the 'spooks paranoid about everything' course haven't you?" Chris climbed into the car and shut the passenger door. By the time Mike got in, Chris had already done up his seat belt and was going through the daysack that had been under his legs. His head came up with a smile and his right hand produced an unopened packet of biscuits. "Result!" he stated as the car moved off. "By the way, you didn't answer my question!" Chris stated between mouthfuls. Mike thought for a moment before he answered.

"What question?"

"Wonder Woman or Batgirl? Which one would you date?" Mike looked around the outside of the car and sighed. "Well," Chris continued, "which one?

∞∞∞∞

Dermott looked in his rear-view mirror, the layby was already out of sight, he replaced the communicator back into his right ear. The overwatch was informing the farm of their movements.

"Roger, collapsing down then foxtrot to our transport, over".

"November, Delta," Dermott spoke.

"November," the overwatch replied.

"Delta, thank you, see you back at the farm," he looked at the passing countryside, his eyes glanced at the parked tractor in a field, a female voice came up on the communicator.

"Juliet, that is November passing my location,"

"Roger," the communications building at the farm replied, "keep an eye for any others following Charlie One over," The tractor had been there since yesterday and two of their farm hands were on it, the farm was tasking them to see if anyone was following the car that Dermott had just met.

"Juliet," she replied, the instruction was received and understood.

"November, can you tell control I have what they wanted and need to chat as soon as I get there,"

"Roger November," Dermott slowed down as he came to a junction, there was no other traffic, so he turned and headed off towards the farm.

∞∞∞

Grishin reached out his right-hand which Tyler took in a firm handshake. Tatamovich nodded once but was already heading for the passenger door of the high-performance car they had hired. The car was parked outside the farmhouse, Paul was standing by the door, there was a 4x4 with four farm hands in it waiting for the council members to leave, they would escort them to the Irish border where a team from the Southern Dun would be waiting for them.

"Thank you for today and thank you for being so honest about the current situation," Grishin stated.

"No problem," Tyler spoke quietly as she released the handshake.

"We will spend the rest of the evening and tomorrow with Connor, I will get him to inform you where we will all meet, and we can deliver our resolution."

"We are not going to his farm," Tyler stated, "if we did, there would be a danger to us from other pack members!" Grishin thought for a moment.

"Yes, I see, I will inform him of that," Grishin turned and walked towards the driver's door of the car, "until tomorrow then," he said without turning around. He opened the door and climbed in. As the engine started. Grishin did not close the door. He leaned out and looked towards her, "I forgot to ask, what did you name your child?"

"Kyle," she replied. Grishin thought for a moment before he replied.

"Why Kyle?"

"I named him after his father,"

"I did not know you and Foster had a relationship!" Grishin stated.

"We didn't" Tyler shrugged, "we only got together once after a dance and …. The baby is the result!"

"Well," Grishin smiled, "that can happen." The car door shut then took off at speed, the waiting Land Rover went after them, Paul waved at them as they headed off down the lane.

"Well," he breathed a sigh of relief. Tyler turned and stepped towards him.

"They did not seem very happy with any of that!" she stated.

"Everything we told them was true," they looked at each other.

"Yes, which means Connor has some explaining to do!" She said with a smile.

"They did seem pleased at the amount of Nocs we've taken down," he stated.

"But not at our involvement with the military," she added.

"No, but we have helped each other quite considerably." Paul said, "do you think they believed us about this Apollyon fella?"

"Well, if we can present more facts about him them maybe we can find out more about what he actually is!" Tyler said as she turned and headed back towards the farmhouse. Paul followed her inside, Tyler turned and held a finger up to her lips, telling him to be quiet. She turned towards the kitchen just a Rhydian appeared, cradling a sleeping baby in her arms. Tyler

61

and Rhydian closed in, they shared beaming smiles, a loving touch, and a caress. Tyler reached in and pulled back the white woollen baby blanket back to reveal a sleeping face.

"He has been fed and changed," Rhydian whispered.

"Thanks," Tyler whispered in reply.

Paul took a step backwards towards the door. "I will come and find you when Dermott gets here!" he stated. Tyler briefly looked over, nodded and all her attention returned to the child. Paul turned and headed back outside. As he closed the entrance door, he turned to face the farm hand that was walking from the communications building towards him.

"Dermott says he needs to talk to you when he gets here; he got what he went for."

"Good," Paul walked towards the communications building, the farm hand walked beside him as Paul continued. "Let me know when he gets here, any problems with the meet?"

"None," the farm hand replied, "just one of the soldiers and a Special Branch guy."

∞∞∞∞

Chris Abbey was restless. The hotel room seemed smaller than it was, he looked at his watch again as he walked over to the only window. It was nearly seven in the evening. He looked out over the view of Belfast. The meet had gone ok, he had given Steve a back brief on it, Steve was not surprised that the wolves had surveillance on the journalist, and he thought it odd they had spotted Lucy and Sam. Mike was gone for a meeting with Darren; they had more work to do on the weapons find earlier in the day. Steve told him it was being dealt with and all he had to concentrate on was their dealings with the farm. He asked for the rest of the night off, and Steve had no problem with that. Chris reached into his pocket and pulled out his phone. He scrolled through his messages. Her real name was not saved, in fact it was abbreviated so it looked like one of the other soldiers. He re-read her last message – 'OK, SEE YOU SOON.'. He sent another message 'WHAT TIME WILL YOU GET HERE?' The message had been sent, but not received or read, her phone must be off. His mind flashed to the last time they had met, he felt his body react to the lustful memories, tonight was going to be the third time they would meet up and there probably wasn't going to be much sleep tonight. The tv was off and there was a siren outside, that was the only noise. He was agitated, and this was not like him. He sat back on the bed. His mind went back to how sensual it felt moving his fingertips down the side of her neck and along her naked shoulder. He could feel his heart quickening at the thought. The siren was joined by another, it made him look out the window again.

The soft knock at the door made him jump up, he almost ran to the door. He placed one hand on the door and the other on the handle as he looked through the peephole at the woman standing on the other side of it. No, he would not be getting much sleep tonight.

Chapter 11 – Hill of Tara, Co Meath, Republic of Ireland.

Paul looked at the clock in the dashboard, it was nearly 4PM, they were right on time. He followed the road that led up to the car park beside the pub near the entrance to the Hill of Tara, he glanced at Tyler who was still reading over the information they got from the military the day before. Paul spotted the parked car near the previous junction; he had not waved at the Southern Dun's surveillance, but they watched them drive past, they would report they had not brought the usual security with them. There were several cars, vans, and minibus's parked along the wall of the church yard and several people standing around, Paul recognised Garou when he saw them. A hand was raised in welcome and pointed towards the verge on his right. Paul left a small laugh; it made Tyler look up.

"What?" she asked as Paul was parking the Land Rover.

"The last time I was here was with Kyle when he did his procession."

"I wish I could have seen that" Tyler remarked. Tyler looked around, most of those there were looking at them. "Well, we better get this over with!" Tyler released her seat belt then opened the door. She was wearing her walking boots, and before she closed the door she reached in and grabbed her padded blue jacket. As she zipped it up two young faces walked towards her, Paul came round the front of the Land Rover as they all caught sight of each other.

"Uncle Paul,"

"Saoirse!" Paul exclaimed, the two jumped towards each other and embraced, Tyler watched as the warm greeting continued. "Jack!" Paul said as they also hugged.

"Uncle Paul, it's great to see you!" Paul stepped back and turned toward Tyler.

"Saoirse, Jack this is Tyler, Tyler ...." The three closed in, Saoirse had a wide grin on her face, she extended her right hand in welcome.

"It is so nice to finally meet you properly, we didn't get a chance to speak when we were up north after ...." Saoirse stopped from saying Kyle name, Tyler took the offered hand.

"Hi, you are related to Paul?" she looked over at Paul, changing the direction of the conversation. "I didn't know that!" she exclaimed.

Jack stepped forward, "Hi," he said as they shook hands.

"Well, we are not blood related," Saoirse looked over a Paul with a warm look on her face, "we just feel we're family!" they exchanged a wide grin, they were obviously close.

Tyler looked at Jack. "So, since we have not met properly before, where do you fit in with the pack?" she asked as Jack stepped back.

"Connor and Orla are our parents," he stated. Tyler's eyes widened as she remembered the exchange in the barn back at the farm with the pack Alpha and his wife.

"How come you never came to train with me when I was on Skye?"

"Dad said I did not have to," Jack looked at Paul, this conversation was making him uncomfortable. "Dad and the others are waiting for you over by St Patrick!" Jack pointed in the direction of the old church building.

"Tell him we will be right over," Paul stepped close and placed his hand on Jack's shoulder, Jack smiled back and lowered his gaze, then smiled as he looked up.

"Sure, it is good to see you Uncle Paul!" Jack turned to walk away then turned back and looked at Tyler. "I heard you took down the one they called 'Sabine' in a one on one." Paul and Saoirse turned and looked at her. A small smile spread across her lips.

"I did,"

"I heard you were not there when Foster took down nearly twenty of them!" it was more of a statement than a question.

"I wasn't," The look on Jack's face changed, he was about to say something when his sister cut him off.

"Jack," he looked at her, she stared back, there was silent communication between the two siblings. Jack nodded then walked away, Paul took a breath in.

"You better not forget the stuff we got on Apollyon!" he stated,

Tyler nodded and turned back towards the Land Rover. "Yes, of course,"

"He's real?" Saoirse asked with disbelief.

Paul stepped closer to Saoirse. "Yes, he's real," he replied.

"You have actually seen him?" she asked.

"Not only seen him but we had a full conversation with him," Paul said as Tyler closed the door. She had a large brown envelope in her hand.

"I mean, he survived a Noc attack and didn't turn?" Saoirse again spoke with an unbelieving tone.

"Pretty much," Paul placed his hand on her shoulder as Tyler stepped closer as well.

"I think we better get a move on, don't want to keep his Lordship waiting!" she stated. Tyler still had the small smile on her face which changed when Saoirse glared at her.

"That is my father and in case you need reminding, your alpha!" She had not liked Tyler's comment and it had obviously touched a nerve.

"Hey," Paul injected. Saoirse looked at him and the annoyance fell from her face. She nodded without speaking and turned away from them.

"They are over here," Saoirse walked briskly away from them and headed towards the metal entrance at the end of the stone wall.

"Ever had the feeling this is going to be a heated conversation?" Tyler whispered to Paul as they walked beside each other. Paul looked at her and smiled. He looked around and picked out the security that was standing around. To the casual observer, they were small groups of two or three, some around the cars, some by the corner of the pub, others near the hedgerow. But to the trained eye, each was placed to identify any threat and mutually support each other in defending their alpha. They had all practiced it, and yes as there was council members, they would have done a rehearsal as well, if not here, then back at the Southern Dun. Some looked, some glared, one waved, another smiled as the two from the north walked past and then through the gate. Saoirse led the way up the dirt path then they headed towards the small group of people who were gathered near the tall statue of Saint Patrick, she paused then stopped when they got close. Tyler and Paul walked a few paces past her then stopped themselves. Connor was standing in the middle of the circle of the higher members of the Pack, who all turned to look at them as they approached. Some of them stepped back forming a semi-circle behind Connor. Tyler looked around; the two Russians were not there.

"Connor," it was Paul who spoke, he bowed his head as he did so. Connor did not acknowledge him, but he did glare at him, His gaze moved to Tyler who bowed her head once but did not speak. Tyler noticed he had clenched fists, he was furious, and she would have to watch that, a furious alpha surrounded by his own pack, this could go very wrong for both of them. Saoirse turned and walked away, Jack came from her left and stepped towards her, he held out his right hand.

"You are to hand over your weapons!" he demanded.

"I am not armed," she said when she looked at him, she turned and looked at Connor, "I didn't think I would need it here!" Jack relaxed his arm but did not move. Paul felt his eyes move from Jack to Tyler, he did not say anything, Tyler was not armed, but he was, Jack had not asked him so he would not volunteer it.

"Fine," stated Connor, he was angry and wanted to vent that anger. Tyler looked at the sullen faces of the senior members of the pack, none of them were happy. Tyler glanced at Paul, he looked at her but said nothing. Tyler made a point of looking around the churchyard.

"Where are the council members?" she asked. Connor turned his back to her and pointed towards the door of the small stone church.

"Having a look around while they were waiting for you!" Connor looked over his shoulder at Jack. He nodded towards the church. Jack nodded once and walked around the back of the semi-circle of pack members, heading towards the church door, leaving the rest in silence. He did not get far when Grishin and Tatamovich appeared. They were both wearing business suits and looked totally out of place among the A Rua Pack who were all dressed for the outdoors. The two Russians confidently headed straight towards them. The senior pack members parted to let them walk past and into the space between Connor and Tyler. Paul took a small step back; his alpha was in charge. Grishin politely smiled as he greeted her.

"Tyler," Tyler bowed her head once, Grishin looked over and smiled at Paul. "So," he continued as he turned where he was standing, Tatamovich did the same, so they were a few feet apart yet facing each other. Tyler recognised what they were doing, she was directly facing Connor, but they were separating them. Connor faced her directly, she was trying not to smirk, whatever had happened between them it must not have gone well for Connor, Grishin continued, "did you get information on this 'Noc Killer?" Grishin was looking at her, she glanced around, everyone was staring at her. She spotted that Jack had walked up and stopped near Tatamovich. He was not a senior member, but Connor had not sent him away.

"Yes," she said as she raised the envelope.

"Well, hand it over!" Connor demanded as he stepped forward. Grishin raised his right hand, stopping him. Grishin glared at him then turned towards Tyler.

"Thank you," he said as he stepped towards her with his left hand held out. Tyler handed the envelope over, Grishin removed the sheets of paper and the photographs.

"He really exists?" Orla stated out loud, several heads turned towards her.

"He does," Tyler confirmed.

"And he survived a Noc bite?" came from another,

"Yes,"

"And he didn't turn?" Orla asked,

"No,"

"And he didn't die either?" This time it was Tatamovich who spoke, the difference with his Russian accent and that of the Southern Irish around him was vast.

"No, he didn't." Tyler confirmed.

"How is that even possible?" Connor demanded.

"I have no idea," Tyler responded, she raised her right hand toward what she had given Grishin, "That's what we got on his background!" Grishin was reading one of the pages.

"And how did we not know about him already?" Connor asked as he turned to one of the others.

"I don't know," was the sullen response.

"So, what is his background? What do we know about him?" Connor turned and demanded of Tyler.

"It is all in there …." She started. Connor stepped towards Grishin and held out his hand to take what he was reading. Grishin stopped and looked directly at him. Connor was used to having his own way. Grishin stared at him, stopping him, Connor paused and lowered his hand, it was a clear message, Connor was not in charge here, Grishin was. Grishin looked back at what was in his hands and turned the page.

"He certainly has a past, doesn't he!" Grishin stated as his eyes darted over to Tyler.

"He does," she confirmed. Connor stared at her. Tyler did not budge, he was pushing her, but she was not responding. Grishin started reading.

"Born 14th September 1961, Ontario, Canada," Grishin's eyes moved down the page as he continued, "1966 – 1975 Alexander Dunn school, Borden, Ontario, then Woodroffe High school, Ottawa," Connor moved as if he was about to say something, Grishin looked up, that stopped him. Grishin looked back down and read more. "1979 – 1981 3 RCR Petawawa, Ontario ..." Grishin looked over at Tyler, "3 RCR?" he asked.

"Royal Canadian Regiment," she replied, she looked at Connor then the others as she explained, "Light Infantry, fast moving, hard hitting," All eyes looked back at Grishin as he read aloud again.

"1982 – 1993, Canadian Airborne Regiment then from 1994 – 2000 – Joint Task Force Two!" Grishin looked up at Tatamovich, who reacted, he understood what that meant. Connor looked between them both.

"So? What is task force whatever!" Tyler looked at him, he was not being obnoxious, he really didn't know.

"Tier one Canadian Special Forces," she explained, Grishin kept reading aloud.

"Advanced Military Freefall, Basic Sniper, Master Sniper, Close Quarter Combat instructor, Survival instructor, Signals, Pathfinder and ...." Grishin looked up at Tatamovich, "Completed the US RANGER course with distinction!"

"What does all that mean?" Orla asked, Tatamovich looked over at her.

"It means he is good, very good," Tatamovich looked at Grishin, "he knows how to stalk, he knows how to hunt, he knows how to kill!"

"When we met him our overwatch and security said they did not see him get close to us or see him leave!" Tyler stated, she turned towards Paul who nodded in confirmation.

"You let him get close to you?" Connor remarked.

"He is no threat to us," she stated, "and he has lost all hint of a Canadian Accent, he sounds local."

"MMMM," Grishin murmured "Almost as if he was trying to hide." He looked up at Tatamovich who took a single step closer, Grishin looked down again, "Languages: English, French, German, Serbian and Spanish," Grishin titled his head, glanced at Tatamovich then read some more. "He has a brother and ..." he read the next few lines before he read them out loud, "had an elder sister who died following a severe mugging, the RCMP investigated a group from the military base at Petawawa for taking vigilante action against the four suspects involved after their court case ended on a technicality." Tatamovich shrugged his shoulders.

"So? I would have done the same!" he stated.

"But why is he here, and why is he killing Nocs?" Connor demanded.

"Simple," Tyler stated, "his parents were originally from here," she turned towards Paul, "Antrim if I remember correctly!" Paul nodded in confirmation, "following the death of his sister he moved back here and away from Canada and was married pretty quickly,"

"So?" Connor asked.

"Six years ago, while on a family holiday the cottage they were renting was broken into, his wife and young children were murdered, he was attacked but somehow survived," Connor placed his hands on his hips, he was looking directly at Tyler, she carried on, "no one was ever convicted, or indeed charged with the murders but at the inquest, he kept repeating that the people who carried it out had elongated teeth and bit his neck .... Did the same with his family," There was a reaction from the senior members standing behind Connor.

"Was that all that was said from the inquest?" Connor asked, he lowered his voice as he did so, this was concerning.

"Yes," Tyler replied, again pointing to what Grishin was holding, "it is all in there, the police and Coroner got a dental pathologist to confirm that the injuries to the victims were not human, the rest ...." She stopped and lowered her arm, "is history, he has been hunting them ever since!"

"So, it's true then, the rumours!" Orla stated.

Connor turned to face her. "The rumours that there is someone hunting Nocs all over the UK and Ireland, has mystical powers and is immortal!"

"Well, I don't know about 'immortal'," Tyler injected, Connor looked back at her.

"We have found out that 'The American' sent a team after a sapien and none returned," Connor glanced at Paul then looked towards Grishin, "we didn't know who this sapien was, but he took down the whole team, including their daylight protection and has left messages that he is after 'the American' himself!"

"So, what are we going to do about this!" all eyes turned to Jack who was standing near Tatamovich. Jack was agitated, "we control these lands, we have to do something about this!" he demanded.

"Who are you?" Tatamovich demanded as he looked back over his right shoulder.

"I am Jack, my father is ..."

"*I KNOW WHO YOUR FATHER IS, ARE YOU A SENIOR MEMBER OF THIS PACK!*" Tatamovich shouted, it stopped Jack.

"I, I mean ..." he stuttered.

"Shut up!" Tatamovich snapped, Tatamovich looked back at Grishin.

"He is no threat to us," Tyler injected, "the footage and transcript of our meeting is all there!" Paul coughed and Tyler looked at him.

"The journalist!" Paul stated.

"Oh yes," Tyler remembered. She reached into her pocket and pulled out the picture of Cara-Marie with Sam and Lucy in the car park. She stepped forward and handed it to Grishin. "Got an update on the journalist," Grishin took the picture, looked at it then handed it to Tatamovich.

"Yes," Grishin asked,

"We have found out that these two, which we have now found out to be from MI5 and MI6, have been meeting up with her and have started to pass her information."

"Information?" Connor raised his voice, "what information?"

"Mostly inaccurate, out of date or useless, they have been telling her what to post on her blog," Tyler stated.

"And from your message last night, these are the same two that want to visit the farm? Yes?" Grishin asked.

"Yes," Tyler confirmed.

"What have you told them?" Connor injected; Tyler looked at him then at Grishin.

"Nothing yet, I thought it best to raise it here first." She spotted the anger in Connor's eyes, he could say nothing to that, she had done the right thing. She spotted a small grin on Grishin's face, was he enjoying this?

"Yes, glad you did," Grishin pointed to the photo, "we will have a closer look at these two, what about the journalist?" he asked.

"*She needs to be taken down!*" Jack injected, "*she has to be ...*" Jack was silenced by Tatamovich spinning around and slapping him with the back of his hand across his face with such force it sent him flying backwards. He landed on a heap on the grass behind where he had been standing. There was a collective movement that was stopped by Connor raising his hand.

"*SHUT UP!*" Tatamovich shouted at Jack. "Are you a senior member of this pack?" he demanded. A shocked Jack looked at his father who wanted to move, to defend him, but

Tatamovich was right. Tatamovich turned to Connor, "why is he even here?" he demanded. Orla moved and walked past them all and helped her son stand. She turned him and started to walk away with him, Jack had a hand to his face, he glanced back, he looked Tyler in the eyes, he was furious. Tyler looked back at Connor. Connor still had an angry look on his face. He breathed deeply; he was restraining himself.

"Right, back to the reason we are here," Grishin started, "I have listened to both the north and the south about what was happening with this Noc Princess," all eyes turned back to Grishin as he looked around, he was getting ready to deliver his ruling, it would be a ruling that would be binding. Tyler and Paul shared a glance then listened to what he was saying, Connor turned towards him as well. "To summarise the events that led to the death of young Foster," Tyler felt her insides churn at the way Grishin described him, she kept her face motionless and still as Grishin kept talking.

Chapter 12

Tyler looked at herself in the mirror, then at her watch, it was almost 10AM She adjusted her hair, gave herself a little shake then looked herself up and down. Her eyes came back up and she stared into her own eyes. She looked around the living room of the farmhouse, it was quiet. There was movement outside as people migrated towards the barn. Rhydian appeared in the doorway of the kitchen; Tyler smiled as she walked into the room.

"He's asleep," Rhydian whispered.

"Thanks," Tyler turned and moved towards her, the two shared a warm hug.

"I will stay here," Rhydian stated as she snuggled in, Tyler's arms closed around her.

"No problems, the briefing will not take long," she reassured. There was a knock at the front door, they separated turning towards the door as Dermott stuck his head in.

"Everyone's here ... ready?" he asked. Tyler nodded and Dermott retreated leaving the door open.

Tyler looked at Rhydian "Well, best get this over with." Tyler turned to leave.

"Mum!" Tyler stopped and looked back at her, Rhydian paused, her eyes moved around, looking at everything, yet nothing. Tyler looked at her, Rhydian was trying to speak but nothing was coming out. The pair looked into each other's eyes and the two shared a moment. Tyler smiled nodded once then turned and headed through the doorway. Tyler walked briskly towards the open door of the barn; Paul was waiting for her.

"Are they all here?" she asked as she slowed down to a stop as she reached him.

"Mostly, got a few out on security, two in the communications room and a few doing farm jobs," Paul looked at her, department heads will back brief them afterwards," Tyler looked inside the arena, the pack and their families were gathered, most standing around in groups chatting, the level of conversation filled the arena. As Tyler started to walk towards the raised platform Paul pulled the main door closed. Tyler stepped up and walked to the centre of the platform as all conversation ceased, there was a group movement towards her.

"Well, as you all know Paul and I went down south for a meeting with Connor and the two council members yesterday to try and resolve all the events involving us for the last year or so," she looked around at the expectant faces, she saw hope, she saw anxiety and concern, "the council members delivered their ruling and," she paused, her eyes did not mean to glance at Paul standing at the side but she did, they then focused on a single member standing at the rear of the pack, "the ruling very much went in our favour!" there was a collective response, the weight had been lifted, they were going to survive as a northern dun.

"What was said?" came one voice, Tyler tried not to smile as she answered.

"For starters Connor admitted that he allowed a Noc princess to go to the southern dun for a face-to-face meeting with them and agreed to terms, allowing them to move against us here in the north ...." The pack responded, there were gasps and a reaction of shock.

"That is against the law!" one voice protested.

"Yes, it is, and Connor was furious that he had been duped," Tyler explained.

"He should stand down!" shouted another, there was a collective agreement.

"No, he isn't, he has made a declaration that he will never stand by again and allow the Nocs to do anything on clan lands," Tyler glanced over at Paul again, then looked back at the pack in front of her, the resentment against Connor was growing. "He made an 'unto death' oath, in front of the council members and Paul and I and as all of you know, that means, he will personally lead any action against the Nocs himself," Tyler breathed for a second, heads looked towards each other, comments were passed, this had not been done in living memory.

"How does that affect us?" a voice asked.

"Well," Tyler spoke, "the council has ruled that because of his actions, we will separate directly from the south," again there was a turning of heads, whispers of conversations, "we will remain part of the clan, which, Paul and I agreed to," her eyes looked around again trying to gage the crowd, "but here, the northern dun will be a separate pack, under our own leadership!" the noise from the pack was almost a cheer, "Connor accepted the ruling for breaking the law, he has stated he will not intervene in pack business but wanted us to keep him informed of any situations with either, the Nocs or other wolves. "We have been given a gift," Tyler extended her left hand towards Paul who turned and lifted the framed picture that had been up against the wall. He held it up, it was a charcoal sketch of a figure of a man, up against a tree, holding a sword up in the air in a declaration, everyone knew it was a representation of Kyle. There was a spontaneous cheer from the pack. "I think this will look good in the bar!" Tyler said above the noise of the crowd, most turned back towards her. "A couple more things, we ...." she paused, "are to be recognised by the council for, in their words, '*achieving a great victory in the face of an attack by our enemies!*" the cheer went up again, Tyler raised her hands, the pack quietened down. "Every wolf of every pack across Europe knows what we did here, every pack knows that we, the Northern Dun, stood against everything they threw at us," there was a growing excitement in everyone who was in front of her and she could feel it, "Every pack knows of our loss, but also what we gained!" she felt her voice raise slightly, "the south are to hold an 'extraordinary dance' next month and invites to several other packs have gone out and the council members stated they will inform the Higher Council of everything that has happened, one of them said afterwards it may be possible that we may get recognition from the Higher Council!" there was clapping, a cheer and an euphoric feeling sweeping through the pack, this was a good time to be a member of the Northern Dun. Tyler spotted Paul raise one finger from his right hand, it was to remind her of what else she had to speak about. She nodded and raised her right hand again, quietening the pack. "One thing still remains," she started, the arena fell silent, Tyler relaxed her arms. "One thing we still need to take care of is the one who started all this!" again there was a collective movement and whispers, "we know, 'The American' is still somewhere here," the room hushed, "but, when we find him, we will take him down for all the hurt and pain he has caused us!" the pack responded with a single yelp.

"Take him down!" a younger male voice shouted.

"*An Rua!*" she shouted, "*we will defend these lands from whoever comes against us!*" another cheer went up, Tyler lifted her right hand again, she lowered her voice, "it is a good time to be in the North!" another cheer followed by applause, Tyler turned and walked off the platform, she was surrounded by smiles, handshakes and excited comments, the pack was in a good place. Tyler walked towards Paul who was handing the picture over to one of the security team.

"Make sure this goes up in the bar today will you!" he said just as Tyler approached; they had an excited look on their face as they took the large frame in both hands.

"Certainly!" they exclaimed, "I am on it!" The door to the barn opened and pack members started to file out. Tyler looked at Paul just as Dermott walked up beside them.

"Anyone fancy a cup of tea?" she asked.

"Yeah," Paul smiled.

"Never say no to tea!" Dermott remarked. The three of the turned and headed outside along with the rest of the pack. Most followed along the side of the barn and headed back to the different parts of the farm where they either worked or lived. Tyler looked over to her right, everyone was smiling, there was an excitement in everyone that made her smile with a deep happiness. The door of the farmhouse opened, and Paul walked in first, followed by Tyler. Dermott closed the door. Paul landed in one of the chairs as Tyler headed to the kitchen.

"Tea?" she said.

"Yes thanks," replied Paul.

"Perfect, you know where everything is, I need to check on the baby," she patted him on his shoulder, "make it will you!" then she darted through the door. She heard a laugh coming from Dermott as she went through the kitchen then up the stairs. She slowed down as she got to the top; Rhydian was standing by the door of the spare room. After she had packed away all Kyle's pictures and prints, she made it the baby's room. Rhydian had her finger to her lips, telling Tyler to be quiet, Tyler slowed and quietly walked along the short hallway, stopping by the door. They both looked at the sleeping baby.

"He is still asleep," Rhydian whispered. The two shared a smile and a loving look. Tyler placed her hand on Rhydian's shoulder then turned and walked back downstairs. Paul was standing in front of a kettle that was starting to boil, she spotted the three mugs standing in a line in front of it. Dermott was in the doorway between the kitchen and the living room.

"Got an idea about what to do about 'The American!" Dermott stated.

"What is that?" Tyler asked. Paul glanced at her then at Dermott.

"Well to be honest," stated Dermott, "it isn't actually my idea," he turned and headed back through the living room. Tyler walked over and stopped by Paul, she faced the doorway where Dermott had just been standing, she folded her arms then glanced at Paul.

"Any idea what he is about to do?" she asked, Paul started to pour the boiling water into the first of the mugs.

"Well, he ...." Paul was cut short by Dermott walking back into the kitchen. He was followed by two of the older men from the pack. She recognised Ian Silver and John Gold instantly. They were both late fifties and both were dressed for working on a farm, if you walked past them you would see two farmers, and they liked that. She greeted the two men with a smile and a handshake, they both politely smiled and slightly nodded in greeting.

Tyler stepped back as Dermott stood beside them, "The idea ..." Dermott started.

"Use us!" Ian Silver spoke. He was wearing a thick dark coloured woollen jumper, he was slightly shorted than John, but was stockier in build. Tyler glanced between the three of them as Paul stepped past her and handed Dermott a mug of hot tea.

"Would you two like tea, I'm making some." Paul injected.

"No thanks," replied Ian.

"Yes, thank you," John was more politely spoken than Ian, his was less of a country accent. Paul placed a mug in front of Tyler, she looked down at the steam as it rose from the open mug. She knew both of these two, they were the fathers of the two sets of twins the rabid had torn apart in the mournes, she remembered the joint grief the two families went through at the four funerals.

Tyler looked at them. "Ok, tell me your plan!" she said.

"Simple really," Dermott started, "we task these two with one job, track and find 'The American'."

"And how would you do that?" Tyler asked.

"In the early 1980's the two of us tracked down that rogue Noc that was running around Belfast!" Ian stated. Tyler thought of a moment, she did not know about that, she was still in Canada at the time.

"We did it again when one of our teenagers took off by themselves," John added, Tyler remembered hearing about that one. "We know 'how' to track, we know 'how' to look, and," John injected, he glanced at Ian then looked back at Tyler, "we have done this before, we know how to do it!" John had a calm look on his face, almost reluctant.

"So how would you start?" she asked.

"Research first," John stated, "review everything we know about him, places we know he has been, sapiens he has killed, etc, then look for patterns. Nocs as we all know," John explained, "if not in a set coven, migrate, we look at where he has been, pick up the trail and narrow down where he is!" Tyler glanced at Dermott who was nodding in agreement.

"We can do it low key, without attracting any attention to ourselves, if we run into trouble," he turned to Dermott, "we can call here for support!" Dermott nodded.

"What would you need?" Tyler asked.

"A Land Rover, surveillance kits, places to stay, weapons," John explained.

"Weapons?" Tyler's question surprised them.

"Well, yeah, if we came across him suddenly, we may have to take him down there and then!" Ian stated, again Dermott agreed.

"What if you need to cross the border?" she asked. Ian looked at Dermott, Ian had obviously expected a different response to what he was proposing, Tyler continued, "what if you track him across the border into the Republic and get stopped by the Irish police," Tyler looked at Dermott, "and are caught carrying firearms, which would be illegal down south!" she looked back at Ian, "if that happens you are going to prison."

"Unless" Paul started, "we register a pistol and a shotgun each," he looked at Dermott, "they are kept out of sight and only used as a last resort."

"Yes, yes, that can be done," Dermott looked at them then at Tyler, "low key, and they have done it before, they know what they are doing.!"

"I take it we are not being asked to take him alive!" John stated. All eyes turned towards him, there was silence for a few moments in the room. It was Tyler who answered.

"No, you're not!" Dermott, Ian, and John all smiled, Tyler raised her right hand, "first of all I want to see a plan, course of action etc, then," she looked over at Dermott, "I want to see a plan for here on how we will react, different scenarios ...." Dermott nodded, "and," Tyler carried on, "a communications plan, what comms we will use, set timings that you two will be in touch with here and an overdue plan," Tyler looked at Paul, "just in case it all goes wrong!" Paul nodded. Tyler looked back at the three of them, "how long will you need to do that?" she asked. Dermott, Ian, and John all looked at each other then back at her.

"A few hours, we will have that done today!" Ian stated.

"Great, let me know when it's done!" Tyler smiled, the three of them relaxed then they said their farewells, and all there headed back through the living room and outside. Dermott closed the door behind him as they left. Tyler and Paul exchanged a glance.

"So," Paul said.

"So," she replied stepping back and leaning up against the sideboard, "what do you think about that?" she asked.

Paul pulled back one of the chairs and sat down, facing her. "Well, they are two of our most experienced trackers so if anyone can do it," Paul shrugged, "I guess they can."

"Two grieving fathers going after the son of a bitch who brought a rabid wolf over here, the same rabid who tore their kids to shreds," she glanced over at him, "and letting them loose, with guns, and a mandate to hunt down the Noc who did it .... Does that sound dangerous to you?"

"Glad you are thinking like that!" he replied.

"Like what?"

"Thinking of the bigger picture," he paused, she waited for him to continue, "it is not just sending two Garou to hunt down a Noc," Paul sat up in his chair, "yes, the fathers of the Silver and Gold twins going after such a prominent target will go down very well throughout the pack," Paul looked her in the eye, "you know they will never stop, they will stay the trail until they catch what they seek!"

"I am counting on it!" Tyler smiled, "plus the pack will know we are actively doing something instead of just sitting around waiting for that prick to try his next move!"

Paul nodded. "Yes, I agree., There's one thing I do need to chat to you about."

"Yeah, sure, shoot," she replied. Paul looked down, them raised his head.

"There is something that is really concerning me,"

"What is that?" she asked, Paul paused again, whatever was coming, it was obvious that it bothered him greatly.

"It is about that Valkyrie woman!"

"Alison!"

"Yeah her ...."

"What about her?" Tyler asked as she walked towards him and pulled back one of the other chairs tucked under the kitchen table. She sat down and looked directly at him.

"Well," he started, "I am concerned ...." Paul started talking with his hands, Tyler sat and listened. "We don't know much, if anything at all about her kind, I mean, is she a threat to us now?" Tyler looked at him, Paul's eyes moved around the room, he carried on, "is she still working for 'The American'?" then Paul looked directly at her, "plus, you didn't mention her at all, either to Connor or to the two council members!" Tyler thought for a second.

"Yes, you are right, I didn't," she shifted in her seat, before she spoke again, "the subject did not come up, yes, you are spot on, we don't know much about her, or her kind, if she is still with 'The American' then yes, she could be a threat to us."

"I think we should try and find as much of that out as possible," Paul stated.

"I agree," she replied.

"Any idea who we could use?" he asked. Tyler smiled and relaxed in her seat, she reached around and pulled her phone out of her back pocket of her jeans.

"Well, they need to be discreet," she started.

"I agree," Paul smiled as she started to scroll through her phone.

"Someone who knows what to look for and has an understanding of her habits and mannerisms!"

"Yes," Paul smiled as she put her phone to her ear, he guessed where she was going with this.

"And someone who would understand how a former police officer would think and possibly act!" Paul smiled again, Tyler spoke into her phone, "Tony, hi, how are you? .... Great, yes, all good here, ... yeah, the trip down south was certainly eventful. In fact, would you be able to come to the farm, I can bring you up to speed on that one, plus, I may have a task for you!"

Chapter 13

Cara-Marie unlocked her front door and pushed it aside. She stepped in and used her elbow to close the door behind her. Her jacket was hung on one of the rungs she had screwed in place just after she moved in, her shoes were flicked off as she dropped her large handbag on the floor. She pulled her slippers on, they felt comfortable. She lifted her handbag and headed into the living room, dropped her handbag beside the sofa and made her way into the kitchen. She glanced at the clock, it was gone five, she had left the office a bit early and had headed straight home. She was staring out the small window of her kitchen as the kettle started to boil. Her mind wandered. The knock at her front door brought her back to reality with a jump. She was not expecting anyone, she wondered who could it be? She walked back through the flat and pushed her face up against the small view hole on the door, she felt her whole-body sigh and groan at the sight of Sam standing there. He had his hands on his hips and impatiently stepped from one foot to the other. She partially opened the door and looked at him as he stepped forward, he almost barged her out of the way.

"Ok, how did you know where I live?" she asked, he stopped in the hallway and looked back at her, he did not answer her question, but he did twist his face up.

"We need to have a chat about things, and we can't do that in a coffee shop!" he turned and paused at the top of the hallway, he looked into the living room and headed towards it. Cara-Marie thought for a moment, she really did not like this arrogant ass, a lot of the stuff he had passed to her she had not used because it was useless. She walked back into the living room, he was walking around as if studying her flat in detail, she stood in the doorway, the sooner she could get rid of him the better.

"Right, so what is so important that you need to charge around here!" she demanded.

"Well, there is this documentary for starters, I believe you are going to take part," it was more of a statement than a question.

"Of course, I am, why would I not?" she started to make her way towards the kitchen. He turned towards her with an inpatient look on his face.

"Right, well, we need a complete run down on everything you are going to say for starters." She stopped in the entrance to the kitchen.

"WHAT?" she raised her voice, her eyes darted over to look at the boiling kettle that had just switched itself off. He stepped towards her keeping his hands on his hips.

"Yes, we need …" he started to motion towards her with his right hand, emphasising what he was saying, "to know exactly what you are planning on saying and exactly who to!" Cara-Marie was more annoyed now that she was before.

"Are you stupid?" she crunched up her face as she asked the question, Sam stopped what he was doing, Cara-Marie cut him off before he could say another word. "I am going to be *'interviewed'* that means they are going to ask me a series of questions of which, I will not have prior knowledge of …" Cara-Marie pointed at him with her right forefinger, "unless that is why you are here?" she stepped towards him and raised her eyebrows, "well? Have you brought me a list of the questions they are going to ask? Well, have you?" she demanded. His eyes looked around the room then back at her.

"No," he replied, "but we still need to know what it is they are planning on doing." Cara-Marie let out a short laugh, then turned and walked back into the kitchen.

"They are probably going to be journalists," her voice echoed around the small kitchen, Sam walked over and stopped in the doorway, he watched as she started to make a mug of tea, she carried on, "and be investigative journalists at that," she said as she started to pour from the kettle. Sam looked at her hands, he had not been offered anything and she was not making him one.

"Well, we are concerned about some of the things they may be looking at.?" he spoke quieter than before. Cara-Marie turned and opened on the door of the fridge, as she lifted out the large plastic bottle of milk, she glanced over at him.

"What exactly do you think they will be looking at?" the door of the fridge closed, she spun around and poured some into the single mug.

"We are concerned about some of the things they might be looking at in detail."

"Such as?" she butted in.

"Such as some of the things that were in your statement about the riverside murder."

"What about it?" she looked at him with a confused look on her face.

"Well, let's go over it and some of the things you should stay away from."

"My statement was part of the inquest into the deaths at the riverside, it was read out in full at the inquest and is now in the public domain …. What precisely shall we 'go over'?"

"In that case, we feel," he paused, Cara-Marie looked at him, he carried on, "it would probably be better if you withdrew and were not involved." Cara-Marie stood up.

"What?"

"It's just, this is not the kind of thing …."

"*Are you fucking kidding me!*" Cara-Marie had raised her voice, it stopped him cold. He looked at her, moving his hands in front of him in a patting motion trying to calm her down.

"Look, Cara,"

"*Don't call me that! It isn't my name! you call me 'Cara-Marie' or better still!*" she took and single step back as she finished her sentence. "Don't call me at all!"

"Look, I didn't mean it like that!"

"Well, what did you mean?" Cara-Marie folded her arms,

"What I meant was, I am just trying to help you as this could get quite emotional and we all know you can overreact from time to time,"

"*Pardon???*" Sam did not notice her face was starting to turn red as he carried on.

"I mean, I am just looking out for your career."

"*My Career?*"

"And we think it is better if you don't do the interview as they may 'push your emotional buttons' as they say."

"Wha …" Cara-Marie's mouth opened in disbelief.

"I am just trying to prevent you from saying or doing anything that could harm what we are trying to do here," she stared at him, he carried on without pausing, "and they will try and get a reaction from you, which, being a woman … will probably be easy, then …"

"*GET OUT!*" Cara-Marie jumped forward and slammed both of her hands into his chest, Sam fell backwards through the doorway into the living room.

"Now wait …" it was almost a whisper compared to the volume of her voice. Her right hand grabbed his left shoulder and spun him around.

"*GET OUT!*" she pushed his back towards the entrance to the doorway.

"Cara, wait," two hands slammed into his back again pushing him into the hallway.

"*I said, get out,*" she pushed him again, "*Get out.*"

"Ok, Ok," he held his hands up in a mock surrender, "I'm going," he reached up and unlocked her front door. The door opened and another push sent him outside. The door could not have been slammed any harder. Standing outside, Sam looked around and composed himself. He turned and looked all around, there was no one to be seen. He adjusted his top and walked back over to his car. Sam did not acknowledge the car that was parked a short distance away until he was driving past, the driver nodded once in return, it was time to go. Cara-Marie was standing by the window in her living room in a rage. She fought to control her breathing; it took a couple of minutes for her to calm down. She paced, something about his whole visit was not right. She was concerned. Then suddenly her eyes widened at the realisation in her head. Slowly she walked over to her handbag. She found her phone then looked around again, she was now convinced. Cara-Marie headed to her front door and as she opened the door held the phone to her ear, she heard the ringing tone then the voice as it was answered.

"Hi, before you ask, yes I am still at my desk as I didn't bunk off early!" Mark joked.

"What are you doing right now?" she demanded.

"What?" he sounded almost sheepish.

"What are you doing '*right now!*" she repeated.

"Err," he paused, "about to go home, why?"

"Right, come round here as soon as you can,"

"Ok are you alright?" he asked. Cara-Marie was walking away from her front door.

"Yes, yes, I am fine!" she looked around, there was no one sitting in parked cars, no one standing around, everything seemed normal.

"Well, I was just about to head home, can it wait?"

"No, it's just ...." She thought for a moment, "I am having a takeout and I know you would love some!"

"Err, I already have some chicken left out .... Are you sure you are, ok?" he asked again. She was getting frustrated again.

"Look, just come around here and I will tell you all!"

"Ok, I'm on my way." She did not say anything else and ended the call. She paced up and down for a while outside the building where her flat was, a passing car beeped their horn and from inside a hand was raised in greeting, Cara-Marie waved back, but she did not recognise the car, it carried on to the main road heading back towards Coleraine.

It seemed like an age before Mark pulled up, she stomped towards him. As he was opening the door to get out, she arrived beside him.

"Where is your phone?" she demanded; Mark was a little taken aback.

"It is in my pocket!" he replied. Mark had a confused look on his face, it was obvious Cara-Marie was furious about something, she looked around again. As she looked at him, she gave him the first instruction.

"Right, leave it in the car," she reached into her own pocket and pulled out her own phone, "if fact, lock this one in the car as well!" Mark took her phone and released his seat belt.

"Ok, sure, we can do that, are you going to tell me what is going on?" he asked as he started to get out of the car.

"In a minute," Cara-Marie stepped back as Mark stood up. He looked at her, he was concerned. "Right lock your car and come over here," she instructed as she turned and walked towards her flat. Mark glanced around then shut the door of his car. The central locking bleeped, and he walked over to where she was standing looking impatient. It anyone was walking or driving past it would have looked like two people just having a conversation, but there was only one person doing all the taking, anyone watching would have seen the man agree with whatever the woman had just said then watch as the two of them walked over to the small set of steps that led up to her front door, no one would have thought anything else.

The front door opened, and Mark slowly walked in. He stopped halfway up the short hallway, Cara-Marie walked in after him and shut the door behind her. Neither of them spoke. Mark looked back over his shoulder and nodded once before he slowly started to walk towards the living room. Cara-Marie took deliberate steps but stopped in the doorway, she watched as he slowly started to walk around the living room. He would stop and look back at her, Cara-Marie pointed with her right forefinger exactly where Sam had been, Mark nodded then started to look around. Cara-Marie watched as Mark slowly made his way along where she had traced, he would stop and lower himself down and look under the coffee table. He rose and looked at the light shade on the light above him, he slowly went over towards the tv. He looked underneath the wooden stand it was on, he looked around one side, then the other. This time he stopped. Cara-Marie felt herself breathe in as Mark stood up, he had something small in his right hand. He held his grip tight. Mark looked at her and nodded once, he then carried on with his slow search around the living room, Cara-Marie pointed towards the kitchen, Mark's head looked over towards the door, then he looked back at her, again only nodding once. He moved slowly, as if he was walking through something delicate. As he got to the door of the kitchen he stopped as Cara-Marie joined him. She stood beside him and traced with her right finger again, where Sam had been, Mark again nodded and stepped into the kitchen. He moved slowly and quietly, kneeling, and looking around. He moved the small bin, then quietly replaced it exactly where it had been. He moved over to the counter and lowered himself down, so he was on one knee. Cara-Marie saw him stop. He slowly reached out and extending his fingertips, reached towards the underside of the counter. Cara-Marie again took a small breath in when he removed the small electronic item that had been placed there. Mark stood up and looked directly at her. She stepped back and allowed him to move past her. She followed him back through the living room and back outside. Mark stopped her from leaving her flat. He held a single finger up to his mouth; he moved his lips as if to make the 'ssshhh!' sound but no sound came out. She looked at him and watched as he turned around and made his way down the steps and over to near his car where there was a public bin attached to the side of one of the lampposts. She watched as he opened his hands into the mouth of the bin then step back. He waved to her to approach as he walked towards his car. He opened the driver's door and reached in to pick up her phone. As he turned around, she was trotting towards him with a smile on her face.

"So," he said as he held the phone out to her, she smiled as she took it.

"Thanks, I guessed that sneaky fucker was up to something!" she said, looking at the screen of her phone.

"So, what are you going to do now?" Mark asked.

"Well, I was thinking of getting in touch with my friend Fiona, from the forensic labs down in Belfast, or" she paused as she looked at the screen of her phone.

"No, I meant, what are you going to do for dinner now?" the question made her look up, her eyes widened again.

"Oh, I hadn't considered that!" she exclaimed. Mark grinned sideways.

"Great," he said as he climbed into his car, "I still have chicken out, so," he reached for the seat belt and as he pulled it around him, he looked at her, standing there, mouth open and mind blank. He looked straight at her. "Cara!" her name made her react.

"What?"

"My house, chicken, dinner," he put the keys into the ignition, "get in!" he instructed, and he shut the driver's door. As the engine started Cara-Marie came back to life, then ran around the side of the car and jumped into the passenger seat. Chicken for dinner sounded ok.

Chapter 14

Lucy was sitting in the reception area of the hotel at the top of the Lodge road in Coleraine. She had walked in, turned left, and sat in the large seat that faced the entrance. The seat was uncomfortable, the table was dark stained wood and did not fit with either of the two chairs sitting either side of it. She had been approached by a member of staff who politely took an order for a soft drink from her.

"Yes, I am meeting someone here, it is a business meeting," was how she answered the young man in the fake bow tie, white shirt, and yellow waistcoat with the silver tray when he asked if she was staying at the hotel. The young man said something, but his accent was strong, and she did not understand what he said. He smiled and turned away; it was not long before he had returned with her drink. She had consumed only some of the drink, when one of the phones in her handbag started to buzz. She reached forward and fumbled around until she found which one had the illuminated screen. She lifted it out and read the short message. She dropped the burner phone back into the handbag without replying to it. Lucy sat there and quietly observed different people coming in and out, she looked out through the windows. As she sipped her drink, a figure appeared behind her only a few feet away, she looked up at the older man in a suit.

"Hi," he started, he walked closer to her chair, she moved her arm before he could brush against it, "May I join you?" he said with a smile on his face that made her skin crawl. It was a light-coloured suit, with a cream-coloured shirt that was open at the neck, he was plump around the waist as the belt of his trousers were strained around him. He pushed the chair back and sat down; the chair moved a few inches rearwards with his weight. He had a sleezy smile and he had not shaved that day, his skin was slightly darker as the result of a recent tan, his hair had been dyed but his eyebrows had not, he was trying hard to hide his age, her eyes darted to the single white band on his finger where his wedding ring had only just been removed from.

"No," she stated. She placed her glass on the table as he sat back in the chair.

"Well, darlin …. I don't think such a good-lookin' lass like you should be left alone!" he ogled her up and down. Her face was emotionless.

"No, you cannot join me, so," she looked directly at him, "leave me alone, besides I am waiting for someone." The man smirked, the difference in their accents was vast, she was not from around here, he liked that.

"Well, if they are stupid enough to leave such a fine-lookin' woman alone in a bar, then hey, fair game!" He went to sit forward when Lucy turned in her chair and raised her left arm. The young waiter who had served her earlier walked towards her. Before the waiter could speak, she raised her voice, several heads around the reception turned towards her when she spoke.

"Yes, can you call the police, this man here," her right hand had the palm uppermost with the fingertips pointing towards him, "has sat down uninvited and is harassing me and making me feel very uncomfortable …."

"Hey, wait a minute …" he started to protest, the young waiters mouth opened, he had obviously never been in this situation before, "you obviously don't know who I am!" the man continued, turning his face up.

"Please leave me alone!" Lucy raised her voice again, this time she sat back, pulled her legs towards her, and wrapped her arms around her torso, as if she was giving herself a hug.

"Aaaahhh," was the only sound the young waiter was able to make, his head looked back at the reception for support. One of the senior members head had shot up at what Lucy had said, in fact, every head in the reception looked over at them. The waiter stepped back, the senior staff member spoke to another member of staff and motioned for the waiter to return to reception as they headed towards Lucy's table.

"Hey, listen here love …" the man sat forward, there was anger in his voice now, his drink landed on the table and both of his hands were above the edge of the table, "I was just wanting to give you the chance to have a drink with me …" The waiter had backed away, the senior staff member was walking straight toward them, Lucy looked the man in the eyes, and she had a stern look on her face. She spoke no more than a whisper without moving her lips, it was loud enough for him to hear, but quiet enough that the waiter didn't.

"*fuuck ….offff!*" The man's eyes widened, just as the staff member arrived and Lucy's demeaner changed to seeming relief.

"Excuse me, Ma'am, but is there a problem?" the senior staff member stood near her chair and leaned forward slightly, Lucy raised her voice and her pitch, she extended her left hand so it touched the arm of the sleeve of the staff members blazer.

"Oh, I am so glad you are here," she looked slightly shocked and motioned with her right hand towards the man sitting opposite her, "I was just sitting here, waiting for my friend when this brute just decided to sit down and start harassing me!"

"Hang on here …" he protested as he sat up,

"I mean you can check you cctv … he just accosted me, totally uninvited!" Lucy looked almost childlike, "all I want is for him just to leave me alone!" Lucy looked up at the receptionist, who had a stern look on his face.

"I never did any of that …." The man continued to protest.

"Mr Hutchins," the receptionist interrupted him, "I have to ask you to return to where you were seated and leave other patrons alone, please!" The receptionist started to raise his voice as he did so.

"What!" Mr Hutchins exclaimed.

"Just please make him go away," Lucy added, making sure the other tables heard her.

"Now just hold on a minute!" Mr Hutchins was adamant he looked around for support but got none.

"Mr Hutchins, now, if you please!" the receptionist stepped back and extended his left hand back towards the reception desk. Lucy looked at him. With her right eye she winked at him then turned back to the receptionist.

"He tried to touch me, I said no but …" as she spoke the front door opened and two members of the security team arrived, two more walked through from the bar, everyone stood in a semi-circle around the table.

"*MR HUTCHINS, I MUST INSIST!*" the receptionist raised his voice. Mr Hutchins glared at her then pushed his chair back in anger.

"Fine!" he spat. He grabbed his drink and as he stood up two of the security staff stepped back to allow the angry man past. Lucy again touched the arm of the receptionist.

"Oh, thank you," she said as the small crowd started to walk away.

"It is no problem," he paused, she spotted him glance at her hand and noticed the absence of any jewellery, "on behalf of the hotel I apologise for his behaviour," he continued.

Lucy smiled at him, "thank you again for your help."

"If I can be of any assistance at all," the receptionist straightened up, "you can find me at reception!" he stated. Her eyes glanced at the shiny name badge, but she was not great at some of the Irish spelling.

"Oh, thank you, and who may I ask for?"

"Fergal," he answered with a reassuring smile.

"Well, thank you again, Fergus,"

"Fergal.!" he corrected.

"Oh, sorry," she blushed, she looked away, then looked back at him, "Fergal!"

"Ma'am," Fergal nodded then walked away. Lucy looked around, the two other tables closest to her quickly emptied and Mr Hutchins was escorted out of the reception area. Lucy smiled a mischievous smile then settled back in her uncomfortable chair and lifted her drink.

"Bravo on the over dramatics!" the female English accent made her look over towards the entrance, Lucy smiled but did not move as the shorter woman with black hair walked over and sat on the chair opposite.

"Hi Nikki, you saw?" Lucy smirked. Nikki leaned forward and rested her elbows on the table, she lowered her voice as she replied.

"You do remember we are not supposed to draw attention to ourselves!" there was a small grin on her face, Lucy leaned towards her.

"I just wanted rid of that dickhead, and quickly," Lucy set her drink on the table. "Speaking of dickheads, how did it go?" Nikki glanced around and shook her head at the approaching waiter, he turned and walked away.

"He made a complete mess of it," Nikki was annoyed.

Lucy looked at her, then at her drink, "What happened?" she quietly asked.

"Well, he pissed the journalist off so much she actually threw him out the front door!" Lucy felt her body cringe, "I think we have lost her as a source," Nikki carried on.

"Did he manage to do it?" Lucy asked, Nikki shook her head.

"After she had been screaming at him to 'get out, get out' and shoved him out the front door she called that photographer friend of hers round, and he ...." Nikki reached forward and lifted Lucy's drink.

"Hey!" Lucy responded as Nikki took a mouthful, nearly emptying the glass as she did so. Nikki set the glass back down in front of Lucy as she continued.

"He .... IS electronically aware!"

"What makes you think that?" Lucy asked.

"He found both devices almost straight away," Nikki sat back and shrugged, "he took them outside then through them in a bin." Lucy looked at her.

"Have we recovered them?" Lucy asked. Nikki sat forward again and smiled.

"Yeah, Bob wasn't too happy about it, but yes, we got them." Lucy frowned and looked down at her glass. "We need to get rid of him, he has caused nothing but trouble since he got here!" Nikki stated, Lucy nodded.

"Yeah, but 'Six' demanded to be involved," she said quietly.

"So," Nikki stated.

"So .... What?" Lucy asked. Nikki sat forward.

"May I offer a 'suggestion'?" Nikki raised her eyebrows as she said it.

"You may,"

"You are the team leader, you can go to the chief and ask to get him moved," Lucy looked at Nikki, Nikki shrugged her shoulders again, "call it what you will .... Causing disruption to inter-agency co-operation, for example." Lucy nodded again, "I hear one of ..." Nikki's eyes darted around, there was no one nearby, she then looked back at Lucy. "I hear one of the 'hangar boys' nearly punched him recently!" Lucy smiled at what Nikki had said.

"Yeah, I was there, I thought it would take the coppers to split them up,"

"Well," Nikki asked, "what are you going to do about him?"

"I am in with the Chief 9AM tomorrow morning!" Both of them smiled, then Lucy continued, "but you let me deal with that, I want you and the others focused on this documentary, I want as much detail as we can get!"

"I'm on it!" Nikki smiled "do we know who is making it? Who are the producers?"

"Yeah, I'll send you an email later with what we have so far,"

"Thanks," Nikki replied, she glanced around again, "and 'bravo' on your amateur dramatics, it was quite convincing!" she said with a smile. Lucy just smiled as Nikki pushed the chair backwards, stood up and headed back out the main entrance. Lucy sat back and looked out the window. It would be another ten minutes before she finished her drink and walked back to the car. There was something she wanted to do before she went back to Belfast tonight.

∞∞∞∞∞

It was dark outside as Tony drove along the familiar road heading back to his house. He glanced at the digital display on the dashboard, it was 21:58, there were two more minutes until it would be ten in the evening, and he had told Karen that he would be home by ten. Tony felt safe, the job would not be too much of a problem, but he would still discuss it with Karen. He slowed and turned into the driveway in front of their house. Karen's small car was parked to one side with the Land Rover that Becky and Fiona had beside it which they called 'The Disco'. Tony turned the car around and reverse parked beside them. He trotted up the steps to his front door with the keys still in his hand. Outside was not cold, but the inside of the house was still warm and welcoming. He closed the front door and was able to kick off his trainers as he hung his jacket up. The living room light was on, but there was no one in there. The door to the kitchen was open and there was a hum of conversation coming from inside. He walked up and filled the doorway, resting his hands on the top of the frame. He smiled at what was going on inside. Karen was sitting by the table with the baby car seat in the middle of the table, it faced the other way, he intuitively knew the baby was asleep. Karen had a magazine in her hands and was engrossed in whatever the article was. Fiona stood by the sink washing different trays and baking utensils, Becky was nowhere to be seen. Fiona looked around and her face broke with a huge smile.

"Hiya," she beamed.

"Hi," he stopped by Fiona and looked at what she was cleaning, "and what have you been baking this time?" he asked.

"What has she been 'trying' to bake you mean!" Karen stated.

"Well?" he asked, Fiona shrugged.

"I was trying to do one of those multi-layered cakes like you see on that baking show on TV!" she replied as she returned to her clean-up.

"Let me guess ...." Tony started as he headed towards Karen.

"We need some new baking trays!" Karen stated.

"Why?" he asked, "what is wrong with the ones we have?" Karen leaned over to her left and was looking at Fiona.

"Yes, Fiona, why do we need new baking trays!" Karen was smiling as she spoke, it was good to see her like this. Fiona muttered something Tony didn't hear.

"Well, we can sort that tomorrow," Tony pulled one of the chairs that was tucked under the table and sat down. He looked around. "Where is Becky?"

"Packing," Fiona stated as she lifted a large bowl out of the sink, water flowed off it, then she placed it upside down on the drainer.

"Oh, you know about your move then?" he stated, Fiona smiled at him.

"Yeah, Dad phoned earlier after you had left," Fiona dried her hands on a small towel, "we are not being replaced here and we are needed back at the farm!"

"I agreed," Karen injected, Tony glanced at her, "having the girls here has been great, and they have been such a help with the baby, but it's time for us to do things ourselves,"

Tony leaned forward and slowly pulled the small blanket back from the face of the sleeping baby, he could not help the loving smile that shone from his face. "He is so beautiful," it was almost a whisper, Karen leaned into him, resting her head on his shoulder.

81

"I'll go help Becks," Fiona stated as she headed out of the kitchen.

"It will be nice to have the house to ourselves again," Karen spoke quietly.

"It will," he answered. Karen sat up.

"So, what job have they got for you?" she asked, Tony sat back and looked at her.

"Simple one really," he started as he took her hand in his, she relaxed.

"Ok, don't keep me in suspense then!" she joked.

"They want me to do as much research on Alison as I can,"

"Alison? Which one is Alison?"

"Used to be a copper in Coleraine, the one who ...." Tony felt his voice trail off.

"Oh, her," Karen stated, Tony felt her grip tighten.

"All I have to do is research as much as I can, sightings, movements, etc and see what I can dig up," Karen wasn't looking at him, instead she looked over at the sleeping child.

"He is so peaceful,"

"I can do nearly all of that from here!" he stated, she looked at him, the concern fell from her face and her eyes sparkled.

"Really?" she exclaimed.

"Really, really."

"Do you know where to start?" she asked, her grip relaxed.

"Yes," Tony looked out the door of the kitchen at the burst of laughter coming from one of the girl's rooms, then looked back at Karen. "Tyler gave me a USB drive with photos, a spreadsheet of sightings, descriptions etc. All I have to do is go through it and find her pattern."

"Her pattern?" Karen asked.

"Yeah, where she has been, possible people she may be or have been in contact with, you know, carry out an investigation." Tony smiled as he said the last bit, "remember, what I used to do for a living." He started to lean towards her, Karen leaned in as well, closing her eyes as she did so. The two heads touched; Tony felt the deep connection with his wife.

"Well, Mr investigator," she opened her eyes and straightened up "How about you put your son to bed, then before you start 'investigating' another woman, you spend some time 'investigating' your wife!" Karen had a cheeky smile on her face,

"So, Mrs Fallon," he giggled as the two of them gently kissed, "are you saying you will fully co-operate with my investigation?" the two closed their eyes and kissed again.

"With the second one, yes," their lips met again. The blanket covering the baby moved, a small hand appeared, and a short noise came from the small mouth. The two broke off their kiss and looked at their son, they then looked at each other.

"I will put him down now," Tony whispered.

"I'll be waiting," she whispered into his ear then stood up then walked out of the kitchen. Tony picked up the baby seat by the handle with one hand, he followed his wife out of the kitchen switching the light off as he went. Fiona peered around the half open door to her room and watched as Karen walked into their bedroom, Tony had the baby and slowly went into the baby's room. She looked back over her shoulder at her sister who was sitting on the bed with her phone in her hands.

"Well, they are sorting themselves out." Fiona quietly closed the door and headed to the main wardrobe of her room. "We still have to do the final security checks around the house!"

"Yeah, we can do that in a minute," Becky said as she tapped away at the screen. Fiona opened the wardrobe door and started to rummage through some of her clothes, "I think I need to do some clothes shopping before we head back to the farm!" Fiona stated as she lifted out a jumper and examined it.

"So," Becky stated as she dropped her phone onto the bed, "Tell me about this new man you have then!"

Chapter 15   Limerick City, Republic of Ireland.

She was leaning over the stone wall of the ancient bridge with her elbows resting on the cold stone, the river flowed underneath, to her left was the old castle, it looked like it was from Norman times. Her eyes looked to the right, she looked at the old stone building she had walked past earlier. Traffic moved behind her, the wind blew over the bridge lifting her long jet-black hair out behind her, it flowed in the wind. She looked up at the stars then back down at the water. She pushed back her sleeve, looked at the time. She felt them approaching, she stared forward and took a deep breath in through her nose, she could smell them. They smelt of a pub, she could smell the beer and cigarette smoke from them, and it was getting stronger as they got closer to her. She glanced down at her feet then back up again. She was wearing old running shoes, dark blue trousers that showed off her legs perfectly. The Light blue denim shirt loosely hung from her slender frame; it was open at the front to reveal a light tan top. The wind became still as they approached; she could feel their leering.

"Would ya look at dis!" she looked over at them. Both of them were on a night out, they both looked the same age, similar shoes, and jeans, one had a plain cotton shirt on. The other had a striped shirt on. The one who had spoken extended his arms, she guessed by his accent he was local. "De almighty has blessed us by sendin' down one of his angels," they were both already merry, she straightened up and turned to face them but kept herself pressed up against the stonework of the bridge.

"And a mighty fine wan at dat!" the other spoke, she smiled and seemed embarrassed, her light blue eyes looked down as the ground then back up at the two in front of her.

"Thank you that is very nice of you," she replied.

"You are not from Limerick, are you?" the first one asked.

"The far side of Bunratty, so not that far!" she smiled.

"What brings you into da city den?" the first one asked, she looked at the second guy, he just seemed to smile a lot but not talk much.

"Well, I was supposed to meet someone, but they didn't turn up!"

"What? De fecker, der loss," the first one remarked.

"What are you for doin' now?" the second one finally spoke.

"Well, I was just thinking about heading home,"

"Ah Jaysus sure dat would be a shame," he looked at his friend, "why not come with us?" he smiled, his friend agreed.

"Oh, thank you, well, that may save the night yet," she smiled and seemed to relax, "but first what are your names?" she asked the louder one first.

"King John!" his voice grew louder at the exclamation.

"King John?" she asked, she pulled a quizzical look to add to her question.

"His name isn't John King, but dat is what he tells everyone!" the second one added.

"I am 'King John', King of all Limerick!"

"Yeah, there is even a statue of him in the city!" his friend added, he leaned in closer to her, "you can tell it is him as he is holding the sword the wrong way around."

"I have seen that statue," she smiled.

"And only 'dis' King John would try and fight off the English with a sword the wrong way around!" he was looking at his friend as he joked.

"Ah Jaysus, Michael, would ya do a man a favour and leave him be when he is with a princess!" the jovial John stepped forward and offered his hand, "and who might you be my lovely?" she smiled and slightly blushed at the compliment.

"Megan," the two shook hands,

"Megan Due," she added.

"Well, it is lovely to meet you," John bowed his head as he released the handshake, he straightened up and stepped back and waved his hand towards Michael, "and dis eejit here is the very poor, and very less well endowed, …. Michael!"

"Hey!" Michael protested. Megan extended her hand towards him.

"Nice to meet you Michael," she looked him in the eyes, she saw his eyes widen as they looked back at her, Michael was smitten.

"Ah, nice to meet you as well," the handshake lasted longer than the first one did.

"Hey, if I could break you two up," Megan released her grip and smiled at Michael, John extended his left arm towards the road that led past the castle and away from the bridge. "We were just heading to one of Limerick's finest establishments," he straightened himself up and placed his left hand in the centre of his chest, "and you would be doing us an honour by accompanying us!" John had closed his eyes and had a mock regal look on his face, Megan lifted her fingertips to her lips and giggled at the same time. Michael stepped forward so he was in front of John, he was directly facing her.

"Forget him, would you like a drink?" he asked, Megan started nodding as she spoke.

"Yes, of course, that would be lovely." Michael turned and started to walk along the bridge, Megan walked beside him, smiling at his chatter. John joined them, walking beside his friend. "Hey, I just had a thought," Megan stated, "my car is just over there!" she said pointing further down the road, "I know a wee country pub that I think both of you would love," the two men exchanged a glance and both their eyes widened.

"Ah, that would be grand," answered Michael.

"Being whisked away by a beauty from Bunratty, can this evening get any better?" John almost shouted. Megan nudged Michael, he looked into her smiling face.

"Yes, I am sure this even can get better," she almost whispered, winking at him at the same time. Michael thought he was about to explode with excitement.

It took longer than she wanted to get out of the city, but they were now making speed and distance along the Old Cratloe road. There was no other traffic on the road as they drove past the old country club. They carried on into the night. The open space either side of them was soon replaced by a stone wall on the left that protected a house and a row of tree on her right. Michael was sitting in the front seat with the louder John in the back, she laughed when they joked and blushed when they complimented her. The tree's stood tightly either side of the road, the darkness closed in on the car, the trees were replaced by a thick hedge. Megan slowed then turned into the open gap that led into the field, her headlight cut through the night.

"Ahh, where are we going?" Michael asked. Megan kept turning the car until it was parked along the hedge facing the tree. The headlights went out and she turned off the engine.

"Well, you have come here to party, right?" Megan winked at him as she released her seat belt, "so let's party!"

"Oh, Micky boy!" John exclaimed from the back seat; Michael looked shocked for a brief moment then got excited as he released his own seat belt. John was already fighting with the belt on his jeans. Megan turned in her seat to face Michael.

"Now wait a second!" she held up the palm of her right hand, "not in here," she glanced at John, "and certainly only one at a time!" John bounced with excitement.

"Yes, yes, dat's grand!" John could not believe his luck; Michael was grinning like an excited teenager. Megan pointed with one finger of her right hand.

"Michael, you and I can head over to the corner of the field," she looked at John, "I will call you when it is ok for you to come over,"

"Aye, sure, no problems," John replied, Megan pointed at John.

"No lights, no phones, no cameras, ok!"

"Ok, sure," John grinned back. Megan opened the car door and stepped out into the night. She heard John talking to Michael. "Oh my God, I can't believe our luck in meetin' her, dis is brilliant!" Michael agreed with him. Megan walked in front of the car; she could not hide her own excitement. Megan walked forward adding a slight sway to her hips as she did so, Michael had to jog the short distance to catch her up. She looked at the excitement in his face.

"Megan dis is ...." She reached out and touched his right arm, her face filled with lust and craving, Michael took a breath in when she saw it.

"Ssshh!" she said as she walked on. Michaels eyes moved down her body, he could feel his own excitement growing, his heart was beating faster, and his breath had quickened as well. Megan walked over the grass of the field, her own breathing had quickened, she looked back at him passionately, then looked forward. She opened her mouth to take a deeper breath in, "I am sooo glad I met you," it was just above a whisper.

"And I you," he replied as his right hand reached out, his fingertips brushed over her shoulder and down her arm, a breeze lifted her long black hair. She opened her mouth to suck in the air, her own heart was pounding as she opened her mouth a little further, just to let her incisors in her upper mouth start to elongate, she felt the anticipation that had been rising almost explode. Michael could hear her breathing in and out through her nose and mouth, this girl was working herself up like he had never seen before, then they reached the corner of the field.

John was sitting in the back of the car, he had opened the window when the muffled sounds started, he could hear his friend scream with excitement, it made him more excited than he first was. He felt himself slap his own thigh; it would be his turn with the beauty from Bunratty soon. Then she called his name, King John could not get out of the car quick enough.

∞∞∞∞

Tyler shuffled into the kitchen; her dressing gown was loosely hanging off her with her plain pyjamas underneath. She looked dishevelled with her eyes hardly open. Rhydian walked in from the living room, she had not slept much either, both of them exchanged a nod then Rhydian walked on and headed for the stairs.

"Is he asleep?" Rhydian croaked. Tyler did not answer the question.

"There is some tea in the pot,"

Rhydian turned to walk away, "I am going back to bed!" and with that she was gone, thumping back up the stairs. Tyler stood in the quietness of the kitchen. It was slow movements, shuffling, not walking as she made her way around and prepared her own breakfast. In seemed like an age before she was sitting there with an empty cereal bowl in front of her and a half-consumed mug of tea. She was too tired to even taste it. She raised her head then slowly stood up, with careful shuffling she lifted the bowl and the mug and headed over towards the sink, the rest of the tea was poured down the plughole. She used her foot to open the door of the empty dishwasher. The mug, the bowl and the spoon landed inside, then she closed the door again. She was about to head back upstairs when the front door opened.

"Helloo," it was Paul.

"In here," she said. Paul walked into the kitchen. He paused and looked at her.

"Someone didn't sleep well," it was a statement not a question. Tyler shuffled over and sat down on the chair by the kitchen table. Paul took the chair opposite her.

"The baby was up most of the night," she explained.

"I spotted movement when I was walking past, so I thought I would pop in."

"Anything up?" she asked as she sat back in the chair.

85

"The farm is running ok, minor issues but we are sorting them," Paul looked at her, she was just about registering what he was saying, "I was chatting with John, the paramedic," he paused, Tyler looked up, "he's written an extensive trauma course he's going to run for us, so given time, everyone will be trained instead of just a few!"

"Yeah, that sounds like a good idea!"

Paul pushed his chair backwards as he stood up, "I will leave you to get some sleep then," He headed for the living room, stopping as he got there and looked back. "Don't forget about tonight, we should leave mid-afternoon." Tyler looked up with a blank expression.

"What?" it was louder than a whisper, but only just.

"The South is holding a Grand Moon Dance tonight hosting the two council members and they've invited several other packs to attend. We chatted about this yesterday!"

"Yes, yes," she placed her hands on the table and stood up, "I remember,"

"They have sorted accommodation for us but want us there before teatime."

"Yeah, sure," her accent was tinged with Canadian; that happened when she was tired. She blinked slowly, "no, problem, I will see you later then."

Paul turned and walked outside into the warm summer morning. He looked around after he had closed the front door of the farmhouse, as an old Land Rover came around the corner, then reverse parked by the barn. Two farm hands were heading out towards the fields. The barn door opened, and a farm hand walked towards him. "Dermott is looking for you,"

"Where is he?" Paul asked, the farm hand pointed back at the open barn door.

"In there,"

"Thanks," Paul headed towards the open door. Dermott came out just as he was getting there, he had a serious look on his face.

"Ah, great," Dermott started.

"What's up?" Paul asked.

"Just heard from the South, possible Noc killing near Limerick last night,"

"So," Paul shrugged, "isn't that their problem?"

"Aye, but this wasn't done by any Nocs they know about!"

"Ok," Paul paused, "if it isn't our problem then why are they telling us about it then?"

"Well, since the ruling they tell us about all Noc activity down south," he started.

"So?" Paul repeated.

"They've had several Noc attacks the last few years by an unknown Noc.

"How does that affect us? "We are dealing with Noc activity on our lands!"

"They asked us to keep an eye out, in case it migrates,"

"Which for a Noc outside of a coven is normal," Paul added.

"Aye, it is, but this one is different!"

"How?" Paul asked.

"All the victims are male between the ages of twenty to thirty years old,"

"The only thing we have had recently was the couple down at Murlough! And the ones that did that got taken out by that fella Apollyon!"

"Aye, they did," Dermott looked down, then looked over to the farmhouse, "are they up yet?" he asked. Paul turned and looked back at the front door of the farm as he replied.

"Yes and no, by the looks of it, the baby had both of them up all night."

"Glad I had my kids years ago!" Dermott stated, Paul looked at him and nodded.

Chapter 16

Paul spotted Tyler as soon as she walked in. Her hair hung down over her slim shoulders and her face was lit with a beaming smile. She was greeted by several members by the door. Paul lifted his hand, she waved back and headed towards him. The bar was not packed but it would be soon, there was a level of excitement you could almost taste. Tyler arrived beside him, Paul was wearing black tie and seemed almost relaxed up against the bar.

"I have never seen this before!" Tyler stated, Paul smirked.

"Not surprising, it was only built about five years ago," Paul used his thumb to point to the double doors at the far end of the bar, "the big hall as well, it was made to look medieval."

"Can't wait to see it," Tyler turned towards the bar and attracted the attention of the bar staff, "Hi, what Gins do you have?" she asked, then looked at Paul, "what do you fancy?" she asked, pointing at his nearly empty glass.

"Brunettes mostly," he smiled as he spoke, "but there has been a couple of blondes though," Tyler looked at him and raised one eyebrow.

"I meant, 'what would you like to drink?'" she asked.

"Oh," he laughed, he pointed to the glass, "same again please!" a long howl echoed through the open windows and the room exploded in cheering.

"THEY GOT THE KILL!!" one excited voice shouted, *"WELL DONE,"* one of the women who was standing near them stated, both Tyler and Paul could not help but join in with the emotion in the room. The bar man placed the two drinks in front of her and Tyler held her credit card towards him, the bar man stood back and raised both his hands.

"Connor says the four from the North are not to pay,"

"Oh!" Tyler exclaimed, she looked at Paul.

"Oh yeah, something else I forgot to say, don't need any of your cards tonight," as Paul lifted his drink he nodded towards the far end of the bar, Tyler lifted hers and followed him through the smartly dressed pack members in the bar. Tyler could easily pick out the small groups of four who were not part of the southern An Rua pack, Tyler was about to say something when the double doors opened, and a single figure walked out. He looked late fifties and was immaculately dressed, he had black polished Brogues, white woollen socks nearly to his knees, Tyler spotted the small, ceremonial dagger that was sticking out the top of one of the socks, His kilt was plain green, with a small broach on it, she recognised the traditional emblem of the An Rua clan. He had a plain white cotton shirt with a draw string front, it was a traditional 'Jacobite' shirt His silver hair was combed back, and he had a very proud look on his face.

"AN RUA ...." He started, *"AN RUA, HONOURED GUESTS, LADIES AND GENTLEMEN,"* his accent was local, the room fell silent as heads turned towards him, *"MAY I HAVE YOUR ATTENTION PLEASE!"* he looked around, and continued, his voice boomed. *"ON BEHALF OF CONNOR O'CONNOR, ALPHA OF THE AN RUA, MAY I WELCOME YOU ALL TO THIS JOYOUS OCCASION!"* Tyler looked around, it was a sea of smiling faces, she looked back at Paul who had just raised his glass in recognition to an older couple who were standing at the bar. *"MAY I INVITE THE HONOURED GUESTS TO REMAIN IN THE BAR AND AN RUA, CAN YOU TAKE YOUR SEATS PLEASE!"* He stepped back and moved to the side of the open doorway as the members moved towards the entrance.

"Guess that's our que!" Paul stated, he nudged Tyler; they followed a group headed in through the entrance. The huge room had a stage to the right, with lights and curtains. It was only slightly raised and the space in front of it had circular shaped tables dotted around it. to the left was the straight top table, there were four steps up to the platform it was on.

"Where are we going to be seated?" Tyler asked. Paul pointed to the steps.

"On the far side of the top table,"

"Really?" her head spun round to look at Paul, "we are really top table tonight?"

"Yes, really," he held his drink in his left hand and extended his right, "after you."

"Thank you," Paul followed her as they made their way along the row of high-back chairs. Tyler noticed the cutlery was polished and set neatly, there was a small plate with a buttering knife placed exactly horizontally on it, there were bottles of red and white wine between every pair of places. She looked at Paul, "you'd think this was one big wedding if you didn't know what it really was!" she walked on, reading the place names as she did so.

"I hear it's used for that as well" Paul stated.

"Really? Wow," they were not at the end but close to it. Tyler stood behind the place setting that had her name on it. Paul walked past and stood behind the next one. Both set their glasses down and watched as the room slowly filled, it did not take long. The room had dark walls with beams of dark stained wood made to look like support struts, the lights hung in small clusters, the tables also had candles surrounded with a floral display; the straight top table had a display the entire length of the front edge.

A couple walked behind the and took up the last two places at the end of the top table. "I'm excited about the show tonight, they have put so much into it!" the woman remarked.

"Oh, I didn't know there was a show as well!" Paul stated.

"Oh yes, it's a new one called 'The Night the North Fought Back!'" Paul and Tyler exchanged glances before all heads turned back to the entrance door.

"AN RUA, PLEASE WELCOME OUR COUNCIL MEMBERS, COUNCILLOR GRISHIN AND COUNCILLOR TATAMOVICH, WITH OUR ALPHA," he stepped back as the sound of bagpipes started, "CONOR AND ORLA O'CONNOR!" The applause started as the piper entered the room, his playing echoed around he marched in and turned to his right, he marched forward a short distance then turned to face the main room, the applause became a rhythmic clap in time with the tune. Behind him was Connor with Grishin, the two were smiling and chatting as they slowly made their way towards the steps, Orla and Tatamovich were right behind them. The piper continued until the four were standing behind their chairs. Connor looked towards the piper who finished his tune and looked towards the top table. As Connor sat down, the room rippled with the rustle of everyone doing the same. Wine was opened and drinks were poured, the room had an excited feel to it. Tyler did not know the one seated beside her, but he knew her, the two stated chatting and she was introduced to his wife beside him. The entrance doors opened again, and Connor rose to his feet, the room went silent again.

"An Rua," he turned and nodded to both council members as he introduced them, "Council members," he turned towards the open doors, "May I ask you to welcome our honoured guests," the applause started again, the entrance door was filled by two young couples, both had white hair, piercing light blue eyes and stern looking faces, all were slim but heavy built, the men's hair was shoulder length and flowed neatly from their heads down onto their shoulders, they held the hands of the women beside them, their hair was the same colour and flowed the same way, they were slim yet powerful, Connor introduced them. "From Siberia, the Siberian Wolves!" the applause grew louder, the first male stopped and nodded towards Connor before smiling and leading the others to four places at a table near the stage, the pattern continued for each set of four pack representatives, each had their own physic and dementor, "All the way from Australia, The Diamondback Garou! ..... from India, The Sikhandi!" Tyler watched as the two couples entered, the darkness of their hair matched the deepness of their skin.

"Wow, those Sari's look amazing!" Tyler commented to Paul.

"I don't think I would suit one!" he replied, Tyler giggled as she imagined it.

"From the Balkans, we are honoured for the first time to welcome, The Silver Eye wolves!" Tyler's head shot up, as four women walked in, stopping as they nodded towards

Connor. All had jet-black hair, even from this distance she could see all four had piercing light blue eyes, there was several shrieks from the gathered pack, Tyler leaned towards Paul.

"I have heard of them, but never met any!"

"Yeah, the only 'all female' pack in the world!" he replied.

"You can nearly smell the testosterone rising!" she stated out loud, the two men either side of her turned and looked at her, neither could reply before Connor spoke again.

"From England, The Iceni Wolves!" The applause continued as the two couples walked in, nodded towards Connor then took their seats, *"From the Russian plains, The Mongol Garou!"* Tyler glanced at Paul, she noticed they were the only ones he did not applaud. *"Finally, from Bavaria, The Magna Germania!"* Tyler looked over at the four Teutonic people who walked in and stopped. None of them were holding hands, unlike the others, they were all dressed the same, none of them smiled. The nod was given and returned, then they quickly headed to their seats, all eyes turned back towards Connor. *"Unfortunately, none of the Great packs from across Canada, the US or from the Middle East could make it this evening, but"* He turned and looked at Grishin, *"we have received messages from all the main packs worldwide! All who could not be here have sent us their best wishes,"* there was a murmur of conversation around the room, *"The first part of our celebration is we have added five new members to our clan!"* there was a cheer from one of the tables and an applause from around the room, Tyler clapped as Connor raised his right hand, *"BRING FORTH THE BEAST AND THE SUCCESSFUL – HUNTING PARTY!"* Everyone turned to the entrance doors as they opened and the piper started to play again, this time Tyler thought she recognised the tune. She watched as four people carried a large wooden platter at shoulder height. The well-prepared body of a deer lay over most of it and was surrounded by garnish, the head wasn't cooked and probably was the beast that had just been culled. Behind it walked five people who were already dressed for the feast, they were all young, if she had to guess late teens, possibly early twenties. All looked proud as they walked in one after the other behind the beast. The platter stopped and the five turned and faced the gathered crowd.

"May I ask our honoured guest to carry out the marking ceremony!" Connor was smiling as he turned to Grishin who nodded and pushed his chair back, smiling as he did so. Grishin walked behind the top table and headed straight for the stag's head. The piper started another tune as Grishin lifted the ceremonial knife and taking a grip of the fur of the neck sliced more than a handful off. Another cheer when up. Grishin placed the knife back on the platter and stopped in front of the first of the hunting party. Quiet words were exchanged, smiles, and handshake then Grishin wiped the fur down both sides of their face, leaving a small trace of blood there. Grishin made his way down the rest of the party repeating the marking on each one. The piper stopped after the last one and Grishin stepped to one side.

"AN RUA!" he shouted, *"your hunting party!"* and the room exploded in joyous applause, From the far side of the room people starting to stand, the movement swept over the room like a wave, Tyler rose as did Paul, the applause continued. Tyler spotted the distinguished man who had started the evening step forward and warmly embrace the youngest of the party, when he stepped back, he was fighting back his tears.

"That is his youngest one there!" Paul said as he leaned towards her. Tyler looked at him and nodded once. The applause died down and everyone started to retake their seats. the beast had been taken to the kitchen and Grishin was just getting back to his seat, Connor was still standing, everyone looked towards him.

"Honoured Council members, honoured guests .... An Rua ...." He raised his glass above his head, *"Tonight! ..... we FEAST!"* The room again started to applaud as he sat down. Tyler's eyes shot to her left as the double doors opened and a steady line of young teenagers

wearing black shoes, black trousers and white shirts all walked towards each table. Each one was carrying a tray with the first course of the meal on it. The feast had begun!

ᗜᗜᗜ

The lights of the Land Rover cut through the night, Ian Silver was driving, John Gold sat quietly in the passenger seat observing everything. They nearly missed the turn off for Dunserverick harbour but found it just in time. The small winding road forced him to slow down even further as they rose up over the crest of the small hill, then the harbour was in front of them. The single building at the harbour was unlit, no one was home. Ian turned the Land Rover around, so it was pointing back out the way they had come in, 'always know how you are leaving' was something both had taught their children. The lights of the Land Rover went out and the engine went quiet, both men got out at the same time, closing the doors without slamming them. John Gold had a small zip bag over his shoulder; he would only remove the shotguns if they needed them. Slowly the two men walked up to the front door of the dark house, Ian went down on one knee and studied the ground, John had stopped several feet back, if the door suddenly opened, he could deal with anything that came out. Ian looked back at him and shook his head, he rose and slowly made his way along the front of the door then around the small wall that surrounded the parked caravan without making a sound, again John kept off to one side. They moved in silence. Ian swept around the side of the wall then under the yellow metal frame that was the entrance to the car park. John looked around, his eyes looked over the empty car park, the building at the rear, the hedgerows, and the hills behind them. Ian slowly made his way along the inside of the wall, He stopped near the small gate that broke the wall, he went down onto one knee, again he studied the ground then looked up, John stepped closer.

"Three," he whispered, John came down beside him and looked at the tracks on the ground. Ian started to point at what he was seeing. "Two male and one female Noc," he looked at John, "but not recently,"

"How long?" he asked.

"At least a week,"

"We can still track them from here," John straightened up and looked at the direction of the tracks. "Looks like they went up behind the toilets!" he stated, Ian stood up.

"Yes, it does," he replied as John stood up beside him.

"Shall we?" John smiled as he slipped the bag off his shoulder.

"Damn right we shall!" They followed the tracks up the wall past the wooden dingy that was upside down and looked like it had not been moved in some time, Ian concentrated of following the tracks, John kept an eye on everything else around them. The sea crashed into the rocks around the small harbour behind them and the wind gently blew. It took another fifteen minutes of slowly moving, tracking, and observing before the two of them where back inside the Land Rover. Ian started the engine as John took out his phone. Ian turned the heater on as John held the phone to his ear.

"Hi Dermott," he started, Ian looked around the outside of the Land Rover, then over as much of the greyness of the night as he could make out, John continued, "aye, we found three sets of tracks and a lair behind Dunserverick harbour, but it was only temporary..." John glanced at Ian, "yeah, at least three weeks, we have put a motion sensor in place if they ever come back .... Ok, yes, we know where to look next .... Aye, all the best," John ended the call then Ian switched on the lights and the Land Rover jumped forward.

"They must be closer to Tony's than we first thought!" Ian stated.

"Aye, must be," John agreed. Ian drove on into the night, this was going to take time.

Back at the harbour among the rocks a figure moved. Jason Apollyon had watched the two wolves sweep the area but had remained hidden. It was obvious the sea had helped cover his presence. He slowly stood up and lifted the large rucksack onto his back. He carefully made his way onto the stone jetty then towards the single house, it only took him seconds with the simple lock on the front then he was inside. The heavy rucksack landed with a thump on the floor, no one had been in here in over a month. He would sleep warmly tonight.

stage. He had fair hair that moved as he danced, he also looked like he was also in his early twenties, but his skill as a dancer was clear. Tyler leaned towards Paul.

"Looks nothing like Kyle! Was Kyle an Irish dancer?" she asked.

"No, watched him try it once at one of our dances …" Paul looked at her face, he smiled as he answered, "let's just say, it didn't go well!" there was a laugh at the end. They both looked back at the stage as he came to a stop right in the middle, the music was perfectly timed to stop just as he did. He looked straight at where Connor was sitting, the applause roared and was mixed with cheers. The dancer stood and accepted the well-deserved adoration of the audience, he was the hero of the story after all. He stood with his arms outstretched, fighting for breath at the same time. As the applause started to quieten down his left hand moved to his hip, and he extended his right hand towards the side of the stage where he had entered from. The music started again, the tune was a softer one, it was introducing another dancer. She came on the stage and danced her way across towards where 'Kyle' was standing, she had a black velvet dress that stopped just at the top of her thighs, her thin legs were covered in thick black tights. The front of the dress had an embroidered Celtic pattern of many colours. Her hair was short and blonde and did not seem to move, but the smile shone from her face, her arms were by her side as she danced her routine, Tyler did not notice that her feet had started to tap along.

"The alpha had chosen one to be by his side," the female dancer stopped right beside him, the mist from earlier had gone, the stage was clear, the intricate footwork was for all to see. The two looked at each other, smiled, their hands reached out and their fingertips touched, then their arms slammed against their sides and the two started dancing in perfect unison. The music picked up pace as they playfully danced around, their faces full of joy as they faced each other, a love story was being told. Tyler and Paul looked at each other and they both said the same thing at the same time.

"Amanda had black hair!" the two shared a laugh as the dance continued. The 'Kyle' dancer left the stage the way he had entered from, and the female dancer continued. Her dance slowed, her movements were slower, she used her arms a lot more. She was being sensual with her story; Tyler was smiling watching the graceful performance. The music flowed with the rhythm of the dance, here was another very skilful dancer. She danced from the centre of the stage over towards the side of the stage, she slowed and moved her hands as if she was touching the tree silhouetted at the end of the stage. The music changed back to the tune of the Nocs.

"They waited until she was alone, defenceless, then they struck!" Tyler felt her eyebrows raise as 'Sabine' and the Nocs jumped back onto the stage.

"Of all the words I would have used to describe Amanda, 'defenceless' is not it!" Tyler laughed. 'Amanda' danced back towards the centre of the stage, her smile was gone, she looked concerned, she looked from side to side as the Noc dancers formed a semi-circle behind her, 'Sabine' stayed to one side as 'Amanda' danced towards one side, she would be challenged by two Noc dancers who would force her back to the centre, this was repeated several times until all the Noc dancers stopped. 'Amanda' was still and looked at 'Sabine' 'Sabine' stepped towards her and started a dance, the two danced in unison moving for one side of the front of the stage to the other, battle had commenced. The mist again flowed over the stage, 'Sabine' withdrew, and 'Amanda' danced towards her when all of the Noc dancers joined in, they all moved towards her, then throwing her arms up, 'Amanda' disappeared into the mist. There was a noise of disapproval from the audience, the dancers all formed up again and danced around.

"They struck at beauty, they thought they had beaten us," the mist started to clear as the dancers all left the stage, the music changed again, it was slow and sombre. 'Kyle' slowly walked forward, he stopped at each step, he looked distressed, he looked from side to side as if searching, Tyler felt herself well up, he searched to the left, he searched to the right, then he

stopped at the spot-on stage where she had fallen. He went down on one knee, his fists touched the floor either side of his feet, he stared at the empty space.

"*But he was strong,*" he slowly stood up right, but still looked down, "*he drew on the strength of his ancestors,*" he slowly raised his head, the look of sorrow slowly changing to a look of anger, "*he knew he could call on his own,*" His head shot over to the side of the stage as he stretched out his right hand, calling on someone hidden from view, "*there was a warrior who would stand with him, to fight as a pack!*" The music bounded in excitement; a loud cheer went up as he shouted from the centre of the stage.

"*TYLER ... COME FORTH!*" Tyler felt herself move in her chair as the young dancer leapt forward. She landed on the stage and started a dance as she moved towards the outstretched hand. Her hair was dark auburn, similar to her own, but the dancer, like the others was very young. Her dress was similar to 'Amanda's, her dance was energetic and full of vigour. Her hands and her feet moved at such speed, her energy followed from the stage, the audience was captivated. Paul leaned in to say something, but Tyler spoke first.

"God, I wish I was that young!" she smiled. 'Kyle' pulled the dancer closer to him, like a puppet master he turned his finger, and she spun around, she moved up beside him then stopped, both dancers looked at each other then they looked towards the audience extending their hands as they did so. The room exploded in clapping and cheering. When the clapping quietened down, the music started again and both dancers ran off the side of the stage. The music changed back to let everyone know that the Nocs were about to appear back on stage. 'Sabine' led the group dancing their way to the middle of the stage, they formed up behind her and danced a short routine. Tyler looked at Paul, he was staring at the stage, there was a grin on his face but there was still a stern look in his eyes, the dance continued.

"*They gathered their strength ... they gathered for a strike, but near the sea is where they would fall!*" The music changed again as 'Tyler' led several dancers, all of whom wore black trousers and light green silk shirts, 'Tyler' was at the front of the green shirts and 'Sabine' in front of the dark dancers. They all danced in unison then all stopped. 'Tyler' and 'Sabine' looked at each other on stage, Tyler shifted in her chair, Paul spotted it, he glanced at her.

"Not exactly White Park Bay is it!'" He stated, he heard her let out a short laugh.

"No, it isn't!" The two groups started a dance off, then they all joined back together, Tyler watched as the wolf dancers slowly one at a time danced towards a dancer with a black shirt, when they danced past them, the dancer with the black shirt would turn their back to the audience and go down on one knee. This happened until 'Sabine' was standing on her own over at the edge of the stage. 'Sabine' looked at 'Tyler' and held up one finger.

"*The challenge was made,*" The narrator stated, the dancer who was playing Tyler answered by holding up one finger of her left hand in reply, "*and the challenge was accepted!*" the voice of the narrator increased with excitement.

The dancers in the green shirts moved towards the back of the stage, the lights dimmed, and two white lights shone down on each of them, the dance off started. Each took turns, they danced towards each other, then backed off as the opposite one stood still. They both performed high kicks and a very technical dance. The dances got faster, each out doing the other when finally, 'Tyler' stopped and pointed directly at her opponent who fell onto one knee.

"*VICTORY!*" The narrator shouted, the dancers all crowded around 'Tyler' and the room cheered, they all stepped back as a smiling Kyle walked forward and hugged, her, the dancers stepped back as she bowed her head. "*She had done enough, her alpha was pleased,*" the narrator continued as she skipped and headed off the stage. The dancers stood around, the music started again, 'Kyle' led the dancers in a short routine before they slowly made their way off stage. The lights dimmed and the mist reappeared, slowly dark figures stepped out from the right-hand side of the stage, silhouetted by the back of the stage being slowly lit up. They were hunched over, their elbows pointing to either side of the stage with their fingers outstretched towards the floor, each took a large step then stopped, looked around, then another step, the music announced that the Nocs were back.

"They had been dealt a blow, but our enemies had laid a careful trap,"

There were boos and hisses from the audience as they stepped towards the middle of the stage. Tyler smiled as the left side of the stage was illuminated and two dancers in green appeared. They both walked on stage then looked towards the advancing Nocs, both looked shocked, they stepped further onto the stage, one beckoned other green shirt dancers from their side of the stage to join them. The dancers lined up, one behind the other, the first two looked at each other and smiled, they started to dance where they were, then the dancer behind the joined in, then the next, this carried on until all the green shirts were dancing the same. They all moved as one towards the centre of the stage and the Nocs started to retreat, Kyle appeared at the left-hand side of the stage, everyone was smiling as the group danced towards the front of the stage and moved into a diamond shape, the dancers continued on. The lights focused on the dancers as the Nocs all stepped back into the darkness. The music stopped as the darkened Noc dancer appeared at the rear of the stage, she lifted her arm, there was a crash of drums. A small pyrotechnic went off and a green dancer at the rear of the diamond turned and felt down into the following mist. Another dark dancer appeared in front of her, and it was repeated until there were six Noc dancers standing pointing towards the few green dancers. The surviving dancers helped wounded comrades limp off their side of the stage, the mist started to clear to reveal Kyle kneeling over a fallen dancer, they lifted their hand to touch Kyle's face, quiet words were spoken, and the arm dropped, Kyle bowed his head. The dark dancers started to dance to their music again, they moved forward, all facing the audience and danced as Kyle opened his hands and spread his fingers. His fingers reached upwards, he lifted his face, which was full of rage as the narration continued. *"The trap was sprung, but there was one they had not counted on, and the strength of one would prevail over all!"* the narrator let out a small cheer as Kyle stood and stared at the Nocs who had all stopped dancing. He strode towards the Nocs, the wolf dancer who had been on the ground behind him was helped away. Kyle turned to face the top table and pointed with the fore finger of his right hand at the ground in front of him. He drew the finger across himself, drawing a line. The music jumped and he started to dance, the Nocs danced as well. Tyler and Paul exchanged another glance,

"This was nothing compared to what had happened for real," Paul stated.

"But it makes a good stage show," she smiled, Paul smirked, as she spoke again, "I am pretty sure that the real story of 'Phantom of the Opera' is nothing like the stage show!"

"The Phantom of the Opera' was real?"

"Apparently," she replied, as Kyle jumped in the middle of the Noc dancers, dispersing them, he kept his right arm straight with the finger still pointing at head height, moving it as if it was a sword. He danced around a dark dancer, he swished his arm and the dancer fell, another danced towards him and with a swish of his arm, fell into the mist. He danced around until all the dancers had gone down on one knee, then ran off the stage until there was only one left. She slowly walked onto the stage, she was wearing a plain black velvet short dress and thick black tights. Her face was white, and her black hair was tied back behind her head. Again, Paul and Tyler glanced at each other, she looked nothing like Dani! The dark dancer danced forward as Kyle performed a jump then turned and danced towards her, pointing at her with his finger. She stopped and pointed back at him. Her feet moved twice, the drums crashed twice, the pyrotechnics went off twice. Kyle turned holding his hands to his chest, the Noc danced another two steps, both matched with the crash of the drums, Kyle limped back to the far side of the stage, falling onto his knees. The dark dancer knelt down at the right-hand side of the stage and picked something up. Kyle was joined by two more who helped him stand. The dark dancer held the small blade up for all to see, she looked over at Kyle, licking her lips opened her mouth and a loud hiss came over the sound system. It echoed around the room,

"*Help me stand!*" The narrator spoke. The Noc dancer danced towards the centre of the stage, facing the top table but pointing the knife towards the three at the side. "*Tie me to the tree!*" The two either side of Kyle brought a single white rope around his waist, the Noc danced closer. "*Leave me,*" the voice commanded, the two dancers with Kyle shook their heads so all could see, Kyle pointed with his right hand, directing them off the stage, slowly they walked off out of sight. The dark dancer danced around the centre of the stage, brandishing the knife as she did so. Kyle pointed up towards the heavens.

"*IS MIS AN RUA!*" he shouted, looking skywards as he did so, "*IS MIS AN RUA!*" he repeated. Tyler's eyes moved to the main audience, several were on their feet, some punched the air, the cheering was building with the tension. The dark dancer lunged at Kyle who suddenly pointed at her with his arm. His hand was between her body and her left arm as she stopped. The knife was dropped, and she fell to the ground.

"*Their princess who started this had fallen,*" the narrator stated as she fell to the ground, several dark dancers ran onto the stage and formed a semi-circle all pointed with one finger towards him, Kyle pointed skyward again.

"*IS MIS AN RUA!*" he shouted defiantly. Drums and pyrotechnics went off again.

All the lights went out. Slowly the empty stage was illuminated, mist flowed like water as Kyle jumped forward, arms outstretched dancing all around the stage. The narrator spoke, "*The blood of his enemies flowed from his sword, but his soul dances on!*" Tyler could picture him, not the dancer, him, Kyle, she could see his smile, hear his laugh. "*He stood his ground, fearless to the end,*" the dancer performed a high kick, then spun around, "*to him we see new strength,*" the dancer walked towards the front of the stage, knelt onto one knee. "*He gave his all for his pack,*" the dancer bowed his head then he jumped up and pointed towards the heavens with the fingertip of his 'sword', "*HE WAS AN RUA!*" the narrator shouted. Tyler felt her insides tighten; the room exploded in rapture. Tyler's realised what had just happened. The performance had been outstanding, she could feel herself welling up with tears at the story of Kyle Foster, her lover of just one night, the father of her child, the alpha of the Northern pack had just become the one thing she never could have ever expected.

THE TALE OF KYLE FOSTER HAD JUST BECOME LEGEND

Chapter 18 – Newtownards airfield.

He stood and watched the twin-engine Piper Navaho touch down on the main runway of the small airfield. He glanced at his watch, it was just before midnight, the pilot had made it with minutes to spare, there was no flying after midnight. He watched the plane start to slow as it hurtled along the runway, he glanced over his shoulder, the engines of both of the 4x4's started and there was movement from the rear vehicle as it reversed and turned so it pointed towards the exit. He was casually dressed, as he had been instructed. 'No suits don't want to make the security obvious!' so they didn't. Their weapons were concealed as well, the firearms certificates had been rushed through for the pistols, the long weapons, well, they could deal with that if they had to use them. The plane taxied towards them, one of the other members of the security detail walked forward and held up a torch that had a red filter on it. He pointed toward the plane and flashed it twice, the place turned towards them, from inside the cockpit came the response, also through a red filter, two brief flashes followed by a single flash. He looked around, everyone was doing what they were supposed to, the third 4x4 was by the main entrance, it would be opened for them so they could be on their way without any delays. The engines on the plane shut down as it came to a stop near them, he walked towards the side of the aircraft where the door was, the 4x4 slowly moved up and came along side of it. The door of the aircraft started to open so he walked over to the rear door of the 4x4 and opened it, it was only a short distance between the two. The door of the aircraft jolted as if it was stuck then came down, the thin white rods snapped into position, holding the door in place also acting as handrails for anyone leaving the aircraft. Martin Hanna appeared in the doorway. He held the door of the 4x4 as Martin made his way down the steps then trotted the short distance between the aircraft and the 4x4. He shut the door of the 4 x 4 then walked around and climbed into the front passenger seat, he nodded once to the driver as he closed his door. The vehicle took off, it did not speed away as that would attract attention to them, but it was fast enough so they could deal with any threats they may come across, the 4x4 was the first and best weapon they could ever use. They drove past the second vehicle that took up a position behind them. He touched the earpiece and listened to what was being said, he nodded without speaking.

"Glenn?" Martin asked from behind him, he turned his head slightly, so he was pointing his right ear towards him.

"Yes Sir," Glenn Nendrum had looked after Martin for some time, but he was still the client and Glenn was always the professional when it came to business, especially this business. In close protection he had been schooled from the very start to 'always maintain a professional distance' but the first rule of close protection was 'dead clients don't pay!'

"So, tell me the set up!" Martin asked. Glenn turned and looked out the front of the 4x4, his eyes never stopped moving.

"We have four vehicles, all prepared," he started.

"How?" Martin asked.

"All have been fitted with 'Run Flat' tyres and we had the armour fitted by Elephant Armour Group with a vehicle communication system linked and controlled by the safe house," he looked back at him, "that is where the base station is at!" he looked forward again.

"What level of protection is the armour?" Martin asked.

"Level three, so small arms up to seven six two and shotgun," he looked back at him, "but not solid slug at point blank!" The driver did not flinch, but he did slow as they passed through the main entrance to the airfield, the main headlights cut into the night. Glenn noticed the driver had raised the fingers of his right hand off the steering wheel in an acknowledgement to the team member who was standing beside the smiling uniformed airfield guard, a wave from the guard went unreturned. Glenn glanced into the side mirror; the second vehicle came in behind them as they headed towards the main road. He looked at the small sign in blue letters that advertised 'ARDS AIRPORT'. He had been through a lot of airports; he was not sure how something that small and with so few amenities could describe themselves as an airport.

"What about the windows?"

"Elephant did a special on them for us, new stuff from America, UV protection included, rear windows tinted."

"Is that it?" Martin asked.

"No," Glenn continued, "each vehicle has smoke and noise distraction dischargers underneath so if we need to cover ourselves and get away quickly, we can," Martin looked around the inside of the vehicle, it was comfortable, he liked that. "And the engines are all upgraded and fitted with internal snorkels so they can wade through water up to a depth of five feet. We can outrun anything currently on the roads here!" he stated.

"Who is team leader?" Martin asked.

"Mark Castle with Dan as two eye sea,"

"When did you all get here?" Martin asked as the vehicle jumped forward.

"Early yesterday morning, the vehicles and kit all arrived yesterday afternoon, the house is secure, we have two there running the security room we all did a drive through of the route with the third vehicle acting as a Resident Escort Section for this move tonight." Just as he spoke the second vehicle roared past them, Glenn sat back in his seat, he guessed the next question, "they are heading up to the next check point to do A.S. just to make sure there is no one behind us!" Martin nodded again; Glenn had gone through all the usual Anti- Surveillance that the team would normally carry out, "twelve other team members so fifteen of us in total."

"How long until we get to the safe house?" Martin asked.

"Thirty-eight minutes," Glenn reached up and touched the earpiece.

"How did we get out of the airfield so quickly?" Martin asked, he spotted a quick smile on Glenn's face.

"Simple, it was an approved Aviation Authority flight plan, from inside the UK, so that was a big help."

"Are they not curious, even slightly?" Martin butted in. The driver smirked and let out a short laugh through his nose, Glenn looked at him then back outside the vehicle.

"Yeah, but there was no baggage, so that helped as well; all your baggage arrived this afternoon, it is in the house already." Glenn turned back to what he was doing. "So, we said that guy you're a film producer looking at locations for a big Hollywood blockbuster and you don't want anyone knowing you are here ...." Glenn paused, "he seemed ok with that."

"Really! He believed you?"

"Well, that and the £300 in cash I slipped him did help make up his mind." Martin let out a short laugh. Silence fell over the inside of the car as they made their way along. Martin could make out constant transmissions in the earpieces of both the men in the front, but he found all that chatter to be annoying and did not want to listen to it. He settled back and looked at the passing countryside. Martin's mind focused on the reason he was over here, he had work to do, and he was already having ideas about what he wanted for a prize this time.

"Oh, the two that you wanted to speak to are already there," Glenn stated. Martin let a wry smile spread over his face, then it fell when Glenn finished his sentence, "and they seem absolutely petrified of some bloke called 'Jason'.

∞∞∞∞∞

Tyler looked around the busy bar, there was such a feeling of excitement, the stage show had been a hit. Tyler looked at her watch, it was after midnight, but she was tired of the constant flow of congratulations, the first couple would have been enough. Her eyes moved to the parting crowd as Paul made his way towards her. He was excited and his face was flushed, as he approached, she could smell the shower gel, he was not long changed.

"Did you enjoy the run?" she asked as she lifted a drink from the bar and handed it to him.

"You didn't go on the run?" he asked.

"No, I ..." she was cut off by a loud voice, everyone looked towards where Connor was standing. He was slightly raised above the crowd as he was standing on something that lifted his head and shoulders above the crowd.

"Everyone .... Hello, everyone may I have your attention for a moment please ..." the music in the background was turned off and a hush came over the room, the well-dressed patrons of the bar all turned towards him. *"Thank you, Councillor Grishin would like to say a few final words ..."* Connor stepped down and out of sight, Grishin stood up, smiling as he did so, his accent was a marked contrast to Connor's.

"Connor, first of all I would like to thank you and all An Rua for hosting such an amazing event ...." There was a cheer and applause, Grishin lifted one hand and motioned for quiet, he continued, "I believe we can all agree Connor, you can certainly put on a great show!" There was another cheer and applause, "the tale that was told was one that certainly will be retold worldwide," Grishin looked around where he was standing, "and I challenge all gathered here tonight to do so ... take this tale and tell it to all our kind. Our enemies tried to divide us ... they tried to overwhelm one of our smaller dens by moving a hunter force to these lands, but true to their long clan history, the An Rua rose and did not just meet the challenge .... They fought them!" Grishin's tone changed, the volume of his voice raised, "Foster and the Northern Dun took down one of their Princess's and one of the most celebrated hunters!" The cheer this time was louder, fists punched the air again, Grishin was tapping into the euphoric feeling in the room. It took a few minutes for it to quieten down again, Grishin held his hand aloft. "Where is Reynolds?" he asked, his eyes looked around, Tyler felt her insides turn at the mention of her name, Paul stepped back, and a small space formed around her.

"Over here!" came one shout, Tyler felt the eyes of the room turn towards her.

"Tyler, please, come forward," Tyler felt her body react to the command. She handed Paul her drink and she walked forward along the path through the crowd. Grishin was smiling as she approached, he placed his hand on her right shoulder, she stopped beside him and turned to face the room. Grishin looked at Connor, "I can see why you are known as the 'red haired warriors!'" there was another cheer. Grishin looked at Tyler, he raised his voice again, "Tyler Reynolds of the An Rua ..." she felt her eyes look up at him, "I do not think you fully realise the service you have done, not only for your clan, but for all Garou around the world!" Tyler looked away, she had a polite smile, but she was far from comfortable. Grishin lifted his hand from her shoulder and turned towards Connor again, "Your alpha, Connor was correct in recognising you and your great achievements earlier ...." Grishin looked back over the bar. "So, to add to that, I am formally inviting you to be recognised in front of the entire High Council later in the year!" Tyler felt her eyebrows shoot up, the room reacted with a joyous explosion, like a pond that just had a rock thrown into the middle of it, Grishin lifted his hand again and again the room fell silent. "As you all know, the truce has been in place between us and our enemies, we know that this was organised by one who would see our kinds at war once again," there was a murmur of conversation which stopped when he lifted his hand again. "The example of Kyle Foster of the An Rua is an example to us all!" Tyler looked at the faces that beamed with pride, the electricity flowed through the room, fire burned in the eyes of nearly everyone in front of her, "Foster stood his ground, his actions not only saved Garou that would have been lost, but the blood of his enemies flowed from his sword ...." Tyler glanced at Connor, he was looking at Grishin, he looked over at her, their eyes met. Connor's eyes had a red rim, he was nearly in tears, Connor looked away, "I charge you all, everyone here ... to tell all Garou, around the world of the feats of daring and bravery performed here in the green land ..." Grishin's voice was rising again, he was letting his own passion flow through his words, "let all know that we will never again stand by and allow them to act against us *ever again!*" the cheer echoed through the room, he held his hand high again, he then turned towards Connor. "Connor O'Connor of the clan *An Rua!*" Connor looked up at him, "I charge you, from this night, in the spirit and example of Foster of the Northern dun, to go forth and rid this land of all our enemies!" Tyler watched Connor; the cheering that started drowned out his reply of 'I will' Tyler understood what that meant. Grishin again lifted his hand and the room fell silent. "So, An Rua ..." Grishin started, "all Garou will find new strength in what you have achieved here .... And may the memory of Kyle Foster be a blessing to his clan," Grishin suddenly stepped back and down from the small stool he had been standing on, he extended his hand offering it to Tyler. Tyler looked at him and started to shake her head.

"Tyler, step forward!" it was Connor who spoke. Her body reacted to the command. Tyler lifted the sides of her long dress from around her knees and she took the careful steps up onto the stool. She straightened herself up, balancing as she did so, she could now see every face in the vast crowd in front of her. Grishin carried on from behind her.

"*I, Edward Grishin of the High Council of the Garou, recognise a Red-Haired Warrior of the clan ... AN RUA!*" The room exploded in joy once more. Tyler steadied herself on the small stool, she looked towards the back of the room, she tried not to look into the many rapturous faces in front of her. There were cheers and tears, glasses were raised, smiles were shared, her eyes found Paul standing at the far end of the bar, his smile beaming from his face. He nodded once, she replied. As the cheering died down Tyler looked around herself and choosing her footing very carefully stepped back. Connor stepped forward and offered her a hand. There was a pause between them, he was being gracious, she nodded and accepted his offer of support with her right hand, her left hand hitched up the figure-hugging dress. Tyler walked through a sea of smiles, handshakes, and hugs of congratulations until she got back to Paul. He lifted her drink and handed it to her as she arrived beside him.

"That looked painful," he stated as she turned so her back was up against the bar.

"You have no idea!" she answered as she lifted the drink to her lips. Paul turned so he was standing beside her facing the rest of the room.

"Connor did not look too happy about you being invited to the High Council," Paul drank from his own drink as she looked at him.

"Has he ever been invited himself?" she asked.

"Nope, don't think anyone here has," he looked towards her, "to be recognised by the High council ...." Paul was interrupted by the excited face coming through the crowd.

He had dark hair and looked to be mid-forties; he was wearing the same black tie as everyone else. Tyler looked into his dark eyes; she recognised the wolf that was holding his hand out towards her. His grip was firm, he was taller than her and he locked eyes as he introduced himself.

"Hi, I am Rich, Rich Turpin," he offered Paul his hand, again looking directly at Paul as he did so, "I am Iceni," Tyler noticed that he had an accent, but she could not place it yet.

"Hi, Rich, I met your alpha once, John, a few years ago," Paul replied, Rich stepped back, he was in a very good mood.

"Yeah, John is still there,"

"Where is 'there'?" Tyler asked.

"Norfolk," Rich spoke with his hands, they did not stop moving as he spoke, "and respect from us," he slightly bowed his head, "that was some feat you achieved!"

"Not without cost!" Tyler lifted the drink to her lips.

"Anyway," Rich instantly changed the conversation, "you guys are from the Northern Dun, yes?" he asked.

"We are," confirmed Paul.

"Great," Rich reached into his pocket and handed a folded piece of paper to Paul. Paul opened it and read the contents. "Can you please pass my details on to Tony Fallon?"

"Sure, may I ask how you know Tony?" Paul looked up from the note.

"We served together, well sort of,"

"Sort of?" Tyler asked, Rich smiled back at her.

"Yes, he was in One Para and I was in Three Para .... I was never sure if he was Garou or not, only got it confirmed after he had left and I kinda lost touch with him ...." He looked back at Paul, "I have been trying to find him for the last couple of years, ... He isn't on any social media and I kinda hoped he would have been here tonight!" He shrugged.

"Sure, I will give him this when I see him." Paul held up the note before he folded it and placed it in his pocket, "he has been busy of late," Paul added as a female figure in a black cocktail dress reached out of the crowd and tugged at his sleeve. She had streaked hair and had a very defined shape, Tyler instantly looked her up and down, this girl liked to lift weights.

"Dick, come on, he wants to chat to us!" she demanded, she had the same accent as he did. Rich Turpin looked back at them both then smiled again.

"Looks like I gotta go," he looked at Tyler, "Respect again for all you have done and," he glanced at Paul, "thank you, please let Tony know I would very much like to hear from him," Rich kept smiling as the girl tugged at his arm again.

"Dick, come on," she insisted.

"Gotta go," he repeated then disappeared back into the crowd.

"I wonder if he owes him money?" Paul suggested.

"What?" Tyler asked.

"Normally if someone is looking for someone else that desperately it is normally because they owe them money!" Paul laughed at his own joke. In the corner of the room, out of sight from where she was standing, a group of musicians started. It was a lively traditional Irish tune that she could not name but she recognised it, it nearly drowned out all conversation.

"Well, at least we know his parents had a sense of humour!" she drank from the glass again. Paul looked at her with raised eyebrows.

"What do you mean?" he asked, her head spun towards him with an unbelieving look.

"You never heard of 'Dick Turpin'?" Paul went to answer but Tyler laughed then carried on, "you know, the eighteenth-century Highwayman, Dick Turpin, used to hold up stagecoaches and steal horses," Tyler emptied her glass, "ended up getting hung in York, if I remember correctly," she turned and raised her hand to attract the bar staff.

"Steals from the rich to give to the poor kind of guy!" Paul said as he turned to the bar. ""Looks like this will go on for some time yet!" he stated.

"Not for me," Tyler was still facing the bar.

"What?" Paul asked. Tyler looked at him.

"After this one I am off to bed!" She looked down the bar then at the large painting that hung on the wall near the corner of the room. "I am not as young as I used to be anymore," Paul leaned in and nudged her.

"Someone to see you," he whispered. Tyler turned as four tall women came out of the crowd and formed a semi-circle in front of them. It was the four from the Silver Eye pack. All four had a piercing look in their eyes, from a distance it was light blue, but up close, it was almost silver. They smiled then one spoke in a language Tyler did not understand. Tyler recognised the alpha as the one on her right-hand side stepped forward, smiling as she did so.

"I am sorry, but she does not speak any English," a hand was offered, which Tyler took, "I take it you do not speak any Serbian, with your permission may I interpret for her?" Tyler released the handshake.

"You do not need my permission for anything," Tyler smiled.

"Firstly, may I introduce," she turned and extended her hand towards the first one who had spoken, "this is Jana, our alpha has asked her to represent the Silver Eye here in the green land at this event." No handshake was offered, Jana slightly bowed her head, Tyler responded in kind, the introductions continued, "this is Katya," a hand was offered, "this is Petra ...." again a firm handshake was exchanged, "and I am Debbie."

"Debbie?" Tyler was surprised, Debbie smiled back.

"My mother was English, from Somerset actually," she twitched her nose in a playful way. Jana stepped forward and started speaking, as she paused, Debbie translated what was being said. "On behalf of the Silver Eye Wolves our alpha would like to extend to you .... our congratulations at your great victory and offer you this gift ...." Jana looked to her right, Tyler had not noticed that Katya had kept her left hand behind her, Jana started talking again as Katya presented a small wooden-framed pencil sketch of a tall tower, Tyler took it and looked at the picture. Debbie continued to translate as Jana spoke, pausing only to listen to what Jana was saying next. "This is the tower of the Cathedral in Belgrade ...." Debbie listened again, "it is traditional for us to gift a gift to recognise a true warrior ...." Jana started smiling as she continued speaking, Debbie paused, there was a reaction of the other three, whatever Jana had just said none of them knew about it. Debbie had a shocked look on her face as she turned towards Tyler. "Our Alpha would like to honour you with an invitation to attend a dance at our den," Jana spoke again, cutting Debbie off, Debbie looked at her then back at Tyler, "which dance can be decided by yourself of course ...." Debbie glanced at Jana then spoke to Tyler. "I cannot stress enough the honour this is," Debbie glanced at Jana then looked back at Tyler, "this invitation has never been made before to someone outside of our pack!" Tyler stepped closer to Jana, she did not look at Debbie, she looked Jana in the eyes and spoke directly to her.

"The Silver Eye are known throughout our history for their skill in battle," Tyler slightly bowed her head as she continued, "it will be my honour to share a dance with such warriors," she paused as Debbie translated, a broad smile spread over Jana's face. Tyler stepped back and turned towards Paul. "May I introduce, Paul Hawkins from the Northern Dun of the An Rua ..." Paul straightened up, there were nods but no handshake. Jana looked at Paul then back at Tyler. When she spoke, Debbie smiled.

"She asks is this is your mate?" Tyler and Paul looked at each other, Paul felt his eyes dart away, Tyler let out a short chuckle.

"Good Lord, no," Tyler touched Paul's left arm with her hand. "Paul has been a faithful member of the An Rua for many years," Tyler relaxed, "and he has a family of his own." Paul went to say something, but Debbie started to translate what Tyler had just said. It was Jana's turn to look surprised, she instantly started saying something, Debbie smiled, and the others relaxed. Jana looked at Debbie who then let them know what had just been said.

"Jana apologises as she did not mean any offence,"

"There was no offence," Tyler smiled. Jana looked serious again and looked directly at Paul and started speaking, Debbie nodded as she finished.

"Jana states that unfortunately, the invitation to attend a dance can be extended to female Garou only," Debbie looked directly at Paul, "she is sorry, but" Debbie tilted her head slightly as she continued, "clan rules .... No men!"

"That is not a problem," Paul stated. Paul felt a poke from behind him as the barman set two drinks in front of him. Jana spoke again, again Debbie nodded and waited until she had finished before translating.

"Jana again extends her congratulations," Debbie listened as Jana smiled and spoke again, "she says she would like to hear the details of your fight with the Noc Hunter sometime!" Tyler's eyes bounced from Debbie then back to Jana.

"Of course, I would be happy to do so," Tyler stated, Jana spoke again.

"She says she hopes you enjoy the rest of the dance and is looking forward to receiving you at our own den soon," Debbie translated.

"I look forward to it!" Tyler smiled as she spoke. The four nodded then started to make their way along the bar, for them, drinks were next on the agenda. Tyler and Paul turned towards each other.

"I see why they are called 'Silver Eye!" Paul stated, Tyler again looked at the picture. She ran her fingertips over the ornate carving of the frame.

"This is lovely," she answered. Paul handed her the drink, she sipped from it then looked around, "time for bed I think!"

"You can finish that first!" he stated, laughing as he did so.

"Yeah, ok," The four Silver Eye where directly behind Paul as two eager young male An Rua, with drinks in hands made their way through the crowd to confront the four women at the bar.

"Well, '*hell-o ladies!*" stated the first one, four heads turned, three voices all answered in unison.

"PISS OFF!"

Chapter 19 - MI5 Regional Headquarters, Laganside, Belfast

Lucy waved at Nikki as she closed the door to the small office she'd been working in. She was neatly dressed in a dark navy-blue open jacket with a red top, jeans and a pair of deck shoes that matched the colour of her jacket. She held the brown folder in her left hand as she walked along the corridor and headed towards the large office at the end. She glanced at her watch; she would arrive at the exact time the senior MI5 case officer in Belfast had requested her to. It was a gentle knock at the door. There was a pause, she stepped back as the door opened, she did not recognise the first person who appeared in the doorway, behind them she could hear the voice of the senior case officer bidding them a goodbye.

"Hi Lucy, come in, come on in," he stepped back and extended his arm, welcoming her. The desk was at the far end and faced the door, there were two monitor screens that faced the single chair was behind the desk. To her left was a view of Belfast lough, her eyes moved around the room, there were two chesterfield chairs in front of the desk, behind her and along the rear wall was a chesterfield couch with a small coffee table in front of it. Beside it, near the windows was the stylish cabinet the same height at the side of the couch. The wall on her right was bare, no pictures. The top of his desk was also devoid of any personal items, she knew he was married but things like that were never discussed, he never mentioned it, so she would not. There were two phones on top of the desk, both different types of secure phones, the keyboard for the desktop that was internal to the desk was in front of the monitors and a single wire tray, that was empty was all that was visible on the top of the dark stained wooden desk. She recognised the type, all station chiefs had them, it was what was internal to them that made them important and not obvious to the untrained eye that made them look so normal. She stopped when she got to the chairs, she waited until he had walked around his desk. "Sorry I could not meet with you the other day, but ...."

"It's ok," she smiled. Johnathan moved quickly, he looked like he was a middle-aged man who had a career in business; the fact was, he was one of the youngest 'head of station' so far in the Security Service, but then, a life undercover is a stressful one. He landed on the swivel chair, sat forward, and rested his arms, Lucy sat down on one of the chairs as he did so.

"So, are your update reports done?" Lucy stood and stepped forward and handed him the folder she was carrying.

"All done," she re-took her seat. Johnathan took the folder, dropped it on the desk and opened it. He flicked through a couple of pages then looked up at her.

"So, short version, he completely made a mess of his surveillance ...."

"Alienated a source that we had been cultivating, upset the police and I am pretty positive that one of the SAS guys was about to hit him the other day ...." She looked directly at her boss, "since then, they have not exactly been 'helpful and co-operating". This is hindering our investigation into this whole situation."

"Normally, if it was one of our own, then I would move them, but in this case ...."

"What? just because he is MI6, he can carry on any way he likes? This is still 'our jurisdiction', our investigation, not theirs!" Lucy looked annoyed; Johnathan glanced down at the folder in front of him.

"No, that is not it," he looked back up at her, "for the time being we need to facilitate them, there *is* a world-wide factor here and we can use their help with the Russian connection ...." He glanced down briefly, "two ex – GRU Colonels have come up on the radar I believe?"

"Yes, one called Tatamovich, and another called Grishin," she nodded then pointed towards the folder, "it's all in there," Johnathan nodded.

"Ok, can you email a copy of this please?" he asked.

"It is already in your inbox," she smiled.

"Ok, I will speak with MI6, but for the short term, just give him something to do and keep him out of the way until I can sort it out for you."

"That will be difficult, he is in charge of this task!" her statement made him sit up.

"No, he isn't!" Johnathan replied.

"That is what I was briefed by them in London just before I flew over." Lucy looked at his face, Johnathan's face did not move, he did not react to what she had just said.

"Wait a minute," Johnathan turned and picked up the handset of one of the phones, he paused before tapping in a short number. Lucy relaxed as he sat back in his chair, holding his phone to his ear, he looked out the window. The call was quickly answered. "Hey Wendy, Johnathan here, over in Belfast ..." his face changed at whatever had just been said, "no, it is not currently raining here!!" there was a short laugh as he listened to something else being said. "Yes, of course that is no problem," he nodded then glanced at Lucy before looking back out the window. "Right the reason I am phoning, your guy over here ...." Lucy watched as his face contorted as he held back another laugh, "yes, he has 'been a bit of a prick' .... One of the military lads nearly slapped him the other day ...." Johnathan looked directly at Lucy and held the mouthpiece away from his mouth, "from London, next time, let them!" Lucy politely smiled as Johnathan looked away again. "Sure, sure, what I want to confirm, I have just heard from my team leader here that he is currently in charge and that cannot be the case ...." he nodded again, "that's great .... May I leave that with you to sort with your guys? .... Perfect, cheers." Johnathan took the phone away from his ear, turned in his chair to face her. When he replaced the handset, he looked directly at her. "You are in charge, and you have always been in charge. He will be told that, this evening by London and their first question was ...."

"Is he being a 'bit of a prick?'" Lucy injected.

"'Complete prick' was the actual words used but, yeah,"

"Thank you," Lucy had a small smile of her face at the news.

"Oh, speaking of this documentary about our furry 'friends, when is it going out?"

"Tonight, just after teatime," she answered.

"Anything we should be concerned about?"

"Not as far as I know, there is currently no connection with us and anything going on here over the last two years." Lucy was confident in her answer. Johnathan sat back in his chair.

"Brilliant, you can tell me all about it tomorrow then!"

∞∞∞∞

Tony turned the keys in his front door, he looked around, the sun was low in the sky, the door jolted then it opened. He stepped in and closed the door. The living room was dark, the light from the kitchen flooded into the hallway. He could hear the baby gently crying, but it was coming from the spare room, not the kitchen. He dropped the holdall on the floor underneath the various jackets and coats that hung from the rungs on the wall. He slipped his jacket off and followed the noise, he turned down the hallway and stopped by the open door where Becky had been staying, it was now the baby's room. Karen was standing in the middle of the room swaying gently, cradling the baby in her arms.

"Hey," he said as he propped himself up against the door frame, she smiled back.

"Hey," she looked into the small face wrapped in the white baby blanket. "So, how did things go today?" she asked, Tony stepped forward, moving closer to his wife and child.

"Well, Tyler and the others got back just after lunch time, from all accounts they put on quite a show down there,"

"Really?"

"Yeah, Paul was saying that Tyler was honoured in front of everyone by Connor, and they wrote a show based on what happened here," he paused, "no one expected that!"

"No, I guess not," she replied.

"Connor has been tasked with clearing all of Ireland of Nocs, once and for all!"

"About time, the sooner the better if you ask me," she sighed.

"And there were several other packs there as well, including four from the Balkans!".

Karen looked at him, "You're assuming I know who you are talking about!"

"The Silver Eye!" Tony smiled again.

"And ... who are they? Remember I don't know your clans as you do!"

"They are quite unique as they are the only 'all female' clan of wolves in the world!"

"All females?" she asked, "bet that went down well with the guys down south!"

"Yeah, they really keep to themselves' they do not normally leave their clan area,"

"Why are they called 'Silver Eye' then?"

"Well, from a distance, their eyes look light blue but close up they look silver!"

"Mmmm, a bit like your lot with red hair!" Karen answered as the baby went quiet, "he is falling asleep," she whispered.

"Everyone is buzzing about this documentary," he whispered.

"When is it on?" she asked.

"8PM tonight,"

"Do we know what is going to be said during this programme?"

"No, but the police don't seem to be very worried about it."

"They wouldn't be, they haven't been attacked in their own home ...." Karen stopped herself, Tony reached forward and placed his hand on her shoulder. She looked at the baby then at him. "This whole, werewolf – vampire war thingy is getting to be more of a problem!" she stated. Tony paused, he was going to say something, then didn't.

"I will put the kettle on," Tony spoke quietly.

"Dinner will be an hour, at least," she stated. Tony nodded and stepped closer, he looked down at the small face with adoration, he then looked into her eyes. He closed his eyes and gently kissed Karen's forehead.

"I'll do dinner." He smiled then walked back into the kitchen. The phone in his pocket started to ring, jolting him back to the present., He held the phone to his ear.

"Hi John," he said into the phone as he answered the call.

"Hi Tony, just a quick call to let you know t we have finished our sweep,"

"Ok ...... where are you two at the moment?" he asked.

"Errr, not that far away from you,"

"Then pop round, better to have this conversation face to face than down a phone!"

"Yeah, sure, we can be there for about half seven! If that is ok with you guys?"

"Yes, in fact, that will be perfect, we will have finished dinner and the wee man should be asleep by then!" there was a chuckle down the phone.

"I don't miss those days, yeah sure, half seven then." Before Tony could answer, John cut the call. He put the phone in his pocket.

Karen appeared in the doorway of the kitchen. "Who was that?".

"Ian and John are going to call round later," he stated as he opened one of the cupboards and lifted down two mugs.

"Not for me thanks, are they going to be here for dinner?" she asked.

"No, after, said they would get here after 'half seven',"

"Good," Karen turned and headed back to the baby's room, Tony watched her go, as she disappeared from view his phone rang again.

"Obviously forgot something," he muttered out loud, he lifted the phone to his ear without noticing that it was a withheld number. "So, what did you forget this time?"

"Tony," the female voice was not the voice he expected, he reacted to the voice.

"Err, hello," he stuttered, he was not sure if he recognised the voice or not.

"Hi Tony, it's me, Alison, Alison Wallace," the name hit him like a brick.

"Alison!" he was not sure of what to say next.

"Yeah, I thought you would have kept this number .... Look, the reason I am calling .... We 'need' to talk, quite urgently in fact,"

"Do we ...."

"Yes, we do .... It is a matter of life and death!" He felt his wolf awaken; anger started to rise in him.

"Really? Well, I currently don't think my life is in danger .... Your life however ...."

"Tony, please .... I just need some help,"

"HELP?" he did not notice he had raised his voice, "and why should I help you? The last time I saw you, you tried to kill me!"

"No, I didn't,"

"Actually .... yes, you did, it was at your house if you remember!" Tony was now pacing around the kitchen, he did not notice Karen quietly walking up and stopping by the entrance to the kitchen, watching him.

"Actually, I didn't, you arrived with a gun out, you had hostile intentions, I was just defending myself," Tony stopped, that was not how he remembered the fight at the rear of her house. "But that does not change how much we need to talk right now,"

"Yes, it does, I don't have to talk with you if I don't want to."

"Tony, stop being a prick, this is serious, we need to talk, I really need your help! This is serious, serious business." Tony noticed she had used the word 'serious' twice.

"Ok, what can we possibly have to talk about? As I cannot think of a single thing, I want to discuss with you?" there was a pause, for a moment Tony could hear her breathing.

"We can't talk down the phone, can we meet face to face?" now that he was listening, he could hear the anxious tone in her voice.

"Ok, we could meet at the farm, there are several people there that would love to have a chat with you. .... Just to clear a few things up!"

"Are you kidding me! If I went there, I would not leave alive!!"

"Ok, how about we meet outside the police station in Coleraine, I am sure they would like to chat to with you, after the footage from the Mussenden temple car park ...." He injected.

"Stop being stupid," she spat. Tony felt himself smile, was he getting to her? He stopped pacing and looked at Karen. She mouthed 'who is that?' without speaking, he responded, 'Ali-son Wall -ace," her eyebrows shot up, then she turned and walked away.

"Ok, what do you suggest then?"

"I could come to your house, I am not that far away,"

"Not a chance in hell is you coming here!" his reaction was instantaneous, there was another pause down the phone.

"Ok, not tonight, but can we meet tomorrow, do you know Ballintoy?" she suggested.

"Of course, I know Ballintoy, I was a copper in Coleraine a lot longer than you were!"

"Ok, how about down at the harbour, say 2PM?" there was a long pause before she spoke again. "Tony, I desperately need your help .... He *will* kill me if he finds me ...." The tone of her voice had changed again, she even sounded desperate.

"Who?"

"I cannot say down the phone .... Look Tony .... I don't know what else to do ...." Tony turned and walked towards the back door of the kitchen; he looked out over the landscape.

"Alison, if you can't say anything then there isn't much, I can do …. You understand I need to get permission first!" again there was a long silence before she replied.

"Ok, but if your pack of wolves are there then I am gone!"

"Who is trying to kill you Alison?" he repeated the use of her name. He listened to her breathing for a few moments, she lowered her voice.

"Do you know who 'The American' is?" Tony felt himself straighten up.

"I know of him …. But I also know a great many people who really *want* to meet him!" again she paused, Tony carried on, "Ali, if you want our help, then there has to be something you can do for us! This isn't a one-way street you know."

"I, …."

"Look, let me phone the farm and see what we can do and what they will want, can you phone me back in say," Tony turned and looked at the clock on the wall, "five minutes?"

"Yeah, sure." Before Tony could say another word, she hung up the phone. Tony walked over and switched off the nearly boiling kettle and scrolled through the contacts on his phone. He lifted the phone to his ear and listened to the ringing tone.

"Hi, didn't you just leave here?" Dermott replied.

"Hi, yeah, are Tyler and Paul near you at the moment?"

"Spookily enough … yeah, they are both here, why? What is up?"

"Right, put me on speaker phone, you are not going to believe this!"

∞∞∞∞

Lucy was sitting up with her legs stretched out along the sofa in the living room of the house she had been given to stay in. The TV was on, but she was not really watching it. The empty pizza box was on the small coffee table. She set the large glass of cola on the coaster on the small table and reached for the buzzing phone in the pocket of her jeans. The simple message stated she had received an email. There were no other details. She dropped the phone on the sofa and reached around to the side of the sofa where her small open daysack was. She moved her personal laptop out of the way and grabbed the thicker, 'Toughbook' laptop she had for work. It was a lot more secure and was scanned regularly for any security problems. She had the Toughbook on her legs then she logged into her work emails that were below the 'TS' or Top-Secret classification that she could view when outside of a secure location. She had one new email. She recognised the bland email address of the sender; the time and date were only several minutes ago. She clicked on the email and read the short paragraph.

TELECOM TRACE: ALISON WALLACE/ANTONY FALLON
PAIR TO MEET AT BALLINTOY HARBOUR TWO O' CLOCK TOMORROW
WALLACE REQUESTING HELP IN RETURN OF INFORMATION ABOUT THE AMERICAN

Lucy reached for her phone and scrolled to a name; she tapped out a short message. 'NIKKI, COFFEE, MINE, NINE AM TOMORROW. FANCY A DRIVE UP THE COAST???'

Chapter 20

Cara-Marie's phone was sitting on the far side of the coffee table in her living room, and it was on speaker.

"So, how did the interview go?" Mark's voice asked, there was noise in the background, Cara-Marie had already guessed he was driving.

"We only did it this afternoon so I will be surprised if they use any of it," she replied.

"What did they want to cover?"

"Well, we went over the body we came across in Coleraine, talked through the Castleroe murders, but they kept going back and forth about if I believed if werewolves were real .... And if so, how could I convince them of that!" She reached forward for the remote for the TV then her glass of wine.

"And did you?"

"Did I what?"

"Convince them?"

"Their interview technique was sloppy, they were not listening to what I was saying, they certainly had their own agenda and kept trying to put words in my mouth!"

"Isn't that what 'tabloid and scandal journalism' does?" Mark responded. If he had been sitting at his desk, she would have thrown something at him. She stared at the phone for a few seconds before she answered.

"Sometimes I cannot believe we are part of the same profession!"

"I am a photographer; we are not the same profession!" he retorted.

"Not you, him!"

"Oh, so you wouldn't kiss him under the mistletoe then?" Mark laughed as he spoke.

"I wouldn't kiss him under a general anaesthetic!" she protested. Her thumb pressed the button on the remote and the screen burst into life, "anyway, this is about to start, so I'll say goodbye .... Are you not watching?" In the background of the call a car door slammed.

"I will be in a few minutes!"

"You only have a few minutes,"

"Coolio, chat afterwards then." The call ended and she sat back, she scrolled through the channel index until she found what she was looking for. She looked at the time, then at the screen. She reached for the wine glass; she would at least be comfortable for the show.

∞∞∞∞

Rhydian was on the sofa as Tyler walked in from the kitchen. Rhydian had the TV on and firmly held onto the control for the TV.

"Is he asleep?" Rhydian asked.

"Yeah, just," Tyler replied as she landed in the big chair. Rhydian looked at her, Tyler looked exhausted.

"I think nearly everyone on the farm is watching this!" Rhydian stated as she turned the volume up slightly.

"I think you may be right," Tyler replied.

"Do you know what would be nice!" Rhydian stated.

"What?" Tyler asked.

"A glass of wine to go with it!" Rhydian smiled; Tyler looked at her.

"Do you know what would also be nice?" Tyler asked.

"What?" Rhydian replied, a smile starting to appear across her face.

"If you were to get us both a glass!" Rhydian did not need to be told twice, she jumped up, dropping the tv controller onto Tyler's lap as she ran into the kitchen. Tyler smiled then sank a little more into the chair. She was looking at the TV, but not registering what the images were. She could hear Rhydian moving around the kitchen. Her eyes blinked slowly then looked over at the baby monitor on the side, she had gotten little sleep last night and the baby had kept her busy all day, she felt drained.

∞∞∞∞

Mike Dear was in the living room; he had not been home all that long, but the attitude had started the moment he had closed the front door. His wife was furious with him, and he had no idea why. He had got back earlier than the time he said he would, she already knew he would not be home for dinner. The TV was on, but it was set to 'mute'; she had stormed out of the kitchen every time he had walked in. He had asked what was wrong and he was met with a chorus of 'Fine', 'Nothing,' and 'Why do you think there is anything wrong!' He had been married long enough to know that things were far from 'fine' there was certainly something wrong. He felt his stomach rumble as lunch had been seven hours ago, and it had only been a small lunch at that. She had already eaten, the plates where in the dishwasher, nothing had been left or prepared from him. The kitchen was clean and looked empty. His eyes looked up at the ceiling of the living room, there was the 'thump, thump, thump' of his wife's stomping around their bedroom. He had a mug of coffee in one hand, so he placed it down on a coaster on the coffee table. He lifted the small laptop that was at the side of the large chair he was sitting in; it did not take long for him to put in an order for a Chinese take away to be delivered. He dropped the laptop back down on the floor and turned up the TV, the phone in his pocket beeped with a message. He pulled the phone from the pocket. Darren's name was over the screen. He tapped on it, then read the message.

'HI, ARE YOU WATCHING? Mike felt his eyes look up at the ceiling again then he tapped in a reply, 'YES, JUST SETTLING DOWN, STARTS IN A FEW MINUTES' He set the phone on the side and reached for the mug of coffee again, as he sipped it the phone buzzed again, 'HEARD FROM 'LUCY' THAT THE AMERICANS HAVE BEEN IN TOUCH VIA THEM AND THEY WANT TO DO AN INFO SHARE, DO NOT THINK LONDON IS VERY HAPPY ABOUT IT' Mike read the message twice. Darren did not say 'MI5', he would not, the Americans must be CIA or maybe FBI, he didn't know. Mike paused, before he answered, he had only seen Darren a few hours ago, why he didn't mention this before mystified him. He waited before he replied. 'OK, WE CAN CHAT MORE TOMORROW, IS SHE GOING TO BE AROUND?' he placed the phone back on the arm of the chair, as he drank from his coffee it buzzed again. 'HOPE SO, SHE IS LOVELY, PLUS, HER AND SAM HAVE HAD SOME SORT OF FALLOUT' again Mike waited before he replied, 'THANKS FOR THE HEADS UP,' Mike kept the phone in his hand as he was sure Darren had not finished. The phone did buzz, but this time it was not Darren, Mike felt his eyebrows raise at Lucy's name on the screen. He opened the message as there was another series of thumps from the room above him. 'HI MIKE, LUCY HERE, ARE YOU WATCHING THE PROGRAMME TONIGHT?' Mike looked up at the TV screen. 'YES, JUST WAITING FOR IT TO START, ARE YOU WATCHING?' He had given Lucy his number, but she had never used it before, it was clear that Darren and the military guys did not really trust the security service as the most common complaint he heard was they would never give the whole picture. His phone buzzed again, 'YES, JUST SETTLING DOWN NOW,' Mike thought for a moment, he nearly answered *'that's nice'* but decided against it, there was obviously a point to her getting in touch. 'GREAT, HOPE THIS IS NOT WHERE WE FIND OUT WE MISSED SOMETHING!' Mike smiled as he placed a smiley face at the end, he wondered what response that would get. He did not have long to wait. 'YEAH, THAT WOULD NOT BE GOOD, IN FACT, I AM NOT THAT FAR FROM YOU, MAY I POP ROUND? I WOULD LIKE TO CHAT WITH YOU ABOUT SOMETHING THAT HAS COME UP'. Mike set the coffee down before he answered. 'OK,' his

111

phone buzzed straight away with her reply, 'THANX, I WILL BE THERE IN TEN,' Mike set the phone down. His eyes looked up at the partially open door to the living room as his wife stomped past. The front door slammed and in seconds the car revved, reversed down the driveway and then drove away from the house. Mike looked at the phone again, he remembered giving her his phone number, but not the address of his house.

∞∞∞∞

Tony glanced out of the panoramic view from his living room before he sat down on one of the chairs, Ian Silver and John Gold were on the sofa, Karen had the baby in the kitchen and was making snacks. Tony had offered but he had been 'shooed' out of the kitchen, both Ian and John had doted over the baby before they had their 'chat' with him. Short version, there were only a few Nocs, two males and possibly one female and they were nearby but did not seem to be a threat, in fact, they seemed to be going out of their way to hide. John was confident they would find them now that the order had come from Connor to first locate every Noc in the region, then in co-ordinated actions take them down, Ian was looking forward to that bit. The TV was on, the titles of the current affairs programme was just starting.

"This is either going to be total nonsense or very cringeworthy!" Ian stated.

"Or both," Tony replied.

"Has there been anything from the farm on this?" John asked.

"No, nothing, as far as we can tell, but let's see what they come up with,". Tony's eyes jumped to the open door as the baby started crying, Ian and John looked at each other.

"I don't miss those days!" John stated Tony was about to say something but stopped himself. He remembered the distraught state both men had been in at the joint funerals of the two sets of twins, an anguish he now understood. The screen changed to a single figure walking along the embankment at Coleraine. He was wearing an outdoor jacket that was open, he was older, his hair was silver from age; he had a serious look; he slowly paced forward as he spoke.

"Here we go," Ian stated, Tony glanced at him then at the presenter.

"*Good evening, in tonight's programme we are going into the realms of fantasy! ….*" John coughed, Tony shifted in his seat, "*tonight we are going to investigate a series of brutal murders over the last few years that has stained Northern Ireland in blood!*"

"Ten out of ten for laying it on," John said out loud, Tony felt himself get annoyed, he wanted to tell the other two to shut up and watch, but he didn't. The presenter carried on, "*Reminiscing of the darkest days in the early part of the troubles, we have seen a new war come to our country ….*" He walked on, the camera walked in front of him, Tony could see exactly where they had filmed it, "*according to official sources, we have been in the middle of a gang war between rival 'Eastern European Organised Crime Gangs', who brought a whole new level of violence with them …. And the police … the police seemingly powerless to stop them.*"

"Maybe you should have stayed in the cops, you could have helped!" John laughed at Ian's comment, Karen appeared in the doorway with the baby in her arms.

"Anything much so far?" she asked.

"Just started," Tony replied.

"*On this programme we will look at the compelling evidence, including several witness statements that there is something more disturbing, more terrible carrying out this seemingly endless series of murders …… as the death toll continues to rise, we discover the truth behind them is far more frightening that any inter-gang war ….*" The presenter stopped and looked straight into the camera; he raised his voice to make his statement stand. "*There is a werewolf loose in Northern Ireland!*" The main titles of the programme started; the music took over where the presenter had been speaking. Karen turned and walked away and the three of them looked at each other.

112

"A ... werewolf?" Ian said out loud, cringing as he did so.

∞∞∞

Rhydian looked over at Tyler, who was nearly falling asleep. Tyler had not touched the glass of wine that was sitting beside her chair, Rhydian had almost finished her own.

"I wonder how many people switched the channel at that statement?" Rhydian stated. Tyler stretched herself, a huge yawn spread from her.

"I am going to bed," she said sheepishly. Rhydian's eyes darted to the full wine glass as Tyler stood up. "Night," Tyler stated as she off into the kitchen.

"Night," Rhydian responded. Rhydian waited until she had closed the door at the far side of the kitchen before she made a move for the glass of wine.

∞∞∞

Cara-Marie looked at the screen of her phone, it was her mum. The main titles were coming to an end, and she knew if she answered this, she would be on the phone for some time. She flicked the side of the phone and turned it too silent. She set the phone back down on the table and sipped at her wine. The presenter reappeared, she glared at him.

"Just over two years ago, the first brutal murder took place. Edgar Trotman, who had just moved to Belfast from Manchester ...." Cara-Marie's eyes flicked back to the flashing screen of her phone; her mother was trying to call again. She ignored it. *"This was followed shortly afterwards by several other very brutal slayings where all the victims were torn limb from limb ...."* She hated this type of 'project fear' journalism, *"the worst of which, happened right here in the peaceful town of Coleraine, where five Innocent teenagers were ripped apart by something, which, for the first time, on this programme we can reveal, was not human!"* She felt herself cringe, she recognised the blurry image on the screen, then she heard Rachel Boyd's voice as she was being interviewed.

∞∞∞

Mike was sitting alone in his living room. He felt his insides turn, he recognised that picture as well, the camera turned to a solemn faced young woman. Rachel Boyd's name appeared across the bottom of the screen. The picture was from her dead brothers' phone.

"So, once you saw this photo, what was your first response?" the presenter asked.

"Well, I was just so shocked, this is obviously what killed them all at Castleroe!" Mike looked at her body language, she had been well prepared, she knew the questions that were coming, this was not an interview, she was reading from a prepared script.

"Did you keep this, or did you show this to the police?"

"Well, I did at first, but they were not interested!" she coughed and twitched, he could see it, why could no one else?

"NOT INTERESTED! Are you saying that the police did not follow up on this vital piece of evidence that could have stopped the brutal slaying that went on afterwards?" Mike looked out his windows as the small car pulled up outside. Inside was Lucy, her hair was down over her shoulders, and she was wearing sunglasses. It had been bright, but Mike did not think it was that hot. She parked half on the pavement and half on the road, he rose to watch her move around and collect some things before opening the car door and stepping out. Mike was no longer listening to the programme; he watched as this tall beauty closed the door and threw the strap of a small leather handbag over her shoulder. She had a black sleeveless sports top on that perfectly sculpted figure.

"Where the hell did you hide them?" he said out loud, Lucy had a larger chest than he had ever first noticed. She was wearing a pair of blue denim shorts that had a small turn up, he felt his eyes moved down the long slim legs as she walked around the car and up the driveway towards his front door. She smiled and lifted her left hand in a wave, the movement jolted him into springing towards the front door and opened it.

"Hiya, thanks so much for this!" Lucy smiled.

"Yeah, no problem," Mike held out his right hand towards the door of the living room. She looked around then followed his direction.

"Is your wife not home?" she asked as she paused in the middle of the room. Mike followed her into the living room.

"No, no, she had to pop out for a bit," he walked over so he was beside her, he again extended his hand to offer her a seat on the sofa. "Can I get you anything? Tea, coffee?" he offered. She turned and glanced at him, smiling as she did so.

"Thank you, no," she looked at the TV, "have I missed anything yet?" she asked as she sat down. Mike for a moment did not move.

"Err, no, not really," Lucy turned and sat down in the middle of the sofa, he was tempted to sit beside her, but changed his mind. He walked over to where he had been. The image from the Boyd phone reappeared on the screen.

"So, we can clearly see from this picture that the children, all who met a gruesome end at Castleroe, were not killed by any European crime gang but in fact by this .... Beast!"

"That looks like a Malamute," Lucy stated.

"What?" Mike asked as he tried not to stare at her. Lucy pointed towards the screen.

"That picture, it looks like an Alaskan Malamute," Lucy smiled, "I used to own one!"

"Oh," Mike responded.

"Well, if you are the only one here, then we can talk," Lucy turned where she was sitting to face him.

"Ok, what about?" Mike did not know where this was going.

"What are you doing tomorrow morning? And would you like to go for a drive up the north coast?" she asked.

∞∞∞∞

Rhydian leaned closer to the TV, studying the blurry image, she recognised the shape of a Garou, then it was gone, and the face of presenter was back. *"Was this the creature that murdered those innocents at Coleraine? So far, no one has been arrested or charged. To add to this growing overwhelming volume of evidence again for the first time on TV we can show other pieces of footage, taken in the Mourne mountains of the victim, a hill walker called Craig Keenan,"* Rhydian sat back, she had seen the footage of the rabid from the mournes.

∞∞∞∞

"Castleroe was where Davidov and the girl Anna had gone at the time when they were still having an affair and the kids surprised them ...." Tony looked over at Ian and John, "they did not want to leave any witnesses,"

"How did you know they were there?" John asked, Tony looked back at the screen.

"We didn't, the three of us went there just for a quiet picnic, heard the screaming and reacted!" The footage from the mournes started, "and this as you know," Tony was pointing to the screen, "was the rabid from Germany." The two men went silent, this was the wolf that had killed their children. Tony glanced at them, John reached out and placed his hand on top of Ian's which was gripping the top of his knee. Tony realised this was the first time they had seen this

114

footage. *"We can clearly see from this footage this is no ordinary dog, or animal attack, listening to the victim's voice, he describes what attacked him and part of this description was 'Oh my God, it has arms!'"*

∞∞∞∞

28 minutes later.

Cara-Marie turned the TV off in anger as the end credits rolled up the screen. She was already upright and flung the remote behind her onto the sofa. Her phone kept flashing with phone calls and text messages. There was a list of arrived text messages and missed calls. She paused, then tapped on the one from Mark. 'WELL, THAT WAS NONSENSE!' she started to tap in a reply but changed her mind, she called him instead.

"Good thing about phones is you cannot throw things at me down them!"

"I don't believe it!" she started, Mark stopped speaking and listened, "they completely misquoted me, and they edited it, so I look like I am some complete idiot that had no idea what she was doing!!! I mean who do they think they are!!!" she was very angry.

"What did you expect, you were not reading from their script, so they edited it to fit what they already had as an end conclusion .... What did you expect?"

"Who is that Detective Inspector Wells?" he asked.

"I think she is the one leading the current investigation into the Murlough murders,"

"She really pasted Parrish, didn't she, almost if she was reading from a script!"

"She probably was,"

"She really pasted you as well," he started.

"I am not bothered by that,"

"Oh, hang on," Mark stated, Cara-Marie stopped.

"Are you OK?" she asked.

"Yeah, there is someone at my door .... call you later," Mark hung up the phone. Cara-Marie then started to scroll through the messages she had been sent. She stopped on a number she did not recognise, she opened it and read the message. 'HI, YOUR MUM GAVE ME YOUR NUMBER AND SAID THAT YOU WERE SINGLE AND I SHOULD GIVE YOU A CALL, SHE SENT ME SEVERAL PICTURES OF YOU, AND WOW, YOU ARE STUNNING, SHALL WE MEET, SAY, TOMORROW EVENING FOR A DRINK? OWEN.'

"What da Fuc ......"

Cara-Marie had just gone from angry to furious in one message.

Chapter 21 Ballintoy Harbour

Tony drove slowly down the steep and narrow road that twisted and turned its way down the slope towards the small harbour. He was in first gear; the road was that narrow only one car could pass, and the twists were almost 180' degrees. The road came around the rock face and dropped down into the open car park that faced out to sea. There was a pavement with a row of spaces that could fill very easily. The other side of which were the rocks that protruded out of the water to defend the coast from the worst of the ravages of the sea. The rocks were covered with small rock pools, some big enough that you could almost swim in them. Tony turned his car around and reverse parked, so he was facing the single road that led back up the steep hill. He glanced at his watch, it was nearly 2PM, he looked around, there was only two other cars, neither of which he recognised. He got out, it was a sunny day, but the wind blew in from the sea bringing a coldness with it, so he lifted his jacket from the passenger seat and pulled it on. That would help to conceal the pistol he had on the belt of his trousers and under his top. He walked around the rear of his car and along the pavement towards the harbour itself. It was a stone harbour that had been built for a small fishing fleet that no longer fished. On his right were two buildings, the first had a slate roof and looked like they were public toilets, the second was much larger and had a flat roof, there were two men walking around, they were taking a lot of interest in both buildings. In front of him was the wide concrete ramp that went down into the water, where the small boats would be launched from. He walked on past the picnic table where a family were packing up, two small children were running around in a game, the young couple seemed happy and enjoying their day out, but it was time to go. Tony walked along the harbour wall towards the mouth of the harbour, the wind blowing gently over him. He stopped at the end, he looked over to his right, at the small stone building that had a large entrance, it had been used for storage at some time in the past. He looked around, the north coast stretched out, the rocky outcroppings and cliffs dominated the coast, he looked straight at Rathlin island in the distance, and he smiled, he loved where he lived. A car roared into life, Tony did not look around as the family drove back up the road and out of sight. He looked at the view again as the wind picked up into a breeze, his hands deep in the pockets of the jacket, the side of the harbour wall came to just about his waist.

"Beautiful isn't it!" Tony did not move. He recognised Alison's voice. He waited for a few seconds before he slowly turned to face her. He had expected her to be pointing a weapon at him, but she wasn't. She was standing nearly ten feet away with her hands deep in the pockets of her Gortex jacket. She looked dishevelled, her hair was a mess, she looked drained like she had not slept in days, this was not the Alison Wallace he had worked with in Coleraine Police Station, always immaculate, always well presented.

"Yes, it is," he spoke quietly. She smiled politely then looked down, she raised her head and looked around. Two men were walking around the far side of the harbour, there was a lot of pointing and nodding, they were obviously not local.

"I wonder what they are up to?" Tony asked as he glanced over at them.

"Location managers," she replied. Alison was staring at them as Tony looked at her.

"What for?"

"Location managers for some TV show they are going to be filming part of here," Alison looked at him but did not maintain eye contact, "something about dragons and zombies," she shrugged, "I was chatting to them earlier."

"That doesn't sound like it will take off!" he injected.

"They seem to think it is going to be the next 'Lord of the Rings!'"

"Selling shares in it were they?" Tony joked. Alison didn't laugh.

"We are not alone, are we?"

"No," Tony paused, she looked up.

"Are you going to let me leave her alive?" Tony looked at her face, her lip was trembling, and her body had just tensed up.

"If we wanted you dead, you would be already!" he stated firmly. Alison looked straight up with her eyes, then look away, there was a shrug as she pulled her hands out of her pockets, Tony's eyes darted to her hands, he relaxed slightly when he saw that they were empty.

"So, how long have you known about me?" he asked, her face reacted.

"About you being a wolf? Day one I met you!" her face lightened a little, "spotted you immediately, Kyle however," she looked away, "did not spot him at all!"

"Well, neither did I to be honest,"

"Even when we were chatting about the riverside murder, did not see it at all, he kept it well hidden,"

"That was because he did not know himself," Tony added.

"No, I don't think he did actually," Alison spoke quietly.

"Are you armed?" he asked. Alison looked around behind her, there was no one there. When she looked back at him, she looked concerned.

"When I said my life is in danger, I wasn't joking, if he finds me, he will kill me!" She had a frightened look in her eyes, she was serious.

"Who?"

"*HIM!*"

"Yeah, I am going to need a little bit more than just 'him'" Tony stated. Alison paused and looked around again, she was obviously uncomfortable with this, "You need to tell me exactly who or we will not help you at all!"

"Ok," she looked up, "it was 'The American',"

"Real name please!" it was not a question, but a demand.

"I don't know,"

"How can you 'not know'?" Tony reacted; Alison took a step towards him.

"Tony, please, I don't know, we were told not to ask, some sort of curse or something." Tony paused, the wind blew around them, he looked around the harbour, the two men were getting back into their car, his eyes followed them as they drove away.

"Not enough," he whispered.

"What do you want?" she pleaded, Tony turned and stared at her.

"Everything,"

"Everything?"

"Yes, everything, who, what, where, what they wanted to do, what the final objective was .... Everything," Alison bit her bottom lip then looked at him.

"Ok, ok," Tony stared at her, she looked up, "Well, all of that is going to take some time, don't think we can do all that here!" she let out a nervous laugh.

"Well to get you started, what was this 'American' trying to do?"

"That's easy, start a war,"

"How?"

"I don't know how he knew both Dani and Sabine, but he knew how much Dani wanted to kill both you and Kyle and how much Sabine wanted Reynolds, he brought them over here to do just that, the others were mostly the waffs and strays from small covens around western Europe," she looked at him, "not much of a force actually."

"What about the one they turned, Martin? What was the story there?"

"I only met him after they had turned him, he turned psychotic and went on a raping and killing spree, when we realised that he could not be controlled he was handed over to you guys ..." Alison held her hand out, "And you guys did not disappoint,"

"What about the rabid? What the fuck was going on there?"

"I didn't know anything about that," she pleaded, "Tony please, believe me,"

"Who did then?"

"Dani, she found out the Germans, once they knew she was infected, forced her out, I honestly don't know how she knew but she did, we organised a car for her, inside was camping gear, food, money, change of clothes and the like ... I never actually met her, once she was here, we had no contact with her," Tony looked up the side of the hill then turned away from her. "Look, The American did it all," she stepped forward so she was standing beside him as he looked out to sea, "he wanted to force the An Rua to react, then he could use that as an excuse to mobilise every one of them in Europe," Tony looked at her, she looked down then reached out and touched his shoulder, "Tony please,"

"Slowly .... Take out your weapon and set it on the wall then step back." Alison paused, then taking slow deliberate movements placed her pistol on the wall, then stepped back.

"Tony, please, believe me," Tony quickly lifted the weapon and tucked it into one of his pockets, he turned and nodded behind her, she turned around, standing over the side of the hill were nearly twenty people, all staring at her, she recognised what they were.

"It isn't me you have to convince ...." He nodded towards the two older men that were standing glaring at her from the stone table at the end of the harbour wall, she had not seen them approach, Tony pointed towards them as he started to walk away from her.

"They are Ian Silver and John Gold; their children were torn apart by that rabid in the mountains. I suggest you don't do anything stupid and do what they say ...."

"Tony please, I just want to live ...."

"Do as they say, and you will, there are a few people back at the farm that 'really' want to talk to you." He started to walk away then turned back towards her. 'By the way,"

"What?"

"What is a Valkyrie anyway?"

∞∞∞∞

Cara-Marie saved what she had been typing then saved the story to the editor's drop box then looked up at the clock on the wall, it had just gone 3PM. She glanced at the number over her own inbox, it had gone from just over two hundred to nearly five hundred, most of them were a result of the programme last night. It had started as soon as she got to work, everyone had watched it, and she vented her anger at how she had been portrayed. The odd one out had been Kevin. He had only mentioned it once, she had expected him to be leading the charge, but he wasn't, quite the opposite in fact. She looked over at him in his office, he was on the phone and the door was closed. Mark walked back up from reception and retook his seat, he moved the mouse and became focused on the screen.

"Can I get your opinion on something?" she asked. Mark stopped and leaned over around the side of his monitor. He had raised his eyebrows; she had her phone in her hand and was looking at it.

"My opinion?" he asked.

"Yes," she replied without looking up.

"You normally give me my opinion first!"

"Mmmm?" she answered.

"Nothing," he said as he went back behind his monitor, "what is it?"

118

"Can you have a look at this for me," she stood up and stretched out her hand, offering him her phone.

"Ok," he took the phone and looked at the screen, "what am I looking at?" he sat back in the chair and started to read.

"Mum gave this guy my number, he started messaging me last night."

"Your mum gave him 'several pictures of you?'" he crunched up his face.

"Yeah, I had it out with her this morning."

"And where did she meet this …. 'Owen'?"

"In the queue in the supermarket when she was shopping."

"In the queue at a supermarket!" Mark started laughing and he stood and handed the phone back, "So, when are you going to meet 'the future father of your children?"

"You think I should? I mean, look at it! That was only the first of several messages I got last night." she said as she took back the phone.

"Hell no, that sounds so creepy it's unreal!" Mark responded.

"He sent friend requests to nearly all of my social media last night, so I blocked him!" Mark started to properly laugh, "told him not to message me and I had blocked him."

"Have you blocked him?"

"Not yet, but I wanted to chat with you first about it."

"CARA!" They both looked round at Kevin who was standing in the doorway of his office, "have you got two minutes!" Kevin turned and walked back towards his desk.

Mark turned and looked at her, he was still grinning. "Guess that is your que!"

Cara-Marie stood up and dropped her phone back into her handbag on the floor.

"I wish he would get my name right!" she tutted as she lifted her notebook and pen then walked over to the office. She stopped in the doorway. Kevin was behind his desk looking at something on his monitor, he looked up as she filled the doorway.

"Come in, come in, take a seat." She closed the door and took sat down. "Right two things," he started as he took his hand from the computer mouse, "I have been chatting with Belfast and they acknowledge you have turned down the position in Belfast at head office,"

"Well, they can't 'make' me go, can they?" she butted in, Kevin paused.

"They could if they really wanted to, but they are happy you wish to stay here," *was he happy or sad about that, she was not sure.*

"Thanks, prefer it here to Belfast," she said, "but you said there were two things?"

"Yes," Kevin shuffled in his seat, whatever was coming was the real reason she was sitting here. "They were very impressed by the documentary last night!"

"Impressed? But they got it all wrong!" she did not realise t she had raised her voice, but Kevin did, he kept his wrists on the desk but raised his fingers to settle her down.

"Well, take it from me, that they were impressed, and as you know there has been quite a reaction from it, so they want you to do another piece on it."

"What kind of piece exactly?" she asked, Kevin looked at his notebook.

"A four-piece article to be serialised over four weeks and distributed over the whole group, each piece to be not less than five hundred words," he looked up at her, "you OK with that?" she reacted with glee, being told to work on her favourite story and on work time no less.

"Yes, of course, brilliant," she was excited, "when do they want it by?" she asked.

"End of the week, I want you to finish that farm story first,"

"Already done," she butted in again.

"And the Jackson piece?"

"In your drop box already, finished it before I came in here!" she was beaming.

Kevin sat back, "Ok, then take two days and get it done," Cara-Marie jumped up and headed for the door, "Cara!" Kevin stopped her, she looked back at him.

"Yes?"

"I want to preview it before you submit it and get Mark to pick out a selection of photos to go with it,"

"Sure, no problems!" she grinned as she opened the door.

"Cara," he stopped her again,

"Yes?"

"I mean it, I want to approve the text and the photos before you submit, stick to facts, that's all!" she got what he was saying, he was still the editor after all.

"Will do," she turned and headed out of the office and back to her desk. Kevin heard the invite for coffee and watched as the two of them headed out the back door of the newspaper. Kevin turned and clicked on an email, he read over then clicked to reply. He typed quickly. 'DONE, SHE WILL BE OUT OF THE OFFICE FOR TWO DAYS' then he clicked on the send button without adding the electronic signature box at the bottom.

Chapter 22 – Limerick City, Republic of Ireland

Grishin and Tatamovich walked across the stone bridge heading back into the city. It was starting to get dark; they had finished re-tracing the steps of the Noc that killed the two men.

"Shall we go back to that pub where we had lunch?" Tatamovich suggested,

"You mean the one with the red headed, large breasted, very strong accented barmaid who took a liking to your credit card at lunchtime and kept repeating she was working tonight?" The two men shared a laugh. Tatamovich's phone started to ring, he paused, Grishin took two more steps then stopped to look at him.

"It is a Russian number," he muttered, he lifted the phone to his ear, "Privyet," straight away he had a stern look on his face, "Da, Da," he nodded, "Spasiba," he lowered his hand, "there's been a death in the high council, we are to return in the next few days!" he stated.

"Who?" Grishin asked, Tatamovich shook his head.

"He didn't say," Tatamovich started to walk forward, "I think the Irish have things in hand here anyway!"

"They do," Grishin agreed, then his phone bleeped with a text message. Grishin took it out and read it, he looked at Tatamovich. "Reynolds has captured a Valkyrie," the two men continued to walk along the bridge.

"I did not believe they actually existed," Tatamovich stated.

"Neither did I, we'll head north tomorrow then fly home after that!" Grishin stated.

"Da," his answer was automatic, he was thinking about the redhead.

"I wonder if they do a bed and breakfast at that pub?" Grishin asked.

"They do!" Tatamovich stated without a second thought.

∞∞∞∞

"Really? This could not wait until tomorrow?" Chris was not happy.

"Apparently not," Mike agreed. Mike looked along the coast, they were in a small car park that was on the edge of a cliff face. It was on the coastal route between Ballycastle and Portrush. The three cars had been there a while, Chris really wanted to be somewhere else, the two MI5 girls, Lucy and Nikki had just been for a little 'walk behind a bush' but were on their way back again. This meeting had been called by Sam from MI6, and he was late.

"What time is fucknuts getting here?" his contempt for Sam was growing, Mike looked at his watch as the smiling girls approached.

"Half an hour ago,"

"Well, where is he?" Chris demanded.

Mike leant up against his car and folded his arms. "Successful walk?"

"Well, let's just say it's a weight off my mind!" Nikki laughed as she answered.

"So, are you saying you are not 'full of shit' anymore!" Chris injected, all three turned and looked at him, he was not making a joke.

"Ok bitchy, who lit the fuse on your tampon?" Nikki replied, her response made Mike giggle once. A car slowed and turned into the car park.

"He's here," Lucy said as the car came into view. When Sam got out of the car, he was not happy. He stomped over to where the group was waiting and had an envelope in his hand.

"Right," he started.

"What fucking time do you call this!" Chris demanded.

"What?"

"Sorry, was the question too difficult for you? What .... Time .... Do .... You .... Call ... this?" Chris was angry. Sam stared for a moment, Lucy tried not to grin, Sam was not used to people speaking to him like that.

"Anyway, he is here now, so, what could not wait until tomorrow morning then?" Mike injected. Sam glared at Chris then looked towards Mike.

"Right, the task this afternoon, what was the outcome of that?" Sam asked.

"Well, Fallon met up with one, Alison Wallace, at Ballintoy harbour, they had a conversation, after that they all went back to the deer farm." Nikki stated.

"And what do we know about her?" Sam asked.

"Alison Wallace, former police officer, retired after thirty years' service, used to live near Bushmills, current whereabouts, unknown," replied Lucy.

"Do we know what they said during their meeting?" Sam asked.

"Yeah, got most of it on audio, the transcript will be ready tomorrow."

"Good, is she currently wanted by the police in connection with anything?"

"Not at the moment," replied Mike.

"What about the footage from the farmhouse where that drug dealer and his girlfriend were killed? Was she not there?" Sam stated.

"The group of people from the CCTV footage is not great, at this moment in time the two tall women remain officially unidentified by the police," Mike stated.

"But she was there?" Nikki asked.

"There was no DNA or scientific evidence that puts her at the scene, the girl in the house was raped and killed by that fella Martin, and the guy was also raped and killed by at least two other people but the DNA there was corrupted," Mike explained.

"What about the footage from the carpark at Mussenden, it was her attacking that woman, Yelina what's-her-name!" Chris added.,

Mike shrugged, "As far at that investigation goes ......" he started.

"It was closed," Sam stated. There was a moment of silence then Sam raised the envelope and handed it to Mike, as Mike took it, "we are interested in these two, both Russians,"

"Grishin and Tatamovich!" Lucy stated, Sam looked at her.

"Right, we need to find out all the farm knows about these two as we are very interested in their activities and their connection with the farm." Sam was about to say something else when an angry Chris stepped forward.

"Hey, can we not do all this crap tomorrow? Some of us do have lives you know!" Everyone looked at him.

"Yeah, we could all meet tomorrow," Lucy looked at Chris as she spoke, Chris nodded.

"Listen here soldier boy, you are here to do what you are told, so, do as you are told...." Sam had not finished speaking when Chris moved. The movement was that fast it took everyone by surprise, he jumped forward, covering the distance between himself and Sam in a microsecond. Sam's body slammed against the side of the car, Chris had Sam's right hand pushed into his chest and his left hand around the right side of his own face, so his own left arm was choking him. Chris had his own face pushed up against his struggling victim.

"You ain't in charge of shit! .... dickhead!" Chris screamed at him. It took a moment before the others jumped forward to intervene.

"Hey, hey, we are all on the same side here," Mike was trying to release the grip Chris had on Sam, but he quickly realised Chris's immense strength and grip on him, it would be Chris's decision to release him. The two girls were on the other side tugging at Chris's arms.

"Chris, let him go, let him go," Chris paused and slowly released his grip, then he stepped back, Sam slid down the side of the car, gasping for breath. Chris looked at him with utter contempt. He then looked at Mike.

"I'm outta here," he muttered as he turned and marched back to his car. As Sam was standing up, he was still rubbing his throat, there were tears in his eyes.

"I will get him fired for that!" he spat.

"You will do no such thing," Lucy raised her voice as the car door slammed and the engine roared into life. The car jumped forward and the wheels spun with a screech, and in moments, Chris had disappeared and was gone. Sam stuttered his words as he spoke again.

"I have been assaulted, and I want action taken against him!" Sam said as he straightened himself up.

"No, you damn well don't!" Lucy stated.

"Look, I ...."

"Have fucked up everything you have touched!" Mike looked at Lucy, she was now angry, he had not seen this side of her yet, Nikki on the other hand was just smiling at what was now happening in front of her. "Get in your car and fuck off .... I will email everything from today when it is ready!"

"But I ..."

"Get in your car and leave ...." Lucy was standing her ground, she was aggressively pointing towards his car, *"if you still want to have a job then do it ...... NOW!"* Sam was still rubbing his throat as he glanced at Nikki, then Mike. Lucy was glaring at him as she shuffled off towards his car. No one spoke as he opened his car door and got in, the three of them relaxed as Sam slowly left.

"Wow, I have never seen anyone move as fast as that!" exclaimed Nikki.

"Me neither," added Lucy.

"Did you get the impression that he has done that before?"

"Well, he is in the SAS after all," Mike added and he picked the envelope off the ground, "and they are very good at what they do!" Mike tried not to smile as he spoke.

"Hell yeah, want to get me some more of that!" Nikki looked excited.

"Well, let's stick to the current task in hand," Lucy had relaxed a bit. She took a deep breath in, "Nikki, we can finish this later," Nikki looked at her then at Mike and smiled.

"Yeah sure," Nikki headed towards the car both her and Lucy had arrived in.

"Well, that was certainly an eventful meeting," Mike stated.

"It was," Lucy turned toward him and stepped closer, Mike noticed she slightly lowered her voice. "His days over here are numbered, but that is not what we needed to discuss," Mike straightened up, whatever was coming he guessed was the real reason for the meeting. "I was going to ask Chris for more access to the farm, as I know, he is closer with them than any of us."

"He is," Mike agreed, "what is it you're after?"

"Our boss wants us to get a video recording of one of them changing, you know," she tilted her head, "into their wolf thingy's,"

"Wolf thingies?" Mike almost laughed, then a serious look fell over his face, "you have never seen one, have you?" he asked.

"Only in still pictures," her eyes looked around, "I guess part of me still doesn't really believe they are in fact real .... Stuff of nightmares you know."

"Yes, I know,"

"When was the first time you saw one .... You know, for real?" she asked. Mike breathed in as the memory came flooding back.

"When they murdered Simon," Mike's eyes looked at the ground.

"Detective Simon McAllister, killed in Castleroe, near Coleraine," she stated as if reading directly from a statement.

"MURDERED," he corrected.

"Sorry, murdered,"

"Yeah, when I found what was left of him, I was in a state of shock, normally when I see dead people, I don't know them ...." Lucy looked at him, he was talking so she let him, he carried on, "his head was on a pole, just the amount of force that would have taken to do in such a short time .... then I looked up, and it was up on top of the hill looking at me, it just stood there," Mike stopped talking. He was staring into nothing; Lucy could see that all he could see was what he was describing. She wanted to comfort him, but she stood there, listening. "I should have raised my pistol, but I couldn't move, it was staring at me, then it just turned and walked away" Mike looked at her, "never seen a dog walk on its hind legs before!"

"That bit was not in your original statement!" she smiled.

"No, it wasn't," he looked down again, "I just could not form the words to ...." He stopped again, this time she stepped forward and placed her arms around his neck and pulled him in to a tight hug. Mike didn't do anything for a few seconds then slowly wrapped his arms around her body, he could feel the tears starting to well up in himself.

Lucy broke off the hug and stepped back, "I cannot even imagine,"

"I hope you never have to!" Mike responded.

"Anyway, if you can, get Chris back on board, we could use footage of a change and information on their 'councils' that were mentioned in the past." professional Lucy was back.

"Ok, I'll ask, but don't expect a positive response,"

"I would like to visit this farm as well,"

"What?" Mike let out a short laugh, "I will ask but ...."

"Ok," she smiled.

"Well, I best get back on the road," Mike stated.

"No problem, we can chat tomorrow then." Lucy smiled at him. Mike smiled and walked back to his car. Lucy walked around and got into the drivers' seat of the hire car they had given her; Nikki was in the passenger seat.

"And .... What are you doing with him?" she said playfully.

"Managing an asset," Lucy stated as she started the engine.

"By screwing him?"

"If we get the result we want, then ... so?" They both watched Mike's car turn out of the car park and head off in one direction, they would go the other way.

"Just because your marriage when down the drain, that does not mean you have to end every other marriage you come across!" Nikki stated. The car moved off.

"It did not 'go down the drain,' he went off with another man for fucks sake!"

"That was a long time ago, Luce,"

"If the next words out of your mouth are that I need to 'let it go' your mouth is suddenly going to start bleeding! I know what I am doing!" she spat. The car accelerated onto the road as they headed for Portrush.

"How many marriages have you ended now .... Ten, eleven?"

"Twelve!"

"You shag them, get them to leave the marriage then dump them!" Nikki stated, she had a serious look on her face as she spoke.

"If they are unfaithful, then how could I trust them! Do it once, they will do it again!" there was anger in Lucy's voice.

"Maybe you should date single guys instead of just going for married ones!"

"Maybe you should shut the fuck up and mind your own business!"

"What! Like you do with Sarah and me? Every time you see her you constantly go on that our marriage isn't legal over here ... how about you take your own advice for once!"

The rest of the car journey to Belfast would be a quiet one.

Chapter 23

Megan Due sped up as she drove across the border between the North and the South. The border was just a yellow box painted on the road. A nefarious smile spread over her face, this was her first time coming this far north, the Irish police in the south would not be looking for her up here, in fact, no one was! She looked at the road sign, the North was in miles per hour, but the South Road signs were in kilometres, that will take some getting used to. As she drove over the bridge her eyes darted down to the river that flowed underneath and as quickly as it was there it was gone, the road was again surrounded by trees as she headed towards the small town of Aughnacloy in County Tyrone; there were trees on her right and open fields on her left, and she felt her excitement growing, she was going to have fun in the north.

All she had to do was find this famous 'Vampire hunter' that no one had ever seen or had any details on him. She heard stories about this man that had been given the nickname 'The Destroyer'. Some did not believe he existed, others lived-in fear in case he came calling. She would throw that back in the face of them all. Scared, she was not, quite the opposite in fact, this was a man she wanted to kill and if the wolves got in the way, well, she would just kill them as well! She did not hear her phone bleeping with the text message, it would be nearly an hour before she found it and read the short message. 'WE NEED TO MEET, YOU ARE TO SEND ME YOUR DETAILS, I AM IN NORTHERN IRELAND NOW ON A JOB.'

∞∞∞∞

"Hey," Dermott said as he walked through the front door of the farmhouse, Paul walked in after him. Rhydian had just come in from the kitchen and Tyler was sitting in the large chair with a sleeping baby in her arms.

"Ssssh!" she whispered as she slowly swayed from side to side.

"I'll take him," Rhydian offered, stepping forward, holding her arms.

"Cheers," Tyler smiled as she spoke. The two exchanged the sleeping bundle and Rhydian headed towards the stairs. Dermott and Paul took off their jackets and sat down. "So, what is up?" Tyler asked, Paul sat back but Dermott sat forward.

"Well, we have heard from Ian and John, and they have confirmed that there are only three Nocs anywhere near Tony's house."

"Do they know where they are sleeping yet?" she asked.

"No, not yet; they are sure it's pretty close but," Dermott glanced at Paul.

"But?" Tyler asked.

"But that isn't the bigger problem currently," Paul stated.

"What is?" Tyler sighed.

"They have sighted a group of guys that are certainly searching around the North Coast, and ...." Paul paused.

"And they have done a drive by of here taking photos and video of the front of the farm!" Dermott stated, Tyler sat up.

"Nocs?" she asked.

"No," replied Dermott, "sapiens, but they are certainly surveillance trained, mostly do their stuff at night, are all male and from what we have so far, probably ex-military of some type!" Tyler looked at them sternly.

"So, what do we know so far? Apart from that?"

"We have one vehicle registration plate so far," Paul stated, he glanced at Dermott before looking back at her, "and that is being investigated, once we know, you will know."

125

"Do you think it is our SAS friends?" she asked.

"Don't think so, but we should ID them before we throw it back at them!"

"Agreed," Paul added.

"And what have we been doing about Connor's declaration?" she asked.

"Well, the two Nocs in Belfast we knew about were taken care of, Ian and John have a plan for what is left in the Northwest and the one that was left down near Newry has left the country," Dermott explained.

"Do we know where it went?" Tyler asked.

"Initially headed over to England," Dermott nodded a few times as he spoke, "we told the Iceni about him, and they are going to deal with that."

"Good," Tyler sat forward, "any fallout about the TV programme so far?" she asked,

Paul and Dermott glanced at each other. "Not so far, very little in the printed press, that fella Dr Burns is still being rubbished, the girl from Coleraine whose brother was killed at Castleroe seems to be getting torn apart online with lots of people saying she is just selling a story of her dead brother etc," Paul replied.

"So, nothing coming our way then?" she asked.

"Not so far, even 'down south' seemed happy with it," Dermott stated with a grin.

"Ok, what about that journalist? You know, McKenna?"

"From the Herald?" Paul asked.

"Yes, her," Tyler replied, Paul shifted in his seat.

"Well, as far as we can tell, very few believe her, so most are ignoring what she is saying and the police keep repeating the 'Eastern European crime gangs' line," Paul looked at Dermott, "that is a lot more believable to most than what she is trying to push!" he added.

"Good,"

"When are you going to meet the high council?" Dermott asked, Tyler grinned.

"When they formally invite me, plus, we don't know exactly 'where' in Russia it is." Paul moved and took out his phone, he looked at the screen. "Well, that maybe sooner than you think!" he stated.

"Why?" Dermott asked.

Paul turned the screen of his phone around to show him a text message. Grishin and Tatamovich are on their way here!"

"When do they get here?" Tyler asked.

"They are just leaving Limerick City, so should be here in about an hour and a half."

"Ok," Tyler stood up, the others did as well. "We better tidy the place up for them." she walked around the chair and headed into the kitchen; Dermott spoke quietly to Paul.

"You did not ask her about the military wanting to bring the MI6 guy here?" he asked, Paul shrugged. "No need, the answer is no!"

∞∞∞∞

He was an older man, enjoying walking his dog, which was an old dog as well. His hair was receding, and his glasses looked as him. He was smiling as he walked along the coastal path, the old black Labrador plodded along beside him, stopping occasionally to look back and wag its tail The old man's jeans were a bit baggy and he was still wearing the old woollen jumper his late wife had knitted for him, and the new bright blue Gortex jacket his daughter got for him for walks like this. The long wooden staff aided his walks these days. He walked like a shepherd of old, yes, there was just him and the dog these days, but that suited him. They had sat beside each other and watched the sunset earlier, the dog, happy to be with him, and him, happy to be where he was in life; they walked side by side, but now it was getting dark and time to get home.

The evenings were not cold, but he would build a log fire when he got in, his dinner would not take long either, yes things for him were good.

He stopped. He was confused. The path followed the coastline and there was a drop on his right-hand side, it was not cold, but it was not warm either, the wind off the sea made sure of that, that is why he had the jumper and jacket on, even the dog stopped to look at the man that was running up the path towards them. He had jeans on and trainers, but he was topless, why would a half-naked man be running along the path at night? He would ask him when he got here, which, at the speed he was running would not take him long. The old dog started to wag his tail; he was always friendly when he was meeting new people, the old man stopped and rested on his staff, the half-naked man was now sprinting towards him, 'what could possibly be going on?' he wondered. He looked around to see if there was anyone else, but there was no one for miles.

∞∞∞∞

Glenn Nendrum was walking away from the parked 4x4's; he had the small backpack over one shoulder as he started to walk along the coastal path, Martin upon seeing the dog walker got very excited, the team had an unscheduled stop and they had been told to wait there. He had guessed why they had stopped, Martin had not fed in a while. He found the discarded top and picked it up, he walked on until Martin was walking towards him out of the darkness. His face, neck and most of his chest were covered in blood, as were his hands, Martin was still excited as they came together. Glenn slid the day sack off his shoulder, and it landed with a thud on the ground. Martin was keen to get at the two large plastic bottles of water, wet wipes, towel and change of top that were inside.

"Where is he?" Glenn asked. Martin dropped down onto one knee and opened the bag; the towel came out first. When Martin spoke, Glenn could see his elongated incisors.

"He is just over that rise," Martin was like a child with a new toy.

"And the dog?" Martin started to wash himself and did not look up as he answered.

"Over the cliff, it was nearly dead anyway,"

"We have the meeting with 'The American' in thirty minutes," Glenn explained,

"Sure, no problem," he sloshed water over his face and neck then opened the packet of wet wipes, "can you sort that out?" Martin motioned with his head back up the path.

"I can," Glenn said quietly. He pulled the metal, screw-topped bottle out the day sack. He walked up the path and just over the rise was the body. There was a lot of blood. The old man's throat was ripped out. His face was contorted, mouth opened in horror, arms outstretched with clawed fingers grasping at nothing. He opened the metal bottle and poured fuel over the torso, along the leg and right foot. He flicked his lighter and the fuel started to burn blue as it made its way back up the leg. The flames had taken hold, so it was not just the fuel burning, then with a flick of his foot the burning body slid over the edge and down to the rocks below. Glenn stood at the edge and looked at the burning body, there would be little to no evidence left. Glenn walked back down the path with Martin was just finishing getting dressed.

"Ok, are we good to go now?" Martin asked as he stood up.

"We are," Glenn replied as he approached.

"Great!" Martin turned to walk away, leaving the day sack in the middle of the pathway. Glenn had a quick look around to ensure that nothing had been left, then he zipped up the day sack and headed back to the waiting 4x4's.

Chapter 24

"Wait here," Martin instructed. Glenn nodded then Martin turned and headed off into the forestry block. Glenn turned and faced the parked 4 x 4's, the security team was doing what they were supposed to be doing. Each vehicle had the driver still behind the wheel, two near the entrance of the car park, two at the far side and all were in touch with their communications.

"Where the hell is he going now?" the voice in his ear asked. Glenn looked at the security team leader who was sitting in one of the 4x4's.

"He did not say," Glenn answered quietly. This broke every rule of what they were trained to do, the client, the person they were contracted to protect, had just got out and ran off into the trees, they did not know where he was going, how long he was going to be or anything. To say that this was unprofessional was an understatement, but then, he had watched him commit a murder on a coastal path less than an hour ago, so this was an unusual task for them. He had been with the client for some time now, he had seen it before, there had been a few glances and concerned looks from some of the team but he had reminded them that they were being paid three times the normal amount so they should have expected it to be three times the more difficult a task. Once the client had arrived and they had him in the safe house they had now been briefed on the 'not normal' security arrangements, but there had been a reaction when it was confirmed that the client was a senior vampire and the meeting, he had attended near Salisbury had been to the site of a large coven of vampires. The next part of his brief was what would happen if any of them spoke out of turn or told anyone about who they were working for, "Your bodies will never be found! Just remember that!" the message had got through. "This lot are very good at 'media manipulation' so don't bother trying to sell any story you think you might get money for, as they will destroy you, I have seen it before, so don't try it, ... however, if you look after them, they will look after you, you are being employed for a reason and they will pay over the odds for it," Glenn had watched their reactions, "you will not be involved in anything that they do, you are here for protection, nothing more!" that had got some nods, "in six months' time you will have so much money you will be able to afford a mansion in any of the posh areas of London, right next door to the superstars and people we normally protect!" that had got what he wanted, smiles and relaxed faces, he had appealed to the very reason they had applied for the job in the first place. He turned his head as the car door closed, the team leader walked around the front of the car.

"Any idea who this person is he is meeting?" Castle asked.

"None," Glenn answered.

"And if something happens to him?" Glenn looked at him but did not answer, "Dead clients don't pay!" Castle added.

"He is more than capable of looking after himself!" Glenn stated.

"Then why employ us? Why expose himself like that to us?" Castle looked around at the other team members.

"Because we do the things he can't!" Glenn stated, the wind picked up.

"You know," Castle started, "if you had told me six months ago that vampires were real ... I would have said you were insane!"

"Noctrailis!"

"What?" Castle asked.

"They call themselves 'Noctrailis', not vampires," Glenn corrected.

"Whatever," Castle snorted, "but we just witnessed a murder,"

"Did you?" Glenn turned towards him, "did you actually see him kill anyone?"

"Well, no," Mark Castle had just become uncomfortable.

"So, what did you see?" Glenn asked.

"He ran off up the path and came back washing blood off himself,"

"He could have killed a stray dog,"

"But he had to change what he was wearing as it was caked in blood ...."

"But did you 'see' him attack anyone?" Glenn asked.

"Well, no, but it was obvious that ...."

"That what?" Glenn was now being defensive, "what did you '*actually see*'? did you see anyone else on the path?"

"Well, there was that dog walker ...."

"And did you see him attack him?" Glenn demanded.

"Well, no, but ...."

"But what?" Glenn stopped; he was staring directly at the head of the security team.

"But nothing," there was a short silence between them before Mark spoke again. "When this is over, am I going to finish it alive?" he asked.

"Well, that is very much up to you, there is a real threat as there is with any high value client," Glenn explained.

"I mean, when this is finished will I be allowed to leave the contract alive and go back to my normal life?" Glenn noticed that he had asked 'I' and not 'we'.

"You are the first security team that they are using, let's not set a precedence shall we!" Glenn turned and walked away; Mark Castle watched him go.

"That didn't answer my question!" he muttered.

∞∞∞∞∞

Jason Apollyon went down on one knee. His right hand stretched out to move the grass in front of him. He breathed in through his nose, he could smell them. He still had his dark green outdoor jacket on, his large rucksack sat comfortably on his back. He stood up and looked around. The gust of wind blew past him, he looked back, he was alone. He went down his knee again and lowered his nose to the ground, his eyes followed the track across the field, there was more than two of them. He rose then slowly made his way across the field, following the young vampires running scared.

∞∞∞∞∞

Martin slowed down as he arrived at the far side of the forest. The security team was still at the other side of the trees, and they had stayed there, exactly as they were supposed to do, he now knew that Glenn could control them to the level that he wanted. Martin slowed down to a walk as he approached the small stone building. It was not made from bricks, but large stones of different sizes, it was done to make it look like it had been made centuries ago, but the structure was more recent than that. The building was at the top of a single track that cut its way down through the trees, there was a gap of nearly thirty metres between the two blocks of trees. The small building had one large door at the front, it had been built as a store house of some description. Martin stopped. He stood perfectly still. He listened. He listened to the wind, he listened to the wildlife, he listened to the trees. The sound of movement came from the far side of the building, he was not alone. Martin slowly went down on one knee as the lone figure made its way nervously around the front of the building. His eyes narrowed and focused on The American as he stopped by the corner that was closest to him. The American was looking around himself, he shifted where he was standing and motioned a greeting with one hand towards him when he was spotted. Martin stood and slowly paced his way towards him.

129

"Hi, are you alone?" The American asked. Martin initially did not answer, he looked up at the trees behind him, before looking back at him.

"What do you think you are doing?" Martin demanded.

"Just making sure you are alone," The American stated, Martin jumped forward, making the American repel back up against the side of the building.

"I meant, what the hell have you been doing over here!" Martin was shouting, he was furious, "Do you realise what you have done! This has been one of our biggest disasters in nearly a century!"

"We need to take the war to the wolves!" The American protested, he stepped forward and waved his hand as if dismissing Martin as he did so. Martin stepped closer, batted his hand out of the way with his left hand and grabbed the American around the throat with his right hand and threw him up against the side of the building.

"You cost us over one hundred of our own," The American slammed into the building, Martin let go of his grip and watched as The American sild down the wall on to the ground. *"You cost us the lives of Sabine AND Dani! Two of our best!"*

"Look, I ..." The American started.

"You what? YOU WHAT?" Martin screamed at him, the American cowered. Martin stepped back and placed his hands on his hips, glaring at him as he did so. The American struggled to his feet, rubbing his neck. "Sabine was one of our best hunters and you sacrificed her for nothing!" Martin spat.

"I didn't tell her to go up against Reynolds on her own, she was supposed to draw her out and into an ambush! Not stand toe to toe with her!" The American had an angry look on his face, Martin turned slightly back towards the forestry block. "If everyone had done what they had been told, the way I had told them, then we would be ruling in Ireland,"

"There is no way you would ever have been strong enough to overpower the Southern Den with what you had; they are too strong for you." He continues, "Look, if Dani had ...." Martin suddenly spun round and slapped him across his face with the back of his hand.

"Don't you dare try and blame her for anything," the force of the slap sent him spinning back into the wall again, he bounced off it and landed face down beside Martin. Martin stepped away from him. It took The American a few moments to right himself, as he stood up the right side of his face was already swelling as a small bit of blood trickled from his mouth.

"Look, I know you had plans for Dani to be your Queen, but" Martin spun around again, but this time The American ducked, smiling as he did so. The smile was wiped from his face when Martin's right foot hit him square in the chest, the force of which threw him rearwards. Martin danced around him, kicking him as he did so, the force of each kick growing stronger. The American tried in vain to fend off the barrage that he was enduring.

"Stop it, stop it now!" The female voice pleaded from the far edge of the tree line. Marin stepped back as the four young figures appeared. Martin knew they were Nocs, they were no threat to him. The girl stepped forward, the three young males stayed back, Martin could sense their fear. "Please stop," she repeated. Martin looked down at the pitiful mess that was lying on the ground in front of him.

"Still getting women to fight your battles for you!" Martin spat at him as he finished. Martin turned to walk away, he did not get far when The American landed on his shoulders, tipping him over, the two started to grapple on the ground, it did not take Martin long to push him to one side then roll away. Both jumped up, the battle between them did not last long, Martin was a hunter, a fighter, The American was not. The four in the tree line watched as The American franticly threw punches hitting nothing but air, however each punch, slap and kick that Martin threw landed and landed with force. The four watched as Martin circled his prey accurately chipping away until the American was down on one knee, raising his right hand as his left cradled his abdomen, he was exhausted.

"No more, please, no more," he pleaded, Martin stopped and stared at the four.

"Any of you got anything to say?" he demanded, all four shook their heads, the three males backed away a few paces, the girl did not move. Martin looked down at the cowering individual in front of him. "I should kill you for what you did to Dani!" and again he spat at him, this time it landed on his head.

"I'm sorry," he whispered. Martin walked around him and stood in front of the four.

"You will take him to where you are all sleeping, he will be collected tomorrow night in preparation of being taken back to Salisbury to answer, publicly for his actions ...." Martin looked at each one in turn, "*Is that understood!*" There was a row of nodding heads. None spoke as Martin turned and slowly walked over to where the American was still on the ground, trying to control his breathing. Martin stopped; he had his back to them. They could tell in the darkness that he was doing something, then a wail came from The American, his hands came up, trying to deflect the flow of warm liquid that gushed towards him. Martin stood and continued, only adjusting his jeans after he had finished, then he walked over to the far side of the track and back into the trees the way he had first come without looking back. The four of them sprang forward to help. They all crouched around him; the strong smell of urine made their faces contort. Two of them helped him stand, The American was almost in tears.

"What are we going to do?" the girl asked.

"We have to go back to the lair; you heard what he said!" one of the males replied.

"No, we can't stay there," The American explained, "if we do, we are all dead!"

"But ...." The male started; The American looked up.

"No buts, we have to go back there, pack up everything and move, as far away from here as we can!" The American pushed two of them out of the way, he started to head back to the front of the building. The three males started to follow him, but the girl stared into the forest.

"Wait, something is there," it was only a whisper, only one of the males had heard it, he looked back over his shoulder towards her.

"What?" he asked. The words had only just come out of his mouth when the front of his chest burst as the arrowhead smashed its way through. He hands came up, gripping the end, his shocked face matched the others as his legs gave way and he crumpled to the ground. She looked on in horror as the figure burst from between the trees, the rage in his eyes was only matched by the rage on his face. Jason Apollyon dropped the crossbow on the ground, everyone's eyes focused on the large hunting knife in his right hand.

"Get him!" screamed the American, her body turned as the two other young males ran towards him, their punches, and grasps in vain as Jason ducked and turned, the bone in an arm cracked, the male squealed, the second one grabbed towards the hair of their attacker. He missed, but the blade that was turned and rammed up under his chin and into his head did not. As the knife was withdrawn, the lifeless figure started to collapse towards the ground, again the figure was turning, the blade sliced through the air, the volume of blood splattered over a large area of the ground. The fear had gripped her, she could not move. The American rolled over and started to grab at the ground as he tried to get away.

Suddenly her body moved. She turned and ran. The fear had her, she had to get away, she had to, her body screamed as she crashed through the trees, her scream was not from the branches that tore at her skin, tore at her face, it was the fear, it was making her run. She could not hear the pleading that was going on behind her, but she did hear a strange 'swooshing' sound, but she did not know what it was, her body was screaming, run, run, run. The blade impacted into her back; it brought her down with a crash. The large piece of metal burned where it was lodged in her back. She could hear him screaming, The American was pleading for his life, then a sound ended it. She tried to move her arms, to crawl but pain burst through every part of her. Her body jolted as the hunting knife was pulled, with no gentleness out of her back. A boot went under her side and the upward force spun her onto her back. Her arms were splayed, all strength from them gone, her chest was panting, trying to force air in, but she could feel her life blood pouring out her back. She looked at the remorseless face. The fear came back. She knew who this was, it was The Destroyer, and no one ever survived meeting him.

"Please, please," she whispered. He knelt pushing his left knee into her right shoulder, his left hand firmly closed her mouth. His face was emotionless, her eyes caught the tip of the blade just before it was rammed into her chest, the blade parted her ribs and forced its' way through her heart. Her body tried to jolt but her strength had gone, her limbs were useless now. The fear would not be with her for much longer.

Chapter 25

Detective Inspector Wells adjusted the hood of the one-piece paper suit before pulling the paper face mask into place. She walked past the row of parked vans and vehicles that were from her own investigation team as well as Crime Scenes Investigation's, there were already a lot of people here. She headed towards the police tape and the uniformed police officer standing at the side, two figures who were also dressed the same way she was walked towards the tape. One lifted their hand in a wave, she recognised both her Detective Sergeants.

"Hi boss, over here!" one of them shouted. Underneath her mask she smiled, she tried to hide her excitement, this was the part of the job she loved the most, the chase was on!

"What have we got?" she asked as she approached, the uniformed officer lifted the tape, and she ducked underneath it. She started to head off along the path marked out. She stopped and looked back at the two Sergeants; they had not moved. "What?" she asked. The two of them looked at each other then walked towards her.

"Right boss, before you go up there, there are a few things you need to know!"

"What are you on about?" she protested. The two stopped either side of her.

"It's about what's left up there". Inspector Wells walked past them; she glanced back.

"Walk and talk, I want to know all before Special Branch puts in an appearance!"

∞∞∞∞

Tyler looked at her watch, almost midday and the Russians were late. She folded her arms and leaned against the side of the farmhouse. She scanned the lane that led from the road to the busy yard, farm hands headed out of the barn, waved, and continued on with their work,

"Any idea when they will get here?" She turned her head and smiled at Tony Fallon as he walked up and stopped beside her, she looked back down the lane.

"They are already late,"

"They seemed to get a bit upset last night when we wouldn't let them near Alison," he stated. Tyler turned and looked behind him before straightening up.

"She has been very co-operative with all our questioning since she got here!" Tyler responded, "especially with you, she obviously trusts you!"

"Well, we were in the same section at Coleraine police station,"

"She did not want to be interrogated by either of them," Tyler continued.

"Have you shared everything we have so far?" Tony asked. Tyler looked at him and nodded without speaking. They both turned their heads at the single car turning into the lane. It slowly made its way up and turned towards them once it reached the top. "One up," Tony said out loud, there was only one person in the car, Grishin waved at them as he turned the car around and parked beside a Land Rover along the side of the barn. "Oh, quick one, Dermott has heard from Ian and John, there was a Noc attack along the coast last night."

"Who?" she asked.

"A dog walker, heard from that Apollyon fella, he has been texting Paul and claims to have taken four of them down and that American we've been looking for!"

Tyler looked at him. "How do we know for sure?"

"Paul has tasked Ian and John to go to the location that Dermott was sent," Tony glanced at her, "he's sent the pictures he got, and they are going to phone once they know what has happened!" Grishin got out of the car, slammed the door, and started to walk towards them.

"I want to know as soon as they do!" she instructed.

"They will phone the farm directly when they know." Tony confirmed. The two of them stepped forward as Tyler held out her hand.

"Good afternoon."

Grishin took her hand "Is it afternoon yet?" he asked as he released the handshake, the greeting was not offered to Tony. Tyler looked at her watch again.

"Just," she stepped back, "shall we go inside?" Grishin nodded once and walked past the two of them, opened the door of the farmhouse and walked inside. Tony smirked at Tyler.

"After you," he whispered. Tyler turned and followed Grishin into the farmhouse, Tony walked in after her and closed the door behind himself.

"I am going to make a pot of tea; would you like some?" Tyler offered as she walked through the living room and towards the kitchen. Grishin turned and sat down in the big chair. Tony paused before taking a seat.

"Yes, thank you," Grishin shouted towards the door after her. He raised himself up and shouted over the top of the chair, "NO MILK!" he turned and sat back, he looked over at Tony, "you Europeans have no sense, you take a perfect oriental drink, and you add cow juice to it!!" Grishin shook his head in disgust, Tony did not know what to say to that.

"So," he started, "Mr Tatamovich not joining us?" Tony was trying to be formal, Grishin looked at him for a few moments before he relaxed somewhat.

"No, he is with the security team that Connor insisted on in Belfast, they are going to look at some 'Blue fish'," Grishin looked away. Tony looked through the door to the kitchen, Tyler had looked around, no one had told her about a security team from the south being this far north, and she looked annoyed.

"The Big Fish," Tony corrected.

"What?"

"It is called, 'The Big Fish' and it is a landmark beside the river Lagan that flows through Belfast, it was built in 1999 and it is considered fortunate if you touch it with your bare hand!" Grishin had an annoyed look on his face.

"I do not believe in superstitious nonsense," he stated.

"Neither do I," Tony was about to say something else but the look from Grishin stopped him. Tyler was walking in carrying a tray with three mugs, a teapot that had steam rising from the snout, a small bowl of sugar and a small jug that Tony guessed would have milk in it. The tray was placed in the centre of the small coffee table then Tyler poured the hot liquid into the three mugs.

"Help yourself!" she stated as she placed the ceramic teapot back on the tray, Grishin reached forward and lifted the mug closest to him, Tony waited until Tyler had poured her own milk before he sat forward and put both milk and sugar into his.

"Did you use teabag or loose tea?" Grishin asked.

"Bags, don't have any loose tea," Tyler stated.

"My Babushka was from Magadan, and she always made a large pot of tea with loose leaves," Grishin grinned at the memory, Tony went to speak but Tyler lifted the fingers on her right hand to stop him. They had never heard Grishin talk about his personal life before. Grishin glanced up. "Sorry, I forget you do not speak Russian, my grandmother!"

"Oh," Tyler stated. Grishin looked down into his drink.

"When we had finished, she would look into the cup, look at the leaves that were left and tell you your future!" Grishin smiled at his own comment.

"My grandmother used to do the same," Tony injected, Tyler looked at him and Grishin raised his eyebrows, Tony carried on. "It is an old Irish tradition for grandmothers to do that!" there was a small smile on Tony's face. Grishin sat forward as the landline phone started to ring.

Tony stood up, "I'll get that!" Tony walked past Grishin and lifted the handset, "Hello," he answered, then lowered his voice and continued with the call.

"So, is the Valkyrie still being awkward?" Grisham asked Tyler.

"Not at all, in fact she has been very free with her information and all they were up to last year!" Grishin looked at her then set the mug down.

"Then I will interrogate her now; we have questions!" he stated. Grishin sat forward as if he was going to stand up but, Tyler lifted her hand.

"No,"

"NO?" Grishin raised his voice.

"We have agreed with her that we will only have 'conversations' not interrogations, we have transcripts of everything we have done so far for you." Grishin's eyebrows lowered, he did not like being told 'no,' Tyler continued, "she trusts Tony and the two of them have been chatting all morning and she is being very co-operative."

"I *will* get the information that I want," Grishin lowered his voice.

"Of course!" Tyler smiled, "this is the first one of her kind that we have had access to, if she was a Noc, she would be dead already." there was another pause, "have you told the high council about her?" Tyler asked.

"Yes," Grishin sat back in the chair and looked at her sternly. "I want to know everything about 'The American' his current whereabouts, his activities, everything!" It was not a question; it was a demand. "Also, we need to know what abilities she has!"

"Well, she is Telekinetic for one!" Tyler replied.

"I want to see it!" Grishin stated,

"You will," she responded.

"As well as the American, I want him!" Grishin's tone was changing.

"He is dead!" Tony said out loud from behind the chair.

"What?" Grishin reacted as Tony walked past and sat down where he had been moments before, Tyler did not react.

"That was Ian Silver and John Gold, they are at a site near where there was a Noc attack last night, they have found four Nocs piled up and burnt and another which they believe is 'The American' nearby," Tony looked at Tyler, "they are taking DNA swabs and collecting all the personal items from the scene."

"Good, send a team to help with the site clearance," Tyler instructed, Tony nodded.

"I want proof it is him!" Grishin stated.

"You will have it," replied Tyler.

"You also said there are sapiens in groups taking picture of here?" Grishin looked from Tyler to Tony.

"Yes," Tyler started, "we have pictures of some of them, one of their Land Rovers so we are using the police to find out who there are!"

"And when will that happen?" Grishin asked.

"Well, I emailed them what we have so far this morning and," Tony paused as Grishin turned and looked at him, "and they are normally pretty good at getting back to us with things like that!" Tony finished off. Grishin looked at his mug and drank some of it.

"Ok," he said as he placed the mug on the table, "let's go see this Valkyrie of yours and find out what else she can do!" he stated as he stood up. Tyler and Tony stood as well; Tyler motioned towards Tony with her right hand.

"Tony, can you bring her to the main area in the barn, we will speak with her there!"

"Of course!" Tony headed for the front door. Grishin gave Tyler a sideways glance, he knew what she was doing, he did not like it, but for now, he would go along with it.

∞∞∞∞

Mike walked into the portacabin and closed the door. Chris was sitting around the small table reading something and had the soles of his trainers on the edge of the table, he was using his legs as a rest for the sheet of paper he was reading from. Lucy was sitting opposite Chris, both seemed to be ignoring each other. Steve Minister was standing with his back to the door, he turned and acknowledged Mike. Mike nodded then headed over to where the other two were sitting. Lucy looked up and smiled, she seemed pleased to see him, Chris just looked nodded once and went back to whatever he was reading as Mike sat down.

"Hi," Mike started, Lucy's smile got bigger as she reached out her hand to Mike.

"Hiya," Mike positioned himself halfway between the two of them. As he sat back in the chair, he opened the hardback folder he was carrying. "I got this from the farm earlier, it seems there has been a group of what they describe as 'professional looking men' taking photographs of the farm and around the north coast." He fumbled with the paper printouts of the pictures he had downloaded from the email; Lucy sat forward and took a handful.

"Mmmm, I wonder who this lot are!" she flicked through the assorted pictures.

"Let's have a look," Chris placed the sheet of paper he had down and sat upright, extending his right hand. Lucy handed him a couple of them as she studied the one in her hand.

"I wonder if they are Russian," Lucy said out loud, she had a concentrated look on her face, "they certainly look military," she continued.

"We have no idea," Mike added.

"I know them!" Chris exclaimed.

"What?" Mike sat forward as Chris looked at the faces of the groups of men.

"Yeah, two of them are ex-para's," Chris looked up and used the corner of one of the pictures to point to individuals, "these two are ex booties, not sure about him ...."

"I'm sorry, 'booties'?" Lucy asked.

"Royal Marine Commando's, also known as 'boot necks," Mike stated.

"Yeah, that's right," Chris commented.

"When the Royal Marines were first formed in 1664 their first role was protection of the officers at sea on board Royal Navy ships, so they had to wear leather straps around their necks to prevent their throats from being cuts by seamen trying to mutiny, and the leather was the same that was used to make their boots, hence the name, 'boot necks'!" Mike smiled.

"How the hell do you know that?" Chris asked.

"When I first left Police college my first station in South Armagh still had Marines there, it was not long before the military were withdrawn. The Commandos certainly made sure we knew their history!"

Steve Minister who had been quiet until now reached out towards Lucy. "Let's have a look then?" he asked. Lucy handed him some of the prints, Chris pushed a picture into the middle of the table.

"Most of these guys are British, not Russian!" he stated.

"So, you know them then?" Lucy asked.

"I know 'of' them, don't know them personally," Chris added.

Steve pointed to one of the faces. "This one was in two para just when I left three para," Steve added, Chris leaned forward and nodded.

"So, any idea what they are doing now? More to the point, what are they doing over here?" Mike asked.

"Yeah, do you know anyone who would know?" Lucy added, "I also want names,"

"Well, last I heard, he was on the circuit," Chris stood up and reached into his pocket, "I will make a call and see what I can find out!" Chris walked to the door and headed outside. Steve started to look over the pictures.

"I would say most of them are probably ex-military, looking at physical stature, clothing etc." Steve spoke without looking up.

"So, what does it mean, 'on the circuit?" Lucy asked.

"The circuit' is what the security and Close Protection industry is called, this could just be a close protection task or something," The door reopened, and Chris charged in, still with the phone in his hand.

"Got it, yeah they are all working for the same firm that only employs ex-military," Chris kept walking towards the group.

"So, why would they be interested in the farm?" Lucy had lowered her voice as Chris sat back down, "have you got real names, etc?" she asked.

"Yup," he replied. Mike's phone buzzed with a text message, he fumbled with his pocket as Lucy carried on.

"Excellent, can you note down as much as you know and I can take it from there," she was being polite, but Chris knew it was an instruction.

"We have a job on!" Mike stated, everyone looked at him as he held the phone up and read from the screen, "from Darren, police are responding to a forestry block near Castle Rock where they have just found four staked and burnt bodies with another nearby with a crossbow bolt through their heart," Mike looked around, "also burnt," Everyone stood up except Steve.

"OK, does he say exactly where?" Lucy asked.

"Yeah, I know that part of the world well, so no problems," Mike responded.

"Ok, let's go," Lucy said with a smile, can I travel with you?" she asked.

"Sure," Mike responded.

"I am going to finish my brew first!" Stated Steve, everyone looked at him as he continued, "every brew I have made over the last few days I have not finished," he raised his small cup, "going to finish this one," Chris landed back down on the uncomfortable chair and Mike and Lucy exchanged a glance. "I mean, the bodies are not going anywhere, are they?" Steve smiled.

Chapter 26

Cara-Marie was sitting in the drivers' seat of her car with her legs out the door and her boots on the ground of the car park. She was looking over her notes on what had happened on the coastal path. She looked up at the two uniformed police officers who were standing by the blue and white tape that blocked the path, the car park was quite busy with police vehicles, there were several people walking around, all busy with what they were doing. The black van with the white lettering of 'Private Ambulance' pulled away. It always surprised her was the number of people who thought it actually was an ambulance, the two people in black suits who were normally in the front did not give it away either. The body had been recovered from the drop over the cliff and had been packed away and was now being transported for the post-mortem. Her phone started to ring, she looked at Kevin the editor's name before she answered.

"Hi,"

"Hi Cara, where are you at the moment?" he asked. His question initially confused her, she tried not to be sarcastic with her answer.

"Where you sent me, to the body found this morning near the coastal path, why?"

"Right, yes, what is going on there?" Kevin had not phoned her to have this discussion, there was another reason, but she went along with it.

"There was a body discovered this morning, initially thought he had just fallen over the edge but once they got to the body, they found it had been burnt, plus massive injuries around the neck, so, yes, it is murder."

"So, what are the police doing?" Kevin butted in.

"Major Investigations arrived, to take over. I was chatting to a station officer from the fire service, and he said there were traces of accelerant on the clothes, and only some clothes and the outer layers of skin were damaged, so it was not a serious attempt to destroy a body."

"Do you have a name yet?" Kevin butted in again.

"Of the fire service guy? Yes," she looked down at her notes and read the name she had scribbled down the side, "Station Officer Crawford."

"No, not him, the body, do you have a name yet?" Cara-Marie felt her eyes look up from her notes, Kevin was being annoying again.

"Not confirmed but I have a name of who it may possibly be,"

"Right, are you all done there?" Here it came, the real reason for the call.

"As much as I am going to get done, yes."

"Right, if you follow the coastal road towards Castlerock there is a forestry block just two miles away from where you are." She thought for a moment as she pictured his directions.

"Yes, I know it,"

"Right, I want you to go there right away,"

"Why?" it was her turn to butt in.

"Police have just been called there, five bodies have been found, one has a crossbow bolt in its chest." Kevin then said something else, but she missed it, her mind was racing again.

"Ok, on my way," and she hung up before he could say anything else. She swung her legs in and shut the door, the seat belt clicked into place just as the engine started, she made her way through the police vehicles, she noticed several of the vans that had been there earlier had left. As she made her way out onto the main road her phone rang again, this time the ringing was coming through the cars media system. She pressed the small green button on the steering wheel and the ringing stopped. The car followed the rise and fall of the road as she carried on. "Hello," she said as she glanced out to sea, she always loved the views from the North Coast.

"Hello, may I speak to Carol Marie McKenna please?" The female voice had a strong American accent. Cara-Marie had a picture of a middle-aged woman at the other end of the phone, a stranger getting her name wrong did not bother her, Kevin even after all the time she had been at the Herald still getting it wrong infuriated her.

"Hi, it is Cara-Marie, not Carol."

"Oh, I am sooo sorry," Cara-Marie felt herself smile at the apology.

"No problem,"

"Well, I am Jenny Max, and I am one of the journalists from the Elkhorn newsletter," Cara-Marie was confused.

"I am sorry, but, where?"

"The Elkhorn newsletter," there was a slight giggle down the phone, *"we are a regional newspaper here in Wisconsin.*

"Cara-Marie felt her eyebrows rise. "All the way over there in the USA!"

"All the way over here in the good' old' US-A," the woman responded.

"And what may I do for you?" Cara-Marie asked.

"Are you able to video chat at the moment? I think face to face would be better!"

"Sorry, no, I am currently driving. I am using the in-car audio for this call!"

"Ok, that makes sense, can we organise another time then?"

"I am sure that is no problem, but may I ask what it is you want to video chat about?"

"Sure, I would like to interview you for a series of articles that I am doing here in Elkhorn, you would get the newspapers fee of five thousand dollars of course," Cara-Marie quickly did the conversion in her head.

"That would be nearly three and a half thousand pounds!" she exclaimed, "may I ask what you want to interview me about as that seems a lot!" There was a giggle down the phone.

"Well, that is normal for international interviews, but yeah, it will just be a chat, probably no more than thirty minutes of your time, I will be recording it of course,"

"Of course," Cara-Marie heard herself say out loud.

"I have been following your articles for over a year and a half now and I think that we are approaching the same subject, just from different places and I just wanted to first get in touch then see how we can help each other." Cara-Marie was defensive again, her car slowed down as she went over a hill, cars sped past going the other way.

"I am sorry, Jenny, but I am not sure that I follow you."

"Oh, I am sorry," Jenny paused and there was the sound of paper rustling, she was searching for something, *"I am very interested in your accounts of your experience when you found a body by 'the riverside' in Coleraine and then your article titled, 'The Castleroe Murders', where five teenagers were mauled ..."* for a moment her mind flashed back to being with Kyle, hearing the scream and then what looked at her. That face, that face that wasn't human, but the eyes were intelligent.

"Yes, yes," she stuttered, "we can do that," there was a pause in the conversation, Cara-Marie wanted to speak but felt she couldn't, it could wait.

"And from what I have seen not just in your articles but on a recent documentary,"

"That was shown in America?" Cara-Marie reacted.

"No, I found it online, well, one of my researchers found it," She has her own researchers? for a moment Cara-Marie was jealous. *"Is it ok just to call you Cara?"*

"Cara-Marie is my first name."

"Cara-Marie it is then, I really love your name, my ex-husband was an Irish-American!" Cara-Marie cringed; this was not the time for 'that' conversation.

"Ok," was all she could muster.

"*So, what time would best suit you,*" Jenny asked. Cara-Marie glanced at the clock on the dashboard.

"Well, it is just after two PM now so,"

"*It is just after nine AM here, so would later in the evening be better for you?*"

"Yes, that would do fine, say, seven o clock, UK time,"

"*Great, I will send a link to this number of some of my work so you can see which direction I am coming from,*"

"And what direction is that?" Cara-Marie asked as she slowly applied the foot brake, then pulled in behind the line of unmarked, but obvious police vans at the side of the road, a lone uniformed police officer was in the middle of the road directing the flow of traffic.

"*For a lot of your work, you have not been believed, ridiculed, well, the same has happened to me,*"

"Why?" she asked as she turned off the engine and the car fell in to silence.

"*For the same reason. I have seen them too; you and I both know 'THEY' are real. All we have to do now is prove it.*" She did not say the word, 'werewolf' she did not have to.

Cara-Marie McKenna of the Coleraine Herald had a new best friend.

∞∞∞∞

The large stone crashed into the side of the arena then fell to the ground. Alison lowered her hand and looked at the ground in front of her.

"Have I performed enough tricks for you yet?" there was growing resentment in her voice. She looked over at Grishin, Tyler and Tony. Grishin had his arms folded and was staring at her, Tony had a sad look on his face, there were two farm hands by the main door.

"How large an object can you move?" Grishin demanded, Tyler looked at him.

"Alison has been more than helpful since she got here," she protested.

"She will answer all my questions," Grishin responded without looking at her.

Alison turned and walked towards the three of them. "Why? have you got a X-wing stuck in a swamp you need moved?" the irritation in her voice was clear.

"A what?" Grishin's face contorted, he did not get the reference.

"I think the Council member is asking if your abilities, are governed by size?" Tyler asked as she took a s step forward. Grishin gave her a death stare. Alison made an audible sigh.

"So far, it has only been smaller things." She turned and motioned with her left hand towards where the stone was, "never tried on anything much bigger than that!"

"Can you move a car? A body?" Grishin demanded, Alison looked at him.

"No, too big," she looked over at Tony, "I can move items that someone is holding, but I cannot move something with a heartbeat," she explained.

"What do you mean? explain!" Grishin was used to getting his own way.

"Well," Alison started, she motioned towards Tony with her right hand, "If Tony had a knife, or in fact any weapon in his hand I could stop him using it, by taking it from him, but I would not be able to control his actual body," Grishin lifted his head.

"Demonstrate," He looked at Tony, "do you have your weapon on you?"

"Err, yes," Tony replied, Grishin motioned with his right hand.

"Attack her," he looked at Alison, "I want to see you take his weapon!"

"I am NOT some prancing pony!" she raised her voice, "you wanted to see what I can do, well, I have done that, and several times, I am not here for your entertainment!" Alison responded. Grishin unfolded his arms and took a forceful step towards her.

"You WILL do as you are told!" Everyone could feel his wolf wanting to come forward. Alison did not move, but Tyler and Tony did move closer to Grishin.

"I am not here for you to control!" Alison was standing up to him.

"And you are *my* guest here, and you will always be treated as such!" Tyler forced a smile towards Alison, Grishin glared at her then back at Alison. The large door of the barn was pushed open slightly and a member of the communications team entered, he was in a hurry.

"Tyler, I ..." he started. All four turned towards him and he stopped. There was a pause before Tyler spoke.

"What is it?"

"We just heard from Ian Silver and he said to inform you at once," Tony and Tyler turned and faced him.

"What?" she said. He looked nervous, Grishin turned his head and was staring at him, and it was unnerving.

"He said to say," he looked down at the folded piece of paper in his hand, "The Noc attack on the coastal path was NOT done by the American or by the ones with him,"

"You know where he is?" Alison asked, "The American?"

"Yes," Tyler said as she looked back over her shoulder to answer her.

"If you know where he is, then KILL HIM!" Alison demanded.

"We think, someone has done that for us already!" Tony spoke.

"What! he is really dead!" Alison walked up to Tony, she stretched out her left hand and touched his arm, the two shared a glance and a smile. Grishin slowly turned and looked at the farm hand.

"Is that all?"

"N-no," the farm hand looked at Tyler. "He said they found the lair and request a team be sent out this evening, Tyler walked towards him, closing the distance between them.

"Great," she looked at Tony, "make sure that happens!" Tony nodded.

"Who killed him?" Alison asked.

"We are not sure," Tyler looked at Grishin, "it is being investigated at the moment."

"He also said the Noc attack on the coastal path, had the body set afire then pushed over the cliff," he stumbled through the rest of the message, "he also said the police have said there was practically no forensic evidence collected at the scene."

"Sapiens!" Grishin stated.

"What?" Tony reacted, Grishin refolded his arms.

"Trying to hide or dispose of a body like that is the work of sapiens, Nocs don't do that," He looked at Tyler, "you have a Noc who has help, and not just daylight guardians!"

"Say one that has a sapien close protection team around them" she stated.

"Salisbury!" Alison stated, Grishin turned his head as the rest looked at Alison.

"What?" he asked.

"The big coven in Salisbury," Alison repeated.

"Yes, but what about it!" he demanded. Alison looked at Tony.

"Something The American started to tell Sabine, the coven in Salisbury were setting up different security companies to do Close Protection contracts," she shifted where she was standing, "he was saying that they were piling millions of pounds into it, different companies, here, the middle east and using ex-soldiers as protection and to dispose of bodies." Alison turned to Tyler, "he was saying that none of them would know where the money was actually coming from, but they would use one of the smaller companies, with hand-picked individuals, here and in England for security for all their safe houses that they have around the country!"

"What?!" Tyler raised her voice, she looked at Tony who looked surprised as well. Tony touched Alison on the shoulder.

"What safe houses?" he asked.

"Sabine only mentioned it once," Alison looked at Tony, "she said that they had been working on their security and now had at least one, if not two houses in every town and city across the country that migrating ...." Alison paused as she thought about how she would describe them, "coven members could sleep in, with full sapien security around them."

"You know where this network is?" Grishin asked, his tone was still forceful.

"No, but I do know that Salisbury was furious with what he was doing over here, last I heard they were going to send some 'Master Hunter' over to deal with him," Alison looked around, "The American," she explained.

"Who are they sending?" Tony asked.

"Some 'Master Hunter' apparently, he had scored some 'great victory' recently and Dani was supposed to be his prize, but"

"But she took off and came over here!" Tony looked at Alison, "Sabine told me,"

"You saw her?" Alison reacted.

"Yeah, these two were old friends!" Tyler injected; Tony looked embarrassed.

"Yeah, we met at Dunserverick harbour, we were trying to de-escalate what was happening, she told us a bit about Dani," Tony looked at Alison, but it was Tyler who spoke.

"Yeah, Tony here gave her quite the drilling!" Tony's eyes shot up at Tyler, his face reddened, and he took a breath in, his insides turned at the thought of what he had done.

"Don't suppose you know the name of this 'Master Hunter' do you?" he asked.

"No, sorry, that was never said in front of me," Alison replied.

"Hanna," Grishin spoke in a lowered voice.

"What?" Tyler asked. Grishin straightened up.

"The 'Master Hunter' from the Salisbury coven is called 'Martin Hanna'" Grishin added. He looked up at Tyler. "The 'great victory' was over four wolves who were only on holiday from Canada, from the Ojibwe clan," he paused.

"Yes, I know them, they looked after me for quite a while, go on," Tyler felt herself straighten up, Grishin looked past her as he continued.

"There were four of them, two recently married couples, who were just on holiday on an Island in the English Channel, but the Nocs discovered them, cornered them, but they were able to fight off the Nocs, so Salisbury sent him in. None survived."

"Killing four wolves? How was that a 'great victory'?" Alison asked. Grishin turned towards her, his tone had mellowed.

"Because two of them, were a son and a daughter of the Clan Chief, they sent them a video of what they did with the bodies after they were dead." Alison went to say something, but Tyler cut in.

"Some Nocs, when they kill one of us in wolf form, like to cut a pelt of fur and keep it as a trophy," Tony shifted where he was standing and there was a visible reaction from the farm hands who were nearby.

"Could this 'Hanna' be here? Could he be the one on the coastal path?" Tony asked.

"Sounds like it," Tyler stated, "and if he is, it will our turn to score a 'Great Victory!'"

"One thing you can answer," Grishin turned back to Alison, all eyes turned to him.

"What?" she asked.

"The American,"

"What about him?"

"His real name .... Do you know it?" he asked.

"Yeah, that has been a secret for like, ever!" Tony added.

"Yes, I do know it," Alison was looking at Grishin as she spoke, "I was told there is some 'curse' or something to do with it,"

"Well, …. What is it?" Grishin asked. Alison looked down and visibly bit into her top lip as she tried to suppress a smile.

"Is it that bad?" Tyler asked, Alison nodded.

"I do not like asking twice …" Grishin stared, Alison looked at Tony as she spoke.

"Sydney Puttman," There was a ripple of laughter between the group. Grishin stepped past Tyler and started to walk towards the door.

"I can see why he kept that quiet!" Tony smirked.

"Yeah, I didn't believe it either until Sabine warned me never to mention it."

"Right, I need to speak with the High Council, we need to find out if this is just Salisbury or worldwide!" Grishin spoke as he walked away Tyler followed him, Tony stayed with Alison. The other farm hands followed Tyler, leaving the two of them in the arena.

"You are safe," Tony stated, Alison looked at him.

"Was I in danger?" she asked.

"Very much so," Tony replied as Alison looked at the closing door.

"I could take him!" she said defiantly.

"No, Ali, no, you couldn't." Tony said as he placed his hand on her shoulder. He turned and started to walk towards the entrance, Alison walked with him. "Did you always know about me?" he asked, "about being a wolf?" Alison let out a short laugh.

"Spotted you the first day you walked into the section room!"

"What about Kyle?"

"Kyle?" she responded.

"Yes, did you know about him?"

"No," Alison gripped the large door and tugged on it. The large door moved on its coasters and opened enough for them to move outside. "Did not see it in him at all," Tony closed the heavy door behind him. "He hid it very well!"

"He didn't know," Tony answered, Alison looked at him.

"That makes sense." It was dark now and Tony looked at the moon. "So," she started.

"So, what?"

"So, what is with the whole 'barking at the moon' thingy with your lot?" Tony looked at her and raised his eyebrows.

"My lot?"

Chapter 27

Megan Due looked up at the darkening sky, her face was still covered in warm blood, and she loved the way this felt. Her whole body still tingled, her teeth were still elongated, and she was still out of breath as she pulled up her jeans. She looked around over the ground for her top she had been wearing, it was here somewhere, the passion of the sex with whatever this guy's name was had just been the foreplay, it was how she fed off him that was what she wanted. His body twitched in the darkness; she did not care about him anymore; he would be dead soon. She spotted her small day sack laying a short distance away. She walked over to it and took out the large bottle of water and a clean top. As she was washing herself, she suddenly became aware she was not alone. Her movements slowed down, she rubbed her face clean with the towel she had stolen from the small bed and breakfast that she had been in, she wasn't going back there so it didn't matter. She pulled the clean top over her head and stood up. She was staring through the darkness, yes, there was someone else there. Her head made a slow sweep, she had a clear view of over thirty metres, but she was being watched. She relaxed slightly; it wasn't sapien. The metallic click made her head spin round.

"And just who the hell are you?" The voice was male and English. She recognised the sound of the hammer on a pistol being pulled back, she slowly turned her body towards the voice. He was standing ten metres away, in the darkness and was aiming the pistol at her. She knew straight away that he was Noctrailis.

"That depends on who is asking!" She looked past him into the darkness, the gentle breeze brought their smell, he was not alone, there was a group of sapiens, not far away, but far enough for them not to intervene.

"I am asking!" he demanded. She smirked and rubbed her face with the towel again.

"Yeah, I am going to need a little more than that," she retorted. He lowered the weapon, but he still stood there, with his arm extended, the pistol firmly gripped in his hand, he could easily take her down if he wanted. She dropped the towel into her daysack and squatted beside it. She sorted through her things, spotting her pistol in the daysack. She did not touch it as it wasn't necessary yet, but she could get to it quickly if she needed to. She looked up at him,

"Well? Aren't you going to introduce yourself?"

"You aren't fully one of us!" he stated, he kept a stern look on his face.

"Ten points, now your starter for ten more .... Who are you? What are you doing here? And I take it that lot over there are your daylight guardians!" She pushed her fingers though her hair then reached back into the day sack. He looked annoyed now.

"I am the one asking the questions, not you! Who are you and what are you doing here?" he demanded.

"Quid pro quo .... If you don't tell me anything then you're getting shit from me!"

"Fine," he quietly replied.

"Fine," she quietly repeated. He took a breath in before he spoke again.

"I am Martin Hanna, Master Hunter to the Queen who sits on the Noctrali throne at the head coven in Salisbury!" Megan squatted again looking through the day sack. it was not the response he had been expecting. "Well?" he stepped closer; he was getting more annoyed.

"Well, what?" she asked.

"Who are you? What are you doing here without permission?" her head bolted up.

"Permission?" she stood up, she had a fleece top in her left hand, the pistol was wrapped in the fleece, but she had a firm grip on it. "Let's get one thing straight bucko, I don't need your permission to do anything!"

"Actually, you do!" he raised his voice, "all Noctrailis must obey all rulings from the Queen and the council!"

"Why?" she asked.

"What do you mean, why? She is queen. They are council and must be obeyed!"

"But you have already stated that I am not fully Noctrailis!" she was poking him.

"I want your real name!" this was a demand.

"Megan," she said with a smile. His body relaxed as he studied her face.

"So, you 'are the famous 'Megan Due' I have heard so much about?"

"Well, I don't know about 'famous'!" she smiled, he didn't.

"I was not sure you existed, heard the rumours of course,"

"Rumours? Oh, I have not heard any rumours?" she relaxed, her left hand flicked the fleece over her left shoulder and her right hand tucked the pistol into the waist of her jeans. Martin's eyes widened; he had not previously spotted the weapon. For a moment, his own right hand tightened the grip on his pistol. "So, you were saying about these rumours then?" she was being playful, but he knew she was a killer.

"Well," he kept his stance, if she was coming closer to launch an assault, he would have a fight on his hands and the protection were too far away to help him. "Conceived by a human mother and a Vampire father, who was then killed in his sleep by the fore mentioned mother when she found out he was planning on using the new-born in a ritual...." He was looking at her, she shuffled where she was standing and she looked down, this was uncomfortable for her so it must be true, he decided to keep going. "The mother who then married into a gypsy traveller family and when she was nineteen her stepdad organised a marriage for her to the son of a rival clan," she shuffled again, he tried to suppress the smile that he now had, he was enjoying this. "A marriage that saw her in hospital on her wedding night after a severe beating by her new husband." She looked up at him and stared at him. He had her. "Is this true so far?" He saw the anger in her eyes, it was!

"You forgot the bit where his 'best man' came on the honeymoon as well as apparently the two of them having 'shared everything' since they were boys!" There was venom in her voice.

"And you killed the two of them for it!"

"So?" she asked. He shrugged and took a step forward.

"No, I don't blame you," he was relaxing around her, she may not be dangerous yet, "in fact, I agree with your actions!"

"I don't need your approval," she stated.

"Would it stop you if I told you the council dis-approved of what you have been doing?" Megan spun on her heels and stomped back to her daysack.

"I don't give a toss about your 'hive' or it's Queen!"

"Coven," he corrected. Megan dropped the fleece into the daysack and leaned forward to pick up the day sack. Martin's eyes focused on her bum as she was bending over. She straightened up and looked at him.

"What?"

"Coven," he repeated, "We are in a coven, not a hive!"

"There is a difference?" she crunched up her face as she asked the question.

"No, I suppose to those outside there isn't." Megan threw the strap of the daysack over her shoulder and looked at him.

"So, what are you doing here? Isn't Ireland outside of your jurisdiction?" she asked.

"We don't have a set 'jurisdiction'," she was agitated, he carried on, "but some of your activities have been causing us problems!"

"Like what?" she demanded.

"Well, I understand you tracking down your father-in-law and then hunting your own father in revenge for what they did,"

"You don't know anything!" she spat.

"Really? You kill the son of the chief of a clan of gypsies and don't expect any response from them?" she looked over her shoulder at him as she squatted again. She forcibly grabbed her items and shoved them into the daysack. It was her turn to get angry. "They would have hunted you down, they take things like that personally!" She did not reply. "Why did you kill your own father?" he asked. She zipped up the top of the daysack the stood up again, she turned and stepped closer to him.

"Are you kidding me? He sold me to that animal for him to use any way he chose to ... what was I supposed to do?" Martin stood calmly in front of her, he watched as her cheeks flushed and her eyes dilated.

"And you have been causing problems since then." Martin said quietly.

"With whom? The weres?" her question caught him off guard.

"The who?" he asked.

"The weres ... you know ... were ...wolves," she demanded.

"Never heard them be referred to as that before!"

"But what of them?" she asked.

"The Garou? They will not bother you, if you don't cause them problems, plus I hear they are currently having enough problems between themselves to worry about us!"

"I wasn't worried about them in the first place, I can spot them a mile away!"

"Well, leave them to us," Martin reassured.

"I was going to!" Megan twisted her face. Martin looked over at the body that was lying on the ground.

"You don't need to feed the same way we do," he looked at her, "so, why kill like we do?" Megan let a nefarious smile spread across her face.

"Well, killing them is only part of the fun," she smirked.

"So, who was he?"

"A married shit that thought he could dip his wick and get away with it!" Megan almost spat at the body on the ground.

"Yeah, I heard you only target married men,"

"So?" she asked.

"So, what are you doing this far north? I heard that you may currently be near Limerick?" Megan looked at him.

"Tell me first what you are doing over here Englishman?"

"Coven business, which means it's none of yours!"

"Then what I am doing is none of yours!" she almost hissed at him.

"I could make you if I wanted to!" He moved closer drawing level with her face.

"You couldn't make me do shit!" she replied, the venom in her voice was back. The two of them stared into each other's eyes, this had become a stand-off.

"Don't push what you don't know," he lowered his voice.

"I could say the same to you!"

"I want you to stay in touch, so we don't get in each other's way. I have a job to do!"

"Are you going to tell me what that job is? And does it involve your little army over there?" her face was almost touching his, both of them tensed up, a fight was imminent.

"Nope and they are here just to protect me!" he stated.

"Well, they ain't doing a very good job so far are they?" before he could answer she lunged forward, and her mouth closed on his. The kiss was deep and passionate. His hands landed on her hips and quickly moved up and under her top, pulling her closer. Her hands came up onto his chest and firmly but slowly pushed him away. Her teeth bit down on his lower lip. She pulled at it until he made a yelp. He released his grip, and his right hand came up and touched the small bleed, because of that he had not noticed yet that her fingernail had drawn blood from a small scratch she had left on his left cheek. He lowered his eyebrows and glared at her. He looked into her eyes and saw what was there, it matched her smile. She reached up and pulled the pistol out from her waist and dropping the daysack onto the ground, she let the weapon fall on top of it, then she started to undo the belt that was around her jeans.

"What are you waiting for? Get'um off then!" she commanded.

Martin had a ghoulish grin on his face. "I am going to enjoy this!" he stated.

Sitting in the front seats of one of the parked Land Rovers, two of the close protection team watched the small screen. The passenger door opened, and Glenn Nendrum lowered his head inside. "Is he still there?" he asked.

"Oh yes!" replied the driver.

"What are they up to? Still chatting?" Glenn asked.

"Nope," replied the second one, "now 'da funky dance of louve!" the two team members started laughing at the way he had finished his sentence.

"What?" Glenn stated.

"Here," the passenger turned the small screen of the monitor towards him. "We have three remote cameras out, to be honest, she is well fit this one!" Glenn looked at the screen then withdrew his head out of the inside of the vehicle.

"Fine, let me know when they are done," the door slammed shut and the two team members went back to their voyeurism.

"Hell, if we were recording this, we could sell it to a porn site!" the two men laughed then the voice of Mark Castle echoed in their earpieces.

"Shut your faces, I can hear both of you from here, so whatever you two are laughing at put a sock in it!" The two men looked at each other, yes, he was right. The rest of the deployed team was spread out in pairs covering the location of their current employer, they would tell the rest later, not that they didn't already know, Megan Due and Martin Hanna were both being very loud.

∞∞∞

Ian Silver and John Gold were lying beside each other along the hedge row. They both had binoculars and were looking at the small farmhouse that was in total darkness. Ian lifted his and looked through the lens, the small battery powered the imagine intensifier that was built into the binoculars, the farmhouse looked grey. John turned his head as Tyler silently approached. She was bent forward and had large woollen socks over her boots. Her padded jacket hid the body armour she was wearing underneath. Her woollen hat covered her head right the way down to her eyebrows. He nodded as she raised her right hand, he turned back towards the farmhouse. Tyler laid down on the grass verge beside him and looked through the hedge line. John handed her the binoculars; she nodded once and took them. She got herself comfortable then looked through them.

The farmhouse was a small single storey building, the brickwork looked like it was from several centuries ago, but the roof was a modern one. She was looking at the single front door with square windows either side, she could almost imagine the layout inside. Ian started to set up the video camera so they could record what they were about to do.

Tyler spoke in a whisper. "Still no sign of the daylight guardian?" she asked.

"No," John also spoke in a whisper, "she took off when the two Nocs got back,"

"And we are sure there is only two in there?" Tyler asked.

"We think so, only seen the same two coming in and out."

"And only one guardian?"

"Yes," John replied. Tyler lowered the bino's and looked over to her right.

"And how far away is Tony's house?"

"Nearly two and a half miles," John turned and looked at her, "as the crow flies."

"Two point seven miles," Ian added as a small red light appeared just at the back of the camera. The small tripod was sitting over an exposed root of one of the bushes in the hedge, Ian looked through the viewfinder then raised his head to look at Tyler, "good to go here!" he stated. Tyler nodded then touched the communicator in her ear.

"Delta, Tango, over,"

"Delta," Dermott's voice echoed in all their ears.

"Tango, all set at this location," As she was telling Dermot that, Ian lifted the stalking rifle that had been at the far side of him. He lowered the small bipod that was at the front of the bolt action rifle then positioned it so he could see the front door through the telescopic sight.

"Roger Tango, Oscar One and Oscar Two, report."

"Oscar one, in position," the voice was a whisper, but overwatch one was ready.

"Oscar Two, in position," the second voice was a whisper as well.

"Roger," Dermott confirmed, "Alpha leader move up to your Final Attack Position," Tyler listened to the two clicks that confirmed the assault group was ready. Tyler lifted the binoculars and scanned over to her right as the line of eight figures, hunched over moved up to the side of the farmhouse. She could recognise the figure of Ruth being the lead assaulter. They all had the same helmets on, with what looked like ski goggles over their eyes. The dark grey boiler suits covered the modular body armour underneath. Tyler spotted another two moving up behind the assault group. They stopped at the far side of the lane, Tyler could easily spot the frame of John, the paramedic from the farm. He had his large trauma bag on his back.

Dermott's voice came over the communicator again. "Alpha leader, Alpha leader, you have control, you have control." Again, Ruth responded with two clicks, she was too close to the target to use her voice, she understood. Tyler watched as Ruth stopped by the single door. her weapon pointed towards it, each of them moved under the single window on that side of the door. Ruth's left hand touched her helmet and the third assaulter moved out of the line to the far side of the door, this was the 'Breacher'. Tyler watched as 'The Breacher' slowly allowed their rifle to hang by their side as they took out a small item from their vest and then pulled a covering off one side of it. They placed it just above the lock of the door then stepped back along the wall The Breacher took control of the rifle and held up something in their left hand, to show it to Ruth.

"*All stations, this is alpha leader …. Stand by, stand by, stand by,*" she did not have to say the next word of 'go'. There was a small noise and the door swung open. As it did so Ruth was already through it closely followed by the rest of the assault team. The Breacher turned and knelt down on one knee, raising their rifle up, to stay there for the assault. Tyler lowered the binos; all they could do now was listen to the commentary from the assault team.

"*Alpha leader, living room clear,*"

"*Alpha Two, moving towards door one,*"

"*Alpha Four, moving towards door two,*"

"*Alpha Six, bedroom two, clear,*"

"*Alpha two, firing,*" Tyler and John exchanged a glance, all they could do was listen to the engagement. "*Alpha Two, Bravo down, bedroom one,*"

"*Alpha Leader, firing!*" Ruth was no longer whispering, "*Alpha Leader, Bravo down, main kitchen,*" Tyler could not help but smile at what she was hearing.

"*Alpha leader, Alpha Two, bedroom two clear but …*" There was a hesitation. Ruth's voice came up next.

"*Alpha Two, roger, what have you got?*"

"*Alpha two ... two yankee's down and one Bravo severely injured on the bed!*" Again, Tyler and John exchanged a glance.

"Two dead sapiens and an injured Noc?" John stated out loud, it was one more than what they had expected.

"*Alpha two, Alpha Leader, Is the room secure?*" Ruth asked.

"*Alpha Two, yes yes, over,*"

"*Alpha Leader, roger, Delta, site is secure, Mike One Four, to our location over,*"

"*Mike One Four, moving,*" Tyler's eyes darted over to the sudden movement of John the paramedic rising up and running forward and in through the front door.

"*Oscar One and Two, Delta, is the site secure?*" Dermott asked.

"*Oscar One, no movement,*"

"*Oscar Two, no movement,*"

"*Roger, site is secure, Alpha team start site sensitive exploitation,*" Dermot instructed. Tyler pushed herself up then spoke into the communicator.

"Alpha team, Tango, now mobile to your location,"

"*Tango, Roger,*" Ruth replied.

"We will wait here," John stated, Tyler nodded then turned and started to run along the hedge row. It did not take her long before she reached the lane that led up to the old farmhouse. She ran past the team member who had been with John the paramedic then past the Breacher who was still by the entrance. The living room was a square shape with a single sofa in the middle. The large open fireplace was on the right with a small tv on a stand to one side of it. To her left in the corners were doors that had an assaulter standing in each one. Either side of the fireplace were two other doors, again with assaulters standing in them.

"Over here," one of them stated and motioned with their left hand. They moved out of the way to let Tyler walk past. She walked in and John the paramedic walked out back into the main room of the farmhouse. The small bedroom had a double bed pushed into the far corner, the duvet was caked in blood, the young male Noc was curled up against the wall, he was cradling his abdomen and was in pain. Ruth was standing by the top end of the bed, she had lifted her goggles and pulled down her scarf, she still pointed her rifle at him, another assaulter was standing at the end of the bed also pointing their rifle at him. Tyler glanced at the dead body that was lying under the bed, their arm reached out from underneath towards the other body that was face down and up against the far wall. Tyler looked at the young face, his neck had been ripped out. She stopped at the side of the bed and stared at what was there. She felt her hatred building.

"Yo-you," the Noc fought for breath. Tyler glared at him.

"What are you doing here?" she demanded.

"Ka – Kill me," he whispered. Tyler raised her eyebrows.

"Oh, don't worry, that is going to happen," Tyler said with a smirk.

"Make it quick, please," he stated.

"First you are going to answer some questions," Tyler walked up and stopped beside Ruth, the Noc winced in pain.

"Please," he whispered.

"What? like you did for these two?"

"I didn't feed off them, I swear,"

"You 'swear' and why would I believe you?" Tyler's voice was getting angry as Dermott walked into the room.

"And just who the hell are you?" Dermott demanded, Tyler looked at him and smiled, the smile fell from her face when she looked back at the Noc.

"Adrian,"

"And where are you from?" Tyler asked. The Noc looked up at her.

"Isle of Wight, just off the southern coast of England," he crunched up in pain again before he could look up again. "If you are looking for him, he should be back soon," the Noc forced the words out.

"If you mean 'The American'? he isn't going anywhere!" Dermott almost laughed, Ruth and Tyler smiled as well. The Noc looked up, there was a shocked look on his face.

"You killed him?"

"No, we didn't, but someone else did?" Tyler answered.

"But what about Sue? She was with him?" the Noc pleaded.

"Their burnt bodies were found earlier!" Tyler stared at him as she spoke. He lowered his head and started to cry.

"What are you doing here?" Dermot raised his voice to ask the question. The Noc looked up, tears started to flow down his face.

"He brought us over here to start a war with the wolves," he lowered his head, then looked up at Tyler, "we went to the house of the ex-copper, Fallon to draw you out,"

"Why?" Dermott demanded. The Noc winced again then looked at him.

"Dani ...." He looked over at Tyler, "she wanted you dead," he looked down again, "we were expecting you to follow us, not Foster."

"And you got quite the surprise there!" Dermott joked, he was smiling as he looked at Tyler then Ruth, Ruth smiled back, Tyler didn't.

"We were told you were just a pack of dogs, we were armed, it would be easy," he winced again.

"What was 'the American' going to do next?" Tyler asked, she continued to stare at him. The Noc looked up and nodded.

"He was meeting someone,"

"Who?"

"Someone from Salisbury, he had heard from one of them that they had sent over the 'Master Hunter'," Tyler and Dermott looked at each other, the Noc was confirming what Alison had told them. Tyler looked back at the Noc.

"Why?"

"To take him back there; he had heard from someone there that The Queen had ordered it, they aren't ready for the war yet,"

"What war?" Dermott leaned forward and placed one of his hands on the bed. The Noc turned his head.

"The war with the wolves, they are not ready yet. 'he' stepped over the mark, shouldn't have come here and done what he did." The Noc opened his eyes and looked defiantly at Tyler. *"Your days are numbered, assassin! The ones who walk by the night are coming for all of you!"* he crunched up in pain. Tyler unzipped her jacket and took out her Sig Pistol.

"Well, that isn't something you will ever see!" the unsuppressed shots echoed around the room, the Nocs head rocked and exploded as several bullets slammed into it. Tyler stepped back and looked at Ruth. "Have you finished with the SSE?" Ruth leaned forward and looked at the door of the bedroom at the assaulter who was standing there with a black plastic bag in one of his hands, it looked quite full.

"Is it done yet?" Ruth shouted at him. The assaulter lifted the heavy bag to show them.

"Yeah, as much as we are going to get!" Dermott had stepped back as Tyler stepped closer, so her legs touched the side of the bed. She stared at the dead Noc lying there. She turned and looked at Ruth.

"BURN IT,"

Chapter 28

Rupert Baskerville stopped the old series two Land Rover in the layby he had been told he would be met at. It was dark and there was a nip in the air, but he did not feel the cold, his mind was elsewhere. He turned off the engine and lights; the road was in darkness. It wasn't a busy road but there was occasional traffic back and forth. He opened the door and got out, reaching back inside he lifted the dark green Barbour jacket on the passenger seat. He pulled it on but left it unzipped. He walked to the front of the Land Rover and pushed his hand into his pockets, he did not know how long this would take. The layby was long enough for several trucks, with a small, grassed area separating it from the main road. The road was lined on both sides with trees; behind the trees was farmland.

"Are you armed?" the voice asked. Rupert spun around and there, standing near the rear of his Land Rover was a single male figure. He was young, mid to late twenties, wearing old trainers, jeans and a jacket zipped up He had not shaved in a few days and his hair was a mess, in fact, he looked ill. Rupert looked him up and down. Rupert then looked behind him, there were no other cars, he must have been waiting out of sight and seen him arrive.

"And who are you?" Rupert demanded.

"Answer the question, are you armed?" the young man demanded.

"No," Rupert's eyes moved over him, 'belts, buckles and bulges,' the obvious places to conceal a weapon on a human body, there wasn't anything obvious. "I wasn't planning to hold a meeting under arms," he stated. The young man hesitated, before he spoke again.

"You will be picked up from here shortly, leave the keys for your car with me!"

"Not a chance in hell am I doing that!" Rupert almost shouted.

"But I ...."

"But nothing, I have come to have a meeting, not to be taken as some sort of hostage!" Rupert walked towards the young man and pointed at him with his right forefinger, "now you tell whoever is in charge that!"

"I ... ahh ..." it was not the reaction that the young man had expected.

"Well?" Rupert placed his hands on his hips, the young man was intimidated.

"I ..."

"Look, go and speak with whoever is in charge and let them know I am here OK!" Rupert barked the order and the young man nodded, then turned and scurried away. Rupert watched him walk to the very end of the layby, then climb over the small wire fence that ran along the outside of the trees. Rupert looked around; the young man was obviously not alone. Rupert was alone. His head ranger knew about the meeting and where he was now but there had been nothing about him being collected and taken somewhere else. A single car drove past, Rupert watched it head off into the night. He looked around and studied the darkness, 'let's see if I can spot them' he thought to himself. A truck drove past going the other way. Rupert first looked around the layby, nothing, he then looked closely at the far verge, his eyes moved over every detail he could see, but there was nothing out of the ordinary. He turned around and stood up when a dark coloured car pulled into the layby, it turned its lights off; it was an executive high-end model. Apart from the main windscreen all the other windows were darkened, the driver and the man in the passenger seat were smartly dressed but had stern looks on their faces, Rupert recognised security personnel when he saw them. The car drove past and pulled in nearly thirty metres away, if anything was going to happen then there was plenty of space for it to happen here. Rupert noticed that the brake lights did not illuminate when it stopped, a standard fixture in vehicles used for protection. The front doors opened, and the two men got out, 'definitely security' Rupert thought to himself. One of the rear doors opened and the principal bodyguard got out. The two-security walked forward as the BG walked around the car and opened the other door. The man who got out was shorter than the rest, he was smartly dressed in a suit but seemed out of place in the country. The BG shadowed him and the whole team walked towards him in an obvious practiced move. Rupert straightened up and walked towards them, closing the gap between them quickly. The security team stopped, so Rupert did as well, he knew what they were doing, he had done it so many times himself.

"Lord Baskerville, it is a pleasure to meet you," the man was well spoken. "I must say, I've heard a lot about you!" the smile on his face was not one that Rupert would ever trust.

"Good evening, you have me at a disadvantage, may I ask who you are?" Rupert stated, his eyes fixed on the person the security team was here to protect. There was a long pause before the question was answered.

"My name is not important, but my position is 'Protector' so you can call me that!" the Lord Protector studied the sapien in front of him.

"Protector?" Rupert crunched up his face.

"That is my title, but names are not important, I hear you are having problems with some wolves on your land, and you would like our help?"

"I came here to find out 'if' you could help first of all,"

"Well, dealing with wolf problems has been something we have had to deal with for a very long time Mr Baskerville," the Lord Protector took a single step forward as he finished his sentence, "a very long time indeed!"

"Have you now? OK, give me a recent example of how you have been 'dealing' with them then." the Lord Protector paused, the mischievous smile came back over his face.

"Recently we sent our Master Hunter to Ireland to deal with the problem there!"

"Master hunter?" Rupert asked.

"Yes, one of our best in fact!" the Lord Protector stated, "I gather you have been over there recently yourself!"

"Yes, I have,"

"Was the trip, beneficial?"

"Not really,"

"Tell me about your wolf problem then,"

"First tell me exactly what your organisation is, what are your capabilities and how do you think you can help me?" There was a movement from the security team, their boss was obviously not spoken to like that. The Lord Protector straightened up at Rupert's comment. "You approached me, not the other way around".

"Yes, yes we did, your 'fire force' idea certainly has some real potential to it," The Lord Protector stated, Rupert's eyebrows raised.

"May I ask, how you know about that?" Rupert fixed his gaze on the protector, who smiled and slightly shrugged.

"Well," he started as he took a single step forward, "as you know the Close Protection world is a small one, so when we heard about the Earl of Baskerville setting up a new security company with a whole new idea we were certainly interested!" Rupert did not take his gaze off this man, there was something about him he did not trust, he now regretted not bringing some of his rangers with him.

"May I ask who 'we' actually are?" Rupert studied his instant responses, this 'protector' liked being the one in charge and he did not like having to answer questions. It took the protector a few seconds to answer so Rupert was guessing that whatever was about to come out was probably a lie.

"The stockholders,"

"Of?" Rupert asked.

"Our company,"

"Right, tell me exactly who it is you work for or this conversation is over!" Rupert raised his voice to make sure this 'protector' got the message. The Lord Protector straightened up and looked directly at Rupert.

"Maxx Investments,"

"Never heard of them!" Rupert replied, the Lord protector smiled.

"Good, I am glad you haven't, and our stockholders like it like that, but have you ever heard of Naiad Securities?"

"Yes,"

"Thalassa security solutions?"

"Of course,"

"Despina Protection Limited?"

"Yes, they are all part of the Hippocamp group of security companies!" Rupert stated.

"Well, at Maxx .... We own all of them!" the Lord Protector smiled his nefarious smile again, "so you can see, we have access to vast resources worldwide with considerable experience in all aspects of close protection and asset protection." The Lord Protector smiled.

"So, how do you know about the wolves then?" Rupert asked.

"At Larissa Group, we have a whole department of that company whose sole task is counter surveillance and counterintelligence," the Lord Protector shrugged, "we like to know who is watching us and listening to us, 'Industrial espionage' is big business as you know."

"It is," Rupert started, "but you didn't answer my question, how do you know about the wolves?" he said sternly. The Lord Protector again took a moment before he answered.

"We have had run ins with them in the past!"

"Really! Where?" Rupert prodded.

"The side of a road is not the place to hold business meetings to discuss such things,"

"You are right, where are your head offices? I can meet with you there!" Rupert suggested. The Lord Protector looked down before looking up at him.

"Unfortunately, we do not allow visitors to our head offices, we can send our head of security to your home and discuss how we can be mutually beneficial for each other." Rupert felt his insides tighten, this lot had an agenda, they knew about him, but he knew nothing about them, and it would take time to find out.

"I am sure that would be fine,"

"Great we will be in touch then!" As he spoke the Lord Protector turned and walked away. In a well-practiced move the security team moved as one, and escorted him back to the car, in less than a minute he was in the car, and they were off.

"Goodbye then!" Rupert stated out loud. The dark car headed off down the road; it did not go back the way it came from. Rupert looked around, there was no sign of the scruffy young man that first approached him. The night suddenly felt cold, a coldness he had not noticed before. Rupert walked to his car, removed the Barbour jacket and tossed it onto the passenger seat. He climbed in and shut the door. As the engine started, he went into the main pocket of his jacket and pulled out his mobile phone, he plugged in the earpiece then scrolled through the numbers before driving off. Rupert would do some basic anti-surveillance to make sure he was not being followed before he pressed the call button on the earpiece.

"Hello Boss," the male voice had a thick accent.

"Marcus, I have a job for you!"

"What kind of job boss?" Marcus replied.

"The type you are good at," there was a short laugh down the phone.

"Sure, what do you need?" Marcus stated.

"Have you ever heard of a company called 'Max investments'?" Rupert stated.

"Nope, can't say that I have, why?"

"What do you know of Hippocamp group?" Rupert asked.

"Hippocamp? Yeah, I've heard of them, they control a load of different companies, each one does something different, close protection, Marine, anti-piracy, you know, stuff like that, why? What do you need?" Marcus asked.

"I need you to look closer at them, apparently 'Max investments' controls them."

"Ok, do you want me to look at anything specific?"

"No, I want to know as much as I can about them, they seem to know a lot about me. They want to send their head of security down for a face to face so we can discuss the possibility of working together," Rupert replied.

"Isn't that better done in their head offices?" Marcus suggested.

"Yeah, I said that, apparently they 'don't do visitors.'"

"What?" Marcus replied.

"Yeah, which makes me want to know 'why' they don't do visitors!"

"Mmm, what was the name of this guy you had the meeting with?" Marcus asked.

"Another weird thing, he just called himself 'The Protector'!"

"What?"

"Yes, said his name wasn't important, so I want to know it, I got the plate from their car as a start point."

"Ok, if it was a firm's car then it will be registered to that firm," Marcus replied, "how long have I got?" he asked.

"As soon as ..."

"Ok, boss, I'm on it!" the line went dead., Rupert settled down for the drive back; it would take just over two hours and the old series two Land Rover did not have an audio system. The traffic on the road was picking up as he approached the feeder road to take him onto the motorway. The phone started ringing, it was a withheld number, which meant it wasn't Marcus. He pressed the small button on the cord of the headphones.

"Hello,"

"Rupert Baskerville?" The voice was male, deep and an English accent.

"Who is calling?" he answered.

"I don't have much time, but the person you just met in a layby wasn't human!" Rupert's body reacted, his eyes narrowed, his body tensed, and the grip of the steering wheel tightened, ready for an attack, the voice seemed scared.

"Who am I speaking to?" Rupert asked.

"Look, listen to me, the vampires only want your land, your property, if you let them in then you are a dead man ... don't you understand!"

"I don't know who you are, or what you want ..."

"The one you met tonight is their 'Lord Protector', he is beyond evil, you, your family, you are all in danger, don't you understa ....," suddenly the call was cut short. Rupert would have to wait until tomorrow to try and trace where the call had come from.

Chapter 29

Cara-Marie walked into the coffee shop at the bottom of Long Commons in Coleraine. She was mostly pleased, the interview with the journo in the US had gone well and it had been posted online. Cara-Marie had added a link to her blog. Her 'new best friend' had seen what she had seen as well, the descriptions were too close for her to have made it up, it was confirmation, there were werewolves all over the world. The coffee shop downstairs was busy but there were only a few ahead of her, the two staff were working their way through the different orders. Cara-Marie slowly moved forward until a smiling face greeting her.

"Good morn-un, would you be wantin' any food taday?" She had a country accent, Cara-Marie guessed she must be a student from the local university.

"No thank you, just a caramel latte please," The oven behind her pinged and she turned towards it.

"Caramel latte," she repeated to the other member of staff who was busy preparing the order ahead of her. He looked up and nodded without speaking. It did not take long before Cara-Marie was walking up the single staircase to the upper floor. When she walked into the upper room it was empty except for the woman with long blonde hair sitting at the far end and facing the entrance. Lucy sat up and smiled as Cara-Marie approached. Cara-Marie spotted the nearly empty ceramic mug in front of her. Lucy was wearing a dark blue blazer with a thin dark top underneath, her white training shoes were in contrast to the light blue of her tight jeans, she was neat and tidy, just like a businesswoman on a day off. Cara-Marie had dark shoes, loose light-coloured trousers, a thick jumper, and an outdoor jacket on. They were quite different.

"Hi,"

"Hello," Lucy's English accent stood out even more, "it is so nice you were able to make it!" Lucy held out her hand, Cara-Marie didn't want to shake it, but did out of politeness.

"I take it that idiot will not be joining us?" Cara-Marie asked, Lucy looked at her as she sat back down.

"No, no he will not,"

"Good," Cara-Marie replied as she took off her coat, she dropped her handbag on the floor beside her as she was hanging the coat of the back of the chair Lucy had some good news.

"He's still part of the team, but he will have no further contact with you."

"Great!" Cara-Marie sat down, "right, so what do you want to chat about?" Lucy rested her elbows on the wooden table, it was straight to business for the journalist.

"Just about the spate of recent killings that have occurred,"

"Ok, what about them? None of them point to or seem to have anything to do with our 'furry' friends!" Cara-Marie stated, she did not touch the mug of hot coffee in front of her.

"We don't think they did either," Lucy responded.

"So, who was it? The police don't seem to have much,"

"So, what have you got?" Lucy asked, taking the conversation away from her.

"Well, there was a 69-year-old man walking his dog, who for no apparent reason was murdered, then someone tried to conceal it by setting the body on fire!" Cara-Marie started.

"That is a very difficult thing to do," Lucy injected.

"What is?" Cara-Marie asked.

"To burn a body, it takes time and a lot of heat!"

"The five that were found a few miles away in a forestry block were nearly ash when they were found," Cara-Marie corrected, "three were stacked up, one was laid out on the ground and another was separate from the others with a crossbow bolt through his heart ... the police say they are not linked, but they cannot explain the burning as there is no evidence of any accelerant or fire, the body's just seem to have 'combusted'" Cara-Marie was reciting her notes and from what they had published, this is all stuff Lucy would already know. Cara-Maire looked at the Englishwoman in front of her, she had stopped talking, so Cara-Marie pushed. "Is there any light you can shed on that? Do you know if any of them have been identified yet?"

"The dog walker, yes, the others, no, all the police know so far is they were not local!"

"Who were they?" Cara-Marie asked softly. Lucy sat back in the chair.

"We don't know 'who' they were, it is 'what' they were that interests us,"

"They were not werewolves," Cara-Marie stated.

"No, they weren't,"

"So…" Cara-Marie pushed again, "what were they?" Cara-Marie could guess what was coming, but she wanted to hear the words.

"Noctrailis,"

"Vampires," Cara-Marie stated.

"Apparently they don't like being called that!" a small smile spread across her face.

"So, what precisely is going on then? Six murders all on the same day?"

"Seven,"

"What?"

"There was another one found a few hours ago," Lucy explained, Lucy spotted the physical reaction from the journalist.

"What? where?"

"Out past the white rocks, the far side of Portrush."

"Who?"

"Don't have a name, but 'he' was human," Lucy was looking into Cara-Marie's eyes, this journalist certainly wasn't a poker player she thought to herself. "Killed the same way, throat ripped open, but different from the others, so we think there is more than one of them."

"Oh my God, just what the hell is happening!" Cara-Marie reached for her phone.

"We think there is some sort of feud going on currently," Lucy stated.

"Between the werewolves and the vampires?" Cara-Marie asked as she looked at her phone, there was nothing there.

"No, between different covens of the Noctrailis," Lucy corrected.

"Covens? You mean like witches' covens?" Cara-Marie asked.

"Wolves come in packs, Noctrailis come in covens," Lucy explained.

"So, there are different 'covens' in Ireland that are in a feud at the moment, is that what you are saying?" Cara-Marie stated.

"No, we don't think there are any covens left here in Ireland, this conflict is between a coven in England and one in America," Cara-Marie sat back.

"What? now how the hell do I prove that … Kevin will never let me run any story like that without references!"

"No editor would," Lucy smiled, "you have a friend in America do you not?" Cara-Marie looked at the MI5 case officer in front of her.

"Did you see the interview that we put up recently?" Cara-Marie asked.

"Yes, but you were speaking for some time before that were you not?" Cara-Marie was suddenly not surprised that Lucy knew that.

"Yes, yes we were,"

"And you're both trying to prove your work is correct?" it was Lucy's turn to push.

"Yes,"

"Great, get her to help you then!" Lucy suggested.

"With what? I don't have anything for her, apart from hearsay," Cara-Marie sat forward again, "I mean, what you have said here, is just that, just hearsay." Cara-Marie explained, "I would need to be able to give her something more, do you have anything I can use? For example, any idea where this American coven is?" Cara-Marie demanded.

Lucy fixed her with a polite smile. "We think ... there is a large coven somewhere in Southern England and they are at odds with a large coven over in America!"

"I am going to need more than that." Cara-Marie stated. Lucy stood up and lifted the small shoulder bag she had brought with her, she was leaving, Cara-Marie stood up as well.

"Does the name 'Sydney Puttman' mean anything to you?" Lucy asked.

"No," Cara-Marie replied. Lucy smiled and stepped away from the table.

"We think he may be from, Little Rock in Arkansas," Lucy headed towards the exit, "have your American friend start there." Cara-Marie watched her leave, then sat down and thought for a moment what she had just been told. Isn't that something that MI5 could do for themselves? she wondered. She had been given the lead and yes, she would, of course follow it, but why would they help her? Her phone started to ring, she looked at the screen, 'KEV WORK' filled the screen. She tapped the green button on the phone placed it to her ear.

"Hello,"

"Cara, where are you right now?" there was an urgency in his voice.

"Just finishing off, still in Coleraine."

"Right, there has been another murder,"

"Male, out by White Rocks?" she said as she was standing up.

"Yeah ... how ..." he cut himself off, "good, you already know, so head there now."

∞∞∞∞

Chris Abbey was looking out of the window in the hotel, his eyes moved over the rooftops of Belfast. He was wearing one of the dressing gowns that had been folded in the drawer. He looked over his shoulder, the bed was still a mess and the sound of the shower starting came from the small en-suite. He smiled, it had been a long time since he had been with a girl like her, there had not been a lot of sleeping last night. She had arrived just after teatime last night. He had said to her to have eaten before she got there as he did not want to try and find somewhere to eat. They had ordered some room service late in the evening, but they did not leave the room, they did not have to, there was only one reason they were there. The mobile phone on the sideboard started to buzz. It was on vibrate and he thought about not answering it, then changed his mind. He slowly walked over to where it was sitting, she had not noticed how much of what they had been doing last night he had been recording, the footage he would watch several times more. He picked the phone up, it was a withheld number.

"Hello," he quietly said as he answered it.

"Chris, where are you?" Steve Minister asked, Chris looked around the room.

"Err, still in Belfast,"

"Right, well get off your chick and get back here, things are happening!"

There was an urgency in Steve's voice. "Ok," Chris replied, "I will,"

"Great," then Steve hung up. Chris repositioned the phone so it could record some more. He was in no rush, he had the room for another two hours so, whatever it was, both 'it' was going to wait until after sex in the shower with a brunette and probably again on the bed before he would even think about checking out of the expensive room.

Chapter 30

Rhydian was dressed in a baggy tracksuit; she was pacing around the kitchen when Tyler entered from the stairs. Rhydian stopped pacing, she still looked concerned.

"Come here, you," Tyler stepped forward and held out her arms, Rhydian ran towards her and the two embraced in a tight hug. "You are going to be fine tonight," she reassured.

"But mum," Rhydian stopped what she was saying, Tyler released the hug.

"This is a natural part of growing up, you *can* do this.

"Ok, I suppose," Rhydian looked to the floor as Tyler let go, both turned towards the front door of the farmhouse, several people had just walked in.

"Hello!" It was Dermott.

"In here!" Tyler shouted. Dermott was dressed formally. He was followed by Paul. Tony, Ian Silver, and John Gold stayed in the living room; everyone was in black tie.

"So, howz you?" Dermott asked, "all set for your first hunt?"

"Yeah, I suppose," she repeated.

"You will be grand!" Paul stated with a grin.

"I remember my first hunt; I was scared stiff!" Tony added with a short laugh.

Paul turned and looked at him. "Yeah, I remember your first hunt, you wanted someone else to clean up the mess you left!" there was a chorus of laughter from the others.

"Where are the rest of the hunting party?" Tyler asked.

"Outside," Paul replied. Tyler placed her hand on Rhydian's shoulder.

"Right, it's time." Rhydian and Tyler locked eyes and for a moment, they were the only two in the room, Tony went to speak but Paul raised his hand to stop him, there was subconscious communication between the two. A smile broke on Rhydian's face and the moment was broken. Paul and Tony stepped back to allow her to pass.

"Go get them!" Tony smiled as he encouraged her. Rhydian darted past and headed outside. The three men turned towards Tyler and the mood changed. Tyler looked at them.

"What?" she asked.

"We have a problem," Dermott stated.

"Can it wait until after the Moon Dance?" She suggested.

"We have heard from the South, the Noc that killed two sapiens in Limerick a few weeks ago, they think has come north," Paul added.

"When?" she asked.

"They think about a week ago," Paul replied.

"Which kinda makes sense, all the Noc activity we've seen, wasn't done by the ones we were tracking," Dermott added. Tyler straightened up; a serious look fell over her face.

"A WEEK AGO! And they are only telling us now?" She was getting angry.

"They said, they thought she had gone further south, West Cork direction," Paul said.

"Do they know '*anything*' about this one they let slip through their fingers?" Tony looked at Paul, Tyler was getting annoyed.

"They said *her* name is Megan Due, and we are to look for male sapien slayings," Paul looked at Dermott, then back at Tyler, "it appears she has it in for men!"

"Is that it? No description, migrating habits, background, I mean, what can this Noc do?" Tyler placed her hands on her hips.

"They are going to email me what they have this evening," Paul added. There was a pause, Tyler stepped closer to the kitchen table which she started to tap with the forefinger of her left hand, Tyler's mind was in several places all at the same time.

"Ideas?" she asked. Paul turned towards the living room.

"Ian, John, can you come in here please!" Both, like the others were dressed for the formal dinner, both stood side by side and had serious looks on their faces, Paul motioned towards them. "Both Ian and John here have volunteered, now that the American is taken care of and the Nocs that were with him," Paul turned to Tyler, "I suggest we deploy them again, same brief as before," Paul turned towards Dermott, "they are our best option for finding this Noc," he looked back at Tyler, "and quickly!" Tyler straightened up at addressed Ian and John.

"Gentlemen, your thoughts?" she asked.

"Leave it up to us," Ian stated,

"We will find her!" John added.

"Same brief as before, regular reports, etc, Ok!" Tyler instructed.

"No problem," John stated.

"Right, deploy tomorrow then,"

"We will," Ian answered.

"I will go over everything with you tomorrow morning," Paul said.

"Right then," Tyler stepped forward, "we have a hunt to hold,"

"And a dance to have!" Tony added. The mood in the room relaxed.

"Is Karen attending tonight?" Tyler asked as she stopped in front of Tony.

"No, she is staying at home with the baby, her mum is there tonight with her."

"That's nice for her," Tyler smiled.

"Speaking of babies, where is yours? Who is with the wee man himself?"

"Upstairs, Lynne M'Kane is babysitting tonight,"

"Great!" Tony moved out of the way as Tyler headed towards the living room, "let's get this party started!" Tony grinned as they all filed out after their alpha.

∞∞∞∞

Most of the crowd outside the barn were dressed for the formal occasion, but some of them were still dressed for farm work. There was a space in the middle where the stag was.

"Release the beast!" Tyler shouted, there was a cheer, then the crowd parted, and the deer was led towards the entrance to the field. Tony watched as Tyler again placed her hand on Rhydian's shoulder and offered words of encouragement. Everyone slowly followed as the deer was led through the gate then released into the field. The five teenagers of the hunting party all came together in a small circle inside the field. Tony watched as the final brief was given, and heads bobbed in understanding, then they started undressing. The deer ran off into the field and Tony looked up at the full moon. It felt like it was as bright as the sun, he felt its heat and closed his eyes momentarily and basked in its warmth. Tony opened his eyes as Alison Wallace walked up beside him on his left side. She was wearing a cocktail dress, he looked at her face, she was staring into the field. Tony looked in the same direction and watched as the five teenage werewolves all stood up together, then paced around, some shook their limbs, one opened their mouth as wide as they could in a stretch. One turned and looked towards Tony; he had never seen Rhydian as a wolf before. She looked radiant, then he realised she was not looking at him, he glanced over to his right. Most of the crowd had turned and was walking away but Tyler was standing there, the fingertips of her left hand just touching the wall, her bottom lip was wobbling, and her eyes were red, Tony had never seen her like this before.

"So, what happens now?" Alison asked as the hunting party split into two pairs and the leader in the middle. Tony looked back at her.

"What?" he asked.

"What happens now?" Alison repeated her question as she pointed to the wolves, one pair headed towards the far side of the field, the other pair started towards the near side and the leader, walked upright, slowly up the middle of the field.

"Oh, they hunt as a pack, for each of them it is their first hunt." Tony explained.

"How long will that take?" Alison asked.

"As long as it does," Tony replied, "but we," Tony started to turn away, "can go to the bar," Alison did not move, she just stared as the wolves disappeared over the crest of the hill, all heading towards the small forest.

"I had no idea," Alison spoke out loud. Tony stopped; he glanced over at Tyler who was also staring after the hunting party.

"No idea about what?" he asked. Alison turned around.

"I had no idea your pack was as strong as it is,"

"Would that have changed things?" Tony asked.

"Are you kidding me? There is no way they would ever have been strong enough to take you all down!"

"Do you think he knew that?"

"Who?"

"The American, do you think he knew that?" Tony looked into her eyes as he asked the question. Alison looked away.

"A lot of people died because of him,"

"But do you think he knew?" Tony repeated his question. Alison looked up.

"I think he came here to start something big, and he got a reaction from all of you!"

"That he did,"

"You know," Alison stated as she turned and looked back into the field, "I had never actually seen one of you change before," Alison looked back at him, "it is quite impressive!"

"Well," Tony smirked, "wait until after dinner when you will see us run as a pack!"

"What? all of you?" Alison looked surprised.

"All the ones at the dance, yes," Tony turned and held out his hand, palm and pointed to the front of the barn, "shall we?" Alison smiled and the two started to walk in that direction.

"That Russian fella, is he still here?" Alison asked.

"No," answered Tony as he looked back at the single figure of Tyler still staring into the field. "They have both gone back to Russia, there is a council meeting they have to attend!"

∞∞∞∞

A long howl echoed through the bar from outside; the bar exploded in joyous rapture.

"The kill, they got the kill," one excited voice shouted. Alison and Tony were standing at the far end of the bar.

"Was that ever in doubt?" Alison asked as the cheering started to quieten down.

"It isn't 100% certain, if the deer gets away from them, then it is allowed to live out the rest of its life in peace." Tony explained.

"So, why kill one? What does it achieve?" Alison asked, Tony drank from his glass.

"It is all about herd management," he looked towards her as he continued to explain, "it is called 'animal husbandry', all herds, no matter what species need to be managed when they are being farmed." Alison raised her glass to her lips, her eyes then looked over at the sketch drawing that was in the ornate frame on the wall. The figure was standing beside a tree with one hand in the air, the sword in their hand was pointing towards the sky.

"So that was 'Kyle's last stand then?" she asked. Tony looked over at the drawing, there was a pause before he answered.

"Yes, yes, it was," Suddenly Tony's head spun round as everyone in the bar looked towards the entrance door and the voice that was shouting from outside.

"Where's John? Where is John the paramedic?" Alison spotted the atmosphere in the room change, there was a collection of voices around the entrance door.

"What is going on?" Tony asked to another who was rushing past.

"One of the hunting party is hurt!" said the voice as they headed into the crowd and towards the door. Alison's eyes spotted Tyler dropping the glass in her hand and rushing towards the entrance. The level of conversation in the room was now louder than the background music, there was now only one topic of conversation.

"Any idea who it was?" Tony asked another.

"It is Simon's youngest, John is on his way, doesn't sound too bad," Tony relaxed a little, it wasn't Rhydian.

Chapter 31

Martin Hanna looked up at the night sky, it was a cloudless night and that made things more difficult. There was a noise from behind him, he turned around from where he was kneeing beside the large oak and looked at Glenn as he made his way through the trees.

"Everyone else is back about one hundred metres," Glenn stated as he approached. Martin turned back towards the path that led to the clearing.

"What are they doing?" Martin asked. Glenn went down on one knee beside him.

"They have secured the car park," Glenn looked up at the sky as well, "less than an hour until sunrise, we should be heading back!" Glenn looked at the stern face of his employer.

"Yeah," Martin whispered.

"Isn't that the last night of this cycle of full moons?" Glenn asked. Martin slowly turned his head and stared at him, then he looked back up the path towards the shapes he could make out in the clearing.

"Yes, the wolves would have had their Moon Dance either last night, or the night before," he spoke softly.

"Right, about them ...." Glenn started.

"Not here," Martin cut him off. Glenn looked down the path that cut through the forest. There was an obvious clearing up ahead and, in the moonlight, he could make out the shapes of the two domed tents.

"What are you thinking?" Glenn asked. Martin did not move, there was a long pause before he whispered his reply.

"Something is wrong here."

Glenn looked at him, then slowly turned his head to look around him, nothing moved in around the trees. Glenn's right hand reached up and touched the earpiece in his right ear, he looked at Martin. "There is some movement on the road by the car park,"

"Alright," Martin said, and he slowly rose then turned and headed back down the path he had approached from. Glenn followed; he was still looking around himself.

"Something isn't right here," Glenn said out loud.

"What?" Martin asked, Glenn's comment stopped him. Glenn had stopped beside him, both tensed up. "What do you think is wrong?" Martin asked, Glenn seemed transfixed with something off to their left. Glenn slowly placed his right hand on Martin's left shoulder.

"We are not alone," he whispered, "you said that something was 'wrong' at the tents, what was it?" Glenn asked.

"The tents are empty," Martin replied. Glenn pushed on his shoulder, and they quietly went down on one knee again.

"Possible threat, three o clock from our present position," Glenn whispered as he depressed the 'push to talk' button.

"*Roger, team one now mobile to you,*"

"Why would the tents be empty?" Glenn quietly asked, Martin looked at him.

"I tracked four scents to them, there should be four female hill walkers in them, but there isn't," Martin stated. Glenn was still staring off between the trees in the same direction.

"*Principal, team one, state location over,*" the voice was moving at speed, Glenn momentarily glanced in their direction.

"Follow the path you are currently on, we are now stationary, less than seventy metres in front of you." Glenn spoke into the small microphone, then he looked back through the trees.

"I don't see anything!" Martin stated, Glenn kept his hand on his shoulder.

"If this does turn noisy, you'll do exactly as we practiced," Glenn didn't take his eyes away from the threat, the sound of the team crashing through trees echoed through the forest.

"What do you see?" Martin asked.

"There is something there, and it is not female hill walkers!" Glenn stated as he slowly and very quietly moved his hand from Martin's shoulder and under his own jacket. He removed his own Glock pistol then placed his hand back on Martin's shoulder. Four security members came running through the woods towards them, they were in an extended line, it was a deliberate move to create noise and distraction to let the threat know help was there, it was an overt deterrent. They did not have their weapons drawn. Three members of the team ran past as one stopped; they formed a diamond shape around them. When they saw that Glenn had his pistol out, they each withdrew their own. Everyone was down on one knee and the four of them all pointed outwards from the principal, there was a short pause as they all drew breath.

"Situation?" One of them asked, Glenn slowly straightened himself up.

"Possible threat, three O clock from this location." Three heads all turned and looked in that direction, "we will move in slow time, from here, back to the vehicles," Glenn continued. Glenn looked at Martin and nodded once. All of them slowly stood and Glenn put himself between Martin and the direction of the threat. The security team stayed in the diamond formation; everyone knew what to do. Everyone's head all turned at the same time.

MOVEMENT

Something passed between them. There was a sound of crashing wood and several eyes focused in on the crossbow bolt that had pierced the trunk of the thin beech tree near them. The head was sticking out the far side of the tree with the small, feathered end still sticking out of the near side of the tree.

"GO!" Glenn shouted as he grabbed Martin by the shoulder. The security team closed in on their principal, they were all running at speed, pushing him forward. Martin was hunched over with Glenn beside him, one team member a few feet in front and another a few feet behind, the other two closed in to form a protective barrier around the principal.

"Target not seen!" one of them shouted. Martin was roughly handled all the way up the path in the dark, back to the car park. The two 4 x 4's had their lights on and engines running, they were ready to move. The team had closed in on the vehicles, their weapons drawn and pointing in different directions, they were ready to repulse any attack from any direction, but the main focus was to secure the principal and get out of danger. The rear door of the second vehicle was open, Glenn ran with Martin towards it, Martin was thrown face down across the rear seat, the driver revved the engine as Glenn jumped in the back and slammed the door shut. In seconds all the team had loaded up and both vehicles screamed away into the night.

Jason Apollyon cradled the crossbow in his right arm as he slowly walked towards the tree that had the bolt still in it. He swung the strap of the crossbow over his shoulder and used two hands to push the bolt through the tree and remove it. The tree easily gave way. He blew wooden fragments from the head of the bolt and slowly walked up the path towards the now empty carpark. He took his time; he was in no rush. When he reached the edge of the trees, he stopped. He looked around and a small smile spread across his lips, he had learnt a few things about this Noc. His security team were good, and they were armed and from what he had seen, they knew what they were doing. He turned and slowly walked back towards where he had hidden his rucksack. Jason traced his steps back towards the clearing where the tents were, he would leave them there, he had no further use for them, the scent bottles he had used had worked, but he doubted if they would be as successful again. At the clearing he turned right and headed to where his rucksack was, this whole thing had been a good idea.

At the far side of the clearing, high up in one of the trees, clinging to the main trunk and trying her best not to move, Megan Due fought to control her breath. She opened her mouth;

her teeth were elongated. Her lustful eyes studied the way Jason walked. She tried to breathe though her nose, she slowly wiped her salivating mouth with one of her hands. She could feel her own heart thump inside her chest, the tips of her fingers quivered, she had to have him. Megan bit her bottom lip as she watched Jason disassembling his crossbow, then pack it away in his rucksack. It was nearly sunrise as he trudged away from her. Megan squeezed the tree, her own lust was almost boiling over, she would have him, and she would enjoy him so much, the very thought excited her. Megan slowly made her way down the tree and scurried over to the tents to have a look around. She unzipped each one in turn and looked inside, both were empty. Her heart was still thumping inside her chest as the forest started to brighten, the sun had risen. Her head turned and she walked through the trees to the edge of the forest, drawn by the noise she had heard. In the field beside the wood was a tractor. It was chugging along, over the field. The tractor was pulling a machine along behind it with a large rotor that was turning, it was spreading something, but she had no idea what. Her eyes focused in on the young man who was driving. He looked tired and he looked bored. She looked around, there was no one else around, her heart started to thump harder at the thoughts in her head. It would take her seconds to get naked, and it would only take a few moments for the young farmer to see the naked woman that was waving at him from the edge of the forest, beckoning him over. The sex in the tent would be fast and furious as would be his death shortly afterwards. Megan Due would fulfil all her lust, and this young farmer would be the release that she wanted. He would already be dead when she used her knife to remove his heart, she loved the fact that she knew the hunter from Salisbury would probably get the blame for this as well. Today was going to be a good day.

∞∞∞

Tyler raised her hand to wave goodbye as Ian Silver and John Gold drove off down the lane and away to their new task. They were confident it would not take them long to track down their prey, Tyler believed them. She looked around the front of the farmhouse, she was wearing her running leggings and a small top, her hair was tied back into a ponytail. It was a fresh morning; the sky was clear, and the sun was up. She started to walk away from the front of the barn towards the front door of the farmhouse.

"Tyler!" she stopped and looked towards the far corner of the barn. Paul walked directly towards her; he was dressed for a day on the farm. "Tyler," he said again as he approached, Tyler put her hands on her hips as she became focused on the line of running teenagers who had started to appear behind Paul. one at time they arrived at the end of their run. Some bent over as they fought for breath, others walked around, it had been a close fought race. Some had leggings on, others were in shorts, all had mud over their training shoes and up their legs, part of the race had been cross country.

"Hang on," Tyler said to Paul as she walked towards them, more arrived, sprinting then slowing down at the end of the race, Tyler looked at her watch. "Right, that was only a five K, you need to be doing better than that!" she barked at them. Paul looked at the red faces, Rhydian was one of them, she looked down as she breathed heavily. One of them raised his hand and stepped forward to speak, Tyler cut him off before he could. "Right, it is nearly nine by my watch, you have an hour to get showered and changed and I want all of you in the barn with your training swords, we have a long day today!" Exhausted teenagers grumbled behind her, then slowly all started to head off in different directions.

"Day one of the training going well then?" Paul asked with a smirk.

"Just a wake up to blow out some cobwebs, "we could have started yesterday!"

"The morning after a moon dance! Are you that cruel?" Paul asked.

"Sometimes I think I should be!" she responded.

164

"Did Ian and John get away?" he asked.

"Yeah, you just missed them, it was the right call not to send them yesterday."

"Did we get the photos from down south?" he asked.

"Yeah, after I read that email they sent you I phoned Connor, he said they would send up everything they had, as soon as I got it, I shared it with them."

"Do you think this 'Megan' is a threat?" he asked.

"To us?" Tyler turned towards him, "no, I don't think she is, I am more concerned about this 'Noc Master Hunter fella!"

"Well," Paul started, "he has been busy again,"

"What? when?" Tyler reacted.

"I just came from the communications building and the police are responding to a body of a young farmer out near Ballycastle,"

"What happened?" Tyler asked.

"From what we can glean from the police comms at the moment, it seems he was found naked and staked out and has 'serious bodily mutilations'" Paul was looking at her, she was absorbing what he had just said.

"Ok, do Ian and John know that yet?"

"Not yet, no,"

"Ok, can you pass that to them and get them to look at it for us?"

"Sure,"

"Oh, something else,"

"What?" he asked.

"Connor said he has sent four of his north, they are doing their own search around the border areas, to see if they can spot this 'Megan' character in case she heads south again!"

"Do you have a problem with that?" Paul asked the obvious question.

"One less job for us to do!" Tyler shrugged.

"If that was the other way around, he would be furious!" Paul pointed out.

"I know, but I suppose he has to do something, they lost this Noc, and if she had not come North then we would probably not know anything about her."

"Aye, I suppose," Paul agreed, "some tale she has though," he added.

"What? basically sold by her father into what can only be described as 'modern day slavery', used and abused by her captor then goes on a revenge killing spree against her new family then her own father for doing that to her? I can understand why she is upset."

"They knew who the sapien mother was, did they ID the Noc father?" Paul asked.

"Not to my knowledge,"

"What about that fella, Apollyon, what are we going to do about him?"

"Well, he has taken down a few Nocs for us,"

"Agreed, but we have someone who survived a Noc attack and as far as we know, he did not turn ... that has never happened before."

"No, it hasn't," Tyler conceded.

"Grishin did not seem overly concerned by him either!" Paul added.

"No, he didn't, but then, he had Alison to concentrate on."

"What are we going to do about her?" Paul asked.

"She is sacred stiff, that is for certain!"

"Agreed,"

"And she has been helpful since she got here,"

"She has," Paul nodded as he responded.

"And she does not seem to present a threat at the moment."

"But what if she does? What if ..."

"What if ... what?" Tyler asked.

"What if, her being caught was all planned?"

"Planned?" she asked.

"Yeah, a deliberate act, she did get in touch via Tony," Tyler face reacted, her eyebrows shot up, she was thinking about what Paul had just said. "What? like some kind of double bluff thing?" she suggested.

"I don't think we can cross that off just yet!" Paul stated.

"Ok, get communications to keep an eye on her phone and internet activity."

"She doesn't have either," Paul replied.

"What? no phone? Nothing?"

"Nope,"

"So .... What are you thinking?" she asked.

"I don't know ...." Paul seemed unsure, "there is something I just can't put my finger on about her, something does not feel right about the whole situation."

"The fact she kills like a Noc and in her recent past she helped the Nocs against us?"

"Yeah, something like that," Paul replied.

"Ok," Tyler stepped closer and lowered her voice, "give her something to do on the farm, but not with farm security, keep her out of the armoury and keep an eye on her,"

"Will do," Paul replied.

"Plus," Tyler added,

"What?" Paul asked.

"Try and get back in touch with that Apollyon guy and find out what he is up to, I think we should keep an eye on him as well!"

"I agree," Paul replied, "but he did not seem overly warming when we met up with him at Black Mountain!"

"No, he didn't," Tyler thought for a moment, "but if we can use him to at least track this Master hunter that would be something, wouldn't it!"

"It would," Paul agreed.

"Has there been any more problems with that journalist recently?" Tyler asked.

∞∞∞∞

Detective Inspector Wells was in her office with the door closed. She had the folder open on the desk, she was reading over the data again. She had answered the email from Chief Anderson, she was to take the lead on TV interviews, but he would still lead all press conferences. He had repeated the instruction that the term 'serial killer' was not to be used. She did not like the way this was going. The knock at the door was rapid.

"Come in," she shouted. The door opened and Eddie Cargill partially leaned in.

"Ma'am, there has been another one," Eddie looked directly at her, she stood up.

"Where?"

"Near Ballycastle, a farmer this time," she was already walking around her desk as he continued, "looks like it is the same as before, first reports are 'severe neck injuries!" As she lifted her coat from the back of the door, Eddie stepped back.

"Did that go over the open police channel?"

"Yes Ma'am, it did," She walked past him, pulling her coat on as she did, the whole team stopped what they were doing.

"Shit, that means Special Branch already knows," she stopped in the middle of the room and looked at the team who were at their desks. "WELL! DON'T JUST SIT THERE!" she shouted.

Chapter 32

Cara-Marie looked at her watch as she was standing at the traffic lights across from the brown coffee shop at the bottom of Long Commons, it was nearly 6pm, she was right on time. The lights stopped the traffic and the beeping started indicating it was safe for pedestrians to cross, she went straight for the door of the coffee shop. The coffee shop was packed, there were several people in the queue, she now regretted not leaving the office sooner. The young girl in the queue in front of her turned around and looked her up and down with a disapproving look, Cara-Marie felt her face crunch up, 'just who the hell are you!' she thought, she was about to say something when there was a female voice behind her.

"Cara!" she turned and there was the smiling face of Laura Patterson.

"Hi," Cara-Marie held out her hand which Laura took, it was a firm handshake.

"Hiya, it's been a while!" Laura seemed happy about something. The line moved and the two shuffled along. Laura was wearing jeans and a fleece top, her bobbed hair was neat and tidy, she was trying not to look like an off-duty police officer.

"You are a long way from home, were you working today?" Cara-Maire asked, Laura's smile answered before she did.

"Yes, finished at 4PM, had a few things to do first, but glad I caught you," Laura was certainly pleased about something.

"What can I get for you today?" the girl behind the counter asked,

Cara-Marie turned and placed her usual order. "Vanilla latte please," she turned towards Laura, "what would you like?" she asked, Laura paused for a second.

"Oh, that sound nice," Laura looked over the counter at the young face that looked back, "may I have the same please?" she asked.

"Sure," the girl turned and started busying herself with the order. The two people in front of them lifted a small tray with drinks and a single traybake and left the line.

"Would you like any food today?" the young guy appeared from round the side of the large coffee machine. Cara-Marie looked at the adolescent face for a brief moment, she wanted to ask him 'are you old enough to be working here?' but she didn't, that conversation would take too long.

"No, thank you," she turned her head towards Laura, "would you like something to eat?" she asked.

"No thanks," Laura replied. Both drinks were placed on a tray, Laura lifted out her purse, but Cara-Marie stopped her.

"My treat,"

"Thanks,"

"I can put it on expenses!". Cara-Marie lifted the tray and Laura followed her up the stairs. The upper room was nowhere near as full as the downstairs, which was great when you do not want the person sitting next to you listening to your conversation. Cara-Marie headed for the farthest table, then took the side where she could still face the door. She placed the tray between them, then slipped off her jacket, which she hung over the back of the tall chair. Laura unzipped her fleece but did not take it off. As she sat down Cara-Marie glimpsed the Glock pistol she had holstered on her waist. "Here you go," Cara-Marie passed her one of the drinks, then got comfy herself. She lifted the drink to her lips; she got the smell first before the taste.

"Thanks," Laura did the same, "wow," Laura reacted, "this is really nice!"

"You sound surprised, not the usual thing you drink?" Cara-Marie asked.

"No," Laura shook her head, "normally just get a regular coffee," Laura raised the mug, "but I think I may have just found a new habit!" the two shared a smile. Cara-Marie glanced around at the other patrons in the café, the young girl who was dressed for the gym was having a polite conversation with a guy with a hat who had stopped to chat, they obviously knew each other. The table near the door with three older men in suits sitting around it were at the point of having an argument, whatever the business deal was, it was not going well. By the window was a bald man she did not recognise was reading a book about travelling around the middle east. Cara-Marie's eyes looked towards the door at the top of the stairs. A woman walked in wearing sports leggings and a small workout top. Her dark ginger hair hung down touching her shoulders, she had a large leather bag over one shoulder and was carrying a tray with two drinks on it. The shapely girl got the attention of the three businessmen as she walked past, then the guy with the hat paused and looked her up and down. She spotted it and smiled; she was liking the attention. Cara-Marie looked at her face, she knew it but could not put a name to the face. Laura looked over and the two exchanged a smile before she sat down.

"You know her?" Cara-Marie asked.

"Of course, she is one of our physios, Kelly something," Cara-Marie felt her eyebrows shoot up, she knew that she recognised that face. "Can't remember her surname, I think it is fox or something like that!"

"Vixen," Cara-Marie whispered, Laura looked at her.

"Yes, that is it, you know her?" she asked.

"I know 'of' her, cannot say we are friends." Cara-Marie watched as Kelly's attention became transfixed on the man that had just walked in.

"And that is Dave Tattershall, he is one of the Sergeants in the station," Laura lowered her voice. Cara-Marie watched as the two greeted each other, there was excitement, they were obviously pleased to see each other. Dave took a seat beside Kelly and the two faced each other, Cara-Maire looked as he placed his right hand on her leg, she did not flinch, in fact she leaned forward so he could look straight down her top. "I also know his wife!" Laura kept the commentary running, Cara-Marie looked over at her.

"New station scandal?" Cara-Marie asked, Laura crunched up her face.

"Hardly, those two have been at it for a while!" Cara-Marie was going to say something, she thought about saying Kyle's name and the affect that this woman had on him, but he was gone so she decided against it. "And he is still married ..." Laura looked over at her as she raised the mug again, "worst kept secret in the western world."

"But anyway," Cara-Marie changed the subject, "you seemed pretty keen to chat ...." Cara-Marie lifted the mug again and looked over the rim at the excited police officer sitting opposite her. Laura leaned forward and placed her elbows on the table, with the ambient noise their conversation would not be heard.

"What do you know about all the recent murders around the Northwest?" Laura came straight to the point of the conversation.

"I know about them, but the burning questions is, 'what do the police know about them? Have any suspects been identified yet? Any motive? I mean as far as I can tell, none of the victims were linked!" Cara-Marie stated, see could see the reaction in Laura's eyes and her body language, she was exploding with excitement about something, it was clear, this was no poker player.

"No, no suspects, and yes you are right, there seems to be no connection with any of the victims except for the method of death!" Cara-Marie was now in full listening mode, this young woman was keen to share something important, Cara-Marie let her continue without interruption, "they are totally different from the Castleroe murders, they, as you know, were totally ripped apart, whereas this lot ..." Laura drank from her mug, Cara-Marie continued to listen, "all had their throats ripped out, and all in the same way!" Laura was obviously excited.

"Is Major Investigations in charge currently? Or is it still at a local level?"

"Yeah, they took over, it is called 'Operation Abhartach', that is some Irish legend apparently!" Laura explained, Cara-Marie thought for a moment.

"Yes, it is, he was a dwarf who ruled over a part of the North Coast and was renowned for being exceptionally cruel. When he was killed, they buried him standing up, but he had magical powers and he returned the following night to drink the blood of his victims,"

"Really?" Laura sat up, "sounds a lot like Dracula!"

"Well, it is said that Bram Stoker who wrote the original book actually based most of the story on the Irish legend."

"But I thought he was real, from history," Laura stated.

"The main character was based on the real, Vlad the Impaler, from modern-day Romania, and his war against the Turks, but there is no evidence that he actually drank blood,"

"Oh, I didn't know that."

"Most people just know the Hollywood stuff," Cara-Marie continued to explain.

"But you don't," Laura was looking at her as she asked the question.

"Well, Hollywood has done a lot to distort history,"

"And legends," Laura added.

"And legends," Cara-Marie repeated.

"Must be frustrating,"

"What?" Cara-Marie asked,

"Knowing the truth when all people will believe is what they see in the cinema,"

"So, any idea what direction Major Investigations are currently heading?" Cara-Marie asked, bringing the conversation back on track.

"Oh, yes," Laura's eyes narrowed, and her voice lowered. "Some of the evidence points towards the possibility there maybe two different offenders on the loose."

"Offenders?" Cara-Marie asked, Laura smirked.

"Yeah, that is their word of choice, they really don't like the term 'serial killer' as they really don't want that getting into the press," Cara-Marie smiled, yes, she knew that.

"What else?" Cara-Marie asked.

"Well, you may not believe this but ...." Laura continued, a small smile spread over Cara-Marie's face, how many times had she heard that said to her. "M.I.T. currently thinks that they are all nearly human bites that are causing the catastrophic injuries ..."

"Nearly human?" Cara-Marie interrupted.

"That was the term I heard them use," Laura replied, Cara-Marie's mind was racing.

"Don't suppose you know who is in charge of the investigation by any chance?" Cara-Marie enquired. Laura reacted like a kid in a school classroom who knew the answer.

"Yes, of course, it is Detective Inspector Wells, from M.I.T. Belfast, she is the lead investigator." Cara-Marie recognised the name, but she would look more into that later.

"Brilliant, thank you," Cara-Marie replied.

"Oh, they have a new nickname as well!" Laura stated.

"And what is that?" Cara-Marie asked.

"Vampire Squad!" Laura smiled. Cara-Marie tried not to laugh.

"And why that?" she asked.

"Well," Laura started, "there was the New Years' Day murders .... All bites to the neck ... the couple down at Murlough ... bites to the neck .... so on and so forth ...."

"But they don't think it is the same person?" Cara-Marie asked.

"No, current thinking is one killer and one copycat doing the same thing,"

"Dangerous,"

"Yes, that's what they think?" Laura replied as she drank more of her coffee.

"Laura," Cara-Marie leaned forward as she asked her question, "can I ask you, since you are not part of the investigation's team how you know all this?"

"Well," Laura smiled, "you know how 'cops talk' between each other!"

"Yes,"

"Well, there is also one of the guys on the team that fancies me, and a little bit of flirting and he tells me all!" Laura finished off with a wink, Cara-Marie could not help but smile at the young face smiling back at her.

"Ok, thank you," Cara-Marie replied.

"Thought that you could use some of this to 'poke' in the right direction,"

"Yes, thank you, I certainly can."

"Well, I best be off," Laura stated as she emptied the last remains of her drink.

"Ok, well, stay safe then," Cara-Marie said as Laura pushed the chair back then headed towards the door. Cara-Marie had her own unfinished drink in her hands as Laura went to walk past the table with Dave and Kelly sitting at it, she made it very obvious she was deliberately stopping to talk; her voice was loud enough for nearly everyone to hear.

"Oh, Hi Dave, hiya Kelly," she had interrupted their conversation, there was a slightly confused look on Kelly's face, which changed as Laura kept talking, "Oh Dave, could you pass a message to *your wife,* that I can make the spin class round at the gym this week, thanks!" Laura then turned and headed towards the door at speed. There was a reaction from the two of them, Dave sat back, and Kelly looked embarrassed. Cara-Marie cast a quick look around, several people looked at them, some smirked, others looked in disgust, Cara-Marie spotted the police sergeant had lifted his hand from the leg of his mistress. '*BUSTED*' Cara-Marie thought to herself, she smiled again as she looked away when she realised she had thought the word in a North American accent. Her phone started to ring so she shifted in her seat and pulled it out, she recognised the name on the screen.

"Hi Mark," she said as she held the phone to her ear.

"Hiya, where are you at the moe?" Mark asked.

"Upstairs in the coffee shop at Long Commons, why?"

"Ok, it's just I have to go to court tomorrow and I was going to buy you an early dinner," She had forgot about his court appearance, it was the next stage in the battle with his ex over access to their child.

"Sure, I will wait here," her eyes looked over towards the entrance as Dave and Kelly walked out, leaving what was left of their drinks.

"Brilliant I am on the way, oh how did your 'meet' go?" he asked. In the background of the call, she could now hear traffic, he had been in the office and was just leaving, she could picture exactly where he was, he would not take him long to arrive.

"Yeah, it was good, got a few things we can use," she replied.

"Brill see you soon," and he ended the call. Yes, she had something she could use.

∞∞∞∞

Glenn Nendrum was alone in the 4 x4. He had gone to the disused airfield himself to collect what the small plane had delivered for them. He turned and headed up the lane towards the large seven bedroomed farmhouse they were using as a safe house. No one knew they were there; he had been careful with his anti-surveillance; he knew he had not been followed. The main door to the garage was open and the response 4 x 4 was parked there, two of the security team were leaning up against the front of it. The other security vehicle was parked by the front door and faced back down the lane, Glenn looked up at the small CCTV cameras, they only had three, which was far from ideal but with the time they had to get all the stuff together it was better than nothing. One pointed down the lane then one off to each side, the only part that was not covered was to the rear of the house. The smallest of the bedrooms had been converted into a mini operations room by the team when they had first arrived. They had set up the communications base system in there so that they could stay in touch with the vehicles when they were out and about, they also had a line back to Salisbury as well. Then there were the monitors for the cameras and well as the weapon rack on the side. The small camp bed had a sleep bag laid out on it, the two team members who always stayed behind took turns to keep watch on the cameras and maintain the radios, one could sleep as one monitored. The rest of the team were split between the other bedrooms, the exception being the client. The small basement had been a recent conversation, but it suited his needs, the thick door could only be opened from the inside, the camp bed for Glenn was outside the basement door, only the client got past him. The team had been 'jittery' recently and he had to remind them there was a reason they were being paid three times the normal rate. 'That meant three times the normal work,' that had put most of them at ease. Glenn raised his hand in a wave as he approached, one of the team waved back as he turned the front of the 4 x 4 towards the edge of the tarmac covered area at the front of the house. He reversed parked so it was facing back down the lane but out of the way of the response 4 x 4 in case they needed to get the client out quickly. He turned off the lights and engine and got out, both the team members walked towards him as he got out.

"Right, let's get this unpacked and the gear inside quickly!"

"What is it?" one of the team asked.

"New gear that we needed, is the side door open?" Glenn asked.

"Yeah,"

"Right, grab a box," Glenn opened the rear of the 4 x 4, inside were four large dark coloured containers. The thick plastic outer was designed to protect the weapons that were inside. The lids were clipped down in place, and each had large black handles at the sides.

"What have we here?" asked another voice from the doorway inside the garage that led inside. Glenn looked over at him.

"Get over here and help with this lot." The first two tugged and slid the first box out. The weight made them almost drop it. "Careful with that!" Glenn shouted; more bodies appeared through the doorway. Three of the boxes were heavy but the fourth was lighter, they were manhandled inside, Glenn locked the 4 x4 and headed inside. The boxes had been taken into the spacious living room. "Right, get them open," Glen instructed. The clips were broken and pushed back; the first lid was lifted off to reveal the new rifles inside. One of the team lifted the first one out. It looked like a small M-16 with new rails along the front stock and Advanced Combat Optical Gunsight on top.

"Wow, the new M-4!" one of the team exclaimed, recognising the weapon. He started to pass them out around the team as the other boxes were opened.

"Yeah, well after the last few days it was obvious we did not have everything we need, so I got these," Glenn started as Mark Castle walked in, Glenn looked at him. "In the last box are red dots, range finders and suppressors, I want them test fired and zeroed as soon as possible." Mark Castle nodded as the rest of the team descended on their new toys. Castle motioned with his head towards the now empty kitchen. Glenn followed him in. Castle stopped by the kitchen table; Glenn closed the door to the excitement in the living room.

"Right," Castle started, "just what the hell is going on here?" he demanded.

"I got new and better weapons for us, what is the problem?" Glenn responded.

"Weapons that are currently 'illegal' here ..."

"Yes, but there are only for use as an absolute last resort!" Glenn responded.

"Are we expecting to be in a 'last resort' situation? I mean, just what the hell is going on here?" Castle was getting irate, Glenn paused before he answered.

"How many clients have you worked for where you demanded to know all their goings on?" he said sternly.

"I have never had a client that is a serial killer before!"

"I would not say that in front of him."

"Look," Castle stepped closer, "I have not got a problem with our clients 'Nocturnal activities' nor do I have a problem with being told he is something I thought was only fiction!"

"But ..." Glenn interrupted.

"But look," Castle was using his hands to make his point, "we have been looking at that deer farm he seems to be very interested in, and no, that place isn't normal either, they have a thirty-metre range, a four hundred metre range and a drive in range that is better than where I did my CP course."

"So?"

"So? Are you kidding me?" Castle raised his voice, Glenn remained motionless, "all I want to know, what kind of threat is really out there?" Glenn did not move, so Castle carried on, "look, the guys here did spot two faces there that they knew,"

"Who?" Glenn asked quietly.

"One, Steve Minister and a Chris Abbey," Castle replied.

"So?" Glenn repeated.

"They are SAS! Some of the team knows them, if you want us to go up against a squadron of them you can count me out!" Castle looked directly at him; he was getting angry.

"No," Glenn spoke quietly.

"No what?"

"No, you are not being asked to go up against them," Glenn stepped closer to Castle and leaned towards him, "our client is tasked with finding one person, once he finds that person, he will deal with that person and then we are out of here," Glenn explained with menace.

"What if it all goes 'noisy'?"

"Simple, we extract to that old airfield and we wait for the aircraft the firm will send.

"But what if the police arrive?" Castle asked, Glenn almost laughed.

"Where and at what? it was used as an airfield during world war two, it has not been an active airfield since 1948," Glenn stepped back. "Look, I understand your concerns, and I am glad that you are thinking like this, it shows me that we picked the right man for the job, is there a threat? Yes! Do I think you can deal with it? Yes! Or you would not be standing here." Castle looked him, he was being buttered up, almost patronised.

"All I really want to know is ..." Castle lowered his voice to ask the rest of the question, "when this job is done, will I get to go home alive?"

"You have a family, yes?" Glenn asked.

"Yeah, and this job is clearing my mortgage and paying off the ex-wife all at the same time!" Glenn smiled and held out his hand, Castle took it. The handshake was firm, Glenn was letting him know who was overall in charge.

"Then you are here for the right reasons, yes, you will be able to do all of that!" Glenn released the handshake as the far door opened and a tired looking Martin Hanna walked in.

"Hi Glenn, did they arrive?" Martin did not acknowledge Castle.

"Yes, the team are getting to know them now," Glenn motioned towards Castle, "they will all be tested and zeroed tomorrow, then we can have a full run through of all our drills,"

"Great, great, first class, well done everyone," Martin shuffled towards the door of the living room, then he turned back towards the two men, "look I don't have anything on for tonight,

Glenn how about you and I stay here, and the team can have the night off ... you know, head into town and let off a bit of steam."

"Boss, I don't recommend ..." Glenn started, Martin waved his hand to stop him.

"Nonsense, nonsense, they have been great, just a little thank you from me," Martin opened the door and smiled, "I mean, I am not doing anything tonight, and we don't want any 'cabin fever' setting in now do we."

"No boss, we don't," Glenn nodded as Martin walked into the living room.

"Well, it looks like all of you have the night off, I suggest you take full advantage." Glen smiled. Castle did not say anything as a cheer came from the living room when they heard the news. He had no doubt that 'the client' had heard their exchange and he wanted them out of the way for a few hours. Mark Castle now feared for his life more now than he ever had before. The sooner this job was over the better, he would never work for this company ever again.

Chapter 33

Chris walked into the empty portacabin. There was a lot of activity outside, the main group had an urgent job on, but he wasn't involved so he wasn't interested. The door closed behind him as he headed over to the table with the kettle, mugs, and the containers for making a hot drink. He slowed as he got there, most of the mugs had been used, but not washed up, the table had dried tea and coffee where someone had spilt some but not cleaned up after themselves. Chris lifted several of the mugs and choose the cleanest one he could find. The water out of the tap at the small sink was cold, he rubbed the mug as clean as he was going to get it then half-filled the kettle. When he replaced it, he flicked the switch on the base and the kettle started to make a small grumbling noise. He looked in the different containers, the sugar was nearly gone and there were only a few teabags left. He lifted the container and smelt the coffee, it repulsed him, so he chose a tea bag, there wasn't a lot of milk left either. The door behind him opened and he looked over his shoulder to see Steve Minister walking in.

"There is only tea!" Chris shouted. The door slammed shut as Steve walked towards him, Chris lifted a second mug then washed it under the tap as he had done with the first one.

"Aye, that is fine," Steve replied as he approached. Steve's Scottish accent seemed stronger as if he had been home, but Chris knew he hadn't been. The kettle started to boil so Chris started to pour the hot water into the waiting mugs.

"So, what is happening out there then?" Chris asked. Steve looked back at the door, the sound of revving engines echoed around the large hangar, then there was a voice shouting instructions and at least one car took off.

"Apparently, there is a car moving a boot full of pistols and other stuff across the border this afternoon," Steve turned back and nodded a thanks as he was handed the mug. Steve turned and started to walk towards where the small coffee table was, he continued chatting. "But I am glad I caught you,"

"Really? How so? I haven't missed something, have I?" he asked as Steve sat down,

"What? no, no," Steve took a sip of the drink and his face contorted, "but you do need to work on your brew making skills," he lifted the mug in a fake salute, "this, this is shit!"

"Thanks," Chris sat back in the chair, "and there was me thinking you have me here for my stunning good looks, wit and charm and brew skills." he said sarcastically.

"Keep dreaming," Steve replied as he took another sip, then looked back over to the kettle, "isn't there any coffee?" he asked.

"Yeah, but it is that crap you get in ration packs," Steve looked over at him as he sat forward, "you know, that crap you wouldn't even give to your dog!"

"Yeah, remember when we were in Bagram airfield at the start of Afghan and the Yanks really kicked off at the ration pack coffee we had!" Steve smiled as he spoke,

Chris let out a short laugh. "Yeah, that was my first Afghan tour, they went metal, they were SEALS, right?" he asked.

"Delta," Steve corrected.

"Either way, they got a supply of coffee flown in all the way from the US because of how bad our coffee was, nearly caused an international incident," the two men shared a laugh at the memory. *Brits drink tea, be patriotic and drink 'real' Amer-I-can coffee!* Chris added.

"MMM, it did not do a lot for 'Anglo-American relations,'"

"Well, I tried to help repair that," Chris injected; Steve sat up.

"Shagging that CIA chick for weeks on end was not helpful to 'Anglo-American relations!" Steve responded.

"*Oh my Gawd, you British guys, I just louve your accents!*" Chris imitated; the two men laughed again.

"Heard from one of the Delta guys that when she moved over to Pakistan, Terry Taliban tried to directly take her out," Steve stated.

"How?" Chris asked, Steve looked at him, was that real concern for a former lover?

"They were waiting outside the flat she was in, the armour in the car saved her life!" Chris glanced away at Steve's description.

"She lived?" he asked.

"Still alive, but back in Langley now," Steve added, "Delta are convinced that she is going to be the one who will eventually find UBL!" Chris looked up. Usama Bin Laden, or UBL as he was known was still the most wanted man in the world.

"Well, if anyone can, it will be her!" Chris stated as he drank more of the tea, he contorted his face at the taste, "you are right, this is shit!"

"I am seldom wrong!" Steve pointed out, "but speaking of Afghan, that's the reason I needed to chat with you?" Chris set the mug on the table.

"We are going back?" he asked.

"Heard via the squadron boss, David Priest has requested at least one more team be sent over there," Steve sat back in the chair, "it seems the Yanks are concentrating on specifics," Chris looked over at him as he continued to explain, "the German KSK has been doing brilliant things in the North and the British land commander wants to dominate the ground in Helmand, so, short version, more work for us!"

"When is the next Squadron rotation?" Chris asked.

"G squadron take over from us in four months' time, so," Steve shrugged, "we are off to join them!"

"Ok," Chris said out loud, "who is taking over this job here?" he asked.

"No one,"

"No one?"

"We are cutting our ties with the farm as it might be a bit of a political 'hot potato' if it became public knowledge, we had been helping train a group of very well armed farm hands!"

"That just so happens turn furry once a month!" Chris injected; his tone had dropped.

"Five is taking over,"

"So, that's, it?" Chris asked.

"That's, it!" Steve confirmed.

"Does the farm know yet?" Chris asked.

"I spoke to Paul on the phone this morning, I am heading that way later this afternoon for a meeting with Tyler and Paul to officially turn things off," Chris sat forward, keeping his elbows on his knees.

"I didn't properly believe it until I first saw them," he had lowered his voice.

"The wolves that attacked us in Scotland were all dealt with," Steve stated.

"Yeah, yeah, I know, it's just ...."

"Just what?" Steve asked,

Chris was uncomfortable, which was not like him. "When David and I found those heads on poles, the bodies laid out, deliberately for us to find, then ...."

"Seeing's what did it!" Steve finished the sentence for him.

"Yeah, when something you thought was only in films turns out to be real," Chris looked up, the tone of his voice raised slightly, "it kinda changes your perspective on things."

"Also, Tim has finished his time down with Two One in London, there is a training warrant officers post there if you would prefer?" Steve asked.

"Three years in London with the SAS Reserves and a promotion sounds a lot better than four months in the dingey; wee, bug infested compound at KAF!"

"I hear there are a load of new coffee shops along the boardwalk at Kandahar Airfield these days," Steve said with a grin.

"Still no," Chris smiled, he then raised his mug in a toast, "to London!" he exclaimed, Steve crunched up his face.

"I am not drinking anymore of that crap."

∞∞∞∞

Mike Dear was walking down Church Street in Coleraine. He glanced up at the sky; it was starting to get dark, and it was only six in the evening. The Church was on his right, he had to step to one side to move out of the way of a shopper coming out of the large newsagents on his left. He was in a rush, he moved closer to the shop front as he slowed down. He glanced around then stopped at the window of the next shop along. He stood facing into the shop, to anyone passing he was looking at what was in the window, what he was doing was looking at the reflections in the window as people passed behind him. He felt his insides churn when he spotted the face again. The man was on the far side of the street and was looking at him. This was the third time he had spotted the same face in half an hour; he was now convinced; he was being followed. Mike slowly moved off and stopped at another shop window further down. The face walked past him again, this time going the other way. He made a mental note of him. The phone in his pocket started to buzz, he had his headphones plugged into it already. It was a withheld call, which meant only one thing. Work.

"Hello," he spoke quietly as he pushed the phone back into his jeans pocket.

"Hi Mike," it was Lucy and she seemed excited, "lost sight of you, where are you?"

"Shirt shopping," he replied. The phone went quiet for a few moments before Lucy spoke again, this time her voice was more serious.

"How many?" she asked. Mike stood and looked at the manikins that did not have any heads or hands, each one in a different pose.

"One," Mike responded. Lucy got the reference, he had learnt it on his course when he was in England, he was using a counter surveillance measure, if you think you are being followed then deliberately stop at similar shops and make it look like you are 'shopping', in this case, shopping for shirts. It was a technique first started in the 1970's to counter Soviet surveillance in London. It worked so well that all members of MI5 and MI6 were taught it. Mike could hear movement in the background of the call, Lucy had given him the headphones, her voice was only coming through one of them, he could still use his free ear to listen to what was going on around him, but to the casual observer, he was just chatting on the phone.

"Go for it," she stated, Mike knew what she was doing.

"Male, age: mild forties, build slim, Complexation: fair, Distinguishing features: nil, Elevation: six foot plus," Mike turned and slowly started to walk along the shop fronts, "grey outdoor jacket, blue jeans and white training shoes." He walked over the junction in the pedestrian area of Coleraine, he looked up the road that went towards Tesco's carpark, he briefly looked over the few people who were walking back and forth, he did not recognise any of the faces there. He turned and headed towards the war memorial. He could hear Lucy's voice in the background, she was passing the information on to someone else.

"Where are you presently?" Lucy asked.

"Passing the war memorial to my left, then down towards the bridge," he replied.

"Right, rolling pick up on the bridge, heading away from the town!" Mike knew which side of the bridge to be on. He looked at the front door of the old building on his right that housed

176

the bank. It closed for the day a few hours ago but there were several young people sitting on the steps at the entrance. One lifted his head in a loud, over emphasised laugh. Mike walked past the statue of a footballer and headed down towards the bridge. The pub on the right was already open and the tables outside were filling up, He walked on then stopped at the crossing at the junction of the road and the bridge, as he waited for it to clear he slightly turned and glanced back up the road, he looked away again when he spotted the face again. He coughed and looked down the road that went over the bridge. "Is he still there?" Lucy asked in his ear.

"Just passing the entrance to the pub behind me," Mike stated, again Lucy's voice spoke to another in the background. "Crossing now," Mike informed her.

"Roger, grey hatchback, just passing Tesco's" Lucy's voice responded. Mike started to walk forward with the few other people who were all walking in the same direction. He slowed, then stopped on the bridge, He looked up the river and took a deep breath in, his eyes darted over to his left when a grey hatchback came up onto the bridge. His head turned and he spotted Lucy at the wheel. The traffic was moving slowly and there was a car behind her as she slowed down but did not stop. In one quick movement, Mike darted over, opened the passenger door, and jumped in, the car speeded up as he was pulling his seat belt over.

"This isn't the car you were driving earlier." he stated.

"That isn't the jacket you were wearing earlier." she responded. The traffic lights at the far side of the bridge changed and the car jumped forward. "So, any ideas?" she asked.

"None, never seen him before," Mike replied.

"When did you first notice him?" she asked as they drove along, the river was to his left, he spied a thin boat with two rowers moving quickly over the surface of the river.

"Top end of Long Commons," he replied. Lucy moved her head slightly; she was listening to her earpiece in her right ear.

"Roger," she replied to whatever had just been said, she looked over at him, "OK, we have imagery of him, it won't take us long to get a name," she smiled. The car came up to the large roundabout, she paused, then joined the traffic heading back over the river.

"So, where to now?" he asked.

"Well, for us, it's 'stand down', nothing else on until tomorrow morning," she stated.

"Brilliant, to be honest, today I felt about as much use as the letter 'G' in Lasagne!" Mike replied, Lucy smiled as she thought through the reference, "so where are we off to now?" he asked as she slowed down at the Lodge Road roundabout.

"Well, I can drop you back at the hangar if you want, or,"

"Or?" Mike looked over at her, her long blonde hair hung down over her shoulders, she had a small smile on her face.

"Well, we were originally supposed to be 'on-site' until tomorrow evening? Yes?"

"Yes," he replied.

"And since we have an unexpected stand down this evening, I was thinking maybe we could get a takeout at mine," she looked over at him, there was a sparkle in her eyes, "it would be nice to have a bit of company for a wee while, for a change,"

"Well, I," he started.

"Oh, if that is a problem, I can drop you home, if you would prefer?" she asked. The car jumped forward then headed past the Causeway hospital. "I mean, Darren isn't expecting you back this evening, is he?" Mike paused for a moment before he answered.

"No, no he isn't!"

"Great!" Lucy perked up, "the house they have put me in is a bit sparse, but at least the TV does have all the satellite channels, we could watch a movie or something," she stated. Mike noticed that the car had speeded up, "it will be nice just to have someone to talk to over dinner for once," she looked over at him again, "they don't let us entertain much."

"No, I suppose they don't, yeah, why not, it will be good to have a night off," Mike looked at the audio system, he did not recognise the music that was on. "Also, what is this?" he asked as he pointed to the dash. Lucy turned her head and had a confused look on her face.

"What? you have never heard of Blue Man Group?" she asked.

"Erm, heard 'of' them, never heard them, what is this?"

"New album, it is a rock tour," she smiled, "I would love to see them live sometime,"

"Err, ok," Mike settled.

"Can't believe you've not heard 'Blue Man Group'," Lucy giggled as she spoke, she looked over at him, "let the education start then!" The drive from Coleraine to Belfast could take an hour, Mike could normally do it in forty-five minutes, depending on traffic. Lucy did it in half an hour, she seemed excited to have some company for dinner for a change.

∞∞∞∞

Cara-Marie landed on the sofa; she lifted the remote of the tv and turned it to the news channel, the local news would be on after the main news. She pulled her phone out of her pocket and dropped it on the table and headed to the kitchen. The news filled the living room when she returned with a glass of wine.

"This is better," she muttered to herself as she got comfy again.

"*And now, for the news where you are, good evening!*" the grim-faced presenter disappeared from the screen, she did not recognise the young face that replaced him. The girl was nervous, her cropped blonde hair did not move, in fact, the only thing that did move was her lips, she was new to the job. Cara-Marie started drinking some of the wine, she was not interested in the main story, but the next did raise her eyebrows.

"*Earlier today the police gave a press conference to follow up on the recent murders around the North Coast, our reporter ...*" Cara-Marie nearly dropped the glass as she grabbed her phone. She first tapped out a text to Kevin, 'why did she not know there had been a press conference earlier?' She then started to text Mark when a stern-faced policewoman filled the screen. She was wearing a well pressed police uniform; her name badge was clear for all to see. She had kept her police hat on, which covered her head, and the peak hid some of her face, Cara-Marie read the name that was across the screen out loud.

"Detective Inspector Wells," Cara-Marie turned the volume up as she spoke.

"Yes, Major Investigations has a well-co-ordinated, ongoing province wide investigation, we have made several advances, and I am pleased with the direction the investigation is going." She stated, there was a voice that was out of shot of the camera.

"Have you made any arrests? Or are there any current suspects you are presently pursuing?" there was no reaction in the face of the detective.

"We are pursuing several lines of enquiry, and ruling nothing out,"

Cara-Marie knew what that meant. Her phone burst into life. She placed the glass on the table, sat up and looked at Mark's name on the screen.

"Hiya," she said as she put the phone to her ear.

"Hi, what press conference?" he asked, Mark seemed annoyed.

"There was a press conference this afternoon and we didn't know about it."

"Any idea what was said?" Mark asked.

"From what is on the news, don't think we missed anything," she drank from the wine glass as she finished her sentence.

"Have you any idea what Kevin wants to talk to all the staff about tomorrow at nine?" Cara-Marie's head came up.

"What?" she asked.

"Didn't you see the email?"

"What email?"

"Well, it may have been after you left, he wants everyone in as he has an announcement to make at nine tomorrow morning."

"Didn't see that," she answered.

"You any ideas what it could be?" he asked.

"None, you?" she replied.

"Nope, none,"

"Well, we will have to wait until tomorrow then,"

"Yeah, like I don't have enough on tomorrow already!" Mark stated, Cara-Marie suddenly remembered his court case.

"What time are you in court for?" she asked.

"Two," his tone of voice lowered, she knew he was not looking forward to it.

"Hey, whatever happens she cannot stop you from seeing your own child!"

"Yeah, my solicitor said much the same," he sighed.

"Ok, 'til tomorrow then," she ended the call. The news had moved on, she had missed the rest of the interview, but guessed there was not much said. She sipped at her wine, what could Kevin want to speak to everyone about tomorrow? She set the glass down and reached for her phone. He had not answered her text, so she would phone him, 'he can't ignore that,' she thought. As it turned out, he could.

∞∞∞∞

Mike's body tensed; he was covered in sweat. Even in the darkness of the bedroom her face was clear. Lucy's legs were wrapped around his, her ankles pressed down on his hamstrings, her fingers dug into his shoulders pulling him down onto her. The sex had been some of the most frantic he had ever experienced in his life. He pushed to lift himself up, but she pulled him back down.

"No, no, no, stay where you are," she whispered. Mike felt his whole body relax as he rested his face down into the pillow with her head pressed up against his. His breathing was slowing, hers was still frantic, both were covered in sweat. He slowly lifted his head, there was a slight glow from the face of small clock on the side, it was nearly 1AM. "Don't move," she whispered. Mike's chin rested on her right shoulder. He was not sure who had made the pass at who. The sex on the leather sofa had been the start, afterwards the tall naked shapely blonde had taken him by the hand into the bedroom and they had continued where they had started. Slowly he could feel sleep creeping over him. The sex the following morning would just be as frantic, the sex in the shower afterwards, however, not so much.

Chapter 34 – Beaghmore Stone Circles, County Tyrone.

The silver car parked in the small car park beside the red one that had pulled in just before. The lights and the engines all went off at the same time. Doors opened and two young men got out of each car. As Rick closed his door, even though it was dark, there was not a cloud in the sky. He looked at the small car already there. Rick was the tallest of the four, he had dark ginger hair and was constantly told his eyes were 'Ice Blue'. He loved rugby, he had played it at university, if he had not been studying Law, he may have gone for the Rugby trials to play at county level. Rick was fast, not just physically, but he could think fast as well, he had found that out at a young age, the joke about him was that he was only fast with a rugby ball in his hands, but he had proved many times that was not the case. He wasn't much older than the others, but Connor said he was in charge of this because of how well he could track. Al was the body builder of the group. He kept his hair so short when you first met him you would think he was nearly bald. Al always walked with clenched fists, no reason, he just did, and he was proud of the weight he could bench-press. Daz was the cool one. Tall and slim, always had a smile and did not have a problem attracting attention from ladies. His thick dark hair had a natural quiff at the front and his smile seemed to melt girls, Rick was envious of him, but he would never tell him. Daz loved rugby as well, he played on the wing where his build was prefect, he was also fast, but not as fast as Rick. Sixty-Nine was the opposite. He always had an intense look on his face, he had a dark monobrow and his eyes were brown, they were such a shade of brown they were almost black. Sixty-Nine was the quiet one, in fact, Sixty -Nine never spoke, he could communicate very effectively with facial gestures and hand motions, Rick was glad he was here because Sixty–Nine was the one everyone who met them would remember.

"I wonder who that is?" Rick said out loud. He walked over to the third car and placed his hand near the bonnet.

"Is it warm?" Daz asked. He looked over and shook his head, the car was cold, it had been there for some time. He stepped back and looked at the registration plate.

"It is from near Limerick," the other three walked over to him.

"What is someone from Limerick doing up North at a wee place such as this?" Al asked. Rick looked over the top of the car, the area was grey through his eyes, there was some natural light from the cloudless sky, but the lights from some of the farms were just bright dots in the blanket of grey.

"Well, let's find out," Rick moved his head towards the other three. "Al, send a data message saying where we are back here and that we are going to sweep the area, whoever this is, they could just be camping." Al nodded, "I will go through the gate and head up the middle of the site, Daz, you go to the left and Sixty-Nine, you go right." Rick continued, the small group all agreed, "we will sweep up to where we had pizza the other night." Rick was answered with a chorus of nods then they started to move towards the metal frame at the entrance. It had been painted green some time ago, the paint work was showing its age. The gate was hinged to the post in the fence and the metal gate swung back and forth inside the large 'D' shape of the rest of the frame, it was designed to let people get past but keep animals from both getting out and getting in. The path was wide enough for a single car, and it led away from the gate straight towards the first of the stone circles. Rick stopped beside the sign on the left. 'Beaghmore Stone Circles, Cains, and Alignments' it read, there was an information board about the site as well, they had all read it previously. The site had the exact same layout as sites in Cork and Kerry, but here the stones were a lot smaller, dating over 6,000 years ago. Rick went down on one knee in the middle of the grass pathway and started looking at the ground, the others followed him through.

"What is it?" Daz asked. Rick studied the ground, then look up the path that headed towards the first of the two circles of small stones.

"Single track," he replied.

"Male?" Daz asked, Rick looked back at the ground, he stretched out his hand, so it was just above the grass, he was measuring the footprints he had found.

"Female," he had lowered his voice. Sixty-Nine squatted beside him, looked at the ground then him. Rick glanced at him, then pointed at the tracks. "The footprint is smaller and look at how the feet naturally point inwards, male prints all point outwards, this indicates that the tracks are female." Sixty-Nine nodded and stood up, slowly Rick rose as well.

"Is it her?" Daz asked, with an excitement in his voice, Rick looked around at them.

"Not sure, but just in case, Al, add that to the data message." Al nodded and turned to go back though the gate. "Al!" Rick raised his voice slightly. "Once it is sent, stay with the vehicles, we don't want to be stuck here, ok!"

"OK, doing that now," Al smiled and headed back through the gate. The three wolves started to slowly walk up the path. Nobody was saying anything, but all three were studying the ground around them, the peatland that was either side of the track, the sound of the wind, then the scents and smells the wind was bringing from the small forestry block at the far side of the site. Rick glanced at each of the other two at the edge of the track, Sixty-Nine on one side, and Daz on the other. The path continued and started to rise and head off to the left of the site, the first of the two stone circles was now on the right-hand side. Each circle was about thirty metres in diameter, and although each stone was different, it had been deliberately placed. With their size and shape each stone would have taken several people to lift it, each one was between a foot and a half thick, and you could sit on it, but the circle was almost perfect. All this was done without any machinery and only basic handheld tools. In between the first two circles was the cairn, this was the burial site, whoever was there, they had been cremated and laid to rest. All the stone circles were in pairs, and all had a cairn in between them. Some had a small collection of smaller stones in the middle, the reasons all lost in time. Several larger stones had been placed in a line between two of the sets of circles, Rick slowed down as he went past them, the other two fanned farther out and again, he knelt down on the ground. He studied the sign that was there, the track in the grass led straight over the site and towards the trees. He looked back down the path, it curved around one of the circles, The wind blew over him and the scent it carried slammed into him. His body tensed, the other two dropped down onto a knee at the same time, they had picked up the scent as well. Rick's body strained, his eyes tried to pierce the greyness and the darkness around them. He knew that scent, Nocs could not hide their smell, no matter how many showers they took, they still smelt the same, sapiens could not pick it up, but for a wolf, it was easy.

Rick focused on the corner of the forestry block; she was in there. He looked over at Daz then at Sixty-Nine, he nodded once at each one of them, then slowly he stood. His movements were slow and deliberate. His jacket slid from his shoulders and dropped to the ground. The others started to do the same as they undressed, they would take this Noc down in their true form. His wolf was already starting to come forward as he pulled the tee shirt over his head. Shoes were flicked off, socks dropped on top of the clothes, the last item to be added were his jeans, which still had his underwear inside them. Rick knelt down and whispered.

"Come wolf, come," either side of him the other two were doing the same. He had changed many times, and he loved the way his body felt afterwards: new, refreshed, but the change was still as painful as it always had been. Rick stood up again, this time as his wolf. Now, the night was greyer and slightly clearer, now the smell of the grass, the peatland, the earth filled him, he loved this, loved being a part of nature, this felt so right, it was meant to be. He paced forward, Daz and Sixty-Nine trotted closer to him, the three wolves now formed a line as they crossed over another two stone circles. Rick breathed in through his nose, the wind carried the scent, she had been here, and recently. The three slowly moved towards a larger cairn, the trees were close behind it. Rick stopped, sixty-nine had gone down on one knee and lowered his nose towards the ground, sixty-nine could smell something he could not. Daz moved closer; he was also looking at what sixty-nine was doing. The sound of the scream made them all spin round; they all recognised the sound of Al's voice. All three jumped up and started running back the way they had come. Even in wolf form, Rick was fast, he got onto the path before the others, the distance to where Al lay on the ground near the metal gate only took him seconds. He slowed, then paced the last few feet to where Al was lying on his back. His arms extended out, but his feet were together, so it looked like he had been crucified. The front of his throat was open, it was not a bite, something had sliced it open. Al was placed on the ground so he would be found like this, the Noc that had done it, knew they were there. Al was dead.

Daz ran past and knelt by Al, he grabbed at his shoulders and Daz made a small yelping noise, sixty-nine stopped beside Rick then turned and faced the opposite direction, so his back was against Rick's, he was being defensive in case of another attack. Daz yelped again, Al's neck still pulsed, the blood splattered over his face and into a growing puddle of blood that was seeping into the ground. Rick stared around him there were no obvious signs of where the Noc was now. Sixty-nine tapped his back with his elbow and growled, Rick turned, the wind carried the scent, then they all heard the crashing sound of someone running over long grass, she was just over seventy metres back up the path and on the far side of the first stone circles. Rick looked at sixty-nine and nodded before looking towards the distinct noise, it was being done deliberately. Daz jumped up, made a loud barking noise, and ran past them in a rage, Rick reached out to stop him, but he was already running away from them. Rick started after him; this was exactly what the Noc wanted.

Daz ran towards the centre of the first circle, he stopped and looked over to his right, Rick and sixty-nine saw Megan spring towards him from where she had been hiding behind the cairn. The Katana sword whistled as it passed through the air. She landed a short distance away from Daz, he managed to spin away, the tip of her blade parted a line through his fur, across his back, Daz squealed in pain. Rick and sixty-nine attacked to draw her away from their injured friend. Megan ducked and rolled on the ground, Rick's bite missed, and he only closed his mouth on fresh air. Megan jumped up again as Rick and sixty-nine righted themselves, ready for their next attack, Daz jumped towards her back, Megan spun where she had been standing, everything slowed down for Rick. This happened on the rugby pitch and anytime he fought, the world moved in slow motion for him, but he could move at normal speed but to everyone else he moved so fast some would miss it.

Rick's right foot dug into the ground as he propelled himself forward, his eyes tightened. Megan turned as Daz's mouth missed her, his shoulder was passing by her hip as the blade came down, swiping through his neck. Life speeded up again as Daz's momentum carried the body forward to land on the ground in front of them, his head bounced and rolled to one side. Rick was already jumping over him, Megan brought the blade up in a swiping motion, Rick was able to move to the side and he had been taught the very same movement with a Katana sword. Sixty-nine also turned so the blade missed him. As quickly as everything started, everything stopped. Megan was standing in an open leg stance; her sword was held in both hands, and it was in a defensive position in front of her. Rick and sixty-nine were standing at angles in front of her, if she was standing in the middle of a clock face, Rick was at ten and Sixty-nine at two. Both stared at her, Daz's headless body twitched on the ground behind them. Megan slowly took two paces rearwards, the two wolves matched. Sixty-nine glanced at Rick, he was waiting for the signal to attack. They had done this before, but the last time, the adversary had antlers.

Rick stared into her eyes; cold motionless eyes stared back. Rick made his move, he first jumped forward and snapped with his mouth, he missed, Megan's downward blow also missed as he moved out of the way. Sixty-nine knew what to do, move more to the side and extend the ground she had to defend. With one attacker she could stand, face to face, but with two he could make it harder for her to fight both of them if he was able to get round behind her. Rick attacked again, again the blade passed though air. Sixty-nine attacked, he jumped forward, his attack was with his mouth, but he saw the way she was turning, it would be a horizontal swipe she would be making, he dropped to the ground and the blade just passed over his head. Sixty-nine instantly rolled over away from where the tip of the blade slammed into the ground where he had landed. His feet dug into the ground, and he launched himself with all of his strength back at her again. Rick jumped towards her, he could see what she was about to do, Sixty-nine could not. Megan rolled sideways over on the ground and when she was on her knee, she brought the blade down the centre of sixty-nine's body in a slice. Sixty-nine howled, his arms grabbed at the long wound he now had along his torso. Sixty-nine landed with a thump on the ground. Rick had to jump over him to get to her. She rolled again and as she righted herself, she launched herself at the largest one of the wolves.

She brought the sword down towards the centre of his head, but his hands gripped at her own wrists, stopping the blow. The force of momentum from both of them collided, and the two stepped around in a small circular dance and each fought for control of the other. Then, for a second the two stood in the darkness, staring at each other, both sets of arms straining against the other, Megan trying to push the sharp edge of the blade down onto his head and his arms trying to stop her. For a moment, the world stopped. Neither body moved. They stood there, staring into each other's eyes. For a moment, the centuries of warfare between the two species came down to the two of them. There was no wind, no moonlight, no sound, just the venomous hatred both kinds had for each other, both, wanting to force the other into extinction.

Megan suddenly loosened the power in her arms and repeatedly forced her right knee up into his side in a series of blows that forced him to start to buckle. Blow continued after blow until Rick was forced to let go of her wrists, that gave her the space to release her sword and turn to her right side and extend his reach. Rick was off balance and the speed of her move propelled him forward. Rick landed on the ground with a thud. He rolled over and looked up as this vampire whose face was now full of rage came towards him. The sword that was above her head had already started the strike that would finish him. Her target was his neck, even if she missed, the sword would cause a wound to his chest that would be fatal. Rick looked at his attacker, she had beaten him, he would not be able to move fast enough to get out of the way of the single blade that parted the air with a whistle.

Megan was suddenly thrown over to one side, tumbling on the ground. Rick's head looked at the space she had been standing in, the space that a wounded sixty-nine now stood. One arm gripped his body where the large open wound was, blood flowed over his arm and through his fingers, he was panting, the effort of his shove had exhausted him. As Rick rolled over onto his hands and feet Megan let out a scream of fury, she jumped forward in a straight strike. Rick watched in slow motion as the tip of the blade pierced the front of Sixty-nine's chest and thrust its way through his body and out his back. Sixty-nine let out a howl of anguish as he fell to his knees, his hand grabbing the handle of the sword that was going to end his life.

Rick jumped up and threw himself at her, Megan dropped to her knees and rolled away underneath him. Rick landed on the ground and spun around, she no longer had her sword, she had lost her weapon, now he would tear her apart for what she had done to his pack. Rick's mouth snarled as he went for her again, he reached out to grab her left wrist to pull her towards his mouth, he was going to rip her throat out, exactly the same way he had torn out the throat of the first deer he had hunted. Again, the world moved slowly, his fingers of his right hand tightly gripped her wrist, his left hand grabbed a handful of hair at the back of her head, he pulled his prey towards himself, yanking her head backwards exposing her throat. He lunged with his mouth just as the knife slammed into the left side of his chest. With speed and uncontrolled fury Megan focused her assault on his chest, the knife slammed between the ribs with such speed and ferocity that it totally surprised him, the blade was ripped out then slammed in again. The grip on her wrist loosened, the grip on her hair released completely as the howling wolf fell to the ground. She landed on top of him as she continued to savage the side of his chest. She could not hear the scream that was coming out of her, but the speed of her stabbing continued until the large wolf went limp. Megan Due rolled off him, it took her a few minutes before she was able to stand. She was exhausted from the fight, but exhilarated.

When she stood, she looked around the stone circle. The movement of the wolf with her sword still in its chest made her walk over beside him, he was still alive. Megan looked at him, the wolf's eyes looked up at her, he was in great pain. She placed her right foot on his chest and gripping the handle of the blade pulled it out. The wolf howled in agony. Megan stepped forward and used her right foot to push the wolf over onto its back. She spun the sword in her hand, so the tip of the blade pointed towards him, she looked into the eyes of her prey, the wolf knew what was about to happen.

"Time to head to doggie heaven for you, puppy!" she said sarcastically. The wolf coughed then lifted his right hand. Megan watched as the wolf formed a fist and turned its knuckles towards her. Slowly the wolf raised its middle finger in one final act of defiance. She looked at him and nodded, for a moment she had respect for him, even when faced with annihilation he was defiant. She had beaten his body, but she had not defeated his spirit. She nodded towards him as he lowered his hand, she would be quick, then she rammed the sword through his heart. The wolf let a final cry come forth, his body jolted, then he was silent.

Megan put her foot on his chest again then pulled her sword free. Megan looked over at the bundles of clothes and slowly walked over to the first one. She lifted the tee shirt and used it to clean the blood from her blade, she looked around, the sheath was over to the side in the grass, hidden, she had removed her sword when she saw them, when they first arrived. They were the wolves she had tracked back to here. The phone was in the right-hand pocket of the jeans, and it was unlocked. The light from the screen lit her face up, but there was no one for miles so it did not matter. She scrolled through the names and stopped at one she recognised.

"Orla O'Connor," she said out loud. She knew the name of the wife of Connor 'O'Connor, the current alpha of the An Rua. Megan turned her head and looked back at the three dead wolves; she looked back down the path where the short bald one was. A smile spread across her lips, Megan Due had a great idea. It would not take her long to arrange and mutilate the bodies, she would enjoy taking the pictures, making sure nothing of her was in them.

The thought of sending the pictures and putting Martin Hanna's name on them would cause such an offence and outrage they would probably forget about her, for a while anyway. The very thought made her laugh out loud.

Chapter 35

Tyler had watched the sunrise sitting on the front of the old Land Rover. She felt at peace, there were some clouds in the sky, but not many. The sun's warmth enveloped her, she closed her eyes and felt her body relax. The sound of a quad bike coming along the wall brought her back to reality. Tyler turned her head at the young face of the farm hand as he slowed, then stopped beside her. He switched the engine off; it was quiet again.

"Paul is looking for you, he said to say he is back at the farmhouse and wants you to head there right away," the young voice stated.

"Did he say what was up?" she quietly asked.

"Sum-tin about 'down south' being furious, didn't get it all." He was only passing on the message, there was no point grilling him further, she smiled and then nodded.

"Ok, thanks, I will head there now," her voice was drowned out by the quad bike starting again, he gunned the engine and it jumped forward and stalled. There was muttered swearing and a polite smile from Tyler as he kickstarted it again. Soon she was alone again. She jumped off the front of the Land Rover and walked up to the driver's door. She stopped and looked at the rising sun again, she hoped it would be a peaceful day today. She opened the door and climbed in. The Land Rover started. She reversed and turned, then headed back along the wall to the gate that led towards the farmhouse.

Tyler walked through the living room and into the kitchen. There was a phone on the kitchen table, and everyone was looking at it. Tyler glanced around the table, Dermott, Paul, Tony, Rhydian, and Lynne M'Kane stood there, everyone was looking sheepish as if they had just been caught with their hands in the cookie jar.

"What's up?" Tyler asked as she walked in.

"*What's up!*" it was Connor's voice that came from the phone, it was on loudspeaker, "*I'll tell you 'what's up' you need to sort this shit out before I head up north and take over up there as you obviously can't control shit!*" He shouted down the phone, Tyler's face contorted.

"What?"

"*You heard me!*" he growled.

"Right, for starters, before you shout your mouth off any more you better hurry up and tell me just what the fuck you are talking about, or this conversation is over!" Tyler was getting angry.

"*You cannot talk to him like that, he is still your alpha!*" it was the voice of Jack O'Connor.

"Listen here, puppy," Tyler's hands slammed down on the table and her face was directly over the phone, "you better take a big mouthful of 'shut the fuck up' before I head down there and 'bitch slap you into next week' and I will do it in front of all your friends!" Everyone the in kitchen looked at each other, no one had seen Tyler this angry, "now, just what the fuck is going on?" she demanded.

"The four wolves that Connor sent north were butchered at a site north of Cookstown last night," Paul explained.

"Who by?" Tyler asked.

"*WHO BY?*" Connor shouted, "*by the very Noc that you have failed to deal with, despite my direct order for you to do so, I want this fucker found and I want him found now, or I WILL come north, do you hear me!*"

"If you are coming north, then it better be in a challenge!" Tyler was shouting directly at the phone now, "Just remember, I put you down once before and I don't have a problem doing it again!" Everyone in the room looked at each other, no one knew that had ever happened, there was an audible gasp by a female voice from the phone, Connor was not alone, Tyler carried on, raising her voice again as she did so. "let's not forget, that YOU let a Noc go from near Limerick, which I gather has come north, so I have to deal with that *AS WELL,*" breaths taken in, gasps could be heard from the phone, "and you ... Connor O'Connor, directly let a Noc princess onto our lands, which in case you forget IS AGAINST THE LAW, you then allowed the same Noc a free reign to take action, against your own ON OUR LANDS, which in case you forget, IS AGAINST THE LAW!!" there were inaudible mutterings from the phone, everyone in the kitchen had tensed up, nobody knew what she was going to do next. Tyler stood up straight, she had fury in her eyes as she shouted at the phone, "We HAVE dealt with every threat that there has been against us, WITHOUT your help, and we shall continue to do so, maybe I should head south and take over down there as you seem to be incompetent in running the clan!" Tyler started to look around the room, "I doubt if I would have any objection from the other Dun alpha's here, or in Scotland!"

"*YOU WOULDN'T DARE!*" Connor's voice boomed from the phone. Tyler slammed her fists down on the table, everyone in the room reacted.

"You are 'supposed' to tell me when you are sending any pack member north, you are 'supposed' to get them to come here and introduce themselves, we are 'supposed' to work together against the Nocs," Tyler looked around the kitchen again, "*Fight as a pack, or not at all, does that sound familiar!*"

"*Do not quote the law at me!*" Connor hissed.

"I think I have to, since you don't seem to be able to understand it, let alone follow it!" Tyler lowered her face towards the phone, this time she lowered her voice. "Anytime ... you send wolves north, you let me know, anything you do in the north, you let me know, you want me to deal with a Noc! Fine, no problems, but I WILL decide how and when, not you, do you understand!"

"*Here is what I understand, four of mine were mutilated, by a Noc, on YOUR ground and you have done fuck all about it, and as Clan Alpha I am ordering you ....*" Tyler grabbed the phone and as she screamed, she turned and threw it, with all her strength, towards the far wall. Everyone ducked as it smashed against the brick work.

"Hey, that was my phone ...." Tony started. Everyone turned to look at him, he looked at Tyler, her hair was down, her fists were clenched, and she had a look of fury on her face. "I'll get a new one," he muttered as he looked away. The room fell silent. Tyler stepped towards the kitchen table and tapped it with her finger.

"Right," she said looking up, "What has happened?" She looked at each one in turn, Paul moved, then answered her question.

"The four from the south were camping near the Beaghmore Stone Circles, near Cookstown, when this 'Master Hunter' found them."

"How do we know it was him?" Tyler asked sternly.

"The fucker took pictures with one of their phones and sent them all to Orla!" Dermott injected; Tyler's eyes widened.

"Yeah, he lined the mutilated bodies up took pictures and sent them to her," Paul glanced at Dermott who looked back at him as Paul continued describing what had happened, "three of them were still in their true form," he looked at Tyler, "he cut their heads off,"

"And ..." Dermott injected.

"And what?" Tyler asked, Paul took a breath in before he answered.

"He cut their genitals off and shoved them in their mouths, took the pictures and sent them all to Orla, with a message he put his name to, Orla, quite naturally, is more than upset."

"Oh my God!" Rhydian reacted, the feeling in the room changed, everyone was becoming angry.

"Just like a Noc," Lynne M'Kane stated.

"Right," Tyler tapped the table again, "this is what we are going to do," she looked at each person as she spoke.

"Dermott, I want a full mobilisation, everyone that can deploy, will!"

"It will be done," Dermott replied.

"Tony, get in touch with Silver and Gold, I want an update on exactly where they are and what they are up to,"

"It will be done," Tony replied.

"Find out if they have found the female Noc that the south let slip by, and, if we can deal with her as well, bonus." Tony nodded at the instruction.

"Paul, get in touch with the military and police, find out if they have anything on this guy and his movements," she stepped back from the table, everyone in the room looked at her, she was alpha, she was in charge and she had just proved it. "Also, Paul can you phone down south, express our deepest condolences and assure them that we 'will' find him, and I promise to deliver him to Connor directly."

"It will be done," Paul replied.

"Rhydian, the training that is to happen today will be sword training in the area, I want all the students to have competed the morning fitness training then dressed and ready to go in the arena, with their training swords by 9am."

"It will be done," Rhydian replied. The sound of a baby crying echoed from the stairs; Lynne stepped forward.

"I'm on it," she politely smiled at Tyler as she walked past and headed towards the stairs and the now awake child upstairs. Tyler looked around.

"Does everyone now what I want them to do?" everyone's head nodded, "right, get to it." Tyler stood still as everyone filed past, except Paul who slowed down as he approached. Paul waited for the front door to close behind the rest as they all left.

"Well done," he spoke quietly, she looked at him, she was still angry.

"I want him found and I want him found today!" she emphasised.

"He will be," he replied, "oh don't forget that Steve Minister is coming here this afternoon." Tyler looked at him, she looked tired, she had forgotten that was happening.

"Ok, what time?" she asked.

"2PM,"

"Any news on that Apollyon fella?" she asked.

"Don't think so," he replied.

"Don't guess, confirm!" she cut him off.

"I will," Paul walked past her and headed into the living room.

"Oh, where did this happen again?" she shouted after him. Paul stopped and turned back towards the door of the kitchen.

"Beaghmore Stone circles," he answered.

"Where and what is that?" she asked.

"It is a series of stone circles that date back 6,000 years, it is a pre-historic burial site just north of Cookstown." Tyler looked down, she was listening to what he was saying, tiredness was creeping over her. "Exactly the same layout as two sites in Kerry and Cork, just smaller stones, only been there once myself," he shrugged, "nice place for a picnic."

"Sound like, 'Head Smashed In, Buffalo Jump!' s stated, Paul was confused.

"You got your head smashed in where?" Tyler looked up at his question.

"It's a place in Alberta in Canada, 'Head Smashed In, Buffalo Jump' an indigenous site from centuries ago, very old as well, I went there once with ...." The smile disappeared. Paul guessed she had just had a memory of her previous life with her husband. The husband she never mentioned, the husband she would spend the rest of her life fulfilling her revenge for. Tyler looked at him, her face lifted slightly. "Do an internet search for it, there is a visitor centre there, you can learn about how the indigenous used to hunt buffalo before the arrival of European settlers." There was a pause as Tyler's mind wandered with a happy memory.

"So," Paul brought her back to the present, "what do you want done with this Apollyon fella?" he asked.

"Find out what he has been up to, any information he has on this prick, locations etc," Tyler stepped into the living room, "if we can use him, then do, just keep him away from here."

"Will do,"

"What were Connor's lot doing there anyway?" she asked.

"Well," Paul stated, "it is quite remote, there are some farms nearby, but not too close," Paul shrugged again, "it is a good place to camp."

"But easy to track someone there?" Tyler asked.

"If he knows how to track a wolf, then .... Yes,"

"Let's assume he does, what do we know about his background?" she asked.

"Before he became a hunter for his coven .... practically nothing." Tyler and Paul looked at each other, they both relaxed. "Find out what you can," she instructed.

"I will,"

"Would you know what kind of flowers Orla likes?" she asked, Paul smiled.

"It is no secret that she is passionate about orchids."

"Great, can you sort a bunch to be sent to her please?" Paul nodded and tried not to smile, Tyler had just said 'please' she didn't have to, he was going to do it anyway.

"Oh, just so you know, Connor sent some of his to collect the bodies from the site before the police get involved."

"What?" Tyler asked.

"Yeah," Paul looked at his watch, "they came up a couple of hours ago, they will probably just be leaving," he looked at her, "he did say he didn't want the police in the north involved with any of his."

"That makes sense," Tyler turned to walk away, then she stopped and looked back at him, there was another instruction coming. Paul did not move. A stern looked fell over her face again. "When you speak to Connor, say to him from me, '*I WILL, give you this fucker's head!*" Tyler turned and headed towards the stairs. Paul stood and watched her go. He believed every word of what she had just said, he would quote her, word for word. Paul walked over to the landline phone and lifted the handset to call Connor.

∞∞∞∞

Eddie Cargill walked up to the closed door of Inspector Well's office. The door was always closed these days, a lot had changed since she had taken over. The coffee machine was gone, only she gave the briefs, everything had to be confirmed, twice, if she was in the office before you were in the morning then you had a shouting match on your hands. The inspector did not hide her distaste for her predecessor. The days of it being a 'good working environment' had gone, in fact, any joviality in the office was put down, '*have you not got serious work to do!*' had become her phrase. Team nights out had stopped, when not on official duty the dress down had stopped, suits always had to be worn as 'the highest standards are always expected'. Eddie knocked the door and looked through the office window at the stern face on the phone. She looked at him and carried on speaking, it was not until she replaced the phone that she spoke loud enough for him to hear.

"Come," it was a simple command. He opened the door and stepped in. The inspector had two open files on her desk, the family pictures that Sean had on the desk, were gone, if it

188

was not work related then it had no place being there. One of the female Detective Sergeants was sitting on one of the chairs, she looked at him but did not speak. Eddie stood at the centre of her desk with the office door left open. He was not offered a seat. "Ahh, Detective Cargill," she closed one of the folders and lifted one of her notebooks, she sat upright in the chair.

"You wanted to see me Ma'am?" He stated, she started to read from the notebook without looking up.

"Two things," she said, Eddie could feel his insides turn, 'two things' that was never good. "First we have a report from uniforms in County Tyrone, they are currently at a possible crime scene, and I want you to go and have a look at it for us,"

"Where is it Ma'am?" he asked.

"Do you know where the Beaghmore stone circles are?"

"No,"

"Well, you are a detective, so 'detect',"

"What has happened?" he asked.

"Uniforms are not sure, that is why they want one of us to go have a look," she raised her head and looked straight at him, "so 'go have a look," her expression did not change. "I want proper crime scene reporting and determine if a crime has happened there," she looked back down at the notebook.

"What about the local M.I.T.? isn't this more for them to look at? I mean, that is a bit out of our area." Her head shot up, she stared directly at him.

"Detective, who is in charge of this team?"

"You are Ma'am," he replied.

"And are we not currently involved in a 'Province wide' investigation?"

"We are,"

"Then, since I am in charge, I am giving you an order and I expect it to be carried out! *Is that clear ... Detective!*"

"Yes Ma'am," He looked up above her head. The framed pictures that Sean Parrish had there were gone, the wall had been wiped clean. There was a tut from the chair behind him, he did not look round.

"Right, the second thing I have for you is that I have the results of your sergeant exam," Eddie felt his eyes looked down at her face. She was emotionless. "You passed by only two points," Eddie felt a small smile spread over his face, he looked up at the wall again as she dropped the notebook on the desk. "I must say, that as a member of this team, only passing by a mere 'two points' is hardly what I would call 'exemplary', would you not agree, Detective?" she was annoyed. She sat back in her chair and placed her hands on the desk, power politics.

"No Ma'am,"

"I expect much better from detectives on this team, only two points!"

"No Ma'am, I don't agree," his statement made her sit forward.

"What?" the tone of her voice raised.

"You asked if 'I agree' with your statement about only passing with 'two points' and no, I do not agree. I do know only three people passed that exam out of twenty-seven who attempted it, but no, I did not know I was one of them until you said." He looked at the face that stared back at him, "and a pass is better than a failure, would you not agree .... Ma'am." Inspector Wells pushed her chair back and stood up. She glared at him. Eddie did not move.

"Detective Constable Cargill, I find your attitude, upsetting," Eddie spotted her glance at the Sergeant sitting behind him, he now knew this was planned. "As there are currently 'no vacant' sergeant slots here I take it you will be requesting a transfer?" she glared at him, Eddie thought for a moment.

"Yes, Ma'am, I will be."

"Well as luck would have it," she looked at her desk and picked up the notebook again, "I have already discussed it with Chief Anderson and there is an open slot with M.I.T. at Maydown," she refolded her arms. He did not speak just nodded once; this 'was' a set up. "Good," she sat back down and shuffled her chair forward, "that is settled then." He looked at the top of her head, there was a small smile on her face as she continued speaking. "I will get that sorted for you," she looked up and waved him away with the back of her hand, "you can go now," Eddie turned and walked through the office door, "I am sure that the sloppiness that was acceptable under Parrish will go down a treat up there." She shared a smile with the sitting sergeant, Eddie spun on his heels.

"Ma'am!" Eddie almost shouted, "How dare you!" Eddie clenched his fists by the side of his trousers.

"What?" she said loud enough for the rest of the team to hear.

"Inspector Parrish was a great detective and an inspiration, and I find it 'INSULTING' that you would speak of a dead officer in such a way!" Eddie stood and stared at her; he was defiant. All movement in the main office stopped, everyone looked towards the open door of the Inspectors office.

"Detective Cargill," she said as she slowly stood up, she looked out of the office at the rest of the team who were all looking at her.

"Ma'am," Eddie replied.

"When you get back from Tyrone clear your desk and hand over your investigations,"

"Ma'am," he responded.

"Until you receive your transfer, after today, you are on leave."

"Yes ... Ma'am,"

"You are dismissed." Eddie Cargill walked to his desk. Everyone watched as he lifted his jacket then walked out of the main office, his career with Belfast M.I.T. was at an end.

∞∞∞∞

Several minutes later Mike Dear pulled his phone out of his pocket and read the message he just received; he started laughing as he read it.

"What is up?" Darren Forrester asked.

"Here, read this," he said as he handed the phone over, "Strumfurher Wells is making friends again." He stated. Darren read the message then handed the phone back.

"I better give Sutcliffe a heads up." The smile fell from Mike's face, again there was obviously more going on there than he knew.

Chapter 36

Cara-Marie was sitting at her desk in the office. It was nearly ten in the morning. She scrolled through her emails, there was nothing about the press conference she had missed, but then, there was nothing on interest from it anyway. Her eyes moved down the list, several were possible local stories for her to cover, she clicked on the one from Kevin, it was an email confirming what he had briefly covered when they all had got in that morning. The paper was expanding, there was to be two people dedicated to research, another photographer and two more journalists were coming in, one was from a newspaper in England, but they were originally from here and it was a move home for them. The point of space had been raised by one of the others, there was not enough room currently where they were, to fit the new team members. Kevin had thought of that already, most of the new team would be in different offices at the far end of Church Street, but everyone would come together for the weekly briefings. Kevin stressed several times there would be no job losses, this was an expansion, not finding staff replacements. The email was just a written reference to what was said. He had tried to put a happy spin on it but some of the other staff were not happy.

"Why was the newspaper group expanding us? None of the other 'herald' newspapers were going to almost double in size. That question had come around several times, Kevin had not really answered it. Cara-Marie had not spoken at all during the brief. Mark was not interested, but he was stressed about the court appearance happening later. Cara-Marie opened a new email to Kevin and tapped in a short message. 'CAN I POP IN; I WANT TO RUN SOMETHING BY YOU' she clicked 'send' and the email went. She looked over the desk at Mark, he had one of his cameras in his hands, but she could tell he really wasn't doing much.

"So, what do you think of the expansion then?" she asked. The camera in his hand bleeped, but he did not look up. "Earth calling Mark, come in Mark .... Your time is up," she spoke slightly louder. He looked up with a blank expression on his face.

"Mmmm?"

"Didn't think you were listening," Cara-Marie started scrolling through more emails.

"Did you just say something?" he asked.

"Yeah," her eyes looked over at him again, his focus was back on the camera.

"What was it?" he muttered. Cara-Marie started typing a reply to another email, she looked at her screen as she whispered her reply.

"I'm pregnant," Mark lost grip of the camera, he fumbled it as he reacted.

"You what!" he almost shouted as he jumped to his feet, his chair was propelled backwards into the open space behind him. "Cara ... I ..." he caught the camera body then dropped it onto his desk, several others looked around, unsure of what was happening.

Cara-Marie was, smiling. She looked over the top of the screen, "I am kidding."

"You .... What?" the surprised photographer exclaimed.

"I knew you weren't listening to me," she smiled then winked with her right eye.

"You ... *are* ... joking?"

"Of course, I am joking!" she stated, "it isn't something I can do by myself now is it?" she asked as Mark pulled his chair back towards his desk.

"I wouldn't laugh, it has happened before," Mark picked up the camera body again.

"Well, that would certainly please my mum to know I was having '*the Christ child!*'"

"Yeah, one problem with that," Mark looked over at her.

"What?"

"Where would we find three wise men and a virgin around here?" the two shared a laugh as the landline rang with one continuous ring, in was an internal call.

Cara-Marie reached over and lifted the handset. "Reporters,"

"Hi Cara, yeah pop in, I am free at the moment," it was Kevin the editor.

"Brill, be right there," she lifted her notebook that had been in her handbag.

"Being summoned to Mount Olympus?" Mark teased.

"Of all the ways I would describe him, Zeus, isn't it!" Cara-Marie laughed again.

"I fear the Greeks, even when they present gifts!" Mark stated.

"What?" Cara-Marie asked as she opened her notebook, Mark looked up at her.

"It was written by Virgil between 29 -19 BC," he shrugged, "classic quote,"

"How do you know crap like that?" she asked starting to walk towards Kevin's office.

"They hide information like that in these amazing things called 'books!" he shouted after her, Cara-Marie glanced back over her shoulder at his smile before she kNocked the door.

"Come in Cara," Kevin replied. Cara-Marie walked in and sat down. Kevin was tapping away at his keyboard. "I will be right .... with you," he muttered without looking up. Cara-Marie pulled her pen from her pocket and glanced over her notes from her last two stories. Kevin stopped typing and placed his hand on the mouse that was attached to the desktop computer, his focus turned to the screen, "and .... send." He pushed the mouse away and sat back in his chair, "right, what's up? are you concerned about the new reporters we have coming in?" Cara-Marie paused, that was not going to be her first question, but it was now.

"No, ... Should I be?"

"No, no, no," Kevin laughed as he sat forward. He was in a good mood, that was good for starters, "the new staff coming in are just an expansion, there is more work coming in than we can cover with our current staff, and ...." Kevin glanced at the monitor, "Belfast agrees," he looked at her, "I'm glad you are here, there is something I want to put to you." Cara-Marie was now defensive, the last time he said anything like that he offered her a job in Belfast that she really did not want.

"What is it?" she asked.

"With more staff coming in, I would like you, as you have been here the longest, to head up the reporting team," he paused, "how does, 'Chief reporter for the Coleraine Herald' sound to you?" he was smiling. Cara-Marie did not realise her eyebrows had shot up.

"Wow, err, yes, I suppose,"

"Brilliant,"

"How is it going to work? I mean what will be my job?" she asked.

"Simple," Kevin was smiling in such a way that she knew some of his job had just become hers'. "You are to split the jobs, one to cover agriculture, farming and the environment, another politics and government stories, another health and communities etc," he looked directly at her as he continued, "and you, crime, police, judicial etc," Kevin was motioning with his hands now, he had already given this thought, "I can let you do the specifics, but instead of having only two journo's to cover everything, we can have four, 'focused and directed' journalists who can concentrate on specific stories," Cara-Marie recognised the brief, it was straight off the larger newspaper groups webpage. She nodded and smiled.

"Sure, I can do that. Do I get a pay rise?" the two shared a short laugh.

"Hell no, are you going to do it?"

"Hell yes, but I want a new coffee machine for the office first!"

"Hell no, if I don't get one, then you lot certainly can't!" it was good, humoured banter, which was a good place to be, Cara-Marie thought to herself.

"Right, there was something you wanted?" Kevin said as he sat back in his chair.

"Yes, it's about the recent murders around here,"

"I got your stories each one," he glanced at the monitor again before looking back at her, "all good, but there was no obvious motive," the smile from his face was gone, the serious editor was back, "have you got something we can use?" he was probing.

"Sort of,"

"Sort of?" he retorted, "that isn't like you."

"No, well, nothing concrete, but"

"If the next sentence out of your mouth contains the words, 'werewolf, werewolves, or any sort of 'were-anything', the answer is NO!" Cara-Marie could not help but smile.

"No, nothing like that," Cara-Marie sat forward, "but they are not being covered by the local Major Investigations but the Provence wide one from Belfast," she stopped.

Kevin's face did not move. "So?" he asked.

"So .... they are going to a lot of lengths not to use the word *'serial killer'* but they are going down the track of 'they are all linked'."

"Two words,"

"What?" she asked.

"Serial killer is two words, but I like your thinking, what have you got?"

"Well," she started, "someone close to the investigation told me the investigators have been officially told not to use the words 'serial killer' in any form and they are trying to suppress that the method of killing is the same." She could feel it, she had him, the excitement was rising in her. She had become an investigative journalist for this, she had a story that she could break, and judging by Kevin's reaction, she had him as well.

"Exactly which ones are you talking about?" Kevin *WAS* interested.

"As far back as the New Year's Day murders," she was trying hard not to smile as she spoke, but Kevin had moved in his seat at what she had just said.

"That was what? two years ago?"

"Yes, but that's not the only one,"

"Go on,"

"Portstewart strand to Belfast, Cushendun to Murlough to the Coastal path – all connected by the same way they were all murdered." Cara-Marie had her hand on her notebook, he was thinking about what she was saying.

"Can you confirm that the police are connecting them all?" he asked.

"They have referenced them in different press conferences and press releases," she watched as he glanced at the monitor again.

"Oh, sorry about that one yesterday, I only got the email after it happened as well,"

"Doesn't matter, I got the highlights, didn't miss much, there was nothing I didn't know already." Kevin sat forward again.

"So, what 'was' the cause of death that links them all?" he asked, "and are they really all the same?"

"Yes,"

"How do you know that?" he asked.

"I have a contact down at the forensic labs, she has confirmed the deaths were the result of 'severe lacerations to the neck, causing the arteries in the neck to be ruptured, causing death by severe blood loss' and another contact in Coleraine Cop Shop told me about the 'not to use the term serial killer' bit." Again, she tried not to smile, she was right, and she knew it.

"Do they know what caused the lacerations? And were they all the same?"

"Yes, and yes, they were all the same and they were all caused by a bite,"

"A bite?"

"Yes," she confirmed, the two looked at each other again. Kevin's face fell, she was losing him.

"Cara," he had lowered his voice, she did not like that, "if the next sentence you come out with involved the word 'vampire' then this conversation is over …. Do I make myself clear?" the atmosphere in the office had changed.

"Yes and no," she smiled, "I am not going to use the word, 'vampire' at all,"

"Good, we don't need any more 'Coleraine's werewolf hunter' taglines."

"So," she pushed.

"So, I think you have something," he looked more positive, "find more stuff out, then write it up," he looked back at the monitor again, "I will see what I can dig up as well," Kevin reached and took hold of the mouse again, his focus turned back to what he was now reading.

"Great, I am on it," Cara-Marie said as she stood up, she got the permission she needed to take this further. Kevin smiled briefly then became absorbed in whatever was on his screen. Cara-Marie walked the short distance to the office door and after she opened it, she looked back over her shoulder, this time speaking loud enough for the rest of the staff to hear.

"I still think a new coffee machine for the good and benefit of all the staff is a great idea!" Kevin looked up as she walked back out into the office, several comments flew about what a great idea it was. As she sat down, she looked at the two top emails, one was from Lucy, *'now what does MI5 want with me this time'* she thought to herself, and the second was from her new best friend in USA, it was titled 'Sydney Puttman.' As she clicked on it Mark raised his head over the top of her monitor.

"Oh, your mum is at the back door." Cara-Marie looked at the door, then at Mark.

"Really? What could she possibly want?" Cara-Marie pushed her chair backwards and headed towards the door.

"Well, it is nearly lunchtime, maybe she wants to treat you," Mark replied.

"She has never done that before; I wonder what's up?" she replied out loud as she opened the back door and stepped out onto the street. Her mother was standing a short distance away, she had her back to the door as Cara-Marie walked outside. Cara-Marie looked at the young man standing beside her. He was taller than her mother, he was wearing black leather shoes that had a shine on them, dark grey trousers that had a crease down the front of them and a plain dark blue jumper and a white shirt underneath. The broad smile opened his mouth to reveal his large gums and crooked teeth. Thin fingers extended the hand that was now being offered in a handshake. Cara-Marie was confused.

"Mum, what is …" Her mum turned; she was excited about something.

"Cara, excellent, I caught you," her mother turned towards the young man as her left hand pointed towards him, "This is Owen and he has been trying to reach you,"

"Oh, Heeloo, it is sooo nice to finally meet the daughter of this lovely woman!" Owen was almost spitting through his lisp as he spoke. Cara-Marie did not take the offered hand, she glared at her mother.

"Mum, you got to be kidding me!"

∞∞∞∞

Steve Minister turned the car into the lane that led up to the farm, he knew even if he had not pre-arranged the visit, they would know there was someone driving up the lane. At the top of the lane, a figure stood up behind the right-hand hedge and pointed to the car parking in front of the large barn. He waved his response and reverse parked up against the barn. Standing by the front door of the farmhouse was Tyler and Paul, he waved a greeting. As he switched off the engine, he noticed Paul smiled back, but Tyler looked furious. Several people went past and headed into the barn, they seemed to be in a rush, an old Land Rover came around the side of the barn and stopped near Paul. He spoke to the people inside then it took off past the front of his car and down the lane and away. Steve got out of the car and as he closed the door two more-armed farm hands came out of the barn and rushed over to the metal ladder that went up the side of the barn to the roof, something was happening here. He started to walk towards the waiting pair, there was a grin from Paul and a polite smile from Tyler.

"Hi Steve, thanks for coming," Paul then pointed to the large, padded envelope in Steve's left hand, "you've brought us pressies I see," Paul extended his hand, which Steve took.

"Well, I can only hope some of this helps," he replied. Once he released Paul's grip Tyler offered her hand, Steve noticed that for smaller hands, the handshake was just as strong.

"Hi Steve, so nice to see you again." She spoke quieter than Paul did, another Land Rover came around the corner and stopped near them.

"Hang on," said Paul as he walked towards the driver's open window.

"Shall we go inside?" Tyler offered.

"Yes," Steve answered, Tyler opened the farmhouse door, Steve followed her inside as the Land Rover took off at speed. "Busy day?" he asked as she walked over to the large chair.

"Busy enough," she replied as she sat down, Paul walked in behind him and offered him one of the smaller chairs, Paul sat down beside his alpha. Steve took off his jacket before he did so, he was wearing a patterned shirt that was tucked into his jeans. His outdoor boots were light tan, clean, and looked like they were new. Steve sat down and opened the envelope.

"You said in your message you are leaving?" Paul asked, Steve nodded.

"Yeah, both Chris and I have to be on our way, so our time here is ending," Steve tipped the contents of the envelope into his hand, there were 8 x 10 pictures and printed sheets.

"Afghanistan 'here we come'" Paul smiled. Steve looked at him, he would never confirm where he was going.

"Well," he started, as he dropped the envelope and started to organise what was in his hands, "there are plenty of places around the world we also go." Steve smiled as he spoke.

"I hear the Americans have a new General in charge, McStanley somebody," Paul added, Tyler looked at him before looking back at Steve. There was a pause, Tyler could see Steve thinking, then a small smile spread over his face.

"Stanley McCrystal!" Steve corrected.

"Yeah, that's him," Paul was connecting with Steve, Tyler let the male bonding go ahead as she really wasn't in the mood for this.

"Where did you see that?" Steve asked.

"Part of a current affairs programme I watched about the Afghanistan conflict, he came across pretty well," Paul looked at Tyler, "he seems to have some good ideas,"

"He does, he spent two years attached with us a while ago," Steve explained.

"Does that happen a lot?" Tyler injected.

"We have a permanent exchange with Delta," Steve nodded, "it works really well,"

"So, who is replacing you guys?" Paul asked. Steve sat forward.

"No one, this is also a goodbye from us, but I hear Lucy is still going to be in touch, from time to time." Paul and Tyler exchanged a glance. Steve reached forward and dropped the photos and paperwork on the coffee table, "oh, nearly forgot," Steve said as he turned and started to rummage through the pockets of his jacket, as he did so both Tyler and Paul sat forwards and started to spread the paperwork over the table. Steve turned around and handed the small white cardboard box towards Tyler. The box was only six inches square and about an inch thick, "This is for you, just a little 'goodbye gift'" Tyler took the box and turned it over.

"Oh, thank you," she was unsure what the box contained. The back of the box had cut folds in it, it was not taped closed so opened easily. The contents were covered in a very thin sheet of paper which fell away to reveal the small wooden shield shape, when she turned it over it revealed the painted regimental crest. The winged dagger had the words *'Who Dares Wins'* underneath it and had a light blue background. The crest had the words 22nd Special Air Service Regiment underneath it in eloquent script. Tyler looked at Paul.

"Wow," Paul said as he took hold of the plaque, "this is really something," Paul looked over at the soldier, "thank you."

"Well," Steve started, "you helped us with that lot from Mussenden temple and this is just a little 'thank you,' from Chris and I."

"Right," Tyler looked at Paul, "I am sure we have something for you as well," Paul looked at her blankly.

"Umm, I am sure .... We have something ...." Paul shrugged; Tyler stood up.

"Right," she stated as she headed into the kitchen. The sound of cupboard and drawers being opened and searched echoed through to them. Paul held the plaque up.

"Thanks,"

"No problem," Steve replied. When Tyler returned, Steve stood up and smiled at the large bottle of Irish Whiskey she was carrying.

"Steve, can you pass on to those that have helped us as well, that they have our thanks and on behalf of the Northern Dun of Clan An Rua, please accept this small gift." Paul stood up as the gift was exchanged, Paul spotted Steve's eyes widen as he looked at it. Paul was guessing he was a whiskey drinker and if so, then he may be the only one who gets to consume the contents, the thought made Paul smile.

"Wow, thank you so much," Steve and Tyler shook hands again.

"Right, so, what is all this then?" Tyler asked. Paul moved his chair closer to the table as Steve started to spread the contents out more.

"Right then, these are the pictures you sent us and yes, we got a load of stuff for you."

"Were you able to put any names to these faces?" Tyler asked, Steve had his elbows on his knees and clasped his own hands together.

"Every single one of them," he stated, Paul looked up as he carried on, "Both Chris and I recognised a few of them, they are all ex British soldiers who are employed by the same security company." Steve reached forward and turned one of the pictures over, stuck to the back was a small printout with details of each face in that picture. "We have the ID of each one, on the back, name, brief military experience and where each one did their Close Protection course.!" Tyler lifted a picture. turned it over and started to read what was on the back.

"Don't suppose you know who they are working for currently?" she asked.

"Currently? Yes," he replied, both Tyler and Paul looked up at the smiling Scotsman. "This team here is led by a 'Mark Castle' former Royal Marine, and they are all currently employed by a firm called 'Naiad Security Solutions' which in turn is owned by Hippocamp Group," Steve explained. Paul began looking over the photos that were spread over the table.

"Any idea who they're contracted with? What they're doing over here?" Paul asked.

"More importantly, *where* are they?" Tyler added. Steve searched through the paperwork and found a picture of one of the 4 x 4's. He picked it up and read off the back of it.

"This vehicle, and two others are currently under contract to a senior board member from 'MAXX Investments,' police ANPR have several registered hits having them concentrating on an area between Bushmills and Coleraine." Steve looked up, "does that help?"

"Yes," Tyler replied, "what capabilities do they have? I mean, are they armed? Etc,"

"I would assume they are armed, yes." Steve set the photo down and moved some of the paperwork until he found what he was looking for, "the vehicle specifics are here, all three were upgraded with run flat tyres, reinforced windows, in car armour ...." He held the paperwork out for her, Tyler took it from him, "it's all there, where the work happened, when, invoices, receipts. Seems the work was rushed as they only had level three armour installed,"

"How can you tell it was done in a rush?" Tyler asked as she looked up.

"Well, it appears they were offered level six, but that would have led to a wait of six to possibly eight weeks, level three was all they had in stock at the time."

"Do you know where the work was done?" Paul asked.

"Yeah, I know the company well, lots of people in the close protection world use them, but this lot seemed to be in a rush to get over here." Steve sat back in the chair, Tyler was studying what was in her hand and Paul was looking over more of the photographs. "They came over on the ferry, via Rosslea in the Republic, Special Branch found hits as soon as they crossed the border, and yes, you were right, they seemed interested in here, the Number Plate Recognition has one of them driving past here several times." Steve looked at the two of them, Tyler was focused on what she was reading, and Paul still looked serious.

"Any idea who they are providing close protection for?" Tyler asked quietly, Steve sat forward and again looked for a specific sheet of paper.

"Err, yeah, there was a name, hang on." He rummaged around until he found what he was looking for, he sat back in the chair as his eyes searched the page, "he isn't of any interest to us, or the police, in fact Lucy's lot didn't have much on him, either." His eyes continued to scroll down the page, "yes, here it is, a Mr ... M. Hanna," Steve looked up, "does that name mean anything to you?" he was not expecting the reaction that he got.

∞∞∞

The room was in total darkness. Martin Hanna stirred under the duvet and slowly reached out for the ringing mobile phone. He slowly looked at the screen, it was nearly 4PM, so it was still light outside, but he knew he was safe in here. The number was withheld, and he nearly cancelled the call, but very few people knew this number, so he decided to take it.

"Hello," he said quietly as he started to sink back under the duvet.

"Martin?" the voice was male and English, but he did not recognise it.

"Who is speaking?" He closed his eyes and stretched out on the single wooden framed bed they had built for him. The first mattress was too thin, but this one was a lot better, in fact, all the furniture in his room had come from the large retailer near the City airport in Belfast and suited him perfectly.

"I am calling on behalf of 'The Lord Protector," the voice stated. Martin's eyes opened and his head straightened up on the pillow.

"And how may I help you," Martin replied.

"I am calling to inform you that you are to make yourself available to receive an urgent phone call from 'The Lord Protector' in exactly one hour," the voice instructed.

"May I ask what the call is about?" There was a pause before the voice answered.

"There is an urgent security task for you to complete, you *will* be ready to receive his call one-hour from now," the voice instructed.

"Yes, I will be," Martin answered sheepishly. The call ended without formality. Martin switched the light on. Well, he was now awake so he may as well get up.

∞∞∞

Tyler walked out of the farmhouse. Paul was standing with Dermott beside the new Land Rover parked directly in front of it. Both turned as she walked towards them., she had a very stern look on her face.

"Is everyone in the arena?" she asked. Dermott looked over at the corner of the barn as a group of teenagers, including Rhydian walked towards the open barn door.

"Nearly all," Dermott stated.

"Can you confirm that!" Tyler spoke directly to Dermott who looked back at her.

"Aye, no probs," Dermott turned and headed towards the open door of the barn.

"Is Tony here yet?" Tyler asked quietly, Paul hesitated.

"Yes, I think his is, he got here just after Steve left," he replied. Tyler nodded once then slowly walked around to the front of the Land Rover. She pushed her hands into her pockets and watched as the group of smiling and joking teenagers made their way, laughing as they did so towards the larger door. Paul walked up beside her. He looked at what she was looking at. Tyler had not smiled all day, and after what the soldier had told them, they now had a lot to do. "By the way," Paul started, Tyler looked at him.

"What?"

"Something you said this morning," Paul added. Tired eyes looked at him, they blinked before she spoke again.

"What?" Paul took a deep breath in before asking his question.

"During the phone call this morning, you told Connor you would put him down, '*again*', I was chatting with Dermott and none of us remember a first time?" A small smirk spread over her face as she looked away.

"Well, it was a long time ago," she whispered. She walked forward a few paces.

"Ok, may I ask, when? And what happened?" Paul's question stopped her, she turned and looked at him before turning away again. Paul walked up beside her.

"It was just over there," she nodded past the barn towards the open field. Paul was going to ask a question, but he stopped himself, he let her continue with her memory. "I was with Kyle's father and there was a few from the south visiting," she turned towards him again, "remember the old tractor that was left in that field, just over there?" Paul thought for a moment.

"Yes, the old grey one, it burnt out, didn't it?"

"That happened the following day when Kyle and his brother were playing on it," Tyler walked towards the hedge separating the field from the yard. "I had just got permission to marry, and a young Connor had a 'serious temper tantrum' when he heard I was marrying a sapien." Tyler pointed into the field. "The tractor had broken down, it was just over there,"

"Yeah, I remember that bit," Paul added, "after we had put the fire out, it sat there for a few years before Carl had it taken away for scrap." Tyler looked at him, then back into the field, the sun was setting over the distant hills.

"The fire was the following day," Tyler paused again.

"So, what happened?" Paul asked.

"Well, we were standing this side of the tractor and Connor really went into one," Tyler stared into the sunset as she recounted the memory. "He swore he would 'take that sapien down, like a hound!" Tyler mimicked his voice. She looked towards Paul, "I didn't like that, so, in front of everyone, I put him on his arse!" Tyler let a short chuckle come out of her, Paul smiled, having seen her fight, he could picture it.

"So that was that then?" he asked.

"Oh God, no, two of his lackeys took offence to a 'northern bitch' slapping him so they tried to have a go," Tyler looked at him with raised eyebrows, "put them down as well,"

"Oh,"

"Yeah, I left for Canada the following day." Tyler looked back into the sunset, there was a moment of calm. Paul let the peace of the moment flow, he felt the warmth of the sun on his face, Tyler had closed her eyes. There was a knock on the metal of the barn door, they both turned around and looked at Dermott.

"Ok, we are all here," he stated.

"Thank you," she replied. Tyler looked at Paul and winked with her right eye, "right, let's deal with this fucker."

Chapter 37

The large clock on the wall ticked as it approached 11AM. Chief Inspector Anderson sat on a chair in the centre of the main office of Belfast M.I.T. facing the main whiteboard. He looked angry. Inspector Wells was standing in front of the main white board with both of her sergeants sitting to the chief's right-hand side. Gareth McHale was wearing a dark suit that he did not look comfortable in, whereas Emma Ford was wearing a knee length skirt and plain blouse and looked like she belonged there even though she was the newest Sergeant to join the new team Mary Wells was putting together. She had made it clear that first names were not to be used at work. Chief Inspector Anderson had demanded an update on the progress of this current investigation, that he was still in overall charge of. Inspector Wells was quite angry when that was put to her. The white board had photographs and notes from each crime scene, and this was continued on the two white boards erected in front of the desks on the chief's left-hand side. He sat up; his facial expression was getting angrier.

"Inspector Wells .... Say that again!" all eyes turned to the Inspector,

"The pathologist confirmed all the victims had the same cause of death. Massive blood loss following the rupturing of the arteries in the neck caused by a *'Nearly Human'* bite."

"And explain to me precisely what is meant by *'Nearly Human'* bite?" He gripped the arm rest of the small chair, his body tensed as if he was about to jump from the chair.

"Those are the words of the pathologist, not us," Gareth McHale stated. Chief Anderson then did jump up, he glanced at him then stared at Inspector Wells.

"If I want your opinion, Sergeant McHale I will ask for it, now Inspector, do I have to remind you that it is your job, at the crime scene, first to assist a coroner then ... gather 'science-based evidence that can be presented to the public prosecutor that will lead to a successful conviction!" The Inspector did not move, he carried on, "we do NOT investigate, 'flights of fantasy' or mythical creatures," he was almost shouting, "am I making myself clear?" She let the words hang in the air. She blinked then when she answered she spoke quietly.

"Chief Inspector Anderson," she paused for a few seconds, then continued, "first of all Detective McHale 'wasn't' expressing an opinion, he was stating what the pathologist has put in his official reports," she looked towards him, "Sergeant McHale, please continue to add any quotes from official reports or interviews we have gathered during this investigation,"

"Ma'am," he nodded in response, she looked back at the Chief.

"Second, do not come in here and tell me my job, I am fully aware of the parameters for my job description."

"We do NOT investigate 'vampires or werewolves'," the Chief raised his voice again. The Inspector did not move. She stood there, for a few seconds and stared at him.

"Sir," she spoke quietly, "during this briefing, you have not heard either of those words, in fact, if you so wish," she extended her right hand, with the palm uppermost and spread her arms in a horizontal motion, "feel free to go through every single file and report that we have collected so far, likewise, you will not find either of those words."

"Explain to me then," his voice raised again, "why it is all over the newspapers that you are running a *'vampire hunting squad?'*" he raised his arms in a motion of derision. His arms flopped back by his sides, she still stood there.

"What is in the newspapers is not my concern, what we present to the coroner, then in a court room, is!" Her face was still emotionless.

"Then what does the DNA evidence point to?" he demanded.

"Well at first ...." Gareth started; Chief Anderson's head spun round.

"I WASN'T SPEAKING TO YOU!" he shouted, then looked straight at Mary Wells, "Well? Inspector Wells, what does the DNA evidence point to?" he lowered his voice.

"At first, it was thought that the full DNA samples taken were corrupted," she looked back at him, his face was starting to redden with anger, she carried on, "but when we cross checked them with samples taken at Portstewart strand, and other murders they were all found to be the same,"

"And what .... were those results?" again he lowered his tone.

"Nearly human, we ...."

"Don't be absurd," The chief waved his hand and turned away from her, he walked the few steps back towards his chair, "the samples were obviously incorrectly taken!"

"Sir!" Mary raised her voice; he turned back towards her. "We thought the same, but the forensic labs confirmed that proper procedure was followed."

"There were three different CSI teams, each with between eight to ten people at four different crime scenes," Gareth had stood up as he spoke. The Chief glared at him, he had his attention, so he carried on. "Statistically you have a better chance of winning the lottery, three weeks running using exactly the same numbers!"

"All the science-based evidence points in the same way," Mary stated. The Chief stepped closer to her, then he leaned forward, lowering his face towards hers'.

"Inspector Wells," he had lowered his voice to add menace, "your job here is ..." Suddenly she stepped forward and walked past him, she looked at the other two detectives.

"Sergeant Ford, Sergeant McHale, inform the rest of the team that the two O clock team conference will go ahead as planned in here," the two of them stood up as she spoke.

"Ma'am," they replied in unison.

"Great," she spun back to the face that could not believe what she had just done. "Chief Inspector Anderson and I will continue our discussion on how we can best continue this investigation .... In my office." She spun again and started to march towards the door of the office at the end of the large room. The two detectives looked at each other then started to head towards the entrance door to the team room. The Inspector stopped in her doorway, she looked back over her shoulder, "Oh, Emma, when you are done would you be so kind as to get me a Caramel coffee, please?" She stepped into her office and gripped the door with her right hand and turned to invite him in. "Chief Anderson, if you please!" he was furious. He glared at the two that were leaving, then stomped his way towards the small office. The office door was slammed shut, but both Emma Ford and Gareth McHale stopped just in the main corridor, the shouting echoed around the small office.

"Well, that is a turn up for the books! Did she just use your first name in the workplace?" Gareth stated. Emma looked at him, then reached forward and closed the door.

"You go chat with the team and I'll get the coffee," she smiled as she started off down the corridor.

"Meet you back here in say," Gareth looked at the watch, "fifteen minutes?"

"Make it half an hour, this is going to take some time!" she said as she pointed in the direction of the office. Emma started walking down the corridor, Gareth smiled then walked in the other direction. She glanced back down to see where he was, once he had turned the corner and was out of sight she stopped. Taking out her phone she scrolled through the numbers, then held the phone to her ear. It was a female voice that answered.

"Superintendent Sutcliffe's office,"

"Hi Donna, it's Emma, is my uncle in?" she lowered her voice to a whisper.

"Yes, putting you through now," Emma waited as the phone went silent, she looked around as a uniformed police officer walked past. He nodded a greeting, but she ignored him. He walked on down the corridor and past the door to Belfast M.I.T.

"Emma! Hi," the voice of Super Sutcliffe echoed in her ear, "how are things downstairs?"

"Are you in your office at the moment?" she was almost whispering now.

"Yes, ... Why?"

"Better if we talk face to face, there is something you should know ......"

"Sure, I am free now." She was smiling into the phone. Yes, there were things her uncle needed to know about what was going on in Belfast's Major Investigations Team.

The team that she fully intended to lead one day.

∞∞∞∞

Rupert Baskerville stood near the old farm building and watched the sun in the distance as it started to poke out from around the side of the cumulus clouds concealing it. He was wearing his old Barbour jacket, and he had his hands in his pockets. The outdoor trousers already had some mud on them, the Gortex gaiters that covered his boots and nearly came up to his knees also had mud on them, if you worked on a farm, mud was a fact of life. His eyes picked out landmarks over the countryside in front of him. He repeated in his last interview with the journalist from London that he did not 'own' this land, he was just looking after it for the next generation.

"Boss, we are ready," Rupert turned and smiled at Marcus.

"Thank you," Rupert paused again before he turned and walked along the side of the old out house. He followed Marcus as he led the way through the stone archway into the large open courtyard. They walked towards the single doorway that led into the rear of the large barn. Rupert closed the door behind him. The barn had a concrete floor and was clean, it was actually a hangar for the dark blue helicopter parked in the middle of it. At the opposite end of the barn were two large doors that opened onto the concrete landing site at the far side of the manor house, this was the seat of the Baskerville estate. The aircraft refuelling site was off to one side of the landing site. Neatly lined up and facing the doors were a line of clean, brand new Land Rovers. Rupert and Marcus walked along the side of the hangar towards the group of people who were gathered to one side of the Land Rovers. The two aircrew were instantly recognised by their dark flight suits, they stood near the helicopter, both with their arms folded, almost if they were guarding their prize from the grubby hands that were in front of them. The map was stuck to the white board on the frame near the wall on the right as they approached.

"Alright, everyone semi -circle here!" shouted Marcus; his accent echoed around the hangar. Rupert stopped beside the whiteboard. The collection of people shuffled towards them. Everyone was dressed for being outside, boots, gortex trousers and jackets, some had beanie hats, others woollen and a few with small baseball caps. Rupert looked over the experienced faces. Some were from England, others from the US, some from Africa, he smiled at the Nepalese faces that always had a smile, but behind that a ferocity that new very few limits. Marcus turned towards him. "Boss," Rupert stepped forward.

"Thank you, Marcus," all eyes focused on him. "As you all now know, I have inherited a growing problem in the northern part of my family's estate," the faces looked back at him, no one else spoke, they all listened to what he had to say. "I have tried before for nearly a decade, to resolve this but, they have been adamant, so I have had to look at other outcomes." He extended his hands, "this is where you come in. You are being formed into a unit that is based on the 'fire force' concept used during the Rhodesian conflict. You will deploy in teams of six, in vehicles and when necessary, dropped off by aircraft to deal with any urgent taskings." Rupert looked around again, "all of you come from various military backgrounds, and it is for your experience you have been brought together," he looked over at the pilots in the flight suits, "for example, our aircrew here, have a great deal of experience flying MI-24's in the Sri Lankan conflict," all the heads turned towards the pilots, who stood with their arms folded. "I know the Augusta One- Zero- Nine we have here is a bit smaller, but as far as using the aircraft goes ... they are the experts." There was a murmur among the group. "You are all employed as 'Rangers', yes, I know we are constrained under UK law with the firearms we can carry, and yes, it will only be stalking rifles and shotguns, but we'll all become proficient in using them."

"What kind of sections will we be going out in?" one of them asked. Rupert looked over the faces and found the face that had asked the question.

"The teams will be made of six, a team leader, a signaller, a tracker, a medic and two rangers, Marcus will head up initial training," Rupert looked at Marcus. His face was expressionless. "Marcus, so you all know, has a considerable amount of experience gained from his service with the South African 'Recce Commandos'," Rupert glanced around, he spotted the reaction in some of the faces. "That I think, speaks for itself. Marcus is overall 'Head Ranger', his voice, is my voice," there was another murmur from the crowd. "We will initially start with a 'six weeks on – six weeks off rotation' with two teams on standby to deploy from this hangar at a moment's notice." A few heads nodded; others looked around. Rupert nodded to Marcus. Marcus stepped forward and raised his voice so everyone could hear.

"Right then, you will have seen the bunk rooms here as well as the toilets and shower block, there will be a briefing here tomorrow morning at nine," Marcus looked back at Rupert, then back at the crowd, he had a serious look on his face. "You will be told timings once. You are expected to be on time ... if you cannot be on time then you are gone, is that understood?" More heads nodded this time. "It will be up to team leaders to back brief each of you for team taskings, one thing I want to make clear!" Rupert smiled, Marcus's accent echoed around the hangar, "if you can't do what you are told, you are gone! If you are not safe with your weapon handing, you are gone, I expect you to engage with the training and then the deployments as if you were still serving in your various units, if you can't ...." Marcus did not have to finish the sentence. Rupert stepped forward again, Marcus took a step back.

"Gents, when you work here, you represent me, in your actions, your turnout, the way you interact with any of the farmers or farm hands who manage any aspect of this estate, there is a reason why you were asked to sign 'non-disclosure agreements', however ..." Rupert paused again, "you will never be asked to do anything you are uncomfortable with...." he paused again, everyone was looking at him, "however, when out and about, if you break the law ... you broke the law, NO alcohol will be consumed when on duty, you are being paid to do a job ... I expect, your very best. I want a good working environment; I intend to fully do my part ... I expect everyone who works for me to do the same, is that understood?"

"Yes boss," The accent that answered was African, Rupert nodded at the African face that smiled back at him.

"Right, first on the agenda, this evening we have booked you all in for a meal at 'The White Hart' in the nearby village," A small cheer went up, smiles broke over several faces.

"The beer is on the boss!" another voice shouted; this was answered by a loud cheer.

"I am paying for a meal and dessert; you lot can buy your own beer!" the atmosphere relaxed. Rupert turned toward Marcus, "are the minibus' sorted?" Rupert asked.

"Yes boss," Marcus replied, Rupert turned back towards the crowd.

"Right, you lot, I will meet you all here in an hour then." There was a small round of applause as the group started to disperse. Rupert started to walk back towards the rear door, Marcus followed and soon caught up with him. As they reached the door Marcus stopped him.

"Oh boss, another thing," Marcus stepped closer to him and lowered his voice.

"Yes?" Rupert asked.

"About that 'other thing' you wanted,"

"Yes, any movement there?" Rupert asked.

"Started to, I have recruited three ex-MI5, two surveillance and one of their tech people to cover that job," Marcus looked back over his shoulder as the pilots were shaking hands with several others who were introducing themselves. "Do you want to meet them? I could bring them down here, for a face to face." Rupert paused before he replied.

"Do they know they are working for me?"

"Nope, well, not yet."

"Good, keep it that way, the less that know the better. Where are they currently?"

"Rented a couple of offices in Putney for them to use, they've already given me a shopping list of what they want," Rupert placed his right hand on Marcus' shoulder.

"First class, I will leave that with you then," Rupert pushed the door open and walked outside. He placed his hands back in his pockets as he walked across the courtyard. The green painted wooden door at the rear of the main house opened and a young girl came running out.

"Daddy, daddy!" she screamed as she ran towards his open arms.

∞∞∞∞

Nikki was glad to get out of the car. She did not slam the passenger door shut, but it wasn't far off it. The car took off with all the distain that Lucy could muster. Nikki walked up to the front door and fumbled her keys, they landed on the step and jingled loudly. As she squatted down to pick them up, it masked her observing the rest of the street, her first line of anti-surveillance was done. She flicked through her keys as her eyes moved up the side of the door, the small piece of tape was still in place, the door had not been opened since she had left this morning. The door closed behind her and she dropped her handbag on the floor underneath the assortment of coats that hung from the wall. She pushed one of them aside and tapped in the deactivation code into the building silent alarm system. She flicked off her shoes then she went about her evening routine of putting the heating on for a bath later then she'd decide from the fridge what was going to be her dinner. It did not take long for her to be phoning out for a takeaway to be delivered. She clicked the kettle on to make a mug of tea but as it boiled, she changed her mind, she landed on the cheap sofa with a glass of wine in one hand, the remote in the other. The TV only had the basic channels but that was all she needed. There was nothing in the house she could not walk or run away from if the situation became hostile.

Nikki was still angry; the wine was not really helping with that. The TV was on, but she was not watching it. She looked over at the small clock above the fireplace that she could not use as the chimney as it was blocked. The takeaway was still over half an hour away. There was no coffee table, in fact there was only the basics, one sofa, no chairs, there was only basic stuff in the kitchen, even for a rented house, there was not much in it. She was not expecting the knock at her front door. She nearly dropped the glass of wine as she got up. She quietly made her way back into the hallway, there was definitely someone at the front door. She was staring at the door as she slowly knelt by her handbag, her right hand reached in and took a firm grip of the Glock pistol. She stood up and made her way along the side of the hallway, her right hand with the pistol was in the small of her back, she looked through the spyhole as the door was knocked again. She relaxed when she saw who it was. She kept the pistol behind as she partially opened the door. The toes of her left foot were pushed down the door so the pad of her foot formed a wedge at the bottom of the door, her body weight was pushed up against it, if he tried to force his way in, she would use the gun in her hand.

"You are not supposed to be here!" she was angry at him. Sam from MI6 stepped forward and tried to push the door open, he bounced back off it.

"Look, we need to talk!" he stated, "just open the fucking door will you." he pushed again but Nikki's foot and body kept it firm.

"What's the magic word?"

"What?" he reacted.

"That's not it, 'what's the magic word?'" she repeated. Sam took a step back; his frustration was evident. *"Please!"*

Nikki pushed the door forward and lifted her foot out of the way. She stepped back and allowed him to barge into the house. She closed the front door as he stormed into the living room. He did not see her replace the pistol back in her handbag, it had been agreed previously not to let 'SIX' know that they were armed, as 'six' was forbidden from being allowed to carry weapons in Northern Ireland. Nikki followed him into the living room, he was pacing in front of the fireplace, she did not offer him any wine. "This whole situation is completely ridiculous," he started his rant as she sat back down on her sofa. She couldn't offer him a seat, there weren't any. She lifted the glass of wine as he carried on, "I mean, who does SHE think she is giving me orders!" Nikki now knew exactly who he was talking about, he spun round, his arms waving in fury, "did you hear that she got the station chief to phone London and make a complaint ... *about me!*" Nikki drank some more of the wine, He rambled on, "I should be the one complaining about her! And this whole situation here ... *I* was the one sent over here to take charge," Sam started pointing at his own chest, "me ... not her ..." he vented his fury on the open space in front of the fireplace. "She is the one that is 'fucking' this whole investigation up ... her!!! Not me, and yet, it is *me* who has to take the fall for *her* mistakes ...." He turned on his heels again and started the short pacing back and forth, Nikki continued to drink more wine. "I mean, look, have we been to inspect this farm yet?" he demanded, Nikki shook her head, the rant continued, "*she* ... has given them information, that they have been using, but have we been there? No! have we got footage of one of them changing? No! I mean, they are 'our' assets, not the other way around ..." the pacing continued, "they follow 'our lead' *WE* are the ones in charge, not them and that needs to be forced onto them!" He stopped and turned towards her, "I mean, you agree with me, right?" Nikki went to answer but he cut her off, "I AM supposed to be the one in charge, not her," he turned and started pacing again, "something needs to be done ... something ..." he started muttering. Nikki watched the rant continue. Sam did not notice her tap out a short text message on her phone. She placed the phone on the arm of the sofa and waited. She cradled the wine glass in both her hands so when it started to ring, she made more of an act of standing up to answer it. As she picked up the phone, she held one finger to her lips, then she held the phone to her ear.

"Oh, hi Lucy," Nikki stared at Sam and raised her eyebrows, Sam stopped talking. "Yes, I am here by myself," Nikki walked a few paces towards the hallway, turning her back to Sam, "Yeah sure, give me ten minutes then you can pick me up from here," Sam reacted. Nikki held her forefinger up to tell him to stop and not to move. "Sure, sure, see you then," Nikki smiled then ended the call. She looked at him. "If you want to raise your concerns directly with Lucy, she will be here in about ten minutes. Sam looked furious, muttered something and stormed past her. Nikki was standing in the living room smiling as the she heard the front door slam shut. She walked over to the living room window and watched him stomping down the street to where he had parked the hire car. Nikki had a short giggle as she looked back at her phone, the name 'DAZ F' was on the screen, she pressed the green call button then held the phone to her ear.

"Ok, going to tell me who you were trying to get rid of there?" Darren Forester laughed down the phone.

"Thanks for that, yeah, the dickhead actually called here and was giving off about Lucy, it was the only thing I could think of, soz," there was a short laugh down the phone.

"No problem, we still on for tomorrow night?" he asked.

"Hell yeah," she replied, Darren could not see the way the smile on her face changed the way she looked.

"Ok, see you then," and the line went dead. Nikki was now excited by the anticipation of her thoughts about tomorrow night. Nikki trotted back to lift her glass then headed into the sparse kitchen to refill it. As she landed back on the sofa, she turned the volume of the TV back up again. As she drank more of the wine, she pulled out her phone and looked at it. She was unsure of what to do, first there was the problem with Lucy, yes Darren had told her one way of how to sort that, but now Sam, and it was obvious he was not going to give up easily and he was going to cause more problems. She drank more of the wine then scrolled through the short list of names on her burner phone. She stopped at one and then tapped in a message. 'HI GOT SOME ISSUES; CAN WE CHAT TOMORROW?' the 'message sent' appeared on the screen. Nikki turned herself around and tucked her feet up on the sofa, she lifted to tv controller and stated to scroll through the list of available channels, there was nothing on she would want to watch. The glass of wine touched her lips again and the taste filled her mouth. The phone shook gently with the arrival of a message. She picked it up and opened the message. 'SURE, 10AM' Nikki smiled, at 10AM tomorrow morning she would tell the head of MI5 in Northern Ireland exactly what Lucy had been up to and the way she was totally screwing up this whole situation, then there was Sam from MI6.

Tomorrow would be a good day.

Chapter 38

Nikki was smartly dressed as she walked down the corridor towards the office of the station chief. She felt confident now with what she was about to do, the chief should know what his case officers were doing with people they are supposed to be working with. She knocked on the door at the end of the corridor and waited for the invite to come in. She opened the door. The chief was sitting behind his desk and had some paperwork in his hand, he looked up as she entered, he smiled as he dropped the paperwork on the desk, he held his right hand out towards one of the chairs in front of his desk.

"Nikki, come in, please sit," Nikki smiled and closed the door behind her. She strode over to the offered chair as the chief shuffled the paperwork and dropped it into one of the drawers on his desk. As she sat down, he sat back in his chair. "So, what has that idiot been doing this time? Has one of those SAS guys hit him yet?"

"No, not yet, well, not that I know of but one of them did threaten to 'rip his arms off and beat him to death with the soggy end!'" the two shared a short laugh, "but he is the first thing I want to talk to you about." The chief had a reassuring smile on his face, he was good at making people feel comfortable, comfortable enough to tell him anything, which was a handy skill to have as the MI5 Station Chief in Northern Ireland.

"Go on, what has the dickhead done this time?"

"Well," Nikki sat on the edge of the chair, she wanted to share this information with him, "first of all, he turned up at my door last night, demanding to get in!"

"How does he know where you are living?" the chief asked.

"I have no idea, I didn't tell him," Nikki used her hands to add to what she was saying. "I wasn't in long when he was banging on the front door," she spotted the chief's eyes looking at one of the secure phones on his desk, "I am sure all the neighbours heard him."

"What did he want?" the Chief asked.

"All he did was complain that Lucy was treating him like a child."

"Maybe if he stopped acting like one, that may change!" the Chief smiled.

"Yeah, he does throw epic temper tantrums!"

"Right, I will deal with that, what else has he been doing?" he asked.

"He tried having a go at Darren a couple of days ago," Nikki smiled as she said the next bit, "he actually shoved him, didn't go well for him, turns out, Superintendent Forester can move quite fast," again they shared a laugh, the chief sat forward.

"Well, the Grey Fox does have a reputation after all!" he joked.

"Grey Fox?" she enquired; "have not heard him being called that."

"The first time I came over here, he had not been in special branch very long, but it turns out he took to the job with a seemingly un-natural ability, apparently, when they deployed out, several of the SAS kept trying to convince him to leave the police and join the army, he was that good," he explained.

"Wow," Nikki's face contorted, "can't really see him doing that," her face relaxed as she thought about her next question, "so, why is he called 'Grey Fox'?"

"You can ask him that yourself!" the chief laughed, "speaking of which, are you still doing that task tonight?"

"Yes," she beamed, "he is coming here, and we will be going over the electronic surveillance on several of our P.O.I.s"

"How many Persons of Interest will you be covering?" the chief asked.

"As many as we can get through."

"Who all is taking part?"

"Me, Darren, three of ours and one from Cheltenham," she replied.

"Which one?" the chief asked. Nikki raised her right hand to demonstrate height.

"You know, the tall one who looks like Igor from the old black and white horror films," they shared another laugh.

"Yes, I know the one," the chief responded.

"He needs to spend more time in daylight," she joked, "and talking to real people!" she laughed a little at her own joke, the chief smiled.

"But listen to him, they guy is an expert in cybercrime and cyber terrorism." Nikki smiled but glanced away as the chief spoke, "you know, the very thing he was recruited to do."

"Yes, of course," she confirmed.

"Right," the chief sat back in his chair, "what is the real reason you wanted to see me this morning?" Nikki paused. Her eyes unconsciously darted around the office behind her chief, then they settled on him, where to start, she had planned this of course, but sitting here, right now in front of him, she was now unsure of how to start, the chief started for her. "What has Lucy done that got you so riled?" her body twitched. She calmly took a breath, this could end Lucy's career, but, since she was sitting here, she had to.

"Right," she started. The chief looked relaxed; this could be a bomb shell for him.

"Is it her work?" the chief motioned with his right hand towards his drawers.

"No, no it isn't that" Nikki was unsure of how to start.

"Something social?" he asked. She tried not to react, but there was a small physical reaction she knew he spotted.

"Ok, you may not like this but ...." She started, the chief did not respond, he was letting her talk, "but she is making a play for one of the special branch guys," she looked down, "and he is married, she is doing it just to wreck his marriage and I think that ...."

"Oh, you mean Mike Dear?" the chief injected, Nikki again tried not to look surprised, but she was.

"You already know?"

"Of course, I do, she is managing an asset!" he stated.

"But she ...."

"Is doing her job."

"Her job is to shag married guys and wreck their lives?" Nikki reacted.

The chief looked at her. "Nikki, you have only been in the service just over two years, Lucy has been doing this a lot longer, what she is doing is 'managing an asset' an asset that it has been assessed, will be of benefit to us, long term,"

"But ..." she hesitated.

"What is our role ... as the security service?" he asked.

"Our role?"

"Yes .... What is our job? Currently?" The chief sat forward as he asked the question, Nikki paused again before she answered.

"The protection of national security and in particular its protection against threats such as terrorism, espionage and sabotage, the activities of agents of foreign powers, and from actions intended to overthrow or undermine parliamentary democracy by political, industrial or violent means."

"Very good, and what would your assessment of some of the P.O.I.s we are currently investigating be? Would you consider some of them a threat?"

"Yes," she had lowered her voice.

"And some of those *are* agents of foreign powers, and threats of terrorism and espionage are they not?"

"They are," it was almost a whisper.

"Lucy came to me with an idea, and I gave her the go ahead to manage one part of an asset and," he motioned again towards the desk drawer, "from her most recent report she is managing it very well."

"I .... don't know what to say," Nikki stated, the chief sat back in his chair again.

"As you know, six are desperate to try and take this whole thing from us," Nikki nodded, "I will deal with this dickhead, and him turning up at your residence and possibly compromising it, maybe what I need is to get him on a flight back to London, but in the meantime, don't give him any excuse to throw crap at us, ok!"

"Ok,"

"Lucy needs your support and I *expect* you to give it, ok!"

"Ok, but what will we do if special branch finds out about this?"

"They already know,"

"What?" Nikki surprised herself with the way she responded.

The chief was smiling now. "Darren is fully aware, he and I discussed it,"

"I ...."

"Nikki, we ... and I do mean the corporate 'we' in that, are investigating people and well," he glanced at the drawer again, "creatures that until not that long ago everyone thought only existed in films," he continued, "we have yet to fully realise both the potential and real threats that exist here, this ... is uncharted territory that we are in," Nikki nodded but didn't speak, he carried on, "with intelligence, we still may never know 'the full picture' but it is our job to investigate and help identify those threats to our nation, and how do we do that?"

"The collection, interpretation, analysis and distribution of gathered, accurate intelligence," she replied.

"And what is one of the best ways of doing that?" he asked.

"Correct management of all available assets," she responded, he smiled.

"And how do we do that?" he asked.

"Follow the MICE principles, the reasons someone becomes an asset," her body relaxed, her shoulders dropped, she understood where he was going with this.

"And MICE stands for?"

"When targeting an asset offer Money, learn their Incentive, or reason why they want to become an asset, followed by the Coercion and Extortion of the unwilling asset," she sighed.

"Ego,"

"What?"

"The 'E' of MICE stands for 'ego', it inflates the assets ego to be working for us."

"Yes, yes of course," she looked down again as she answered.

"So, you did learn something during your training then," the chief was smiling again, she politely smiled back. "Nikki, we are dealing with situations none of us envisaged, and I do appreciate that you did feel comfortable enough to raise what you thought was a problem, thank you for that, but Lucy is currently in charge, she is very good at her job, may I suggest you learn from her." Nikki looked up with a concerned look on her face, the chief read her thoughts, "no, I will never ask you to have sex with someone as part of the job," Nikki relaxed, "but what I do want you to learn is how to correctly manage all available assets so we can gather as much available intelligence as possible."

"I will,"

"If you ever need any help, advice or guidance, Lucy should be your first port of call as team leader, but, if she is the problem then you can always knock this door."

"Thank you," Nikki responded. The room went quiet, Nikki smiled at her chief and he smiled back.

"So, is that it?" he asked.

"Yes,"

"Nikki, don't be disheartened, I like the work you have done so far, you do have a career ahead of you in the service."

"Thank you," she replied.

"I mean, keep going, you could probably end up as the next female head of service!" he was lightening the atmosphere and she recognised it.

"Well, I will not be the first there, it would be nice to be the second female head of service," she smiled.

"Third, there has been two already."

"How many female 'heads of service' has MI6 had?" she asked.

"Currently? none," he smirked.

"Well," she straightened up in the chair, "that needs to be addressed then, maybe I should transfer over to them?" again she was smiling politely.

"Not bloody likely!" he joked, "all this time training you then you bugger off and join them, I don't think so," the two shared another laugh, "anyway," the chief reached over and opened his top drawer, "both you and I have work to be getting on with."

"Thank you," she said as she stood up.

"No problem," he replied as she walked over to the door. She looked back at him as she opened it, smiled, and walked out. As the door closed, he lifted the handset of one of his phones and pressing one of the buttons on it, he took it off speaker phone.

"Wow," the female voice said at the other end.

"Right, you got all that then?" he stated.

"Yeah, ok, I will start the ball rolling and I will get Sam brought back to London; however, he will have to be replaced, we still need to have some eyes on this, the connection with the Russians and all," the female voice stated.

"Of course, that isn't a problem, I just wanted you all to hear that," the chief replied.

"Yes, thank you for that, pass on my best to Grey Fox when you see him,"

"Yeah sure, I will," the chief replaced the handset and ended the call.

Now to phone his own head of service.

∞∞∞∞

Tony spotted Alison coming around the corner as he walked towards the entrance to the barn. He stopped, a smile spread over his face, she smiled back and waved.

"Hi," she said as she approached him.

"Hi," he replied, "how are things with you?" he asked.

"Nothing a lottery win would not fix," she responded, the two shared a short laugh.

"Where are you staying?" he asked.

"Under the ever-watchful eye of Lynne M'Kane," Alison was making light of her situation, Tony thought for a moment.

"You know, I don't think I have ever been in her farmhouse," he stated. Alison turned and pointed through the barn.

"It is over that way," she said, Tony playfully pushed her shoulder.

"Yeah, I know 'where' it is, just never been in it." The shouts from inside the barn echoed out through the partially open door.

"What is going on in there?" she asked, Tony stared as more shouts of exertion echoed again.

"Training," he whispered.

"Is it ok to take a look?" Alison nudged him with her shoulder, Tony smiled.

209

"Yeah, sure." The two walked towards the door, Alison walked in first, then Tony, both stopped and leaned on the wooden barrier at the edge of the arena.

In the centre of the arena were two lines of students, each with a wooden training Katana sword in their hands, each pair faced each other. Tyler had her back to the door and her wooden katana was in her right hand, it swayed by her side. They were all dressed in gym gear, leggings and training tops were the order of the day.

"AGAIN!" she shouted, each pair had a double handed grip on the bottom of the sword, they held the swords vertically in front of them, facing their adversary. Tyler pointed with the tip of her sword towards one of the lines of students. "Team A, you will advance this time and team B, defend, OK!" she was answered with nodding heads. "BEGIN!" she shouted. The one line of students jumped forward, wood crashed onto wood as downward blows were defended, the sound of the swords striking the other swords echoed around the arena. Crack, crack, crack. The speed of the advance was only matched by the speed each blow was defended. "Right," Tyler shouted, all the students relaxed, most were out of breath, some looked tired, others looked angry, "not bad, this time B will advance." One of the students motioned towards Tony and Alison, what the student said, they could not hear, but all heads turned and looked towards them. Tony lifted his hand and waved, Tyler raised her hand and waved back. She turned back to her students, "right, keep going," the students lined up against each other again, "BEGIN," she shouted, attacks were launched, and defended, feet shuffled on the ground as wood flew through the air, controlled by the fingers that gripped each sword. Crack, crack, crack. "Right, ok," Tyler continued to instruct, the students relaxed, Tyler lowered her voice and all the students slowly walked towards her. Alison could hear her speaking but could not hear the words. Several heads nodded, then all the students spread out in front of Tyler who kept her back to Alison and Tony. The students found their own space and adopted a fighting stance, one foot was forward, and the swords were again raised, everyone looked serious.

"What is happening?" Alison asked.

"Sword drill," Tony replied, "this brings back memories," he smiled as he spoke. Alison watched as Tyler started a rhythmic movement, which each student copied, for a moment, the whole class moved as one, slow deliberate movements, swords swiped through the air, engaging opponents, first in front of them, then to either side of each student. The gymnastic dance continued with grace; Alison watched as the class went through each movement, downward blow, side stepping, defending, a slow spin and again engaging another foe, Alison was mesmerised.

"She has taught every single wolf in your clan?" Alison asked.

"In the north, yes, some of down south, but not all," Tony replied.

"She trained you?" Alison asked without taking her eyes off what she was watching, the pace had increased, the strength of the blows increased as well.

"That she did," Alison spotted the little twitch and grimace on Tony's face.

"Happy memories?" she looked at him. Tony looked at her, then back at the group.

"Some ... others .... painful," Alison laughed, both looked up as the group launched their final downward blow.

"*HAI!*" they all shouted as they I came to a sudden stop. The shout echoed around the arena, then everyone relaxed. Tyler nodded her head.

"Well done, everyone, that was a good one." The group started to walk toward her, "You all know the timings for tomorrow?" Tyler was looking over the group, some spoke, others nodded. Tyler turned and started to walk towards the exit.

"So, you can do that?" Alison asked, Tyler and the group approached.

"Damn right I can!" Tony raised his voice, he looked at Alison, "I am really good with a sword," he stated.

"Yeah, …. That's not what I remember," Tyler was grinning as they got close.

"What about you? Can you use one?" Tony poked Alison in the shoulder. Alison looked at him with raised eyebrows.

"Better than you."

"What? not a chance in hell is you better with a sword than I am!" Tony was adamant. Alison pointed towards Tyler's training sword.

"May I borrow that for a second?" she asked, then she looked at Tony, "I have a lesson I need to teach someone!" Tyler spun offered the handle of the sword to her.

"Of course," Tyler looked at one of the students, "let them in." She stepped back as two of the students pushed at the segment of the arena wall that was the entrance out of the way, there was now a feeling of excitement in the group in anticipation of the coming battle. Tyler stepped back and turned towards the group. "Right, hollow square just over here," she looked over at Tony, then looked at Alison, "let us keep this simple, 'guys against the girls," a small cheer went up. Tony started to take off his jacket and looked confidently at Alison.

"Let's do this." Alison winked at him as she pulled her jacket from her shoulders. The two combatants walked into the arena as the group split, the girls stood on one side and the group of boys formed on the other. Alison walked towards Tyler who again offered her the grip of the wooden sword. Alison closed her eyes and bowed her head from her neck.

"Thank you," Tyler then stepped back as Tony grabbed the sword that was thrown towards him by one of the smiling boys.

"Come on, Tony!" one of them shouted, Tony caught the sword in his right hand and smiled at the group of boys, he turned and faced Alison, he spun the sword, by the grip in his right hand then raised it, taking it in a two-handed grip. Rhydian stepped forward and tapped Alison's arm, Alison looked at the smiling teenager.

"He drags his left foot when he turns," she whispered. Alison winked at her in reply, Rhydian stepped back and shouted, *"Kick his ass!"* cheers and encouragement started from both camps, Alison focused on him. She studied his stance, the way he gripped the sword, the way he lowered his head, yes, he had been taught. Tyler stepped back to give them room.

"Right, first to three, one point for a strike anywhere on the upper torso," she held out her hands toward each of them, "Tony, are you ready?" she shouted. Tony glanced at her and nodded. She looked at Alison, "are you ready?". Alison looked at her, her face had a serious look on it. Slowly she raised the sword in her hands, she nodded once. Both the swords were lowered towards each other so the tips nearly touched, both fighters could look over the tips of their swords into each other's eyes. Tyler stepped forward and extended her right hand in a slow karate chop motion. Tyler's hand was just underneath both swords, "fighters," she said softly before she suddenly swiped her hand upwards, breaking the invisible bond between the swords, "BEGIN!" she shouted, jumping back as she did so.

Both Alison and Tony stepped forward with such speed it surprised most of the group. Alison landed the first blow, which Tony defended, the wood of the swords cracked as they collided, the second blow was landed, again Tony defended, but it was done with such speed he could not defend the third blow that struck him on his left shoulder. Tony yelped. Alison straightened up as she stepped back, adopting her fighting stance as she did so. Tyler pointed towards Alison with her left hand.

"One point!" she shouted. Tyler was trying not to smile, the group of girls exploded in joy. Tony righted himself, his face looked serious as he tightened his grip on the handle, he looked at Alison and nodded, then motioned with his sword, beckoning her forward. Alison let a little smile appear at one side of her mouth, no one had expected her to be that fast. Tyler stepped forward again, holding her right hand up, both fighters approached, their swords almost touching again. "Begin," Tyler repeated, as she jumped back, again the two stepped forward and the swords crashed against each other, the speed of both assaults was so fast that the swords were almost a blur. This time it was Alison's fourth blow that landed on Tony's right shoulder, again, he yelped, almost dropping his sword as he did so.

"Nice one Ali!" Rhydian shouted as the group of girls cheered again, there was shock with the boys. Alison stared into Tony's eyes; the pain of the blow was there.

"Two points," Tyler pointed towards Alison.

"Come on Tony .... You are getting your ass kicked 'by a girl'" Tony focused on her. All the noise from behind him faded away. He looked at the way she gripped the sword in her hands, he watched as she breathed in and the way the tip of the sword moved as she did so, he focused on the exposed muscle in her neck tightening in anticipation. Tyler stepped forward again and held her right hand up. Tony stepped forward and looked over the tip of his sword into Alison's crystal-clear blue eyes. She blinked as Tyler's hand swiped upwards.

Everything moved in slow motion. His left foot took the step forward and his right foot shuffled after it, the centre of his body weight moved as his sword crashed onto her sword, she had blocked his first blow, she blocked his second, their swords crashed together in a third clash. He watched as she started her own assault, he blocked her first, then her second and he saw the way she was attacking with her third. It took all of his strength to stop the force of her strike but stop it he did. For a second, the two of them stood there, their swords locked together, each trying to push the other backwards. Both pairs of eyes blinked at the same time and both stepped rearwards. Tony was aware of the movement of the group of excited girls behind Alison, but he could not hear them. He did hear her taking a breath in, his body tensed, she was attacking again and again, their swords crashed together. He stepped forward, she blocked his strike, he twisted the sword as her blow landed and again, he forced all of his strength and power into trying to push her backwards. He felt her sword give way, his sword passed through air as she side- stepped to his right, her sword slammed into his right hand before he could do anything about it. Pain shot through his body as he lost the grip of his weapon. He did not hear the sound that he made but everyone else did. The wooden sword he had been holding landed on the floor of the arena. Tony stepped back, cradling his injured hand, the group of girls jumping around their victor. Tyler was smiling as she stepped forward and pointed with her left hand towards Alison.

"Winner!" she shouted. Alison was smiling as she was patted and congratulated by the girls. The boys looked dejected. Some shook their heads, other looked annoyed. Tony looked down as he stepped forward and held out his right hand. Alison took delight in accepting the offered hand, the pain of her grip just made her victory that little bit better.

"I did not know you were that fast," Tony stated.

"Have you ever seen me with a sword?" Alison asked.

"No, but"

"But maybe you need to re-take some refresher training!" Alison said with a smile as she pointed towards Tyler, there was a collective laugh from behind her. Tyler raised her voice as the two stepped back.

"Right, everyone, what did Tony do wrong?" A space formed in front of her, she had a lesson to teach.

"He wasn't fast enough," one of the boys responded.

"No, there was nothing wrong with his speed or his technique," Tyler looked around, "Well? Anyone?" Tyler was looking at her students.

"I underestimated my opponent," Tony said out loud, he looked over at Alison, "I overestimated my own abilities, which, made me overconfident going into a conflict." Tyler stepped forward and into the middle of the group.

"Exactly," she pointed upwards with the forefinger of her right hand, "yes, be confident in what you can do but never, never ever, expect you have already beaten any opponent going into a conflict," some of the boys nodded and the girls smiled.

Suddenly Ruth McDonal appeared in the doorway of the barn, she was out of breath as she had been running, she almost fell into the barn, nearly all the heads turned towards her.

"TYLER!" she shouted as she landed on the wooden edge of the arena. The group parted as Tyler walked towards her.

"Ruth, what is up?" Tyler asked, Ruth fought for breath between passing the message.

"Dermott wants you .... at the comms building .... He said you have to come now,"

"Why? What's up?" Tyler repeated. Ruth lifted her head and looked directly at her.

"He said to say, 'Heard from Silver and Gold, you have to come immediately'." Tyler stepped towards and placed her hand on Ruth's shoulder over the wall.

"Ruth, what is so urgent?" she asked, "what has happened?" Ruth breathed heavily, but everyone heard what she said next.

"WE HAVE FOUND THEM!"

Chapter 39

Mike jumped into the passenger seat, and even before he had closed the door, Lucy had accelerated away from the junction. The car swerved into the faster lane and as he clicked the seat belt into place, he felt himself being pushed back into the seat with her acceleration. He looked at her, she had her hair in a ponytail and was wearing a grey tee shirt and training leggings, she was dressed down from what she normally was.

"Are we in a rush?" he asked, she did not look at him.

"Sort of," the car slowed down behind the truck that was slowly overtaking the large lorry on the inside. Mike looked to his right; they had not taken the turn off he had expected.

"Since we are not going to your office, may I ask where we are going?"

"Booked us a room in a hotel, we can get some work done and 'relax' a bit as well, can we not?" the truck pulled in and Lucy accelerated towards the traffic lights. Mike looked around the outside of the car as the lights turned red, the car came to a sudden halt. "I have some of the case files we can review, as I think there's a lot more going on than we think!" Mike looked at her, she was poised, ready for the lights to change, her face concentrating on what she was doing. He looked into the back seat; it was empty.

"Where are they?"

"In a bag in the boot," she glanced at him, "not the kind of things you have openly on the back seat for everyone to see now, is it?" The handbrake was off, she moved the car into first gear. Mike looked up at the lights, as soon as they started to change the car jumped forward, soon they were out of Holywood and heading towards Bangor.

"So, what is it you want to go over? Is it something specific?" Mike asked, Lucy didn't look at him as they went over the crest of the hill, then she slowed for another set of traffic lights.

"Well," she started, "I have been going over from what we think is the start,"

"And where is that?" he asked.

"The incident with the SAS guys in Scotland?" Mike looked at her. He studied her face, his eyes moved over the lines of her face, along her cheek, she didn't look at him. "You didn't hear about when they were on exercise with the Americans, and they ended up having what can best be described as 'a running battle' with a group of werewolves?"

"Err, no, when did that happen?" Mike asked. Lucy motioned with her head towards the rear of the car.

"We got them to write reports afterwards, at first, they were not believed, and it was thought they were trying to cover for a helicopter crash that happened, then we got the footage and still pictures from the exercise ...." Lucy looked over at him, "I believe you call them, 'the furry and fang club."

"I haven't seen that" Mike replied.

"No problem, I have it on the laptop, some of the pictures are pretty good as well."

"But *when* did that happen? Was it recently?" he asked. Lucy thought for a moment. She slowly turned left then immediate right into the car park of the large hotel.

"If I remember right, about eight, possibly ten months before the Trotman murder," she looked over at him, "I understand you know that one very well!"

"Yeah, I do," The Trotman murder. For a moment, Mike was back in the alleyway where they found what was left of him, for a moment he was standing in the disposable, one-piece suit and for a moment, both Sean and Simon were still alive. When Lucy tapped his arm, it brought him back to where he was. The car was quiet, and Lucy was standing outside, leaning in through the driver's door, her right arm reaching out to him, her finger tapped his forearm.

"Mike ...." Mike looked around, a bit confused, the moment he was back with his friends was gone and reality slammed into his face.

"Yeah .... Yeah," as he fumbled to release his seatbelt Lucy placed her hand on his forearm, stopping what he was doing.

"You Ok?" she spoke softly. Mike looked into her eyes, there was concern there.

"I'm good," he nodded as the seatbelt retracted. Lucy retreated out of the car then closed the driver's door. As Mike got out of the car, she was already at the rear and throwing the daysack over her shoulder. The boot of the car closed with a slam, she walked past him, motioning with her head towards the reception area.

"Well, don't just stand there, come on then," he took off after her. The black day sack was heavy, but she moved with both grace and purpose.

"Something I was wondering about them." Mike spoke as they walked together.

"What?" she asked.

"You know how chocolate is poisonous to dogs ..." Mike looked at her, "I was wondering if it was the same with them?" Lucy looked at him quizzically.

"Well, next time you see them, you can ask them." The two of them walked in through the entrance and she headed directly for the reception, it was clear she had been here before. Behind the desk there was a young woman sitting and concentrating on the screen in front of her. She was hidden behind the desk, only her head visible over it. Beside her stood an older man, very well turned out. Mike spotted the badge on the lapel, 'duty manager'.

"Miss Burrows!" he exclaimed, reaching over reception extending his hand, "so nice to see you back her again," Lucy took his hand and smiled as she dropped the bag on the floor,

"Hello Malcom, yes, it is so nice to be back here in Belfast,"

"Is it your usual booking?" Malcom asked.

"Yes, thank you," Lucy replied. Malcom turned to the young woman.

"This booking is for Miss Rachel Burrows," he looked over at Lucy, "are you still with KT finance, of Canary Wharf in London?"

"I am," Lucy smiled. The young woman started tapping at the keyboard.

"How is life in the world of finance these days?" Malcom enquired.

"Well, things are still tricky after the crash of oh- eight," Lucy smiled at Malcom, "to be honest, glad I still have a job!"

"As am I, dearest, as am I," Malcom replied.

"Room for one ...." The young woman asked as she looked up at Mike.

"Yes," Lucy turned to Mike, "Malcom, this is a friend of mine who we are working with here, Stephen, this is Malcom, who, may I say, is one of the best concierges in the business!" Mike did not flinch with being introduced by a false name; in fact, he would have been surprised if she had used her real name. The two men shook hands.

"Nice to meet you," Malcom started, with a very weak handshake.

"And you," Mike looked around, "you know, I have never actually been in here."

"Oh, a local accent I hear," Malcom said with a playful smile. The woman placed the sheet of paper that had just come out of the printer on the desk in front of Lucy.

"Can you sign here, and may I see a photo ID please?"

"Oh yes," Lucy turned and ducked down to the day sack.

"Yes, I am from here," Mike smiled. Lucy reappeared with a passport which she handed to the young woman as her fingers tapped away at the keyboard.

"Would miss be requiring any venue tickets for this evening?" Malcom was more camp this time. Lucy smiled, these two had obviously met several times before.

"No, unfortunately, but thank you for getting us into the opera house the last time I was here, I never had a chance to thank you for that, the performance was first class," Lucy was being playful, and Malcom blushed.

"Oh, that is no problem dear, it is my pleasure," he leaned forward and placed his hand on the desk, Lucy playfully tapped it.

"Well, it was a 'sold out' performance, how did you manage to get us such good seats?" Mike listened to her tone of voice, it was as if she was speaking to a child,

"Getting tickets to sold out performances is my superpower!" the two shared a laugh as the young woman stood up and handed the passport and the folded card that had the electronic room keys in it to Lucy.

"Your room is on the second floor, your booked newspapers will be delivered tomorrow morning; the restaurant will be open from five, the bar and the gym are available for you to use at your own pleasure." Mike looked at the face that had a small smile on it.

"I bet you get bored saying that!" he injected. Both Malcom and the young woman looked at him. Mike spotted the woman's eyes dart over at Malcom then look at him and smile without making a comment.

"We hope you enjoy your stay with us," Malcom added.

"I will, thank you," Lucy lifted the daysack and handed the room key to Mike.

"Thank you," he replied as Lucy turned to walk away. Mike followed her over to the lift, neither spoke as a man in a suit with a brief case walked up and stood beside them. The doors opened and the three of them walked into the empty elevator. Their journey to the room was in silence. As they got into the room Lucy walked in first and dropped the daysack on the floor near the end of the bed, Mike let the door close behind him.

"So, Lucy, or is it Rachel?" he was about to say something else when she suddenly turned around and threw her arms around his shoulders, their lips met in a passionate kiss. Mike broke off the kiss and stepped back. She looked hurt.

"What?" she asked.

"What do I call you? Lucy or Rachel?" he asked.

"I have several work names, Rachel Borrows is just one of them, didn't you learn that on your course?"

"Yes, of course, I ..." Lucy cut him off with another passionate embrace.

"and ... I have a surprise for you," she whispered into his right ear.

"Before we begin, I need to use the 'big boys' room,'" he motioned with his head towards the small bathroom.

"Sure," she smiled playfully, Mike went into the bathroom and closed the door behind him. The light automatically came on, he leaned forward, placing his hands either side of the sink and looked at himself in the mirror.

"Do you know what you are doing?" he whispered. He paused before he splashed his face with water, then he took a mouthful of the running water and swirled it around his mouth before spitting it into the sink. He wiped his face dry then he flicked his shoes off. He paused again, then took his socks off and shoved them into the shoes. He opened the door and walked forward into the quiet room. The door closed behind him, then he stopped and looked at the bed. Lucy was lying diagonally across the bed, she was on her back with her arms stretched out above her head, her hair fanned out over the pillow under her head. She was wearing a small black lace bra with matching suspenders and thin silk stockings. She looked at him and winked.

"Are you just going to stand there and gape?" she whispered.

∞∞∞∞

Chis Abbey looked at his watch, it was nearly 7PM. He was sitting in the driver's seat of the hire car He looked around the layby, he opened the door and got out; he slammed the door in frustration. He pulled the phone out from his pocket and looked at the blank screen.

"Where the hell are you?" he shouted at the phone. He paced around looking over the fields, the sun had just set. A car drove by at speed, the lights cutting through the growing darkness. He looked at the two males in it. They were not who he was waiting for. Chris scrolled through his messages stopping at the name '*Darling*' he typed in the short message, 'WHERE THE HELL ARE YOU?' he pushed the phone back into his pocket. He looked up and down the road, no traffic for miles. Chris walked over to the passenger side of the car and stopped at the hedge row. He undid his belt and pulled down his zip. As the liquid started to flow, his phone bleeped with a message.

∞∞∞∞

Mike was sitting on the end of the bed tying his shoelace before he stood up and looked at Lucy who was still under the duvet, he had an excited smile on his face.

"Look, I've really got to get going!" he said. Lucy sat up, hugging the duvet.

"Yes, I know,"

Mike looked at the large ring binder folders that she had unpacked. "And we will have to do the case review at some point as well,"

"Well, I will be up at the hangar tomorrow, maybe we can do it then?" she suggested.

"Yes, we can get Steve involved too, you know, get the military input," he added.

"Yeah, we will need to pounce on them soon, as they are off shortly,"

"Oh, I hadn't heard," Mike stated.

"Yeah, they didn't say exactly where, but I heard f them talking about heading back to Afghanistan." Lucy looked at him, Mike slowly knelt on the bed, placing his hands either side of where her legs were, pushing the duvet down on them, moving his face towards her.

"Better them, than me," he whispered as he closed his eyes and leaned forward to peck her lips. When he opened his eyes, her face was directly in front of his, there was a fire in her eyes that he could not resist. She winked once.

"Definitely," she whispered, she then kissed him again before she flopped down on the bed. "But if you have to go, you better go now or I am going to rip your clothes off again," she was laughing as she spoke. Mike retreated and headed for the door.

"Until tomorrow then,"

"Until tomorrow," she shouted after him as the door to the room slammed shut. She lay there for a few seconds before she flung the duvet off and jumped up beside the bed. She was naked, but she did not care. She walked over to the files and lifted the daysack off the top of one of them. She flicked the binder's cover open to where the small device was, the lens was pointing directly at the bed. She pressed the small button that was beside the small, single red light. As the light went out, she looked up at the door.

"Got ya,"

Chapter 40

Jason rolled over from around the old tree so he could see them. He had built his hide quickly the previous day; he had chosen this tree as it was in the middle of the line of trees that stood along the hillside. They did not follow the crest of the hill but dropped down the side. He had gotten comfortable easily. The netting and drape covered him from view, he could see back up the hill behind him and he had an excellent view of the re-entrant that formed the small valley where the large farmhouse was. The drape also had a thermal lining so anything flying overhead would not pick up his body heat, it also helped keep him warm during the night. His rucksack was only an arm's reach away, he had his crossbow beside him on the ground between him and the rucksack and currently, he was enjoying the food out of the self-heating tin. He looked at the two men who were in the hedgerow at the far side of the field. They were watching the activity around the farm, he had learned their names were Ian Silver and John Gold, he could spot a werewolf in human form just as easily as he could spot a vampire. Jason knew they were trackers and had good navigation, but they were not as good ats judging distance as he was. He had been following them since he spotted them, they were clearly looking for the same prey as he was, so he let them lead him to where he was now. The farm had a lot of humans around it, at first, he thought they had the wrong place, then he spotted 'Him'. The Noc, the vampire, the one who had an entire security team around him, that could only mean one thing. He was important. Yes, he had tested the team and yes, they were good. The way they reacted to his crossbow bolt he fired into the tree showed they were more than capable and that meant they would prevent him from getting to his prey. Yes, the wolves had done a good job in tracking them here, now he would see what they did about it. He ate more of the food and smiled, from what he had learnt from his meeting with the female pack leader near Belfast, the wolves would react, he hoped it would be a good show. If they didn't, then he would not miss the next time he fired a crossbow bolt at him. Jason Apollyon let a small smile spread over his face, one of the wolves had crawled back, out of sight of the farm, but clear to anyone else who was watching them, he had a small device with a keyboard on it. Jason recognised the type of device it was, they were sending a secure data message, he guessed back to their farm, yes, these wolves were good, but they would not stop him doing what he needed to do.

∞∞∞∞

Tyler was wearing walking boots and a camouflaged stalking jacket open at the front, her dark fleece underneath the jacket kept her warm. She had a dark coloured baseball cap with her ponytail pulled out the back. When she walked the open jacket showed off the gun belt wrapped around her waist, the holstered pistol on her right side. She had a serious look on her face. The arena went quiet when she walked in. Dermott was standing at the far side of the two whiteboards that were on stands just on her left. Paul was standing with Tony and Alison on the far side of Dermott with the group of people dressed for the different jobs they were going to be doing. Ruth was standing in front of the assault team, in their dark coloured overalls and body armour and at the far side were Becky and Fiona standing in front of the small group of camouflaged stalkers, their weapons either over their shoulders or in their hands. Everyone had a serious look on their face.

"Right then," Tyler started. She stopped at the near side of the boards and looked at Dermott, "have we got a workable assault plan yet?" she asked loudly for everyone to hear.

"We do," Dermott responded.

"Do we have eyes on the target at the moment?" she asked. Paul stepped forward; all heads turned towards him.

"Yes, Silver and Gold are in overwatch just under a mile away and have been sending up to date data messages with imagery every thirty minutes."

"Good," Tyler looked at the two whiteboards. On the first one was a map with a red spot on a building, there were smaller maps of the larger area to one side of it. There were three large arrows drawn on the main map. The second board had several pictures of different people on it, some of them were carrying guns, with written notes beside them. Tyler looked over the boards, then looked at Dermott. "Ok, let's hear it!" Dermott stepped forward, he had a small notebook in his left hand and a pointer stick in the other. He faced the gathered crowd.

"Two days ago, two of our pack, Ian Silver and John Gold successfully tracked a leading Noc from the Salisbury coven to a remote farmhouse north of Bushmills, we believe that this Noc..." Dermott turned and pointed to the picture at the top of the second white board, "is none other than Martin Hanna," Dermott left the pointer on the picture of Martin. "This *IS* their 'Master Hunter' and a leading figure in the hierarchy of the leading coven in the whole of these islands," Dermott lowered his arm, "This Noc, for most of the last ten years has been the lead in their actions against us, we can only speculate as to the real number of Garou deaths he has been responsible for, but ...." he paused, "it is estimated to be over one hundred." Conversations and comments echoed over the pack, heads nodded, and faces contorted in anger. "We have an opportunity," he glanced at Tyler, then looked back at the crowd, "and we are going to take that opportunity that will have a serious effect on their ability to take action against our kind throughout Ireland and the rest of the UK." Dermott paused, "we believe he has come here to join up with 'The American' and organise other actions in the north. As you all know 'the American' has been dealt with, so before this guy disappears again, we are going to take him down." The crowd erupted in conversation, comments, nods, and observations.

"How many Nocs are there?" one voice asked, the crowd quietened again.

"Presently, just him, *but*" Dermott stepped to one side and pointed to another photograph, "he is surrounded by a close protection team of sapiens that are led by this man ..." Tyler moved around, closer to the crowd to look at the photograph Dermott was pointing at. "This is Mark Castle, sometimes called *'The Castle'* but mostly just referred to as *'Castle',*" Dermott dropped his arm again and looked back at the crowd, "Castle is a former Royal Marine Commando and was a member of their 'Commachio Company', which, as some of you know, were responsible for the protection of the Royal Navy's nuclear warheads when they were being transported between storage sites." There was another murmur of conversation that was stopped by Dermott, "since leaving the Royal Marines he has spent the last ten years on the close protection circuit and is highly experienced." Dermott turned to the crowd, "as for the rest of the team, we have identified a team of twelve that deploys around him, but we estimate at least two, if not four, left in the farmhouse to act as a base control and quick reaction team in the event of something happening." Tyler looked at Paul, he nodded, then looked back at Dermott.

"Are they armed?" one voice asked.

"Yes, Ian and John have sent us footage of them training with modern long barrelled weapons and Glock pistols, and from what we've seen, they know what they're doing.

"How do they deploy?" Tyler asked. Several heads looked at her, then everyone turned back to Dermott.

"They have three armoured 4 x 4, one of which is always in the garage attached to the side of the farmhouse ... here," Dermott pointed towards the photograph of the farmhouse, the crowd all stepped closer as Dermott continued. "The other two will deploy, but only after dark, with the Noc and his bodyguard in the first one and the security escort section," Dermott turned to look at them as he explained, "in the second, all standard BG stuff,"

"So, how are we going to do it?" Tyler's question stopped everything. All eyes turned and looked at her. Her stern face looked at Dermott. Dermott turned back to the whiteboards.

"I have broken this down into several phases, phase one: INFILTRATION: Keith from logistics is currently sorting out the transport for the different teams," Dermott looked over at Matt Cairns and the overwatch teams, "Overwatch will deploy to the drop off point .... here," he pointed at one of the arrows on the map. "You will take up positions, here and here. Your first task will be to take out the drivers of the vehicles and provide ECM cover."

"What distance are they at?" Tyler asked as she folded her arms.

"Four hundred metres,"

"And you said the 4 x 4 are armoured?"

"Yes," Dermott replied, "overwatch will take the .338 internationals, we have been told that the armour is only level three so they should not have any problem with that, plus at four hundred metres they will not have to aim off for wind or any other climatic conditions." Tyler looked over at the overwatch teams, she liked this so far, Dermott carried on, "John the Paramedic will go with overwatch as medical cover and Becky and Fiona, you will deploy with two others to here .... Along the tree line to the rear of the farmhouse, you will act as a cut off and quick reaction team," again serious faces and nods of heads, "that leaves the main assault group, and phase two, EXECUTION:" Dermott motioned to Ruth who was standing looking at the boards in front of her assault team. She had her rifle hanging over her shoulder, her helmet was tucked under her left arm and her assault vest now had armour plates behind it. There was mud on her boots. The rest of the assault team were dressed the same, everyone stood in silence. Dermot motioned to Ruth who stepped forward, into where Dermott had been standing.

"We will insert in two vans to the drop off point here ..." she turned and pointed at the map, then looked back at them, "from there we will silently move up through two RV points, here ...... and here .... Once at the final attack position, we will wait for the EMP to take effect then carry out simultaneous assaults on the farmhouse and the vehicles,"

"EMP?" Tyler asked, Ruth looked at her, but it was Paul who answered.

"Handheld Electro Magnetic Pulse generators, got two of them a couple of days ago,"

"Ok. What does it do?" Tyler asked. Ruth turned towards her and started to explain.

"The handheld generator is a 'once only' device, it creates an Electro Magnetic Pulse that disables any active electrical circuit in a sixty to seventy metre radius," Ruth smiled, "we know they use short distance radio communications, as well as 'in vehicle' comms, with the main base station inside the house, we take out that and all their electronic equipment they have installed, in short, the ones inside the house will be deaf and blind to what is going on outside and the same vice-versa!" Tyler smiled at the confident woman in front of her.

"I like it! So, how will you assault the house?" Tyler asked.

"Team one, led by me, will assault the vehicles at the front of the house at the same time the house itself will be assaulted from the rear," Ruth turned to the map and pointed at the red marker on it, "as we can see here, there is only one entrance to the farm and the single lane driveway is just under one hundred metres long, they only have three CCTV cameras that look down the lane and to each side of the house," Ruth looked around again, "the rear of the house is not covered!" Dermott stepped forward and took over the briefing again.

"Right, the farm house will be known as 'Alpha one, our friend 'Hanna' is 'Bravo one', the two vehicles at the front will be 'Charlie one,' which is this one, that they always park near the front door," Dermott again pointed towards the photographs of the 4 x 4's, "and 'Charlie Two' will be the second vehicle that they park over to the side of the parking area at the front of the house." Dermott turned to the crowd again, "Charlie Three is the one parked in the garage."

Again, heads nodded. Dermot paused to let it all sink in what they had just said. "Ok, phase four, REGROUP: once the assault is complete," he looked at Ruth, "the assault teams will carry out sensitive site exploitation, collect *everything* that may be of use to us, cameras, laptops, any hard drives, all paperwork etc and ..." he looked at the assault group, "make sure you get a DNA sample of every person onsite so we can ID them all, that will give us a better picture of who and what the Nocs are using these days. Only when complete, the assault teams will collapse back to the drop off point." Dermott pointed towards Matt, "Overwatch are to maintain position until all the assaulters at there, then they make their way there as well." Dermott stopped again, first her looked at Tyler then he looked over at Becky and Fiona. "Your team are to stay in place until everyone is off site, then you make your way back to your van," he turned to face everyone, "then everyone comes back here, all kit will be off loaded here, and we can go through everything we got!" All agreed. "Any questions?"

"How will the assault be initiated?" Tyler asked, Dermott looked at her.

"We have a distraction charge at the bottom end of the driveway, where it meets the main road, all their eyes will be looking in that direction."

"What about response from the police?" she asked, Paul stepped forward.

"Well, we have heard that nearly all on duty coppers are being called in to be on standby deal with a public order situation in the Heights in Coleraine," he stated.

"Are we expecting them to be used for that?" she asked, "because if they are all there, then they can all suddenly be deployed out to this?"

"Well," Paul started, "there has been trouble the last two nights and there is a local parade, that has been ruled 'illegal' by the police, so ... yeah, we are expecting them to be used there, and not to be anywhere near us!" All eyes turned towards Tyler, there was a concerned look on her face.

"What about afterwards, the police *will* investigate a shoot-out at a farmhouse."

"First of all, the ammunition we are using is either Spanish or Portuguese, nothing even remotely similar to what we have here, plus .... unless we are disturbed, there will not be any bodies for them to find ..." Dermott explained.

"We have an idea for the bodies," Paul injected as he looked at Dermott, "plus all of their weapons, which the police can trace, when they find them, will take their investigations to England .... Not here."

"Yippee!" exclaimed one of the assault squad, there was a shared laugh that rippled through them, they were confident about what they were going to do.

"What about the assault? What is inside the house?" Tyler asked.

Ruth turned towards her "We have a floor plan of the farmhouse, but it is nearly thirty years old, and looking at the pictures that Ian and John have sent, they show that the garage has been added and there has been some work out the back," Ruth looked over at Paul then back at Tyler, "we have been doing rehearsals on what we do know, apart from the garage, we are not expecting the inside of the house to be much different." "Plus, it is not a 'time critical' assault, so we can take time, be precise and deal with anything they have inside."

"Green light, do it!" Tyler almost whispered her approval, but everyone heard and there was an explosion of joy. Dermott raised his voice to calm them all down.

"Right then, everybody .... listen in ..." the different teams quietened down, and they all focused on Dermott, the difference this time was everyone was now smiling, and the level of excitement had escalated. "Don't forget, the people we are going up against are very good, they are professional at what they do," some smiles dropped to be replaced by serious looks again, Dermott carried on, "however," he smiled, "they have no idea we are coming, they are not expecting us, remember what we trained to do ...." Dermott looked around the faces again, "Remember, S-A-S'" he spelt out, "Speed – Aggression – Surprise, any two of them will produce the third, don't forget, we have two objectives here tonight, ONE: we all come home alive!" Dermott had raised his voice as he spoke, then he pointed at the picture behind him, "and TWO: we take this fucker down!" Tyler smiled as the collective cheer echoed around the arena. As the group started to disperse, Ruth shouted commands at the assault team, they would be doing another rehearsal before they deployed. Tyler stepped towards Dermott, they were joined by Paul, Tony, and Alison.

"Well, that all sounds fun!" Tony joked, "where do you want me?" he asked. Dermott glanced at Paul then looked at him.

"I want you, here, with a small team ready to go, just in case this all goes wrong,"

"I-" Tony started; Paul held up his hand to stop him.

"No, we want you, in a Land Rover, here beside the communications building, with five others, ready to go." Paul's tone made it clear, it was not a request,

"Ok." Tony had to obey.

"You are right about the police," Alison stated, everyone looked at her, "if they get anything about a gun battle, they will deploy everything they have," Alison's eyes darted around them, "What will you do if even one police car turns up?"

"Well," Dermott started, "we 'defend these lands,' not govern them, if a single police officer turns up, every single farm hand knows not to engage them," Dermott looked straight at her, "they are the law after all."

"They are," Alison confirmed.

"Well, we better make sure that situation doesn't happen then!" Tyler stated.

"I will take care of that," Paul spoke softly.

"Ok," Tyler looked at Paul, she was going to ask, then changed her mind. "So, Dermott, where will you be during all this?" she asked.

"Oh, I am setting off the distraction,"

"Oh, ok, and where am I then?" Tyler asked.

"Well, the best place to watch the show will be with Silver and Gold," Dermott smiled, nodding as he spoke, "you should get a grandstand view from there."

"And where exactly are they?" she asked. Dermott turned and pointed at the map.

"Here," he stepped back as she leaned towards the map looking at where she was going. "You can deploy with me, either Ian or John will pick you up from the drop off point,"

"Ok," Tyler now seemed a bit more relaxed. "When do we deploy?" she asked. Dermott looked at his watch. "In an hours' time,"

"What about me?" Alison asked.

"What about you?" Dermott replied.

"What do you want me to do?" she asked. Dermott and Paul looked at each other.

"When the troops get back would you be able to assist with going through everything they collect from the site?" Tyler asked. Dermott and Paul looked at each other again, deploying this one was out of the question.

"Yes, of course," Alison knew what that meant.

"How are you with 'babysitting'?" Paul asked with a smile.

"Well," Alison motioned towards Tony with her thumb, "I looked after this one for two years when he first came out of the training college."

"Hey!" Tony protested as the group shared a laugh. Dermott turned and started to take down the first of the white boards, Tyler and Paul turned to walk away, Alison looked at the picture of Martin Hanna.

"I am surprised the destroyer hasn't got him yet!" Tyler and Paul looked back at her.

"Who?" Paul asked, Alison looked at Paul then back at the picture.

"We called him, 'The Destroyer' as everyone who met him was destroyed, some don't believe he exists, but he can certainly let you know he is there," she looked at Tony, "he was in the woods near my house," then she looked over at Tyler, "he also watched you at White Park bay," Tyler and Paul looked at each other as she continued. "But here is the weird bit, it is like, he can just, *'turn it off'* as he can walk right up beside you without you even knowing,"

"What is his name?" Paul asked.

"Oh, it was weird, something Greek I think," Alison replied.

"Oh, you mean 'Jason'" Tyler smiled.

"You know of him?" Alison asked, Tyler looked at Paul, both smiled,

"Met him briefly above Belfast a while ago," she looked back at Alison, "and yeah, he can just creep up on you," Tyler and Paul let out a short laugh.

"Are you not worried about him?" Alison asked.

"Why should we be?" Dermott asked, "he kills Nocs, he is no threat to us!"

"We have an understanding with him and his little 'crusade' he has got going on," Tyler smiled and turned to walk away. Paul winked at Alison then turned and followed her. Tony nudged Alison and motioned with his head for them to follow Tyler and Paul.

"Thanks for the briefing," Tony patted Dermott on the shoulder. Dermott nodded and lifted the first whiteboard under his arm and started to carry it over to the side of the arena.

"So," Alison asked as they got outside, Tyler and Paul were already at the front door of the farmhouse, "what do we do until then?" she asked.

"Fancy a brew?" Tony asked.

"Sure. You are not concerned about this guy at all?" she asked.

"As Dermott said, he is no threat to us," Tony stated. "And from what I hear about him," Tony looked at her, "kinda glad of that," the phone in his pocket started to ring. He pulled the phone out and looked at the name on the screen. "Hi darling," he said as he answered it.

∞∞∞∞

Cara-Marie looked at the screen of her phone to see who it was that was calling.

"Hi Laura,"

"Hi Cara," it was police officer Laura Patterson, she was whispering, "you probably know already but we've all been called into work this evening,"

"Yeah," she lied, "but I don't know what it's about? Is it something important?"

"Tactical Support is expecting trouble around the heights in Coleraine tonight.

"Ok, any ideas as to what time things are happening?" Cara-Marie asked.

"Laura whispered, *"gotta go,"* and the call ended. Cara-Marie scrolled though her phone then pressed the green call button.

"I'm not in!" Mark's voice answered, Cara-Marie laughed.

"Yeah, I have been convinced that you have not been 'in' for years, but hey-ho," Cara-Marie started to tie the lace on the trainer.

"What cannot wait until tomorrow then?" he sighed.

"Meet me in the office in fifteen minutes and I will tell you."

Chapter 41

Jason Apollyon shifted slightly where he was lying. He lifted the military binoculars' and looked over the farmhouse where the security team were doing a walkthrough drill. They had not spotted what the wolves were doing, but then, the wolves had not spotted him either, they were focused on their prey. He looked over to where the two trackers were, they had gotten a stalking rifle out and had just been joined by the female wolf called Tyler. They were lying along the hedgerow; everyone was looking down towards the farmhouse. Along the side of the re-entrant they had moved two other small teams who had stalking rifles, they were in perfect overwatch positions, the wolves were going to do something. Lights suddenly came on all around the farmhouse, both the 4 x 4s and the two small groups of men could clearly be seen. Jason watched as the team leader shouted commands at the two groups of men, they started their slow walk through again. Jason watched what they were doing, they knew their jobs, but with the lights, illuminating the front of the house like that they were not expecting any company, that would have just destroyed any low light vision with the team members. Jason paused. His eyes moved over to the back of the farmhouse; he could sense there were wolves there, but he could not see them yet. He lifted the binoculars again and watched as a single figure slowly made its way, silently towards the rear of house. He was carrying what looked like a flask in one hand, the G36 rifle was controlled by his right hand, he placed the flask out of sight then moved back into the darkness. Jason smiled; he would enjoy watching whatever they were about to do. He felt the phone in his pocket vibrate. With slow, silent, deliberate movements, he placed the binoculars' down, then rolled onto his side before pulling the phone out of his pocket. He had already cancelled the screen light and it was silent. He read Paul Hawkins name on the screen, he glanced around, no one was near him, then he opened the message. 'HI, CAN WE MEET,' Jason looked at the date and time, it had been sent nearly two hours ago. He would reply tomorrow.

∞∞∞∞

"Ok guys, that was good," Castle started, all eyes turned to him, he reached up and touched the earpiece that was in his right ear, "control, thanks for the lights .... Next time, tell me first as you just ruined my night vision!" There was a collective chuckle. A voice came through the earpiece.

"No problem, thought you all could do with a surprise!" Mark Castle looked up at the window on the upper floor of the large house where the control room was. The window had been darkened so no one could see in, but the two guys in there could see out, he could just picture them sitting at the table with the screens of the three CCTV cameras, looking out the window, smiling at their prank. The table was pushed up against the wall so the one nearest the window had a clear view up the lane to the main road. Behind the two in the control room was a single camp bed with a sleeping bag stretched out on it. The weapons rack was against the wall on the same side as the table, when they were in the house, that is where the rifles were kept, there was no direct threat at the farmhouse as no one knew they were there. Castle looked back at the two small teams, one was gathering around the front of the second 4 x 4 and the other near the back of the 4 x 4 he was at the far side of. The 4 x 4's had their drivers inside, the one nearest him had the engine running as it was starting to get cold at night, they were all relaxed. The 4 x 4 that he was near was close to the front door and pointed down the lane. The other was parked at the side of the gravelled reception area that was outside the front of the farmhouse.

The whole of the front of the house was lit up by the very bright security lights they had installed just before they had come over.

"Right, what do you want us to go through this time?" the team member that was closest to him asked. Castle looked at him but before he could speak there was a shrieking noise that came from his earpiece that made him rip it out, at the same time all the lights went out, the area was in darkness. Everyone suddenly turned to the car that had just crashed into the gatepost at the entrance to the lane. Castle's body tensed, his grip on his weapon tightened.

"Boss, …" another member asked. Castle stepped forward, his eyes searching the darkness, was that a figure running away? He could not tell as his eyes were no longer accustomed to the darkness. Suddenly, the car exploded and a plum of fire rose from it, into the night sky. Castle felt his body tense again, this wasn't right. From the far side of the re-entrant a single bright ball leapt from the hillside and like a small shooting star burned its way through the night until it was over the lane. It burst and night became day. Something buzzed past Castle's head and there was a sound from the front of the 4x4, the distant gunshots echoed around the valley. Castle looked at the smashed glass of the windscreen, the driver was down.

"CONTACT LEFT!" He screamed as he sprinted the short distance to the front of the second 4 x 4, it would be cover for him. Around him team members started screaming commands to each other, everyone had their weapons up, Castle slammed into the front wheel arch of the 4 x 4, he looked around the front of the vehicle so he would not silhouette himself for whoever was engaging them. The butt of his weapon was in his shoulder, his right hand on the pistol grip of the rifle and his left on the front stock. His eyes searched the darkness for anything to reveal the location of his attacker.

∞∞∞∞

Jason kept the binoculars firmly pressed to his eyes. The wolves had got total surprise, he guessed they used some sort of counter measures to knocks out the security lights, then the distraction charge that now blocked their only route in, then the flare. For the sapiens, it was an extremely bad tactical situation. Jason had smiled as the overwatch engaged both the drivers as the flare had gone off, he looked over at the first assault team stacked up at the side of the wall of the farmhouse; the second stacked up on the back door. A small charge had gone off and the assaulters were inside the farmhouse. Jason moved the binoculars as the flare started to burn out and the assault team went around the corner. The first two started to engage the team members that were close to the 4 x 4 at the side, the next two moved, side by side in a fast walk that he had done many times, heel to toe, he recognised the technique of walking very quickly, keeping a rifle in a firing position and engaging targets all at the same time. Jason watched as the last two of the assault team stopped at the corner of the farmhouse, they were the backup. Team members rocked as bullets slammed into them, a few rounds were fired back, but they were inaccurate and ineffective.

Jason watched the security team leader jump up and turn to fire at the two assaulters that were sweeping down the side of the 4 x 4, he rocked, then spun as both G-36 rifles spat at him. The flare in the sky died and darkness crept over the front of the house. Jason relaxed and looked over the top of the binoculars and pressed a small button on them. When he looked through them again everything was green, but it was clear. The passive image intensifier worked very well. Jason watched as the assault team moved over the bodies lying on the ground, pausing before firing one round into each head of the defeated security team. They were not leaving anyone alive. There was movement from where the two trackers and Tyler were. She stood up and started to run along the hedge row to a gap then she headed down towards the farmhouse, both trackers packed up their equipment then followed her.

225

The area to the front of the farmhouse was secure. As some assaulters stood guard, others started to search the bodies that were on the ground. There was a sudden flurry of movement, shouts echoed around as a lone figure sprinted away from the far side of the 4 x 4 that was near the front door of the farmhouse. Weapons were raised, Jason looked at the figure, he was injured and was cradling an arm as he ran, one of the assaulters was waving their arms to stop those who were about to shoot. Jason looked at the way one of them started giving directions and instructions, the smaller wolf was in charge. One of the wolves suddenly started pulling off their clothes, they were in a rush, the young male started to drop his equipment onto the ground. As the female Tyler approached, the young male was struggling with his boots, he certainly was very keen to get naked, now this was something that he had never seen during an assault, why would he suddenly want to take off his clothes? Jason watched as the young, now naked male stood in front of Tyler, there was a discussion and the lead assaulter pointing with their right forefinger in the direction of the sapien that was running away. They then looked back at the male who went down on one knee as Tyler turned and walked towards the front door of the farmhouse.

A small smile spread over Jason face. He had never seen a wolf changing before. Slowly the wolf stood up and looked around, Jason had to admit, he looked a magnificent creature. The assault leader patted him on the shoulder, and he took off after his prey. Jason moved so he could watch as the outside team started to collect the weapons and began to pass bags around for everything that came off each of the security team would be taken and searched. Jason knew what they were doing, he had done it enough times himself.

∞∞∞∞

"Up here!" the sound of Ruth's voice echoed down the stairs. Tyler jumped up the stairs clearing them three at a time. The first patch of blood was at the top of the stairs, Ruth's smiling face was in the only doorway on the left. The landing reached out to the right and had several doors along it. Tyler smiled back as Ruth pulled her helmet off. "Got them in here," she said as she stepped in the room. Tyler looked to her right, all the doors were open and there was movement coming from them, the search of the property was in full swing. Tyler stopped in the entrance to the small room. One body had been dragged back in and was laid along the wall on the left. A second body laid beside it. Ruth was the only one in the room, she walked over to the table with the communications equipment on it. The three small screens of the CCTV were blank. Tyler looked at the splattered blood on the wall to the left of the single window, the second sapien had been at the table when the assaulters entered the room.

"So, what have we got?" Tyler asked.

"We have a well-equipped, close protection team, that's armed with illegal weapons."

"But what of the Noc? Where is he?" Tyler demanded. The smile fell from Ruth's face as a howl echoed outside, it was followed by a cheer from those outside.

"Don't know, he isn't here." Ruth explained, Tyler stepped forward.

"What do you mean? Not here? I thought this was his lair!" Ruth walked towards her, pointing down the stairs as she did so.

"It is, we found it downstairs, got two going through it now, but there is a third vehicle missing as well as the Noc, his bodyguard and a 4 x 4 that was 'supposed' to be in the garage ..." Ruth shrugged, "which it isn't, he isn't here," Tyler took an angry breath in.

"Shit," she spat.

∞∞∞∞

"Kill the lights!" Glenn demanded, "stop here!" he shouted from the passenger seat. The driver pulled the vehicle over to the side of the road, the smell of the boxes of take away food still filled the inside of the 4 x 4 but they no longer cared. Up ahead the entrance to the lane was partially blocked by a burning car and the farmhouse was in darkness. Two vans they did not recognise were out the front and there were several people walking around.

"*Wolves,*" Martin hissed. Glenn looked at him then at the driver.

"Reverse, reverse, extract!" Glenn shouted.

∞∞∞∞

Becky and Fiona were huddled together, the other two were still watching the farmhouse. Becky looked up as the last van started to drive along the lane and headed out past the burnt-out car that had been pushed out of the way.

"Is that the last of them?" she asked. The farm hand looked back at her, cradling the stalking rifle as he did so.

"Think so, hang on," he looked away and touched the communicator in his ear. "Delta, Tango Mike, are we nearly complete ... over?" Fiona snuggled into her sister.

"I hope so, I am freezing," she stated, "how long has it been now?" she asked, Becky looked at her watch.

"Well, the assault was four hours ago, and it is nearly sunrise, so hopefully we'll be moving soon," she reassured. They all heard Dermott's voice in their ears.

"Roger, Tango Mike, stay in location, you will be the last to lift off."

"Roger, Delta," the farmhand confirmed, "how long would you like us to stay in location for?" the farm hand asked. There was a pause before Dermott answered.

"Until just after sunrise in half an hour then follow us back to the farm,"

"Roger," the farmhand replied. He looked back at the two girls.

"Well, we will not be needing these then," Becky stated as she lifted the G36 rifle from her lap and reached for the day sack beside her. She took out the empty flask who contents they had all been consuming with the excitement of watching the assault and then the chase down afterwards. They all now knew the Noc they were after was not there, so they had to look elsewhere now. Becky collapsed the stock down and pushed the rifle inside.

"Yeah, we might as well pack up," the farm hand stated as he turned around. Becky and Fiona stood up and Fiona watched as the last Land Rover from the farm drove away, the fire in the farmhouse had already taken hold, the large farmhouse would be fully ablaze before anyone even phoned the fire brigade.

"Back in a minute, I need to pee!" Fiona stated as she climbed through the hedgerow behind them. The two guys shared a smile and Becky opened her eyes and looked around.

"Better make sure we leave nothing behind," she remarked.

"Hey, isn't that one of the SAS guys?" one of the farmhands asked. They all looked around at the single figure that was walking along the hedgerow. He was wearing boots, jeans and a thick outdoor jacket, the woollen beanie hat was pulled down over his head, his hands tucked deep into the pockets of the jacket. When he looked up, he smiled as he approached.

"Chris!" Becky exclaimed, "what are you doing here?" she asked. He smiled then stopped about thirty metres away without saying a word.

The bullets slammed into her back and sent her sprawling forward into the mud of the field. She could hear the gunfire and the cries of the farmhands but there was nothing she could do about it. Pain rocked through her body as a boot lodged itself under her armpit and with a movement flicked her over onto her back.

227

"Fi, run, run," she whispered as Chris appeared above her. He looked down at her and smiled, then he looked up as Fiona stepped closer and threw her arms around him.

"Hi darling," he said as he kissed the excited face in front of him. Confusion racked through Becky's mind, 'What? No, this didn't make sense', she tried to move her arms, she still had her pistol on her belt, Fiona looked at her sister and stood on her arm.

"Fi .... Why?" Becky fought for breath.

"Oh, you know how you wanted to meet my new man well," Fiona nearly giggled as she stepped back and held out a hand, with the palm uppermost towards Chris. "I believe you know, *my lover,* Mr Chris Abbey of the SAS!" The two looked at each other and smiled, Chris leaned towards her and passionately kissed her again.

"We need to get going," he glanced down at the contorted face of Becky before looking at the stern-faced Fiona. "Good shooting by the way, but get it done," he commanded then stepped out of view, "we need to be somewhere else." Becky tried to breathe, but every movement racked her with pain, she focused in on the face she knew, the face that looked down at her. Fiona shrugged.

"Sorry about this, but hey!" Becky looked at the end of the barrel of the pistol that suddenly came into focus, she could see the blade foresight, the notched rear sight was formed behind it, and it sat in the middle of Fiona's eye. A perfect sight picture. Becky saw the top slide of the pistol move, Fiona went out of focus, she did not hear the sound as the head of the bullet slammed into her face, just under her right eye, the head of the bullet passed through her head and lodging in the soft earth underneath where Becky's head rested. "What shall we do with them?" Fiona asked as she looked around. Chris went down on one knee and unzipped one of the rifle bags. He looked over the pristine weapon. He picked it up and placed the butt of the weapon in his shoulder, he looked through the scope, Fiona looked at him, she walked over to him and caressed his shoulder. "You look like a cat that just got the cream!" she giggled as she spoke. Chris looked up at her with an excited look on his face.

"I have," he stood up and kissed her on the lips again. He then looked at the three dead bodies that were lying on the ground. "Take the weapons, leave the rest," he looked back along the hedge row, "we need to get moving," he looked back at her, "we don't have long!"

Chapter 42

Cara-Marie looked at the screen of her desktop computer. Her right hand moved the mouse, and she saved all three stories to the editors drop box. It was a normal day, the reception staff were busy, reporters engrossed in their work and Mark was staring at his own screen.

"I forgot to ask," she started, Mark mumbled a reply but did not look in her direction. "How did things go in court the other day?" First his eyes darted over to her then his body moved slowly as it leaned over to his left, so he was looking around the side of the monitor.

"I told you last night," he stated as he sat upright again. Cara-Marie thought for a moment over all the things they had done the previous evening.

"When?" she asked.

"Remember when the parade in the Heights started getting lively and the police broke up that crowd about to start a riot?" Mark was looking back at his screen as he carried on.

"Yes," she confirmed.

"During that," music started to come from his desktop, he was looking at footage she could not see. She paused a few seconds; she could not remember if he had told her anything.

"Ok, re-fresh my memory." Mark looked over towards her but before he could answer Kevin loomed into view.

"Oh Cara, have you got the articles from last night done yet?"

"Yes," she replied as she pointed towards her monitor, "I just uploaded all three into your drop box," she smiled as she spoke.

"Brill, something else for you," he looked down at the paper in his hand. I just heard the fire brigade is at a farmhouse near Ballycastle," he handed her the paper "this is the address. I hear it is completely gutted and they think it was started deliberately."

"Yeah, I know where this is!" she stated.

"Great, pop out and see what is going on, then do a couple of hundred words for us." She looked up as he walked away before she could ask the next question. There was a pause, she looked at Mark who again leaned to one side, appearing around his monitor.

"Fancy a drive?" she suggested.

"Your car or mine?" he asked.

"Mine,"

"Lunch before or after?"

"After,"

"Great," he exclaimed as he stood up, "afterwards means you are paying and that is always good!" Mark was smiling as he reached for his coat.

"Yeah, I suppose," she said as she clicked on the 'shutdown' icon. By the time the computer shut down and she stood up to pull her coat on, Mark was already standing outside with his hands in his pockets and his camera bag over his shoulder. As the rear door of the office closed behind her, she stopped beside him, he was looking up at the darkening clouds.

"It is going to rain later," he stated. Cara-Marie felt herself shiver; it was getting colder now. She looked up at what he was looking at.

"Yeah, probably," she remarked, she turned and started to walk away, "are you coming or are you just going to stand there and get wet?" she asked as she looked back over her left shoulder. Mark's mind was elsewhere, that much was obvious.

"Oh, ok," he jumped back into the present then started off after her. They both walked side by side towards the end of the road where the crossing would take them into Tesco's carpark. Mark did not speak as they stopped and waited for the crossing. Cara-Marie smiled and waved at someone walking down the pavement on the far side of the road, Mark did not respond, it was almost as if he could not see anyone. The traffic stopped and the green light appeared. The two people on the other side of the road started to walk towards them before they set off themselves. Mark followed her blindly as she walked across the road and into the car park, she headed directly for her car with Mark in tow. It did not take her long to be settled in the car, with Mark in the passenger seat and the camera bag behind his ankles in the footwell of the passenger seat. Cara-Marie slowly manoeuvred the car through the car park and out the other side. They followed the flow of traffic along past the large Chinese restaurant on the riverbank, straight through the traffic lights then straight on. It wasn't until they got further away from the office that Cara-Marie started the conversation again.

"So, you didn't say what happened in court the other day?" she kept her focus on the road, other traffic and what was going on outside the car, but she did spot the way his body tensed at the question. This was difficult for him.

"You would not believe me if I told you!" he stated.

"Try me," she replied as she slowed down at a junction.

"Well," he shifted where he was sitting, he was now uncomfortable, the car moved off and out into the countryside heading towards Ballycastle. "She has tried to stop all access, she wants me to sell my flat, she wants 50% of all my savings, all my assets and she demanded the judge to order that 50% of my wages, pre-tax go to her!"

"What?" Cara-Marie tensed up. "She can't do that!" she protested, "on what grounds?"

"When the judge started questioning her, she fired back 'he is completely irrational and that she is entitled to everything." Mark looked at her, "that is when it all went south."

"What do you mean?" Cara-Marie asked.

"When the judge asked her to back up her claims, she turned on the judge."

"That's not good,"

"No, I had already been able to show that for the last few months every time I had gone at the pre-arranged time to collect the baby, she had blocked it, refused me entrance or had taken the baby somewhere else," Mark glanced at her again, "even got her mum involved,"

"Really?"

"Yes, really, when the social worker took the stand, she tore into them pointing out I had done everything expected of me and that she was the one being obstinate," a small smile spread over his face, "You should have seen the way she reacted when the judge found in my favour, she jumped up and called the judge 'a fucking idiot' and she wasn't going to be doing anything of the sort!"

"What did the judge do next?" Cara-Marie asked.

"Found her in contempt of court, issued her a fine and all contact between me and her is to be through the social worker .... she sacked her solicitor for not getting her exactly what she wanted, went into a rage and the judge threw her out of the court room," Mark paused as Cara-Marie speeded up on the open country road. "But that wasn't the end,"

"Oh, how so?" she slowed down behind a tractor that had just pulled out of a field.

"The social worker then stood up to make a submission, which the judge allowed,"

"What was the submission?" she accelerated and overtook the slow-moving tractor.

"She put forward that my ex was the main problem and wanted her to be declared an 'unfit mother', which my ex's mother protested,"

"That is to be expected, what did the judge say?" Cara-Marie asked.

"She said the social worker would have to put forward a case highlighting all her reasons for doing so," Mark looked out of the window at the passing green countryside. "Which the social worker is going to do." Cara-Marie felt him welling up, he was trying to stop himself from crying, which was something he had never done in front of her. She glanced sideways at him, then slowed down to take the right turn that would lead down to the farm.

"We are nearly there," she said quietly as the car waited until the traffic had cleared before she turned the car down the narrow road. The two sat in silence as they followed the rise and fall of the country road that was lined with trees and hedgerows. They passed the occasional house, some had pristine front gardens, others did not. The road rose over a hill and the small valley opened-up in front of them. They could see the farm; its roof was gone, and the building was only a shell. There were still two fire engines at the end of the lane with several other vehicles parked along it. But they were all near the entrance of the lane, not close to ruined farmhouse, they both recognised the white truck of the military bomb disposal team at the front of the line of vehicles, Cara-Marie was more interested in this than she had been before.

"What the hell is going on here?" Mark asked out loud. Cara-Marie slowed the car down so they could take a better look as they cruised past. The end of the lane was blocked by fire service vehicles and some others that Cara-Marie recognised as police. There were three more cars parked along the road on the right-hand side that made passing them difficult. Cara-Marie pulled in at the end of the line of cars.

"Right, let us see what is going on here then!" she stated as she released her seat belt, grabbed her large bag with one hand then opened the car door with the other, Mark was already out and reaching for his camera bag that had been under his legs.

"Yeah," he replied as she shut the driver's door. She stopped and surveyed the scene in front of her. The six wheeled remote-control robot from the bomb disposal was making its way along the lane, there were a collection of soldiers at the rear of the white truck, Cara-Maire spotted the two police officers who were with the soldiers then there were both the fire engines with a lot of bored looking fire fighters standing around with little, or nothing to do. The entrance to the lane was cordoned off with tape and was guarded by another two uniformed police officers. Cara-Marie started to walk around the side of her car to join Mark on the road when a single male figure ran from the far side of the fire engines, ducked under the police tape, and jumped into the driver's side of the car that was first in the line. The car roared into life, reversed slightly then shot past them, Mark had to jump into the space at the rear of her car to avoid it. As it went past, she saw the concerned look of the sole occupant. The car sped up the road and away from them. "What the hell?" Mark protested.

"Darren Forester," her response was just louder than a whisper.

"What?" Mark asked. She turned and looked at him.

"Darren Forester, he is in special branch ...." Cara-Marie stepped past Mark and headed towards the two police officers that were on the cordon.

"Hey, wait up," Mark got to her as she started to question the police.

"Well," the older one started, "you will have to speak to the senior fire office," he pointed to the only fire fighter that wasn't dressed to fight a fire. "That is him there."

"I'll get him," the second officer walked towards the group of fire fighters.

"So, what happened here? And why is the bomb disposal here?" she asked. The police officer shrugged and turned to look at the figure approaching. Cara-Marie glanced at the burnt-out wreck of a car in the corner of the field; neither the fire service nor the police seemed to be interested in it. Mark took a step back and swung his camera bag around, she would leave him to take all the pictures they would need. The police officer walked to the far end of the cordon as the short, well-dressed man made his way towards her with his hand outstretched towards her. He was wearing leather boots that recently had a shine on them, his dark trousers she recognised as part of a fire service uniform, his white pressed shirt was underneath the dark coloured waterproof jacket that had the Fire Service emblem on the left-hand side. He had a zipped-up leather folder in his left hand, the small woollen beanie hat covered his bald head.

"Ahh, always happy to talk to the press!" he exclaimed as the two shook hands,

"Hi, Cara-Marie McKenna, Coleraine Herald," she introduced herself. The short man released the handshake and smiled back at her.

"Yes, I remember you from last year, we have met before,"

"Oh," she fought to remember where they had met.

"You meet a lot of people in your job," he chuckled quietly, "don't worry, I would not remember me either!" he laughed as she was taking out her notebook.

"I am sorry ..." she paused.

"Senior Fire Officer Crawford," he injected. Mark walked over to where the police officer was standing and raised his camera, Cara looked at the fire officer and asked her first question.

"So, what exactly happened here?" The short man smiled and took a breath in before starting a well-prepared statement.

"The fire service responded to a call from the police to attend this site, when we got here the fire was well established," she started making shorthand notes, she did not interrupt him as he continued, "the roof and top floor had already collapsed when we arrived and we were informed there was no threat to life, so I established two teams to bring the fire under control. I placed one team at the right-hand corner to control the front and the right-hand side of the building and the second team at the opposite side of the property to control the left and the rear of the house," he turned back towards her, "it took us several hours, but the fire has now been extinguished." Cara-Marie noted what he had said, yes, she now remembered him from before.

"So, what is bomb disposal doing here?" she asked. The firefighter glanced at the police officer then answered the question.

"Well, we had started our clean-up operations when one of our firefighters stepped into a small pit that had been recently dug; that is where we discovered at least ten, military grade M-16 type rifles," he carried on, "we confirmed the find, we cordoned and then controlled the site then informed the police who have called in the army to ensure the scene is safe.!"

"Excellent, so no one was home, any idea how the fire started?" she asked as the second police officer returned and stood beside the other officer.

"We have spoken with the landlord, it was on a long term let but he was not aware of who was staying there, the cause of the fire will be investigated and the result of that will be shared with the police when it is completed," he smiled again.

"Any chance we could get a little closer?" Mark asked.

"Sorry, but this is the safe distance we have to control until the site is declared safe by the bomb squad."

"So, about the guns ..." Cara-Marie started,

"That would be a police matter," the fire fighter replied before she could finish her question. She looked at him then towards the two police officers.

"Is that why Special Branch was here?" she pointed with her thumb in the direction they had watched Darren driving off in.

"You will have to ask them that!" the older police officer replied. Cara-Marie looked back at her notes.

"Unfortunately, I don't drive that fast so I would never catch him up,"

"They haven't gone far," the younger police officer started, both Cara-Marie and Mark looked up as he turned and pointed with his right hand towards the far hillside. "They are at the site of the three murders just over there, you can just follow the road round." Even before she said thank you, she was already running towards her car with Mark running after her as he knew she would not wait. The younger police office shrugged, "well, it got the press out of here, so that means we don't have to talk to them any longer," he smiled.

"Aye, I suppose," the older officer answered as Cara-Marie's car burst into life and took off up the road.

Chapter 43

Darren Forester made his way up the trodden path towards the group of people in white disposable forensic suits. He was wearing the same, his trainers were covered, as were his hands and face. He looked up as the small group of people stopped talking and turned towards the figure, they did not recognize that was coming towards them; he stopped as he arrived beside them. His eyes darted over to the domed crime scene tent covering whatever happened. Nearby two of the crime scene team were taking photographs, there was a small gathering at the entrance to the tent, he spotted movement from the far side of the hedgerow.

"Right, what is happening here?" he asked as he straightened up, he was taking a few breaths, but he wasn't out of breath.

"Who the hell wants to know!" a female voice demanded. It came from the figure directly opposite him. His body reacted to the aggression. He straightened up and looked into the defiant face behind the mask.

"SUPERINTENDENT FORESTER …. SPECIAL BRANCH," he almost shouted as he placed his hands on his hips, others looked down, or away, "and who is behind that mask?" he looked into the light blue eyes, he recognised the face of Inspector Wells, but he was going to make her say it. She pulled the mask down from her face but continued to glare at him.

"Superintendent, this is a crime scene that is under my investigation, and I," Darren cut her off by walking through the centre of the group forcing them to step back, he didn't bump into her but the way she moved to the side it looked like he had.

"Inspector Wells, I will ask you again, 'what is happening here?'"

"Superintendent, do I have to remind you that …." Darren spun round, pulled down his mask and screamed at her.

"INSPECTOR WELLS, DO I HAVE TO REMIND YOU THAT YOU ARE ADDRESSING A SUPERIOR OFFICER! DO NOT TAKE THAT TONE WITH ME! I AM NOT ASKING FOR YOUR CO-OPERATION, I – AM – DEMANDING IT!" Everyone at the scene stopped and looked at them. Mary Wells looked at him, she was obviously choosing her words carefully.

"Sir, this crime scene is currently under Major Investigations," she glanced down then back up at him again, "and since that, this investigation is under my command," she repeated, Darren stepped towards her and leaned forward.

"Inspector Wells, …. I am not asking 'who is in charge' or what department is doing what, what I AM asking, for the third time, 'what happened here?'"

"Sir, I think …."

"I am not asking 'what you think'? I am asking 'what happened here!" Darren was getting angry, he looked over her shoulder at the small group of figures that were behind her. "Sergeant, since your inspector can't answer a simple question, I will ask you, 'what happened here'?" One of the figures moved, then spoke through their mask.

"Sir, three people died of gunshot wounds,"

"Great," Darren straightened up, "that is all I wanted to know." He turned away from them before starting to head towards the domed tent.

"Superintendent," Mary Wells continued, "when this crime scene investigation is complete, I will be happy to share that information with your department, and any help that you can provide in assisting with 'our' investigation will be readily received, but in the meantime may I …" Darren spun round and pointed back towards the farmhouse.

"What just happened down there?"

"What?"

"What just happened down there?" he repeated.

"There was a fire, so? That has nothing to do with our current investigation," Darren turned back towards her and stepped closer again.

"Oh really? What about the fourteen military grade assault rifles that are currently being recovered or the fact that there is also an improvised range out the back of that farmhouse where those weapons have been fired ..." he pointed back towards the domed tent, "they died of gunshot wounds, yes?"

"I, err," she started.

"And a weapons find less than a mile and a half away from three people who died of gunshot wounds could be considered significant, could it not?" Darren's eyes moved to the team behind her who were now looking at each other, none of them knew about that. "And I have no doubt that you will be sending one of your team to liaise with my detective sergeant who is down there currently just to establish if those weapons were involved with your current investigation." He looked directly at her. She paused, then looked back over her shoulder at a figures who nodded, turned, and started back down the path he had come up.

"Thank you," she whispered as she looked back at him.

"Have you identified the three people yet?" he asked the wider group.

"Yes Sir," one of them replied, "they all live and work at a Deer farm near Kilrea,"

"What?" that was something he did not know.

"We have spoken with them already and there are two people on the way to give us a positive identification for them," Darren nodded then looked back at the tent. "Sir, there is obviously something 'bigger picture' going on, is there anything your department can shed some light on that will help us with our investigation?" Darren looked back over his shoulder at where the voice had come from, Mary Wells spun round and glared at the voice as well.

"Of course, happy to help," he spoke softly, but loud enough for everyone to hear, "let me know when you're free. I can drop into your office, then we can chat," Darren smiled. Behind the team a figure who was also dressed in a white disposable suit was walking up the hill carrying empty forensic bags. The young woman shuffled past, unaware of what had just happened.

"The press is here!" she stated. She did not look at anyone, she just walked past them all and headed towards the tent. Darren turned and looked back at Mary again.

"So," he started, "Mary," she looked up at him as he used her first name, he carried on, "shall we start again?" There was a faint smile from her, Darren looked around the masked faces behind her then focused in on her. "so, what has been happening here?" he asked quietly.

∞∞∞∞

Tyler looked tired as she walked into the kitchen of the farmhouse. The sound of a crying baby had now stopped, Rhydian smiled as she walked past and then headed up the stairs. Paul and Tony were standing at the far side of the table, both looked concerned, Paul had his phone to his right ear.

"Hang on, Tyler has just walked in, going to put you on speaker phone," Paul took the phone away from his head and tapped at the screen.

"Who is it?" she asked.

"Dermott," Tony replied, Paul placed the phone on the table.

"Okay, you are on speaker phone now, there are only three of us here," Paul stated.

"What is happening?" Tyler asked, Dermott's voice crackled down the phone.

"Well, it is Becky and two of the over watch, but there is no sign of Fiona," Tyler leaned forward and placed her hands on the kitchen table, Dermott carried on, "the police, currently aren't linking them to the farm, but that fella from special branch is here,"

"What? that Sergeant, Mike Dear?" Tony asked.

234

"No, his boss, the Superintendent, Forester,"

"Dermott, any idea of what happened to them?" Tyler asked.

"They have been shot, close range, the guys were shot in the back and Becky, it looks like she was lying on the ground when she got it in the head," Dermott explained.

"No sign of Fi?" Paul asked.

"None,"

"Could it have been those from the farm?" Tony asked.

"Don't be fucking stupid!" Dermott's voice echoed from the phone around the kitchen, "we took care of all of them."

"Well, not all, the Noc and his bodyguard were not there," Paul stated.

"Could this have been the Noc?" Tyler lowered her head towards the phone.

"Not sure, the police aren't telling me much, they just wanted me to confirm the ID's they found on them,"

"Did you tell them about Fiona?" Tony asked.

"Yes, but there is no sign she was there, plus they did get excited when they went through their pockets Becky had two full magazines for her Sig pistol,"

"Have the police recovered their weapons?" Paul asked.

"No, whoever did it took them as well," Dermott explained, getting angry.

"Dermott," Tyler spoke.

"Yes," he replied. Tyler lowered her head then looked at the screen of Paul's phone.

"From what you can see, what do you think happened? And have you any idea who could have done this?" there were a few moments of silence before he started.

"Just from what I could see, the firing point was from behind the hedge, whoever it was, got the drop on them," Everyone in the kitchen looked at each other.

"Impossible!" Tony protested, "all four of them would have known about anyone getting that close!"

"No sign at all of Fiona?" Paul asked.

"None, I … err, hang on …" Dermott had taken the phone away and there were muffled sounds, he was speaking to someone else, then his voice came back on. "Okay, can I phone you back, the police would like to chat again,"

"Sure, no problem," Tyler stated as she stood up.

"Okay," he replied then the call was cut off.

"So, there can be little doubt then," Paul started. Tyler folded her arms; she had a stern look on her face.

"There are more Nocs than we know about, they 'somehow' got close, and they have Fiona!" Tyler was furious, Paul nodded.

"But why not kill her as well?" Tony asked. Paul looked down and reaching out with his fingers touched the edge of the table.

"They have taken a wolf as a trophy," Paul spoke quietly.

"But why take a girl …." Tony stopped himself as the other two looked at him, he could answer his own question. There was silence, wolves taken by Nocs did not survive.

"She will have a gruesome end, and it will be public," Tyler explained, "they like showing off their victories like that!" there was anger in her words. She unfolded her arms, "how many Nocs do we know about?" she demanded.

"Just two, the Nocs we were after at the farm, Hanna," Paul glanced at Tony before looking back at her, "then this one that slipped up here from near Limerick,"

"Megan Due," Tony added.

"Do we know where she is?" Tyler looked at Paul.

"Well, if I had to guess …." He started. Tyler's hand slapped the table.

"I don't want you to guess, I want to KNOW!" she glared at them.

"Then I don't know," Paul replied.

"Right, I want them both found, and found now!" Paul and Tony nodded, Paul turned and went to walk past Tony. He stopped at looked over at Tyler.

"I will speak to Silver and Gold, and find out everything they have," he stated.

"Okay," Tyler had lowered her voice. Paul headed for the door, "Oh, does their father know yet?" Tyler shouted after him. Paul stopped in the doorway and looked back at her.

"Yeah, as soon as Dermott first confirmed who it was," Paul looked at Tony, then back at Tyler, "he is going out of his mind, he is currently on his way there now," Tyler nodded without speaking, Paul carried on. "Lynne M'Kane is with the rest of the family, Dermott is going to stay at the scene and will look after him."

"That's good," Tyler spoke softly. Paul left the premises. Tony looked back at Tyler. "How is your family?" she asked changing the subject, Tony forced a small smile.

"Yeah, they are good, I came straight here when I heard the news." Tyler turned and walked over to where the kettle was, as she lifted it, she spoke without looking round.

"Well, family is important, we have things sorted here, best you go back to yours," Tyler took the kettle over to the sink and started to fill it. Tony was being dismissed.

"I will, thank you," Tony turned and walked out the same way Paul had gone. Tyler stopped and looked at his back as he left. There was still a part of her that could not forgive him for what he did at the harbour when he met up with Sabine. The front door of the farmhouse closed, and she carried the kettle over to its stand and clicked it on. She stared at it for a few moments. The sound of a baby crying echoed down the stairs. Her tea would have to wait.

∞∞∞

Jason Apollyon pulled the zip up on the tent and crawled inside as the phone in his pocket started to ring. He flopped onto the sleeping bag and pulled the phone out of his pocket.

"Hello," he spoke quietly.

"Jason, hi, it's Paul here from the farm,"

Jason briefly closed his eyes, then as he reopened them, he sat up. "Hello Paul,"

"Right, we have a very serious situation here and we would like to know if you know anything that can help," Paul stated.

"Oh, is it about your assault on the farm last night?" he asked.

"How did you know ...." Paul stated.

"I watched, very impressive by the way," Jason paused, then raised his eyebrows, "are you after constructive criticism of your assault? I only have a couple of points!" he already knew that was not why he was phoning.

"No, no, not at all."

"So, what's up?" Jason asked.

"We have lost four of ours ...." Paul stated.

"Oh, during the assault?" Jason sat upright as he asked the question.

"No, that was all fine, no they were out in a cut off, three of them were killed by shooting and a fourth is missing and we need to know exactly where Hanna and, the other one ... the girl, are!" Jason could hear the rising anger in Paul's voice.

"Why do you think it was either of them?"

"Who else could it have been! Look, where are they?" Paul demanded.

"It wasn't Hanna, in fact you only missed him by a few minutes,"

"WHAT? when?" Paul raised his voice.

236

"During your assault, the third 4 x 4 they had been using stopped just short of the entrance, then reversed away when they saw what you were all doing, Hanna was inside, as for Megan, she is already starting to migrate south again, so it wasn't her, in fact in couldn't have been either of them."

"Why not?"

"You said three of them had been shot?"

"Yes, Paul confirmed.

"Well, neither of them kills like that, Megan only bites, she does not use firearms and Hanna would not have left a living witness alive," there was silence down the phone, "I am sorry for your losses," Jason continued, "but it sounds like they were killed by someone else." He listened as Paul conveyed what he had just said to someone in the background, there was a shout of anger, then Paul came back on the line.

"Right, but do you know exactly where they are?"

"Currently?" Jason replied.

"Yes, currently," Paul was getting more annoyed.

"Well, Megan is migrating away from you into Tyrone, last time I picked her up she was heading towards Enniskillen, but she is no threat to your kind, if you want, I will track Hanna for you as he is."

"Right, but let us know as soon as you find him, we think he has one of our girls!"

"He doesn't," Jason calmly replied.

"Well, we will be the judge of that," Paul spat.

"Ok," Jason smiled and spoke quietly, "I will find this Noc for you,"

"The sooner the better," Paul was irate.

"I'm on it," Jason took the phone away from his ear and pressed the red button to end the call. He looked at the small screen then looked around; it would not take him long to pack.

Chapter 44 – Surgut International Airport, Siberia, Russia.

Grishin and Tatamovich were smartly dressed, their suits were covered by thick, dark coloured, long woollen coats to shield them from the weather, it was not winter yet, but it was getting cold. They were quiet as they walked towards the two large glass exit doors of the airport, towing their luggage behind them. Across the road outside was the main car park waiting there were the two large black cars with a security detail around them. Three smartly dressed men stepped out from the left-hand side, the elder one stepped forward and bowed his head from his neck. The other two stopped behind him.

"Godspodine Grishin," His accent was from the local region, Grishin did not have to ask, he could tell they were wolves.

"Da,"

"Pozhaluysta sleduyte za mnoy" The figure turned and walked towards the waiting cars, the two behind without speaking stepped forward and without looking at their faces took control of their luggage. They had been asked to follow him, they were expecting to be collected, there was nothing to worry about here. Grishin and Tatamovich walked towards the first car, the traffic was stopped by members of the security detail to allow them to cross. The man who had greeted them nodded towards one of the security team who then opened the rear door, their luggage would be placed into the boot. As they climbed into the rear of the car, the security detail closed in on their own vehicles, the black car behind them would stay with them, another would be one hundred metres in front and a fourth car would be one hundred metres behind. The two men sat in silence in the warm car as the small convoy made its way out of the airport then away from the City of Surgut. It would be nearly an hour before they arrived at the complex that guarded the Eurasia Hall, the seat of the high council of the Garou.

The two black cars stopped in front of the concrete steps that led up to the two heavy ornate wooden doors. The rear doors of the cars were opened and they both got out, their long coats were removed and left inside the cars, they would not be needed for some time yet. Heads again were bowed at the neck and as Grishin and Tatamovich started up the few steps, the doors opened outwards and the light of the day cut through the darkness of the inside. As they both got to the top of the stairs there was a well-dressed figure standing in the middle of the doorway. The light from outside cut lines across the floor either side of him. His silver hair was combed back, he looked like he was in his early sixties, his black leather shoes where polished, his clothes clean and well pressed and his hands were behind his back. He spoke with a polite English accent, almost like a butler.

"Godspodine Grishin," he nodded to each person in turn, "Godspodine Tatamovich, welcome back to the Eurasia halls, the High Council is expecting you." He had not looked either of them in the eye, he bowed slightly from the waist, then turned and walked away from them. Grishin looked at the male figure who was standing on the right-hand side just inside the entrance, the figure bowed his head before pressing a button on the small control panel and the two doors began to close. The chandeliers above them lit the outer hall, their shoes clicked on the marble floor decorated in a pattern that covered the centre of the room and went all the way to the outer border of the pattern. Great paintings of their history were on either side, each painting separated by tall columns that had thick, dark coloured curtains hanging from them, it all looked very regal. The outer hall faced the large marble staircase that fanned out at the bottom, the dark wooden carved handrails led up to the balcony that was all dark stained wood. The balcony went both directions around the side of the outer hall, on both sides, doors led to other, smaller rooms. They had been there before, and both had stayed in the many bedrooms that were here, the security was extensive, they were very safe when inside. At the top of the stairs were two double doors that were made out of the same wood as the rest of the outer hall, but unlike all the other doors, these had no patterns or artwork on them. The Englishman knocked loudly on the doors, then stepped back and opened one of them. He stepped out of the way to allow them to pass, the door would be closed behind them, he would not follow. They both stepped into the hall of the high council.

There were no windows. The lights hung from the high ceiling which had detailed paintings on it, each painting was separated by gold painted, ornate patterns, again, each painting told a different part of Garou history. They were standing under the gallery that had the upper seats for hosted formal functions. The thick red carpet covered the whole floor. They stepped forward to the edge of the single set of steps that led from the entrance down to the main floor. Either side of the steps were lines of seats, the main hall could seat nearly one thousand people. At the far end was the small stage, on it, in a line were the five seats of the high council. Each one was exactly the same, dark stained wood with red cushioned seats, everyone on the high council was equal. The sides of the stage were covered with drapes, the lights for the stage were high and out of sight, the backstage was large enough that stage shows had been performed here in the past. At each side of the stage was a small step of steps that allowed access from the main auditorium to the main stage, but the stage was only a short distance up. In front of the stage was the semi-circle of tables and chairs, this is where the main council meetings took place, there were 48 places, but they were rarely all filled, it was normal for one or two to be empty at any council meeting.

On the ground floor at either side of the stage were the doors that led away from the main hall, you could get to the kitchens both ways and also outside, the security on the hall often practiced their response if the hall was ever taken by a foe. Grishin and Tatamovich waited for the four people who were standing in the middle of the semi-circle on the ground floor, the council members were being very informal. One lifted his hand and beckoned them forward. Both of them trotted down the steps to be warmly welcomed by the two men and two well dressed women who made up the high council.

"Edward, welcome," the tall, well-built man extended his hand to Grishin; it was a firm handshake, Tatamovich could tell Grishin knew this one well, no one called Grishin by his first name, no one.

"It is good to see you again," Grishin smiled. The tall man smiled at Tatamovich.

"And this must be the famous, Viktor Tatamovich!" he exclaimed, his hand was extended which Tatamovich took, he had been here before, he knew the council members, but he had never spoken with them so informally.

"Da, Tatamovich, this is Councillor Gun'nar from the Volsurga Saga pack," Grishin explained.

"Councillor," Tatamovich bowed his head at the neck, and they exchanged a very firm handshake.

"So, Viktor, good to finally meet you like this," Gun'nar smiled.

"Tatamovich, please," he did not look Gun'nar in the eye, he was high council and outranked him.

"Of course, of course, have you met the council before?" Gun'nar asked as Grishin shook hands with the others.

"I have attended many council meetings over the years, but not informally councillor," Tatamovich replied. Gun'nar stepped back and extended his hand towards each one in turn, who stepped forward, smiled then shook hands with Tatamovich.

"From Canada, Keria Greyeyes of the Great Plains pack," Grishin smiled, he could see how uncomfortable Tatamovich was with this informality. Tatamovich took the hand of the dark skinned native Canadian. Her hair was jet black and went all the way down her back and she had a serious look on her face, again Tatamovich bowed his head.

"Councillor,"

"Godspodine Tatamovich, my father would like me to pass on his best wishes," Tatamovich looked up, there was a small smile on his face as she continued, "he still tells the heroic tale of the two of you in the mountains with the bear."

"Da, that was a long time ago," Tatamovich replied.

"Also," Keria continued, "you were at my marking after my first Moon Dance!" she exclaimed, he looked up at her as she held on to the handshake.

"I was yes," she released the grip.

"My father would like to welcome you again sometime," she smiled.

"I would be glad to accept," Tatamovich replied, Keria stepped back.

"A bear?" Grishin asked, Tatamovich looked over at him.

"Another time," he whispered, Gun'nar carried on,

"From India, this is Sundeep of the Sikhandi," he shook hands with the tall well-built man, whose eyes were as dark as his hair. Then the shorter of the two women stepped forward. She had bright blonde hair and crystal-clear blue eyes, "and from Israel, this is Cindy of the Shen Tov pack,"

"I have heard a lot about you, Godspodine Tatamovich," she stated, "and how much you have done for this council."

"Spasiba," Tatamovich answered as he could not think of anything else to say.

"Right then," Gun'nar stated, and he turned and smiled at Grishin, "the reason we are here today," it was Grishin's turn to feel awkward. Gun'nar turned towards Tatamovich, "have you ever been to one of these?" he asked.

"No Councillor, I missed the last one as I was in China at the time,"

"Well," Gun'nar started, "all that is going to happen after the informal greeting, with a witness from the council, we bring in the council and they witness Edward here being invited to take his seat. Once we have the five permanent members, we can then hold our first meeting."

"That sounds easy enough," Tatamovich replied.

"Yeah, if you can take your seats then we will bring the rest of them in," Keria said as she turned towards one of the doors at the side and raised her right hand. The doors on both sides opened on the command and the other council members who had been waiting in the passageways started to make their way in. Grishin looked at Tatamovich.

"We better take our seats." As they walked around the tables the high councillors all headed to one side of the stage and waited until everyone was standing behind their own chair. Grishin and Tatamovich looked at each other, it took a while; greetings were passed, hands shaken and wishes passed on as different people passed them, but it was now a formal occasion. Everyone stopped talking and the room fell into a silence as the four council members all walked up the steps and onto the stage, they all stood before the chairs that were on the stage, leaving one empty. When they all sat down, that was the que for everyone else to sit down. Once everyone was comfortable Gun'nar spoke, his voice echoed around the room.

"Members," he started as he gripped the hand rests on both sides of his chair, "we are here today to witness this, high council returning to five members." Gun'nar looked at each of the other three high members, each one nodded in turn, before Gun'nar looked at Grishin. "Then, I am pleased to invite, member Edward Grishin of the Siberian Pack to take his place here," Gun'nar extended his hand towards the empty chair, "on the High Council," all heads turned towards Grishin as Gun'nar continued, *"Councillor, take your place!"* The only sound was the sound of Grishin pushing his chair back and standing up. He winked at Tatamovich before walking behind the semi-circle of seats of the lower council. Some looked at him, others did not, but all eyes followed him as he climbed up the steps at the side of the stage then walked behind the chairs of the rest of the High Council. He knew not to walk in front of them, that would be disrespectful. He stopped in front of the empty chair; he turned and bowed his head to each councillor in turn before he took his seat. He looked around the faces that looked back at him, there were two members from nearly every single pack around the world, they could change, but as a high councillor, he was a permanent member. This was his life now, for the rest of his life. He tried not to smile.

"So, the first order of business," Keria said. All eyes turned towards her, she looked down at Tatamovich, "I raise the motion for the Siberians to elect a new member to their council to replace Councillor Grishin," it was the first time he heard his new rank with his name, again Grishin tied not to smile.

"All in favour?" Gun'nar said,

"Aye," echoed around the room.

"All against the motion?" there was silence, Gun'nar looked at Tatamovich, "the motion is carried, Member Tatamovich can you inform your alpha of this?"

Tatamovich stood before he spoke. "Da Councillor," he retook his seat.

"The next order of business," Keria asked. Grishin looked over as a seat to his right was pushed backwards and the male figure stood, Grishin recognised him as one of the Americans from the Great Winds pack. His mid-west accent stood out against the others.

"Councillors, it is with pleasure that we can report, that the previous problem we had encountered within our lands has now been resolved," he was smiling as he spoke, Grishin looked at Gun'nar, who then addressed the room.

"Member, for the benefit of our newest high councillor, can you recap what the issue was!" Gun'nar looked back at the member who was standing.

"Of course," he looked directly at Grishin, "while you were in Ireland, we became aware of at least one Garou that was starting to cause an issue in our lands in and around a large farming town," he turned and looked over the rest of the lower council, "as it turns out, it was not one, but a whole family, they had no idea of our existence or us of theirs's they had done quite well of keeping their true form secret,"

"A whole family?" one voice asked.

"Yes, a father, three sons and a daughter, they are a family of wealthy art dealers who have their own private estate, but they thought that they were the only wolves anywhere in the world," there was a ripple of laughter around the room.

"And the situation has been resolved?" Keria asked.

"Yes Councillor, my alpha brought them all to our last Moon Dance and things have gone very well," he looked around again, "our clan is stronger, and our true form is secure." He sat down.

"What is the update on the problems in and around Arkansas?" Sundeep asked. Grishin looked at the stern face, then his eyes looked over at a different member who stood up.

"Our enemies have been active in and around the city of Little Rock," the elder woman looked around at those that were seated around her, "as we have stated before, there is a large and powerful coven somewhere north of the city and, I must report, they are very good at locating our kind and destroying them," this caused a ripple of conversation around the room.

"What are you doing to counter this situation?" Sundeep asked. The woman turned back towards him.

"Our efforts to gain intelligence on locations, strengths and dispositions of the enemy have so far, proved to be ineffective, they certainly control the local Police, local Politicians and media, our losses have mounted since our last report." Grishin looked at the other high council members, he had a plan, attack them! But he did not speak just yet.

"What are you proposing?" Sundeep asked.

"We ask this council for help, our members have fallen at their hands and this situation cannot be allowed to continue or we may lose the whole region to the Nocs," Grishin's eyes looked over as another member stood up, they turned towards the member who was speaking.

"We, of the Belgic Gaul's pack, offer our assistance, we have a whole team of specialists who have extensive military experience, at the highest level," another stood and joined the conversation.

"The Tukholtsi of the Ukraine can offer two assault teams to help with your situation," The difference in the accents was vast, but they were all Garou. The older woman nodded to each one in turn, before looking back at the high council.

"We accept these offers of help, we can discuss the details later," all of them sat back down, Sundeep lent back in his chair.

"Excellent, at our next meeting can you give us an update on the situation?" he asked, the woman nodded. Sundeep looked over at Keria.

"The next order of business, what is the situation in Ireland?" Keria asked. Tatamovich stood up but before he could speak Grishin started.

"If I may," he looked at Tatamovich, who then sat back down, everyone looked at Grishin, "since this situation was under my authority it is only right that I deliver the report," he started, he then stood up and looked around.

"Please, continue," Gun'nar added, smiling as he did so.

"Nearly two years ago, a senior Noc from the US made its way first to the UK then over to the north of Ireland, without detection," Grishin looked at the High Council, "how he did this, and how his initial presence went undetected is still under investigation." He looked back at the council who were all looking at him, "he recruited a witch princess from the large coven near Salisbury in England and using her, we now believe they cast a sleeping spell over the clan alpha in the South of Ireland, this allowed the witch princess to nullify the main pack so they could divide and then move against the pack in the North," there was a ripple of conversation from the lower council.

"Where did this occur?" Cindy asked.

"At their den, near Dublin," Grishin replied.

"What?" Cindy sat upright, "they allowed a witch princess into their den?" she raised her voice.

"Connor, the clan alpha of the An Rua, has admitted responsibility and accepted my ruling on the matter," Grishin was shutting her down, she would not go over a ruling that had already been made.

"Did both sides agree to this ruling?" Sundeep asked, Grishin looked towards him.

"They did," Grishin replied, he then turned back to the main room, "but what I would like to make you all aware of was how, the pack in the North of the country, under the leadership of Alpha, Kyle Foster, son of the great alpha John Foster, dealt with them." Grishin had raised the volume of his voice, the chatter stopped to listen. "The Noc brought nearly one hundred others including one of their Master hunters over, they armed them with rifles and shotguns and started a campaign to draw the Northern An Rua out," Grishin looked around them again, a small smile broke over his face, "Foster, deployed his pack and engaged them, outnumbered and out gunned, his head trainer, none other than Tyler Reynolds, who first led an assault on a beach, destroying nearly twenty of them and engaging their hunter, which, I may add, in a one on one combat, defeated her, forcing her to flee," Grishin could flee the atmosphere lifting in the room, they all enjoyed hearing about dead vampires, he carried on, "she then, *fought one on one again*, when they tried to attack the family home of one of our own, who they thought was by himself, with his sapien wife, *who was with child at the time*," another murmur went around the room, attacking an undefended family 'just like a Noc' was whispered several times. "Reynolds, duelled with this one, sword against sword to the death and after a witnessed battle was *victorious!*" a small cheer echoed. "Then, they tried to lure the pack out into a final battle, which Foster, as a true alpha, leading from the front, sprung a Noc trap, then almost singlehandedly fought off our enemies, making a final stand as he did so." Grishin paused, there was a feeling of excitement growing in the room, Grishin looked down at Tatamovich, who let a small smile break from the corner of his mouth, he nodded once, Grishin understood. "Foster, with wounds that would have fallen any less Garou, tied himself to a tree and gave the injured and dying a chance to withdraw then re-group, in doing so he himself in a final act, took down the witch princess *with his own blade!*" Comments were passed between the smiling council members, Grishin turned and looked at the rest of the High Council. "Councillors, with this selfless act, Alpha Foster, stood against an overwhelming force, he demonstrated courage higher than that normally expected of any alpha when facing our mortal enemies," Tatamovich smiled, he understood where Grishin was going with this, he looked on as Grishin carried on. "His actions gave a wounded and hurting pack the strength and courage to charge our enemies and in doing so, defeat them!" Sundeep slowly stood up, he looked at Grishin then looked at the rest of the council.

"Would the members of the An Rua stand," he instructed. Grishin looked as the two figures slowly pushed their chairs back and stood up. "An Rua, what have you to say about this account?" he asked.

"The councillor's account is true, since then, our alpha has issued the order to wipe out all enemies in our lands," they responded.

"And what of that?" Cindy asked.

"It is nearly complete."

"If the Irish can do it, then so can we!" a different member stated, the murmur of conversation started again.

"COUNCIL!" Sundeep shouted, and all conversation stopped. He looked down at the two An Rua. "Reynolds is coming here, is she not?" he asked.

"She is awaiting an official invite," they replied.

"I understand the An Rua have a performance telling this tale to music and dance?"

"We do,"

"Then," Sundeep started as he retook his seat, slowly Grishin sat down as well, "I propose that the invite for the An Rua be issued to invite them here to tell the tale of one of our own," he looked around. Gun'nar moved then spoke.

"All in favour?" he asked.

"*AYE,*" echoed around the room, Gun'nar looked at Grishin, "All against?" the room was silent, Gun'nar looked at the rest of the High Council.

"The motion is carried," there was an approving murmur from the gathered crowd. Gun'nar looked at the two An Rua, "Inform your alpha and Reynolds of the invite to come here," they nodded in response. Cindy stood up as the two from the An Rua sat down.

"In light of this report, I propose that for the first time in nearly one hundred years ...." All eyes turned towards her, "I propose that both, Foster AND Reynolds be awarded our highest honour," she looked over at Grishin, "in light of their actions, in the face of our enemies and as an example to us all." Cindy sat down as Keria lifted her right hand.

"Aye," she said out loud.

"Aye," added Sundeep,

"Aye," Gun'nar, all of them looked over at Grishin, who paused, then raised his right hand.

"Aye," Gun'nar stood up and addressed the lower council.

"Members, a vote has been taken by the High Council on this motion to award these honours, which, has been pointed out it has not been awarded in some time and this decision should not be taken lightly," he looked around, "all in favour?" He looked at the end of the table on his left-hand side. Slowly the first hand was raised.

"Aye," Grishin watched as the raising of hands started to ripple along the members like a wave.

"Aye,"

"Aye,"

"Aye,"

"Aye," the vote was unanimous. Gun'nar looked around.

"Thank you, An Rua." The two members stood up again, "inform your alpha after this meeting I require him to be available as soon as possible to receive a phone from myself!"

"It will be done," they responded, then Gun'nar sat back down.

"There is one thing we must consider," Cindy almost shouted.

"And that is?" Gun'nar asked.

"These actions by the Nocs in Ireland, it obviously was not done on a whim! This was planned, co-ordinated, it took time."

"I agree," Grishin added, "I believe the councillor is correct, all this would have taken a great deal of time and planning, it was not something that was done just by one of them."

"What are you suggesting?" Gun'nar added.

"I am not suggesting anything, I am stating it outright, this was the initial stages in a move against us!" there was another ripple of conversation, Cindy stood up. "We have seen, over the last few years a growing spate of incursions and actions against us, we have seen a great deal of territory, especially in the US and large parts of Europe, lost to them," she looked around, "we no longer have any real strength in South America or parts of Africa, Cindy looked over at Grishin, "I believe that Foster has shown us the example," she looked back over the rest of the council, "we *must* take a stand, we *must* fight back, we *must* ... take inspiration from what the Irish have achieved, if they, as one of our smaller packs, can achieve such greatness ... what can we, as a global family achieve? We MUST defend our kind."

"And how would we achieve that?" Keria asked. Cindy looked at her.

"*If you wish for peace, prepare for war!*" hands banged on the tables in agreement, shouts and yelps echoed around the room.

"Councillors, members," Gun'nar raised both his hands, "declaring a world-wide war against them is not something that can be achieved here at this council, we must," he sat forward as he spoke, "invite all the CLAN Alphas to attend then have an open forum to discuss how this can be achieved,"

"Then I propose such a forum." Cindy shouted, Gun'nar sat back.

"That must be seconded by another High councillor!" Gun'nar stated, "our laws exist for a reason," he explained.

"AYE," all heads turned towards Grishin who was looking at Cindy. "The councillor from the Shen Tov pack is right, we have been under attack, I agree with her, they are moving against us and what happened in Ireland was just the first action to see how we, as Garou will react, I second the motion," he looked over towards where Tatamovich was sitting, "if we do not, then they will seek out weaker packs and slaughter them .... And we cannot allow that!" The room reacted. Slowly Gun'nar stood up and addressed everyone.

"Then .... Let this call to arms go forth ... to all Garou, ...

PREPARE FOR ALL OUT WAR AGAINST THE NOCTRAILIS!"

Chapter 45

"It is him," Martin Hanna hissed. The three men inside the large hedgerow at the far side of the car park watched the single figure walk around their parked 4 x 4, it was the only vehicle in the small car park. It was barely illuminated as only one of the streetlights was working. "That is Apollyon," he confirmed. They watched as Jason walked around, occasionally stopping to go down on to one knee, look at the ground and stretch out his fingers, not touching the ground but moving over what he was looking at.

"How did he find us?" the driver asked, "we only just left the safe house."

"It doesn't matter," Glenn turned and looked back at Martin, "he has found us, if he can, the wolves can." They watched as Jason stood up and headed off towards the opposite side of the car park without making any sound whatsoever, then, after he had gone through the small green painted metal gate, they watched him make his way up the pathway and into the small woods just outside Coleraine. Glenn looked at Martin, as Jason disappeared from view.

"Let's get him," Martin whispered. Glenn looked at the direction he had gone, then pointed towards the treeline at the opposite side of the 4x4.

"If we go up that way we could see where he is going," he spoke quietly, "probably cut him off." Martin liked the idea, the driver didn't. He wanted to run, run far away, as quickly as he could. He had signed on for the wages, for the payday, not for watching the entire team being taken down. Glenn had remotely accessed the CCTV once they had got to the other safe house. They had watched the wolves' approach then suddenly everything was switched off. Glenn had said they had used some sort of counter measures to knock out everything that had an electrical circuit and as they had not heard from anyone that meant that none survived. Glenn seemed calm, Hanna was furious, but the driver was petrified, why had they not driven straight to the international airport and left as soon as they could? His suggestion was put down. He did not care if Hanna was seen on the security camera at the airport, he did not care if they had to throw their guns away, they could get on a flight, any flight, and get out of there, they would, at least be alive. But Hanna had demanded they stay, Glenn had, at least, made a phone call asking for a flight to collect them from the remote landing strip, but that was going to be another two days as there was something happening near Dartmoor involving some Earl he had never heard of. 'Why couldn't they stay at the new safe house?' he had asked, during the day, yes, best to keep out of sight but Hanna had something to do that he thought was worth them risking their lives. He disagreed. Glenn had remained silent.

Glenn's movement out of the bushes brought the driver back to the present. He took off at speed across the short distance towards the tree line, Hanna had gone with him, and the driver had to sprint to catch them up. The long weapons were still in the car, but they had their pistols on them. Glenn and Martin moved through the trees without making a sound, but the driver, however, seemed to snap every branch that hung near him, step on every twig on the ground, stumble and fall every short distance as he made his way through the trees, in fact, he was making so much noise that Glenn stopped and knelt by a tree. Hanna went down beside him, studying the ground in between the trees in front of them. As the driver caught them up Glenn tore into him, grabbed him by his hair and slammed his head into the cold tree.

"Just what the fuck are you doing? You seriously need to get a grip and sort yourself out, you are letting everything with a heartbeat know exactly where we are!" the driver was out of breath and now rubbing his face. He was going to protest but chose not to, both Glenn and Martin had drawn their pistols. Martin raised his hand to silence them, he was staring between the trees, Glenn turned and looked in the same direction. The driver could not see what they could see. Martin did not speak, he started using his hands to instruct them on what to do. He was going to go to the right, Glenn to the left and the driver was to head straight ahead. "I will fire first," Glenn whispered. Martin shook his head.

"Alive, I want this prick alive," Martin's voice was little more than a hiss. Glenn nodded then looked at the driver. He gave him a scornful look, then quietly rose, and headed off to the left. Martin disappeared into the darkness between the trees, again, without making a single sound. The driver was alone again, and still petrified. He fumbled as he drew his pistol and slowly rose then started making his way forward. Everything seemed amplified, even his own breath seemed to be so loud that he thought that every living thing around them knew he was there. He tried to be quiet, he was almost tiptoeing as he approached the small clearing up ahead. He could now see the shape of the domed tent. There was sound of movement from the far side of the tent. He stopped when he saw the figure that had been in the car park. He watched as he knelt at the entrance to the tent, the driver recognised the hiss of a small gas stove, he was either making a meal or a hot drink. He walked forward again holding the pistol in both hands, he edged closer to the clearing, the figure had his back to him. The driver stepped out from between the trees, he had not been seen or heard. He stopped. He glanced to either side, he could not make out Glenn or Martin, but they must be there. He looked at the back of the figure in front of him. He watched as he turned the small stove off and started to rummage inside of a small daysack. The driver gripped the pistol tight.

"Hey," he spoke quietly. The figure turned and looked over his right shoulder. He initially smiled then he saw the pistol. "Stand up," the driver commanded. The figure did so and raised his hands at the same time. "Turn towards me," just at the driver spoke Glenn suddenly flew through the air and slammed into him, the pair landed on the ground with a crash and a yelp. Glenn started to wrestle with him to control him.

"Well, don't just stand there, HELP ME!" Glenn commanded. The driver tucked his pistol away then jumped forward. Martin appeared at the side and was gleeful as Glenn struggled to bind the wrists of the twisting figure that the driver was now pinning to the ground.

"We got him!" Martin was almost dancing as Glenn pulled on the cable ties, pulling the wrists together behind his back. Glenn stood up as Martin handed a heavy kick into the side of the torso of his captive. "Lift him up!" Martin commanded, the driver pushed himself up from the ground and jostled his prisoner up and onto his knees, Martin was almost dancing as he stepped forward. "Got you now, prick," Martin punched him in the face, "You aren't such an ultimate warrior after all," another blow was landed, the driver held the shoulders and the taunting and blows continued, "Well, what do you have to say?" the body rocked with the blow, blood was starting to pour from his nose, "come on then," another punch, "Prick," Glenn stepped to the side as Martin continued his assault. "We finally have the great *Jason Apollyon*," the punch was lighter than the others but still made the driver tighten his grip to stop him falling over. Glenn ducked and looked inside the tent, as he straightened up, he asked a question.

"So, where is your famous crossbow then?"

"Well," Martin spat, "Come on Jason, answer him!" another punch.

"You shouldn't call me that," the bound figure spoke quietly. Glenn stepped forward. "What?"

"You really shouldn't call me that!" he repeated, "my name is Justin."

"Then why do people call you Jason?" Martin asked, looking confused.

"They don't," the bleeding face started to smile. The driver felt his captive start to laugh as the large arrowhead of the crossbow bolt burst out of Glenn's chest. It had hit him in the back and went straight through his heart on its way through his chest. Glenn looked shocked for a moment but was already falling to his knees, clutching at the object that protruded out the front of his chest. The very object that had just killed him.

"WHAT?" Martin reacted.

"Jason is my twin brother," Justin smiled through the blood that was running down his face. The driver let him go and turned towards the figure of a screaming Jason Apollyon that burst out of the darkness. "We are identical twins in fact," Justin continued. The driver grabbed for his pistol as Jason was dropping the crossbow out of his left hand, the driver did not see the large hunting knife in his right hand. Jason had a firm grip on the handle, the top of the thick blade went along the bottom of his wrist, so the sharp edge was uppermost. The driver did not fully see the movement of Jason's right hand as it flashed by, but he did feel something slice his neck, his hands forgot about the pistol as they tried to stem the massive flow of blood from his open neck. The driver spun with the force of the blow and landed on the ground desperately gasping and struggling to control what was happening to his neck. He lay on his side as the warm liquid pumped out through his fingers into the cold earth. The driver did not see Martin's pistol being knocked out of his hand or the blow and counter blow that had started between the two of them. Justin Apollyon rocked over onto his side and started to shuffle his hands under his bum, curling his feet up, he was trying to free himself, but the driver did not care, the fear had gripped him. He did not want to die, he wanted to live, he wanted to go home, he wanted to see his daughter again. His arms were becoming weaker, he had started to sob, his mind remembered the last Christmas they had spent together, before the divorce and before she had gone off to university. He tried to whisper his daughter's name, but he could not form the words, his body coughed, his strength was leaving him, he had never been this frightened before, this was it, he was going to die. He did not care about the ripping sound that came from the tent as one of the two who were fighting where thrown through it. The body beside him still struggled with the plastic ties that kept his wrists behind his knees, he would now need help to get out of them further. The fight continued. It was fast, the knife was sticking in the ground, there was a flurry of kicks and punches that missed or were blocked. The two fighters battled on, but the driver didn't care. His hands twitched and he coughed once more, his lips tried forming the word 'help' but there was no air coming up to help him form the words. The cold ground drank at the pool of warm liquid, the source of the heat would not last much longer.

Justin was stuck, he could not get out of the tight restraints that were around his wrists, he would need his brothers help. He stopped struggling, he was properly stuck now, all he could do was watch the fight continuing around the small clearing. Justin waited; He hoped his brother would win, if he did, he would be released, if he didn't, he would be soon to leave this world like the two other bodies that lay there. Both fighters were fast, both were strong, and both knew what they were doing. For a moment, Justin was reminded of old Bruce Lee films he had watched with his brother when they were young. Bruce Lee was as fast, as these two. Justin had never seen two fighters as matched as these two seemed to be.

Jason had rolled over towards where the collapsed tent was, he could feel the injuries he had, Martin was a lot better than he assumed, but both were now exhausted, both were slowing and this was the moment when a mistake would be made by one of them, allowing the other the chance to finish it. Jason's kick to the centre of Martin's chest had thrown him backwards, Martin had tripped and had landed on his back, but Jason instantly had seen the danger, Martin was near his weapon. The pistol lay on the ground near his outstretched left arm. Jason grabbed the handle of the hunting knife and yanked it free from the earth as Martin had rolled over, then jumped up to his feet, he grabbed for the pistol and as he turned to aim at Jason just as he heard the sound of metal slicing through the air towards him. Jason's aim had been good, the large knife easily parted the space between his ribs. He felt himself gasp at the shock of the penetration. His hands dropped the pistol and gripped the handle of the blade that stuck out of his chest. Martin fell onto his right knee. Blood dripped from his nose and mouth. He looked up at the face of his enemy. Jason Apollyon, the destroyer, as he stood up and walked over to him. Martin looked at his face. It was Jason who spoke.

"Martin Hanna, Master Hunter of the Salisbury Coven," Jason stood in front of him and stared with utter contempt at what was in front of him.

"I see we have heard of each other," Martin replied, gasping as he did so.

"We have," Jason replied.

"Tell me one thing," Martin fought to form the words.

"What?" Jason replied.

"How?" Martin coughed, then fell backwards. He held out his hands to keep himself upright. "How did you survive? And why, since you survived, did you not turn?"

"God works in mysterious ways," Jason spoke quietly.

"What? God? What has God got to do with anything?" it was becoming more of a struggle for Martin to speak.

"I believe the Lord kept me alive so I can be the instrument of his holy wrath, to fulfil the vengeance on your kind for what you did to my family."

"What the fuc …." Martin grasped again.

"Your kind are an abomination," Jason stepped forward and took hold of the handle with his right hand and gripped the hair on the top of Martin's head with his left hand. "An abomination in the eyes of the Lord!" Martin's eyes widened as anger and fury filled Jason's face as he ripped the blade out of Martin's chest. Martin's cry diminished as quickly as it had sounded, it barely echoed around the small clearing. Jason started to shout, *"NOW, GO TO GEHENNA, FROM WHENCE YOU CAME!"* and with one movement, Jason rammed the blade under his chin and up into his head. Martin's hands grabbed at the handle of the blade, then flopped by his side. A last gasp came from him he fell back on the ground. Jason straightened up and stared at the vampire on the ground, his hand still held the blade.

"Any chance of some help here?" Justin's voice behind him brought him back to the moment. Jason stepped forward and recovered his knife from his vanquished enemy.

A short distance away, Megan Due gripped the tree with all her strength. She looked down from the viewpoint she had, high in the trees. It had been an easy climb, she thought that The Destroyer had seen her, but he had not reacted to her being there. She fought to control her breath. Her lips quivered and the tips of her fingers trembled, she slowly wiped her mouth, she was salivating from the fight she had just watched. She tried not to move as that would attract the attention of The Destroyer. Her eyes moved over him as he released his brother, she had never wanted someone more than she wanted him right now. She tightened her grip on the tree, her heart thumped in her chest. She watched as the two brothers hugged, then without speaking cleaned themselves. She watched the unconscious communication between the two identical twins, even from up here, she could not tell them apart. The only clue was the speed of the reaction in The Destroyer, the brother was not as fast. She did not feel the chill in the night, she was too excited for that, she did not move, she just watched. She watched them as they cleaned their faces, The Destroyer was hurt, from the way he was moving and the concern from the brother. He had an injury in the left side of his chest, his left wrist and left knee, she would need to remember that. She hugged the tree; the branch she was standing on was a thick one, she was reducing her silhouette as much as she could, the only part of her that moved now were her eyes. The twins searched the three bodies, there was still very little verbal communication between them, they were happy, that was obvious, but they had reason to be, he had just taken down Martin Hanna, the Master Hunter, and what a fight it had been. She had watched the first sapien appear, he was no real threat, but the other sapien was. He was a sapien, but he moved like one of them and she had never seen that before, the Destroyer had picked his targets well.

Her eyes followed them as they cleared the pistols and packed them away in the day sack, the brother had pulled a larger rucksack out of the tent. They joked between themselves as they packed away what they wanted. She had not heard what the brother had called himself, she did not know his first name, but he was 'the brother' he was not her prey, he was not the one she wanted, her lust and passion focused on the Destroyer, he was the one she wanted.

"What about the car?" the brother asked. The Destroyer shook his head.

"No, there will be a tracker on it, plus, the police will do a full forensic recovery on it, best not leave them any DNA that they can keep on record." Her mind raced, of course, she would never have thought of that, he was right, she looked at him again and she felt her body react, she had nearly reached an orgasm watching them fight, it was building again. She would have him, then she would kill him. Her mouth started to salivate again. His accent made her smile, was it Canadian with a hint of Irish or Irish with a hint of Canadian, she could not tell. The tent was packed away in a separate black plastic bag, it would be discarded later. The unconscious communication continued between the twins with a series of looks and nods before the brother took out a small red metal bottle from the side pocket of the large rucksack. He sprinkled some of the fuel over the bodyguard then the other sapien. The brother pointed towards where Hanna lay.

"What about him?" the brother asked.

"No," The Destroyer shook his head, "let the sun do its work." The two shared another smile. The Destroyer tried to lift the rucksack, but pain shot through his body. He let out a cry of pain and he dropped the rucksack onto the ground. The brother jumped over to comfort him, but the sound of him in pain excited her more, her lip quivered again, her fingers twitched, her excitement grew once more.

"I will take this," the brother stated as the Destroyer sat down on the ground. The brother walked around, searching the ground, she realised what he was doing, he was looking for any evidence that they had been there. He even scrapped up the patch of earth where The Destroyer had bled onto. The Destroyer pulled an outdoor jacket on then slipped the smaller daysack over his shoulders. He limped towards the small path that went near the tree she was in. The Destroyer stopped and looked back as the brother made his final sweep and without effort lifted the larger rucksack onto his back. His last task was to use a torn cloth, that he set fire to. The flames at the end touched the leg of the sapien and it breathed life into the wave of the flame that danced up his body, the rag was tossed onto the bodyguard. She watched as the flames took hold. Her eyes looked over the two burning bodies, the crossbow bolt was gone, she had missed it being removed. The fire would not be hot enough to totally destroy the bodies, but it would destroy enough DNA evidence. Underneath her, the two smiling brothers made their way past. the Destroyer was injured, that, with the brother would be an easy fight. If they knew she was there, they did not react, they carried on in the direction they were headed.

It would be easy to track them, then she would have everything she desired. Her eyes returned to the clearing. Her mind flashed back to when she had the Master Hunter, knowing the security team of sapiens was watching had excited her more. She looked at his lifeless body, lying there, in this small wood. She blinked. She felt nothing towards the body that was already starting to break down, when the sun came up it would finish off what was started. The glow of the other two lit up the clearing, she would wait for the light to start to fade before she would move. If, The Destroyer was watching, he would see her shape against the light of the flames move between the trees, yes, she would wait for the flames to die down some more. It would not take long, the brother had not used much fuel, certainly not enough to burn the bodies completely, it was just an ignition, nothing more, these two knew what they were doing, there would be enough for the police to find and keep them busy, but there would be no connection with The Destroyer, their kind, or the wolves. Perfect.

Finally, the time came when she decided she could move. She swung on the branch, then dropped onto the ground. She instantly lowered herself down and turned her head around. She watched for any sign of movement, any reaction to her landing on the ground. There was nothing, The Destroyer and the brother were long gone. The flames on the two bodies were almost out. She slowly walked over to the edge of the clearing. It had been and epic fight, she looked at Hanna, he had lost. She turned and headed down the path, she soon picked up the footprints of the brother, yes, The Destroyer was limping, it was obvious in the prints which ones were his. She lowered herself down and reached out with her hand. She stretched out her fingers over his footprint, her heart raced, her breath quickened, and her fingers trembled. She was getting excited again, she had to have him. For an instant, the images of him taking her flashed in her mind then the joyous thought of her biting down into his neck. That moment, that joyous moment of that hot metallic taste of his blood splashing into her mouth. Her eyes darted up and stared into the darkness in the direction they had gone. She would have him. She was running even before she realised it, and the thought of his blood in her mouth just made her body run faster.

Chapter 46

"Well?" Mark asked as she got back to the car. Cara-Marie shook her head, "what do you think then?" he asked as he opened the driver's door. Cara-Marie slipped her jacket off her shoulders and got in the passenger side. She tossed the jacket onto the rear seat as she shut the door. She remained quiet. Mark shut his door but didn't start the car. There was a moment of silence. "So," he started, "what bullshit did they say this time?" Cara-Marie was annoyed, she looked at him then looked out the from windscreen at the parked transit vans.

"I think they have no idea what is going on?" she spoke quietly, Mark nodded. "And that Inspector Wells is a control freak, did you see the way everyone stopped talking as soon as she approached? I mean, that says everything!"

"So, what do you think is going on?"

There was a long pause before she answered." That all this is somehow connected." Mark looked at the people in the white disposable suits heading from the rear of one of the vans and back towards the uniformed police officer at the cordon.

"And what makes you think that? From what we just got, the bodies up there were not torn apart, nor were their throats ripped out," he looked over at her, she was staring into the woods, "how can this be connected with what happened before? It is totally different." She did not look round, she was immersed in her own thoughts, he carried on, "what did they tell you at the cordon?"

"Three bodies, one with a fatal penetrating injury to his chest and another with a fatal knife wound to his neck and a third they think had been dead for at least a couple of weeks," she answered. She paused again, then looked at him, "I don't buy it, two people, with no ID, that are definitely not from around here, disposing of a body this close to Coleraine? And in a wood used by dog walkers all day, every day, it would be too easy to find after all." Cara-Marie's tone of voice raised slightly, "I just don't buy it!" she seemed frustrated.

"Ok," Mark replied, "What do you think is happening?" he repeated.

"I don't know yet," she muttered.

"Yet?" he asked, she turned and glared at him.

"Yes, 'yet', but I do aim to find out," she turned and stared out the passenger window, "this 'has to be' connected with that fire the other day, it has to be," she was muttering now.

"Why does it 'have to be'?" Mark asked.

"Special branch only appears when there is something going on, I have heard from a police contact that the guns they found were registered to a security company in the middle east," she looked at him again, "how did rifles that were supposed to be guarding some oil refinery out there end up here, a 4x4 that is armoured with a very expensive radio and the police are convinced there is no paramilitary involvement!" Mark did not answer, she was venting so he let her vent. "Three people from that farm near Kilrea all turn up, with gunshot wounds, the very same farm where I know there is something going on at," Mark looked at her, she was tense, her hands had jointed in with the rant, "this is the same farm that, two years ago, a load of them die in a fire at White Park Bay, Do you remember that?" she was becoming more irate.

"Yes, I remember," he spoke softly.

"There is so much more going on here and I want to get to the bottom of it." Cara-Marie stopped Mark put his seatbelt on. As he clicked it into place, he looked at his watch.

"Well, it is nearly three, so shall we head into town and get lunch?" it was more of a statement that a question. Cara-Marie exploded in a rage.

"*WHAT? FOOD? ARE YOU KIDDING ME? WE HAVE GOT TO GET ON TOP OF THIS, WE NEED TO FIND OUT WHAT THE HELL IS GOING ON HERE.*" Mark reached for the key in the ignition. He stopped. He looked at her, she carried on, she started to slap the top of the dashboard, *"WE NEED TO FIND OUT WHO IS DOING THIS, WE NEED TO ..."*

"Cara," he spoke softly.

"LOOK, WE NEED TO BE ON TOP OF OUR GAME HERE TO CRACK THIS!"

"Cara," he raised his voice slightly.

"WHAT!" she demanded. Mark started the car then he spoke again.

"Cara, have you ever seen a stress councillor?" he quietly asked.

"A COUNCILLOR? WHY? DO YOU THINK I AM LOSING IT OR SOMETHING!"

"No, that's not what I said, I ..."

"THEN WHAT .... WHAT MARK? WHAT EXACTLY 'ARE' YOU SAYING?"

"Cara,"

"DON'T 'CARA' ME, WE HAVE A JOB TO DO HERE," Mark turned towards her.

"That's just it, yes, we do have a job to do," he had raised his voice, but he was not quite shouting. "I am just a photographer and you are a journalist, what are you on about *'investigating'* we do not have to investigate anything," Cara-Marie sat back as he carried on, "you have to report the news and I have to photograph it, investigating is the job of the police, *'not us'* ..." he turned away, "I don't care, 'what else' is going on, I don't care if it is some organised crime gang, or vampires ..." he looked back at her, "or werewolves ..." Cara-Marie went ridged in the passenger seat. "You are my friend, and as your friend I need to say something. You are taking all this far too personally,"

"What?" she replied.

"You need to let this go, it is stressing you out, and has been for years now," Mark reached over and placed his hand on hers'. "And it is getting worse." She looked down at the back of his hand. "You have always been there for me, and I think, as your friend it needs to be me to say something." She looked up at him them back at his hand, he lifted his hand away.

"So, what, exactly are you saying? Do you think I am losing it or something?" She was staring at him. Her body was tense, the coil of anger was building up again, this time it was pointing at him. He did not answer immediately, he was choosing his words very carefully.

"Cara," he placed his hands over the steering wheel, "I think you have been taking a lot of this far too personally," he paused, looking over the steering wheel, "you seem to be so determined to prove what you think is right, and this is at the expense of you doing your own job," his eyes darted over at her. She did not respond. "It is obvious you are really stressed about all this," he looked over at her, "we have seen a lot of bad stuff in recent times, but none of these deaths are you fault." He stopped. He looked away then back at her as she spoke.

"Has Kevin put you up to this?" she asked.

"What? Kevin? No,"

"But you have spoken to him, or you would not be mentioning this now!"

He turned in the seat. "Cara, no, no I haven't, I have not said a word to anyone else about this," she was still glaring at him, he turned away again. "And I won't if you don't want me to," She turned in her seat and looked out the window.

"So, where are you thinking for lunch then?" it wasn't a question, it was a change of conversation. He moved the car into gear and headed off, there was no point in saying anything else about it, she was stone, she would not respond to anything else he could or should say.

Lunch would be a quiet meal before they headed back to the office.

∞∞∞∞

Mike smiled as he walked into the portacabin. It was empty except for Lucy who was standing near the small coffee table with her back to the door. For a moment he felt his pulse quicken. She was wearing a dark blue suit, with a skirt that hugged her figure down her legs to her knees. Her hair hung over her shoulders and as she turned her head and looked back over her right shoulder at him, the colour in her eyes flashed, she had taken his breath away, again.

"Mike, Hi," she extended her right hand to the seat on the opposite side of the table, she looked away, the warmth and passion he had known from her was gone, instead there was a cold serious look. "Please have a seat." It stopped him dead. The door closed behind him. Lucy's high heeled shoes clicked on the floor as she walked over and turned and sat down opposite him, he felt his smile drop. Her eyes directed him to sit down opposite her. There was a laptop sitting on the table, with the screen facing where she wanted him to sit.

"Hi," he started to walk forward, "I got your message; I was really pleased to ..."

"Sit down," she interrupted. He stopped by the chair. He looked at the blank screen, then the stern expression on her face. "I said, sit down," she commanded. As he was sitting down, he looked over at her.

"Lucy, what is going on?" Lucy sat and crossed her legs, she pointed to the laptop.

"Press play," she was cold, the passion, the caress he was expecting was gone, instead this was someone he did not recognise. Whatever was about to happen, she was in charge, he felt his own tension rise. He did not like this. There was a mouse plugged into the side of the laptop, he moved the mouse, and the screen came alive. The screen had a 'play' icon on the centre of it. He looked up at the cold face that stared back at him. "Press – play," she repeated. He looked at the screen, moved the mouse and clicked on the icon. The screen came alive, and the footage started. He felt his stomach curl, his body reacted at what he was looking at. It was from the last time he had been at her house. They were both naked and she was on all fours, he was behind her, the sex was as furious as he remembered. The audio filled the portacabin as he finished, and they swapped positions. His eyes were glued to the screen, bile filled his mouth, his intestines tightened, and he started to feel like he was going to vomit. His eyes looked up at the emotionless face looking back at him.

"Lucy, why?" his voice broke, he was just about able to form the words and he looked back at the continuing footage on the screen. Her hair bounced behind her as she held her head back, he was remembering the way she had said his name, the way she rocked on top of him, the way she had responded to him, "I thought we ..." he started. Lucy stretched out two of her fingers and pushed the top of the laptop. It clicked shut. She looked at him and spoke quietly.

"From now on, you will do exactly as we say,"

"Wha ... what?"

"From now on," she looked up and stared directly into his eyes as they started to fill with tears. "We own you; you are ours, and you 'will' do what we tell you,"

"But"

"No buts," He sat back, exasperated. His eyes looked over at his right hand, his fingers were twitching, he looked over at her, the shock of this realisation was hitting him hard. She was expressionless, emotionless.

"You recorded us every time?" it was a struggle for him to form the words. She looked up, into his eyes.

"Of course, I did," there was no smile from her.

"Why?" he asked. She sat forward, her right forefinger pointed and motioned towards him every time she spoke, as if to reinforce the points she was making.

"From now on, everything, and I do mean everything, that comes across your desk, I want a copy, from now on, every decision that is made, you will tell us, you will follow our direction," his eyes focused in on the finger that was wagging on front of him.

"So, that's what this is, extortion!"

"Coercion," she corrected as she stood up. She unplugged the mouse, lifted the laptop, and tucked it under her arm. "You are the asset, I am the controller," she looked into his eyes and he looked back at the eyes he thought had loved him; there was no fire, just cold blue eyes.

"So, I am your puppet?" he asked. She turned and started to walk towards the door.

"And you will dance for me Pinocchio!" Mike Dear sat in silence as the door to the portacabin slammed shut. He sat and stared. The silence of the room was bethunderous. His world had just imploded, she had him, exactly where she wanted him, and he had no idea of how to get out of the mess he was now in.

Chapter 47   - Belfast City Airport

The two men were both dressed in suits, and both had cases on wheels behind them. Both could be described as 'middle aged' both looked serious as they walked through the sliding doors out of baggage reclaim area and into the busy main concourse. They stopped and looked around without speaking. They both stopped when they spotted the younger man in a suit, they could spot a police officer in a crowd. The younger man walked towards them.

"Excuse me, Superintendent Bolton and Chief Inspector Mullen?"

"Yes," one of them replied. The younger man looked at each one of them in turn, try as they might, they both looked like senior police officers.

"I am Constable McNeill, Police Service of Northern Ireland, Welcome to Belfast, the car is parked outside, will you follow me please?" and he turned and walked away. There was no offer to take their luggage.

"So, this is modern Belfast?" Michael Bolton asked as they walked.

"When was the last time you were here?" Martin Mullen asked.

"Oh, early 1990's, we were in Palace Barracks on a two-year tour," Michael replied. Martin glanced at him; Michael very rarely spoke about his past military career in the Parachute Regiment of the British army. The automatic glass doors opened, and they walked outside. The walkway to their right was covered, it led the way to the main car park.

"Hey, it's not raining!" Michael exclaimed; Martin laughed.

"We are parked over here," Constable McNeill directed them towards the unmarked car that sat in front of a line of taxis across the far side of the road.

"No problem," Martin replied. As the young police officer got to the car, the driver got out and walked around the car popped open the boot. The police officer who greeted them stopped by the rear door of the car and waited for them to place their luggage in the boot. The driver closed the boot and opened the rear passenger door. There was a polite smile and a quiet 'thank you' from the two men as they got into the back seat of the car. Everyone knew no details would be discussed outside of the car. As they got comfortable the driver landed back in the driving seat and the young police officer climbed in the passenger seat.

"So, where first?" Michael asked. As the young police officer clicked in his seat belt,

"Sir, Chief Anderson said we are to take you to your hotel and once you are checked in, he would like to formally greet you in his office." The car sped off towards the small roundabout. As they entered the exit tunnel the two men in the back seat exchanged a glance.

"And did he say why he wanted to see us?" Michael asked. The young police officer looked out the front of the car as they left the tunnel and joined the slip road that went onto the dual carriageway headed into Belfast City centre.

"Sorry Sir, he didn't say," The car moved onto the carriageway behind a minivan, the driver soon accelerated and overtook it.

"Ok," Michael replied. The car remained silent for the rest of the short journey. As they pulled up to the hotel the young police officer got out and opened the rear passenger door for Michael, Martin opened his own door as the driver stayed sitting in the drivers' position, exactly as he should have. The boot popped open and they retrieved their luggage; and, as Martin closed the boot, the young police officer stated what they had already guessed.

"Sir, we will wait here until you are ready," again it was a polite smile.

"Thank you," Martin said, "we won't be long." They headed to the main entrance.

"So, let me guess," Michael started, "Anderson wants to warn us off and 'not to tread on his toes' kinda thing?"

"Probably," Martin responded.

"Does he despise you as much as you despise him?" Michael asked. Martin's face tightened in anger.

"He hounded my friend, constantly, until he killed himself." The anger in Martin's voice was evident. Martin looked away as he continued speaking, "Sean Parrish was a good man, and he had finished his time, Anderson should have been charged with Manslaughter!" Martin looked up at Michael, "Sean was a damn good detective, he ran rings around this prick, and this prick knew it!"

"Ok," Michael started to open the door, "Just so I know what I am walking into."

∞∞∞∞

One hour later.

"His office is this way," Martin directed, he obviously knew this building well. Michael followed Martin up the stairs, past the memorial to the 303 police officers killed during the recent troubles in Northern Ireland. They walked past uniformed police officers, all dress ed for office work. Their uniforms were clean and pressed, all the officers who were out on the streets were downstairs, they had their body armour and guns belts on. Michael spotted how tense Martin was, Martin was expecting an argument with Chief Anderson. It had been clear, there was certainly no love lost between the two and Michael could guess what the Chief inspector wanted. There were two senior officers from another police service coming over to do a case review, and nobody liked it when that happened. It could make or break a career. The case review had been requested by the Assistant Chief Constable who was responsible for this part of the police, a review into a long running investigation, an investigation the senior levels of the police service here in Belfast were unsure if it was going anywhere. Martin slowed down when they got to an office door. "We're here," he spoke quietly over his shoulder.

The door was already slightly ajar, Martin knocked in such a way that the force of his knock pushed the door open. Martin stepped inside without an invite; Michael walked in behind him. The single desk faced to door. It was not a large office, but everything was in its place, a few pictures on the wall all the same size, there were two chairs in front of the desk, by the colour of them he knew that they had been brought in for this meeting as they were out of place here, this was not a welcoming office; Chief Anderson did not entertain much. Behind the desk sat Chief Inspector Anderson, his eyes narrowed slightly before he placed his hands on the desk and pushed his chair backward, the stood up. There was no offered handshake.

"Chief Inspector Mullen," he stated as Martin stopped by the chairs.

"Chief Inspector Anderson," Martin paused as Michael stopped level with him on his left side, Martin extended his left hand towards Michael. "May I introduce Superintendent Bolton, Metropolitan Police," again, there was no offered handshake.

"Superintendent, welcome to Belfast,"

"Thank you," Michael responded.

"I don't know if you remember, but we met briefly once before," Chief Anderson looked at Michael and ignored Martin.

"Have we?" Michael asked.

"Yes, on the Hostage negotiators course at Hendon, you gave a lecture on your handling of the house siege in Woolwich that involved the rival Jamaican drug gangs and an overview of the hostage situation at the Iranian Embassy in 1980."

"I have given that presentation many times Chief Inspector," Michael looked straight at him, "could you narrow it down a bit?" Michael was pushing him; he was letting him know that he did outrank him.

256

"It was eight years ago, I did however," there was a short pause, "disagree with your conclusions to the hostage situation at the Iranian Embassy in 1980, no, I don't think the military should have been used, it should have been left as a police matter!" Chief Anderson looked up, Martin's eyes narrowed, he saw what he was doing, he was trying to bait him.

"Well, as I said in my presentation, in 1980, the police service at that time, did not have the resources or the specialty trained units that we do now, and in 1980, the military were the only people in the world, who were doing that type of hostage rescue," Michael replied.

"Well," Anderson butted in, "I think that it should have been left to the negotiators, they would have ...."

"How many live hostage situations have you negotiated Chief Inspector?" It was Michael's turn to butt in.

"Well, I,"

"How many?" Michael moved closer to the chair in front of him, "I have negotiated over eighty 'successful' hostage situations, and I already know the answer to my question, ... you have not negotiated a single one!" Martin tried not to smirk, but it was hard not to. "But" Michael continued as he unbuttoned the jacket of his suit, "discussing hostage resolutions is not why we are here!" he exclaimed as he stepped around the chair and sat down without an invite to do so from Anderson, Martin follow suit. Anderson looked annoyed. Michael sat back in the chair and looked at him. "Please, sit," Michael stated. Martin could see what he was doing, Anderson was patronising him, and Michael stomped on it. As Anderson slowly sat down, Michael looked over at Martin and smiled, then looked back at the highly polished police officer across the far side of the desk from him. "So, Chief .... You wanted to formally greet us here," Michael glanced at Martin then back at him, "that is the only reason I can guess why you would want to speak to us before we meet your team."

"Well actually I would like to go over some ground rules first," Anderson started. Michael sat up; he had a serious look on his face.

"Ground rules Chief Inspector? I hope you are not trying to influence a case review."

"No, that would be,"

"Illegal," Michael butted in, "Chief Inspector, and if that is what you are asking, I will make it clear from the start that kind of thing will not be tolerated!"

"No, that isn't what I am saying,"

"Then what are you saying Chief Inspector?" Michael was not letting this go.

"Just a few 'ground rules' of the way things are done here," Anderson glared at Martin, "As I am sure, Chief Inspector Mullen has told you, things are done differently over here than in London." Martin glanced at Michael.

"Actually, no, Chief Inspector Mullen has stated no such prerequisites, but then, he has been a Met Officer for over twenty years and is used to doing things properly." Martin again smirked at the inter-police service dig, Michael carried on, "So, what 'ground rules' are you talking about then?" Martin looked at Anderson. To say he was uncomfortable was an understatement, he was used to being the one in charge, controlling the situation, the conversation, and here, a man he had just met had completely turned it around.

"Well, simple really," Anderson started, Michael sat back and crossed his legs, he had a small smile on his face as Anderson continued, "the only thing is I expect co-operation,"

"Of course," Michael butted in, "in fact," Michael glanced over at Martin then back at Anderson, "I am surprised you feel you have to bring it up, I expect total co-operation from both you, and your team, I would think that already part of any case review being done by another service."

"And you of course, will have it, in fact, I am not sure why this case review is even needed, everything that can be done has been, and has been to the highest standards."

Anderson sat back in his chair, "I have ensured correct police procedures have been followed at all times."

"Excellent," Michael smiled as he uncrossed his legs, he then placed his hands on the armrests of the chair and stood up, Martin followed suit. "Then we have nothing more to discuss, I understand we are having a telecom conference with the team leaders and the Assistant Chief Constable?" Anderson pushed his chair back and stood up; he lowered his eyebrows before he spoke.

"Yes, we have, the co-operation I am talking about is between us," he had also lowered his voice, the two in front of him picked up the menace that was there.

"Us?" Michael asked, "that is simple, you will fulfil every request we make and when we detail your team members to complete tasks for us, we will try to keep you informed." Anderson was getting annoyed, both Michael and Martin spotted him clench his fists.

"I meant between us," he stated.

"Us?" Michael asked.

"Yes, this is a major, province wide investigation and I am the senior investigating officer of this investigation and I expect your co-operation with me in that any reports or findings you have come to me first, before they are submitted."

"What?" Michael reacted, his voice raised somewhat, "and why, precisely should we do that?" he demanded. Anderson straightened up.

"I want to ensure that all correct procedures are followed, it is just to make sure there is no, 'misunderstanding' in any findings in your review." Martin glanced over at Michael; he could see the anger in his eyes.

"*CHIEF INSPECTOR ANDERSON,*" Michael's tone was serious, "*if you 'EVER' try and influence any case review carried out by me, or anyone who is working for me then I WILL report you for trying to undermine and interfere with an active investigation!*" Michael reached forward and placed his right forefinger onto the desk, "*do I make myself clear!*"

"Look, I was just ...." Anderson started.

"YES OR NO, *DO I MAKE MYSELF CLEAR CHIEF INSPECTOR!*" Michael shouted this time. There was a pause as the two men stared at each other.

"Yes," Anderson broke the silence.

"Yes, what?" Michael was insisting that he use his rank.

"Yes ... Sir," Michaels body started to turn but his eyes still stared at Anderson.

"Chief Inspector Anderson," he had lowered his voice, so it was quiet, his force of personality was coming through.

"Sir?" Anderson replied, he had also lowered his voice.

"If you *ever* do that again, I will arrest you for trying to 'pervert the course of justice'," the look of shock burst over Anderson's face as Martin tried not to look surprised as well, Michael had made the ultimate threat. Michael looked over his shoulder at Martin.

"Do you know where the investigation team offices are?" Michael asked.

"Yes, of course," Martin replied. Michael pushed the chair forward and marched towards the open door of the office.

"Take me there," he instructed.

∞∞∞∞

Dermot and Paul pulled the main door to the barn open and walked in, Dermott closed the door behind him. They both stopped by the wooden barrier that was the edge of the arena. Tyler's voice echoed around, she wasn't happy with the group of teenagers who were out of breath, most looked exhausted. Everyone was dressed for going to a gym in leggings and workout tops, everyone had a wooden training sword in their hands. The group was in pairs, everyone stopped and looked at the angry Tyler.

"NO NO NO, THAT ISN'T WHAT I SAID, IF YOU CAN'T LEARN THE BASICS THEN YOU WILL LOSE YOUR FIRST FIGHT!" some of the eyes looked over at Paul and Dermott, Tyler picked it up and looked over at them, they wanted to talk. She turned back to the students. "Right, take ten minutes, then we are going to start this again and I WILL keep you here all night until you get this right!" Everyone relaxed and headed of a series of small daysacks that were along the inside of the edge of the area. Tyler spun the wooden sword in her hand and walked towards Paul and Dermott.

"She looks upset," Dermott said quietly. Paul looked at him and smiled.

"DAMN RIGHT I AM UPSET!" she shouted as she approached. Paul giggled.

"You forgot about how good her hearing is?" he was smiling at Dermott, who looked between the two. Tyler stopped inside the area, she was still breathing loudly, she had been working hard as well.

"So," she started, "what is up?"

"We have heard from Silver and Gold, they think this fella Hanna is somewhere around Coleraine, but they are not 100% sure yet," Tyler placed her hands on her hips, her breathing was quickly returning to normal.

"Excellent, once they find him, we can deal with him, once and for all," she injected.

"Yes, we have a team on standby that are just waiting for the go," Dermott added.

"And we still think he has Fiona?" Tyler asked.

"I can't be anyone else," Dermott spat.

"How did they get so close to the four, without them realising it?" Tyler asked.

"We don't know, all we do know is the initial shots came from behind them then he performed a Coup de Grace on Becky as she lay on the ground," Paul added.

"Bastards," Dermott spat. Tyler looked down, shaking her head, then she looked up.

"Something isn't right here, even for a Master Hunter, that isn't the way they hunt, that is what sapiens do, not Nocs!"

"I agree, Becky and Fi were really good, I cannot believe they got the drop on them or the others?" Paul added.

"Have they released the bodies yet?" Tyler asked.

"No," Paul stated, "The coroner still has them."

"How is their dad doing?" Tyler asked with concern.

"Going out of his fucking mind!" Dermott replied.

"Understandable," Tyler added, "what else can we do?" she asked.

"Everything that can be done, is being done, we are a pack, packs stick together," insisted Dermott. She looked between the two of them.

"You said a couple of things, what else is up?"

"The police have asked if we can meet up?" Dermott replied.

"Oh, any idea what about?" she asked.

"Not sure," he answered.

"Are they aware of our part in the assault at the farmhouse?"

"No," Paul answered, "if they were, we would already know,"

"Okay," Tyler took a deep breath in, "where and when?" she asked.

"Tomorrow, in a layby," Dermott shrugged, "I know it, so no problems."

"And the military have definitely gone?"

"Definitely," Paul answered, "which is a shame, I kinda liked them,"

"Oh, any news on that last Noc, Megan 'what's her name'?" Tyler asked.

"Last we heard from that Apollyon fella is she was migrating towards Enniskillen direction," Paul stated.

"And he was going to track her down for us," Dermott added.

"That's good," Tyler nodded.

"I don't trust him," Dermott added, Tyler looked over at him.

"We don't have to trust him, just let him take out Nocs for us," she shrugged, "he certainly has enough reason to hate them as much as we do!" she added.

"Aye, I suppose," Dermott shrugged.

"Oh, that reminds me," Paul stated as he stood upright and looked over at the group of teenagers, "Everyone gather round!" he shouted at them. There was a collective movement as they all headed over towards them.

"What?" Tyler asked as she looked at them, then at the growing smile of Paul's face. Dermott looked at him, then remembered something, he looked back at Tyler and smiled. Tyler stepped to one side as the group arrived. Paul winked at a very tired looking Rhydian.

"Everyone, gather in," Paul was looking at the different faces in front of him, "we have news from our two members who were at the high council meeting a few days ago, and" he glanced at Tyler, "and," he continued, "there are two bits of news I would like you all to pass around the rest of the pack as soon as possible."

"Paul, what's going on?" Rhydian had a confused look on her face. Paul turned towards her; he raised his voice as he did so.

"The high council," he looked into her eyes, "has stated that you, Tyler Reynolds of the An Rua, are to be recognised for your actions, against our enemies, with the highest honour for valour, to be given by the high council." A loud cheer went up, Tyler blushed as her shoulders were patted and handshakes all around., Morale increased in the arena. "Also," Paul shouted, everyone looked towards him. "The An Rua have been invited to present our Moon Dance tale to the high council later in the year," another cheer when up.

"I've never been to Russia!" one exclaimed. Paul watched as Rhydian stepped forward and hugged Tyler. The embrace was as long as it was warm and loving. When it broke the two looked at each other and smiled.

"Right," Paul brought everyone back into order, "we will have a full pack meeting tonight, I want everyone to be in attendance," he looked at Tyler, "we have a lot to celebrate!"

"But that is for later, right now you all have work to do, so back to it!" Tyler shouted.

"When you are done, read over the communique" Paul's mood was more serious.

"Oh?" she replied.

"Yeah," Paul nodded, he first looked down, then looked up at her, "they are calling all pack alphas to a full council meeting as soon as possible."

"That can mean only one thing!" Dermott stated. The three looked at each other, but it was Tyler who stated the obvious.

"A WORLDWIDE DECLARATION OF WAR!"

Chapter 48

Michael Bolton walked along the corridor in front of Martin Mullen. Two uniformed officers walked past heading the other way. Michael paused and looked over his shoulder at the smile on Martin's face. "Is it along here?" he asked.

"Just round the corner, the door is signposted with 'Major Investigations' above the door." Martin also nodded with his head.

"So," Michael said, "is there anything I should know about this, 'Inspector Wells' before we go in?" he stopped again and partly turned towards Martin, "I take it this introduction will not be like the one we just had?" Again, Martin tried to suppress his smile.

"Hell no, all I know about her is she is the granddaughter of a former chief constable, and this is her first appointment as an inspector." Michael looked ahead of himself, Martin could almost hear his mind working and he headed off again.

"Okay," he replied as they walked around the corner. Michael looked up at the small plastic sign that stuck out from the top of the door frame of the office. Michael knocked once and opened the door then walked in.

The main office had workstations around the side with a small, raised area that was obviously used for presentations. At the far end was the small office that would be for the team's inspector. In the middle of the room, two desks had been pushed together and in the centre of the desk was the rectangular shaped multimicrophone device that was used for conference calling. Around the desk were six, equally spaced chairs. Standing between him and the desk was a tall woman who turned around as he had entered. She was smartly dressed and had a serious look on her face. The far side of the desk two detectives quickly stood up.

"Inspector Wells?" Michael asked. The woman stepped forward and offered her hand. It was a firm handshake.

"Yes Sir," she responded.

"Superintendent Bolton, Met Police," Michael stated releasing her grip, he turned and stepped to one side as Martin stopped beside him. "And this is Chief Inspector Mullen,"

"Inspector," Martin politely nodded once as the two shook hands. Mary Wells then turned and introduced the other two as they walked around the desk towards them.

"And may I introduce Detective Sergeant Emma Ford and Detective Sergeant Gareth McHale," hands were shaken, and pleasantries exchanged.

"Would either of you like a coffee before we start?" Mary offered.

"Your predecessor had a machine in his office that seemed to be permanently on!" Martin exclaimed as he unbuttoned his suit jacket. Mary looked at him.

"You knew Inspector Parrish?" she asked. Martin stopped and looked straight at her.

"Yes, yes I did," his eyes made an unconscious look to the floor before looking up again, "we both went through police college together,"

"Oh, I didn't know that" she replied, "but if you went through training at the same time how did you know him and how are you still serving? Have you not completed your thirty years' service?" she asked.

"Yes, before I was a Met officer, I was RUC, and I am currently in extended service." There was another pause before she spoke again.

"I am sorry for your loss, I only knew the Inspector by reputation," she added.

"Thank you, Sean was one of the best," Martin paused then looked around, "well, it has been a few years since I was last in here!" he turned and looked around the blank walls and presentation boards, all were blank so not to distract from the meeting that was about to happen.

"So," Michael stepped past Mary, "how long have you been a DS?" he asked.

"Three years," Emma replied.

"Four years," Gareth added.

"Excellent," Michael turned towards Mary, "and the rest of the team?" he asked.

"You are meeting them tomorrow, I thought it would be best to have this conference with just department heads," there was a polite smile from her. Michael looked straight at her.

"I agree,"

"So, what kind of coffee do you have?" Martin asked. The mood in the room lifted. It would be another several minutes before they were sitting down around the desk, Gareth and Emma fiddled with the microphone system then static came out of it.

"We are live in sixty seconds," Mary stated as she looked at her watch.

"We are on," Emma announced as a red light appeared on the top of the device. Martin looked around the room, his eyes glanced over the two empty chairs, he knew Anderson was supposed to be there, but who was the other one for.

"*Hello,*" a male voice echoed from the box. Everyone got comfortable and pulled chairs closer to the desks.

"Superintendent Sutcliffe?" Mary asked.

"*Yes, yes, hang on .... ok, linking up .... now,*" there was a pause then his voice echoed again, "*Okay, that looks like we are all here, Inspector Wells .... Over to you,*" Mary sat forward, she had produced a large notebook and had a very stylist pen with it. She looked directly at the device as she spoke.

"Good afternoon, Sirs, this call is being recorded," her eyes glanced up at the large clock on the wall, "it is now two minutes past three in the afternoon and this is the initial introduction of a case review of 'Operation Abhartach' which is a major investigation being carried out by Major Investigations Team, Belfast of the Police Service of Northern Ireland," she looked around the room, "currently in the room are myself, Inspector Mary Wells," She looked over at Michael, who nodded.

"I am Superintendent Michael Bolton of the Metropolitan Police Service," he glanced at Martin who spoke next.

"Chief Inspector Martin Mullen, Metropolitan Police Service," Mary looked at the first of her sergeants.

"Detective Sergeant Emma Ford, PSNI."

"Detective Sergeant Gareth McHale, PSNI." Mary looked back at the device.

"And for the benefit of the recording can those who are joining us by teleconference identify yourselves." There was a short pause before the different voices came from the device.

"*Assistant Chief Constable Watt,*"

"*Superintendent Sutcliffe, PSNI,*"

"*Superintendent Forrester, Intelligence Branch, PSNI,*" Michael looked at the way Martin's body had reacted to the last voice, there was obviously history there as well.

"Thank you everyone," Mary started.

"*Inspector Wells,*" the Assistant Chief Constable interrupted her, "*is Chief Inspector Anderson not supposed to be joining us?*" he asked. Mary's eyes darted over to Emma, then she looked back at the device.

"Yes Sir, as far as I know he was."

"*Well? Where is he?*" Mary crunched her face at the question.

"I am sorry Sir, I don't know," there was another pause before Super Sutcliffe spoke.

"*Leave that one with me,*"

"Thank you," The main door to the office opened and an annoyed looking Chief Anderson stormed in. All eyes in the room looked at him as the door slammed shut, he waved his hand towards Mary.

"You may begin!" he stated as he angrily sat down. Mary raised her eyebrows and looked at him as she spoke.

"And for the benefit of the recording, we have now been joined in the room by Chief Inspector Anderson, Major Investigations, PSNI," she was being correct and formal. His mouth opened to speak but he stopped himself as he realised the device on the desk was live.

"Chief Anderson, can you call my office after this conference is over?" The voice of Super Sutcliffe echoed from the device, he may have just asked a question *'can you'*, but everyone recognised it was an order.

"Of course, I would be very happy to," he replied as he shifted in his seat, he then glared are Mary Wells at the telling off everyone knew he was going to get later.

"So, to begin," Assistant Chief Constable Watt's voice came from the device, *"I would like to welcome Superintendent Bolton and Chief Inspector Mullen from the Metropolitan Police and thank them for accepting the lead roles in this case review."*

"Thank you, Sir, we are very happy to assist with this review," Michael replied. He looked directly at the device as he did so. Michael's English accent stood out against the other local accents around him. "Sir, may I state, first of all, my thanks to Inspector Wells for the case overview she sent us, that enabled us to get an insight into the case so far," Mary smiled at him as he gave her a polite nod.

"What case overview?" Anderson sat up in his chair, "I didn't approve any such thing!" he stated. Mary Wells went to speak but Michael answered for her.

"I requested it," he looked at Mary, "and the Inspector completed it then forwarded it to me ... so thank you for that," he motioned towards her.

"You are welcome, Sir," she responded. Anderson's face contorted in anger; he had not known about that.

"So," Super Sutcliffe started, *"initially what is it you are looking at?"* Michael shifted in his seat and again, spoke directly to the device.

"Well, first we will need office space to work out of," Mary sat upright, it attracted his attention, he motioned with his head with a single nod, he was giving her space to speak.

"Yes Sir, I have already got that booked for you," she glanced at Martin, "you requested in your previous emails that you would require space for four detectives in total, so we have that ready for you,"

"And that has I.T. access, landline phones etc?" Michael asked.

Mary looked back at him. "Yes sir, it is the office directly below this one, so it is exactly the same as this," she smiled.

"You said enough for 'four detectives?" Anderson asked as he sat forward.

Michael looked at him without smiling. "Yes, I am bringing two of my DS's over from London," again Anderson went to speak but stopped himself, there was a building fury in his eyes, which Michael spotted. "You have not got a problem with that have you?" Michael asked. All eyes in the room turned towards Chief Anderson, he was now gripping the arm of his seat, Super Sutcliffe's voice came from the device.

"No, I am sure the Chief Inspector is happy to accommodate any team members you see fit to include in your review!" Chief Anderson nodded and sat back.

"So, Superintendent," it was the ACC, *"have you any initial thoughts about how you will start your review?"* Michael sat back in his chair; he was speaking directly to the device.

"Yes Sir, I have only had a cursory view of the case files and what I can see so far is there are over fifteen murders all having the same cause of death as some type of 'bite' to the neck causing a rupture of the arteries, differing completely from animal attacks around the Mourne mountains," Michael was getting into his stride, Martin smiled, he had seen this so many times before, Michael carried on, "these first murders all have similarities but, Inspector, you did state in your initial overview there was incomplete DNA evidence taken at the scene,"

"All proper procedures were followed, I can assure you of that," Anderson injected.

"What was the problem with the collection of DNA evidence then?" Michael asked.

"The collected DNA evidence unfortunately was corrupted; this we have put down to samples being taken incorrectly by the CSI team!" Chief Anderson sat back confidently.

"Really?" Michael cast a glance towards Mary, who looked down, she was uncomfortable with what had just been said and Michael spotted it. "So, Chief Inspector, you are putting forward that up to three different CSI teams, at several different locations all took DNA samples and managed to corrupt them all? That strikes me as 'odd' to begin with. When this was first discovered did you not look into it?"

"ALL PROCEDURES WERE CARRIED OUT CORRECTLY!" Chief Anderson replied adamantly, "I PERSONALLY ENSURED THIS!"

"Okay," Michael looked at Mary and extended his left hand towards her, "that is something we can look at, Inspector Wells, you stated in your overview it is not currently thought any of these murders are connected. Is there any reason you have not looked at the possibility you could be dealing with a serial killer?"

"Don't be absurd! What a ridiculous thing to even suggest!" Chief Anderson butted in, again all eyes turned towards him.

"And why is that absurd?" Michael asked, "you have over fifteen murders, all with the same, very unusual method of killing," Michael looked directly at Anderson, "and from what we discovered as well, there have been others with the same method of killing, one in Dublin in a hotel and ..." he turned and looked at Martin.

"Two men in Limerick," Martin added.

"Ah yes, Limerick," Michael smiled as he turned back towards Chief Anderson, "have you spoken with the police in the Republic to see if there are any similarities?"

"That is outside of our jurisdiction," Anderson added.

"So, in your experience, serial killers stay within police boundaries, do they?" Michael glanced over at Mary; her face was trying not to smile at his dig at Chief Anderson. Had she picked up on what Michael was doing? If she had, she was not saying anything.

"We are NOT dealing with a serial killer!" Chief Anderson ranted.

"And why not?" Michael spoke quietly.

"Because .... There are no connections between any of the victims.,"

"Apart from the method they died," Michael looked over at Mary again, "also that name that was in your overview, someone called 'Martin'."

"Kris Martin, yes," she confirmed.

"Wasn't he connected with the five who were murdered at Portstewart strand, then again in Lisburn, and you have CCTV putting him at the scene of two brutal murders in the bungalow somewhere near Cushendun ..." Michael almost winked at Mary as he continued, "and wasn't Martin connected to one of the victims there?" he asked.

"Yes," she confirmed again, "the girl, we think had a previous relationship with him and she had two different restraining orders on him," she glanced over at Chief Anderson then looked back at Michael, "both of which he had convictions for breaking,"

"Well," Michael sat back, then looked at Anderson again, "I think we 'have' established connections, I think our first order of business will be to look at the possibly there is a serial killer," he glanced at Martin who nodded as he spoke, "or a group of serial killers," he looked back at the device, "as we cannot rule out the possibility that this is the work of more than one person."

"*Well, Superintendent Bolton,*" it was the voice of the Assistant Chief Constable again, "*it appears you are certainly off to a good start.*"

"Thank you, Sir," Michael added, the ACC carried on.

"*Superintendent Forester, have you anything to add?*" he asked. Chief Anderson's face burst with surprise; he had not realised Darren was listening as well.

"*Yes Sir, I have already been liaising with Inspector Wells, their investigation and the ongoing investigation headed by us at Intelligence Branch, and I would like to extend to Super Bolton, any help we can be, then please just ask!*"

"Thank you, Super Forester, I look forward to meeting face to face," Michael added.

"What?" Chief Anderson looked at Mary, "I didn't authorise any contact with Special Branch! What the hell do you think you are doing!" he demanded.

"*HER JOB,*" Darren's voice came from the device, "*in fact it was I who approached her as it seems both our investigations may in fact overlap,*" Mary kept a straight face as her eyes moved from the irate Chief Anderson to Michael.

"And why didn't I know about this?" Anderson protested, "there 'are' correct channels and proper police procedures that have to be followed ... 'at all times!'"

"What? like you trying to circumvent all of that, not half an hour ago in your office!" Michael butted in. Anderson stopped and glared at him.

"Michael, *what are you talking about?*" it was Super Sutcliffe.

"Just before this conference myself and Chief Mullen were invited into Chief Anderson's office during which he wanted us to pass all of our reports to him before submitting them," Michael was looking at the device, Martin spotted the reaction in the two detectives and Mary, they clearly did not know about that.

"*HE DID WHAT?*" it was the ACC's voice. Anderson sat forward; Michael did not look at him as he nearly shouted at the device.

"I did no such thing, I was just welcoming them to Belfast and making clear what correct procedures where,"

"By trying to influence us and any findings that we have during this case review by trying to intimidate two visiting officers as 'things are done differently here in Belfast!' apparently," Martin felt his eyes widen at what Michael had just said.

"*CHIEF ANDERSON!*" The ACC shouted.

"I assure you, Sir," Anderson looked over at the stern face of the Met police Superintendent looking straight back at him, "I have not tried to influence anything!"

"What? are you saying you didn't say that?" Michael injected. Chief Anderson glared at him; he could not say what he desperately wanted to. "In fact," Michael carried on, "such was the seriousness of what the Chief tried to do I had to caution him on trying to 'pervert the course of justice.'"

"Sir, I ..."

"*CHIEF ANDERSON!*" the ACC shouted.

"No Sir, all I was trying to ensure with the Superintendent was that ...."

"*SUPERINTENDENT SUTCLIFFE,*" The ACC's voice cut Chief Anderson off.

"*I want to speak to you and Chief Anderson in my office 'IMMEDIATELY'*" All eyes in the room turned to the face of rage that was sitting at the end of the table.

"*Of course, Sir,*

Chief Anderson, report to my office at once,"

"Super, I ..."

"*At once, Chief Inspector,*" Anderson glared at each face, everyone except for Michael and Matin looked away. The ACC carried on, "*for the benefit of the recording, Chief Anderson is just leaving the room!*" Again, it was not a request, it was an order. Chief Anderson stood up with such speed the chair was sent backwards several feet. He turned and stormed out of the room, this time the two detectives sitting beside Mary could not mask their reactions to what they had just heard. The 'met police guy' had just dropped the big one, and this was a tale that would be recounted many times; and it would not be long before whispers echoed throughout the Police Service of Northern Ireland.

"*So, if I may conclude,*" The ACC's voice was once again calm, "*Superintendent Bolton, I look forward to reading your review and any findings you have and I wish you all the success in helping us gain a successful outcome to this case,*" The ACC was being formal, Michael straightened himself in his chair.

"Thank you once again Sir,"

"*Inspector Wells, I can give control back to you, any problems then I am sure Superintendent's Forester and Sutcliffe would be very happy to help!*"

Mary sat forward, "Yes Sir, that will be fine,"

There was a beep from the machine that indicated that he had left the conversation, Mary looked over at Michael. "Conference closed down," she glanced up at the clock on the wall, after she repeated the time, she reached forward and pressed a button and the red light on the device went out. They were not being recorded anymore.

"Right then," Michael said as he stood up, everyone in the room followed by standing as well, he looked at Mary and smiled, "you were offering a coffee if I remember correctly?"

"And don't forget biscuits," Martin Mullen added, smiling as he did so.

Chapter 49

"May I ask everyone to take their seats, we have a lot to discuss," The Lord Protector shouted. There was various movement around the great hall and everyone who was standing in gathered groups broke up and soon all the seats were filled. He waited for the hall to quieten before he looked at each of the others who were sitting on each of their thrones, the only two vacant were for the King and Queen. He looked towards the rear door and waited for the raised hand of the security team member to indicate she had arrived. "Can we be upstanding for the arrival of The Queen of the Black Witches!" The whole room moved and the others who were on the stage all rose as the two doors opened and she walked in. She strode confidently up the middle isle, every eye in the room was on her, and she was loving it. She was wearing black leather boots that went up to her knees, her jeans were black, as was the patterned leather belt that was around her waist. The black silk blouse moved as if it was in wind, but there was no wind. Her hair hung down and rested over her shoulders, The Lord Protector looked at her. She was a stunning woman, he could see how she was the biggest 'madam' in southern England, nearly all of the illegal brothels were controlled by her. Her beauty was only matched by her viciousness, if you crossed her, well, your body would probably never be found. He watched as she walked around the front of the stage and headed over to the stairs at the side that led onto the stage. The coven lords all bowed as she walked onto the stage and stopped in front of her throne. She turned and sat down. Once she sat down, the Lord's did too, then the room filled with the sound of shuffling as everyone else took their seats. The Lord Protector stood up and stepped forward. "Ma'am, coven members, you have been called here tonight to discuss a very serious situation that has developed," he paused, the Lord Mason behind him coughed. "I bring the saddest of news, that one of our own, the Master Hunter himself, has passed over," there was a collective gasp, comments and mutterings started.

"What of his task?" The Queen asked, all heads turned towards her as she sternly looked towards him.

"We believe he was successful in his task of stopping the American, but in doing so, unfortunately he alerted the wolves,"

"Was it the wolves that killed him?" the Lord Mason asked.

"No, it was not, in fact we have discovered several of ours have been taken down by another, who is not connected with the wolves at all!" the Lord Protector stated.

"Then who did kill him if it wasn't the wolves?" The Lord Mason sat forward; anger emanated from him. The Lord Protector looked at him then turned back towards the Queen.

"Ma'am, I can confirm that The American is dead and is no longer a problem for us," The Lord Protector spoke directly to the Queen.

"That doesn't answer my question! 'Who killed him if it wasn't the wolves?'" The Lord Mason spat. The Lord Protector glared at him, nodded towards the Queen, then half turned so he was nearly facing The Grand Room.

"We have learnt that we have a new enemy, there is an assassin called 'Jason Apollyon' and we believe it was he who tracked the Master Hunter and killed him and his bodyguard." The Lord Protector stated.

"*Impossible!*" The Lord Mason almost jumped to his feet, "he had an entire close protection team around him, how could anyone has gotten that close to him?" he demanded. The Lord Protector took his time. He slowly turned and addressed the Lord Mason directly.

"Lord Mason, we received a distress call from the Master Hunter, the wolves had launched a full assault of the primary safe house, only the Master Hunter, his driver and his bodyguard managed to get away." He stated.

"They 'managed to get away' from a wolf assault? I find that hard to believe." The Lord Mason sat back in his chair.

"Well, from what the Master Hunter told me himself, they were out getting pizzas and the assault occurred just as they were getting near the safe house," The Lord Protector turned back towards the Queen, "he stated that he believed this, Apollyon, led the wolves to the safe house and let them carry out their assault," he paused, then turned back towards the main room, "They then went to the secondary safe house, we could not deploy an aircraft with a team that night because you," he turned back towards the Lord Mason, "Lord Mason were taking your time with this approach with the sapien Earl in Dartmoor," he then looked at the other council members, "an approach, from what I can gather has come to naught!" The rest of the room echoed with the whisperings and mutterings between all of those in the main room.

They were silenced when the Queen raised her right hand. "And what do we know of this, 'Apollyon'?" she asked. The Lord Protector turned to face her.

"Ma'am, we believe this is the same one who is nicknamed 'The Destroyer' who has been on a personal vendetta for several years. Until now, we did not know his real name."

"And he is working with the wolves?" The Lord Mason interrupted what The Lord Protector was saying, slowly the Lord Protector turned towards him.

"Quite the contrary, we understand that they have made an approach, but he refused, but since he is only killing our members and wants nothing to do with them, they are happy for him to continue!" The Lord Protector stated.

"Why would they trust him?" The Lord Mason again demanded.

"They don't, but they are happy for him to continue killing us,"

"So, they are helping him then?" again the Lord Mason interrupted.

"Again, no," this time he looked directly at the Lord Mason.

"So, what do we know about him?" The Queen asked.

"Ma'am, he is a former member of the Canadian Special Forces called JTF 2, he is a Master Sniper and is fluent is several European languages," he looked at the other council members, "I have compiled an extensive file on him that I am happy to copy for each of you,"

"Thank you," The Queen replied.

"How do you know it was him who killed the Master Hunter?" the Lord Mason asked. The Lord Protector again looked over at him.

"By the way they were found," he replied.

"What do you mean by 'the way they were found?" the Lord Mason asked, his tone of voice again showing how annoyed he was.

"Simple, I have seen a copy of the Crime Scenes log, first of all, the bodyguard, was killed by a solid object piercing his heart, the driver had a fatal knife wound to his neck and the Master Hunter had been left out for the sunrise." He looked around the rest of the council, "only a sapien would have killed like that, if it had been the wolves, they would have destroyed the bodies completely and they would have told the other packs about taking down one such at the Master Hunter," he looked at the Lord Mason, "in fact, they would not have shut up about it!"

"But how was he able to best the Maser Hunter?" The Lord Inquisitor asked, "surely it would have taken more than one to achieve a feat like that!" The Lord Protector looked at her before he answered her question.

"I believe it comes from how he turned," he replied.

"Turned?" she repeated, "are you saying he is one of us?"

"No, no, not at all,"

"Also, why does he hunt us? How does he know of our true existence?" she enquired.

"All I know is ..." the Lord Protector started, "is that a small group of teenage Vampiri attacked his family, killed his wife, children, and they thought they had killed him," The Lord

Protector again turned back towards the Queen, "he was bitten, but, unusually he didn't die and he didn't turn, we believe whatever he has now become, he has what can only be described as 'un-natural' abilities in hunting and fighting."

"What?" The Lord Councillor sat forward as he asked his question, "he survived a bite from one of us and did not become one of us?" There was another ripple through the room.

"Yes, it appears that is what has happened,"

"So, what is he then?" the Lord Advocate asked. The Lord Protector opened his mouth to speak but the Queen answered for him.

"ABOMINATION," all heads looked at her, there was shock in the room.

"So, what are we going to do about him then? Since he is such a threat to us?" the Lord Mason asked. The Lord Protector turned back towards the Queen.

"Ma'am, with your permission, I would like to pass his name and all the information we currently have around our network of worldwide covens, I believe that while this person lives, we are all under threat." The room fell silent. Everyone looked at the Queen, slowly she nodded her head but did not speak. "Ma'am, again, with your permission, there is something else I need to inform you of." Again, she nodded then he turned and faced the room. "We have learnt the wolves 'High council' will be honouring Reynolds and the An Rua for their actions against us over the last few years in Ireland," there was another ripple around the room, "and most recently, they have requested that all pack alphas, from around the world are to attend a meeting of their 'high council' before the year is out." The room exploded in conversation.

"But that has not happened since before the last truce!" the Lord Advocate stated. The Lord Protector turned towards her.

"I believe you are correct; it can mean only one thing!" the Lord Protector replied.

"How do you know all of this? Where has this information come from?" The Lord Mason demanded. Everyone looked at him, then at the Lord Protector who smiled at him.

"Simple really," he looked at the Queen, "I have had an undercover operative working alongside the wolves for some time now." He seemed really pleased with himself,

"Impossible!" the Lord Mason nearly shouted as he slammed his hand down on the armrest of the chair, "the wolves would easily pick up any of our kind, we would not get that close to them!" he was defiant.

"Oh no, Lord Mason," the Lord Protector started, "I have not been using a Vampiri, I have haven using a sapien."

"A sapien?" The Lord Mason reacted.

"Yes," the Lord Protector continued, "and the only reason they would be gathering all of the pack alphas is to declare a worldwide war against us!"

"War? But the truce still holds, why would they do that?" the Lord Inquisitor asked.

"Because they feel they are in the right to, after everything 'The American' has done, they will feel that it was 'us' who broke the truce and after what Foster and Reynolds were able to do, each alpha will feel confident to be able to do the same in each of their own pack areas!" The Lord Advocate stated as she looked directly at the Lord Protector, "They are animals after all, and each alpha is always trying to outdo the others," she looked directly at the Queen, "it is in their blood." The Queen nodded and looked concerned.

"Your undercover, with the wolves, what else can they tell us?" the Queen asked the Lord Protector directly. He smiled.

"We can ask him now," he turned towards the entrance door at the far end of the Grand Room, "let him enter!" he shouted. The two-security detail at the entrance stepped forward and opened the doors. All heads turned towards the entrance as the single figure walked in. Some rose to get a better look at the man who had just walked in. He was wearing jeans, a fleece top and an outdoor gortex jacket. He stopped at the top of the aisle; the Lord Protector raised his right hand to beckon him closer. As he started to walk forward, the Lord Protector introduced him. "Ma'am. Council members, Vampiri, may I introduce one of our greatest undercover assets: this is Chris Abbey of the British SAS," the Lord Protector smiled as Chris came closer. "Come, come," the Lord Protector beckoned again so Chris walked over to the steps and trotted up and headed toward the centre of the stage, he stopped right beside the Lord Protector who smiled as he approached.

"Lord Protector, I must protest, it is again our rules to bring a sapien in here!" the Lord Mason looked at the Queen, "no sapien can ever walk here," he leaned forward to say something, but the Queen raised her hand and stopped him. She looked at the Lord Advocate who was tilting her head rearwards, as if to sniff the air. The two caught each other's eye.

"Well?" the Queen asked. The Lord Advocate looked back at Chris who stared back at her. She looked back at the Queen as she placed her hands on the armrests of her throne.

"Yes, he is sapien, but there is something else," she looked back towards him, "he has been here before." All eyes turned towards Chris as a small smile spread over his lips.

"Well, Mr Abbey? Have you been here before?" the Queen asked. The Lord Protector looked at her, he spotted the little smile on her lips, her eyebrows had lowered, and he saw the way the tips of her fingers had started to dance on her armrests, she liked him.

"Yes, your majesty, I have," there was a ripple of laughter around the seated Lord's, the Lord Protector nudged his side.

"Our Queen is addressed as 'Ma'am'," he corrected.

"Sorry, Ma'am," Chris looked at her face but dropped his gaze, his eyes moved down the front of her silk top, along her jeans and stopped at her boots.

"How and when?" the Lord Mason demanded; Chris looked over at him.

"My grandfather brought me here as a boy," Chris stepped forward as he spoke.

"I find that very had to believe," the Lord Mason continued.

"I don't give a shit what you believe," Chris started, there was a reaction of shock from the others.

"Don't you speak to me like that, worm, I am a Lord of the Noctraili Vampiri!" the Lord Mason almost shouted at him. "No one speaks to me like that!" He was gripping the ends of his armrests; it looked like he was about to jump forward.

"Who was your Grandfather?" the Lord Inquisitor asked. Chris looked over at her then pointed towards the empty throne.

"My grandfather was Sir Hugh Coldstream-Abbey," he glared at the Lord Mason as he raised his own voice, *"and he was the last king to sit on that throne!"* The Lords reacted, the Lord Mason sat back, his face wide with shock as Chris lowered his arm. The room exploded in conversations and passing comments. Everyone reacted except the Lord Protector.

"QUIET!" the Queen commanded. The room fell silent.

"So, Lord Mason," the Lord Protector started, "he can walk here," he turned and addressed the Queen, "his genealogy allows it." The Queen nodded once and waved her right hand with a circular motion from her wrist, her approval was given.

"So .... Mr ... Abbey?" The Lord Mason started, "what can you tell us about the wolves?" there was obvious sarcasm in his voice. The Lord Protector stepped back so that Chris stood in the middle of the space in front of the thrones.

"Well, the northern den of the Irish pack has separated from the control of the south, the pack in the south broke some major rule or something and two of their council members made a ruling that they could spit from the main pack,"

"Dissent among the wolves, I like it!" the Lord Advocate smiled as she spoke.

"And we just have to 'believe' everything that you have to say and claim, without any form of proof, do we?" the Lord Mason demanded, he looked at The Queen, "How do we know if any of this is actually true, how was he able to gain all this information?" The Queen nodded once then looked back at Chris.

"Well," Chris started, "I have been shagging one of their female members of their security team for nearly a year and well, 'pillow talk' is normally accurate." The Queen looked over at the Lord Mason then back at Chris, smiling as she did so.

"Continue," she commanded.

"A direct assault against them would be pointless, they are very well trained and armed with modern weaponry," Chris looked at the other Lords as he spoke, "they have a very good defensive plan that has a competent and capable surveillance edge to it," he looked back at the Queen, "you would not get near without substantial losses to your attacking force." He glanced back at the Lord Protector then at the Queen. "A force of Russian wolves tried a direct assault on them just over two years ago and the Irish wiped them out!" there was a reaction from the entire room, "but of recent times," he carried on, "the actions of 'The American' and his group did bring them out and away from their main defence. They lost over 15 and had over twice that injured, that took down, nearly half the overall fighting force of the northern den."

"And we lost over one hundred," the Lord Mason shouted," everyone turned to look at him, "those are not sustainable odds by any stretch of the imagination,"

"No, they aren't," Chris added.

"We cannot continue to suffer losses like that!" the Lord Mason sat back on his throne, he looked at the other Lords then at the Queen.

"No, you can't, but then, they were led by an idiot who had no tactical understanding, was seemingly in love with his own ego, and did not know the capabilities of his opposition," Chris added. "That kind of thing has happened before and normally ends badly."

"Where?" the Lord Mason demanded.

"The Battle of the Little Big Horn," Chris replied. The Queen smirked.

"What? and you think you could do a better job?" the Lord Mason baited him.

"I am a Staff Sergeant in the SAS ... damn right I could!" the Lord Protector watched the growing body language between the two, this situation was growing and becoming more tense, something was about to happen, and he was not going to intervene. His mouth was starting to salivate at the coming conflict.

"No sapien can ever lead our hunters," the Lord Mason was almost shouting again. Chris stepped forward and pointed at the empty throne.

"But if I am sitting there, I certainly could,"

"*Don't be absurd!*" The Lord Mason shouted, "*no sapien can ever sit on that throne!*" Chris looked at him then back at the Queen.

"Why not?" he pointed with his right hand at the Queen, "she is human, are you not?" he tucked his right hand into the pocket of his jeans as he took a step closer.

"I am, yes," she replied. The Lord Protector looked at her, she was loving this.

"Can I claim that throne because of my ancestry?" Chris stepped towards it.

"*NO FUCKING WAY!*" The Lord Mason screamed as he launched himself at Chris. The Lord Protector's gasped at what he was watching. The Lord Mason had pulled out a small knife that was now in his right hand, he screamed as he lunged towards where Chris had been standing. All the other Lord's sat back in their chairs, there was a reaction of shock from the room behind him as the blade passed through the space where Chris had been standing. Chris not only had ducked, but his body rotated as he passed under the outstretched arm of the Lord Mason. Chris's right hand had come out from underneath his clothes and slammed into the Lord Mason's chest, then he rotated on his fast-moving feet into the space away from the now crumbling body of the Lord Mason. There was a squeal of terror as the body landed on the floor and rolled onto his back. Chris stepped back and looked at the Lord Mason then up at the Queen.

Everyone in the room could see what was sticking out of the Lord Mason's chest. His fingers toyed with the solid circular end of the wooden stake; his face looked like a ten-year-old boy who was seeing his own blood for the first time. His face quivered, the tears and the sobs quickly passed, and the body went limp. The Lord Mason was dead.

"A wooden stake through the heart," the Lord Protector quipped, "how decidedly old fashioned!" gasps and comments sounded from the room behind them. Chris stepped forward and stood directly in front of the Queen. When he shouted, the whole room heard.

"MY NAME IS CHRISTOPHER JOHNSON ABBEY, AND I CLAIM, MY RIGHT THROUGH MY GRANDFATHER, THE RIGHT TO ASCEND THIS THRONE," Chris pointed at the empty King's throne, "as is my right," he spoke directly towards the Queen.

"The claim of the right to ascend the throne is made before this council!" the Lord Protector shouted. He watched as each one nodded and looked at the Queen. "The council recognises the claim, but the ascension can only be granted by the sitting monarch. Chris took two more steps closer, so he was standing almost in front of her.

"And I will *take* my Queen before this night is through," he spoke quietly enough that only the Queen and the councillors heard him. The Lord Protector could see the excitement in her body, the silk blouse moved with each breath she took. She motioned towards the empty throne. She did not take her eyes off him as Chris walked over to the empty throne, turned, and sat down. There was a nefarious grin on his face as he looked over the Grand Room.

"And what is your first order of business ... Sir?" The Lord Protector was joyous. He bowed from the waist as he asked the question.

"Well, first thing, there is a female wolf waiting for me in a bed and breakfast in the local town," Chris watched the reaction. The Lord Protector straightened up.

"May I make a suggestion, Sir?" he said.

"Of course," Chris replied. The Lord Inquisitor looked at the two of them, what was happening now was obviously scripted, she glared at the Lord Protector.

"Then Sir, I suggest we send a team to collect the wolf and we hold her here until the next solstice when we can anoint your ascension." The Lord Protector said.

"Let it be so," Chris replied he had been well briefed on what exactly to say.

"But what of the wolves? What of the growing actions against us? What are we to do?" the Lord Inquisitor asked.

"I agree," the Lord Advocate added before everyone looked towards the throne.

"Then we must make the necessary preparations we can," the Lord Councillor added.

"Your turn to speak," the Queen whispered. Chris looked at her, winked then stood. He paused as the rest of the Lord's stood as well. His voice echoed through the Grand Room.

"THEN PREPARE .... FOR THE WAR AGAINST THE WOLVES!"

Chapter 50

Mike Dear was sitting on the front of the car they had given him to drive for the day, for one of the police 'pool' cars, it wasn't that bad. He looked around the layby the farm had chosen for this meet up. As usual, it was remote, it was not on a busy road and there were plenty of places for the meet to be observed from, and they would be observing it. He remembered what Darren had said, *'Don't bother taking your own mobile phone, they will be using countermeasures to ensure you don't record them!'* All the other 'meets' had gone well, and Lucy made a point of saying they wanted the meets and flow of information to continue but going to the farm was to stop as they thought the military had gotten too close with them.

Lucy. The very thought of her made him shiver. His mind flashed back to how passionate they had been, but to find out it was all just a setup cut him to the bone, she had recorded every time they had met up and had sex. He could not believe he had been that stupid to think it was something else. It was a warm afternoon, but he still shivered again. She had him, and there was nothing he could do about it. She made it clear she could not only wreck his marriage, but his career, public profile, any standing he had in his wider family, in fact, she had boasted she could, and would, destroy him if he did not do what he was told. He was trapped, she had done her work well. Mike waited, the large brown envelope with the picture and details of what he was to ask about were all there, he sat on the corner of it to stop it blowing away in the mild breeze. His mind wandered, various scenarios came and went of what he could do, but all had the same ending, and it was an ending that was bad for him. He looked up at the nearby trees, he could not see the birds, but he could hear their song. A small smile came over his lips, he spoke out loud without even thinking about it.

"Sean, if that is you .... I could do with your help, I have kinda fucked up!" he spoke towards the birdsong, which went quiet then burst out again. He smiled, "No problem mucker, hope you are good, wherever you are." The sound of a car coming up the road behind him made him look over his right shoulder. He stood up as the Land Rover pulled into the layby, he lifted his right hand in welcome as Dermott drove past him, the wave was not returned, in fact, Dermott looked furious. The Land Rover pulled in directly in front of him and stopped. Mike watched as the lights went out, Dermott was doing something in the front of the car, Mike looked around him, they were not alone. Mike lifted the envelope with his left hand and stepped towards the back of the Land Rover as the driver's door opened.

"Hi," Dermott almost grunted as he walked towards where Mike was standing.

"Hi, good to see you," Mike started, Dermott looked disgruntled and didn't take Mike's offered handshake.

"Look, we got loads going on so can we get to what it is you want?" Dermott looked at Mike, Mike paused and reached for the envelope.

"Yeah, okay," he opened the envelope handed an 8 x 10 colour picture to Dermott. The picture was of a headshot of a middle-aged man, with a bald head who had a phone to his ear, he looked angry in the picture. Dermott took the picture and studied it.

"Who is this?" Dermott asked without looking up.

"Dominic Boat," Mike replied.

"And why are you showing me this?" Dermott asked.

"We are trying to find him, he has been spotted around Dublin the last two weeks and we think he may be heading north," Mike responded. Dermott looked up and shrugged.

"So? Who is he and why do you think we know him?" Dermott looked at him sternly.

"Russian national, little brother of the notorious Vincent Boat,"

"And who the hell is Vincent Boat?"

"You have never heard of Vincent ..." Mike started, he stopped himself then pointed at the picture, "Vincent Boat was head of the largest network of non- government, illegal arms dealers in the world. He and his little brother have been supplying arms to every single conflict around the globe for the last thirty years, Vincent is currently in a federal prison in the USA after a multi-agency investigation." Dermott looked at the picture again as Mike carried on, "Over a thousand AK-47's, three hundred heavy machine guns, two tonnes of mines and explosives and, the bit that really got the Americans going bananas was over fifty surface to air missile launchers," Dermott looked up at him, "Most of the anti-narcotics busts are going on in central America, all the aircraft are flown by American pilots," Mike pointed at the picture again, "after the big brother was jailed, the little brother took over the business."

"Never heard of either of them," Dermott held the picture in both his hands and stared at the face on it. "Why would he interest us? And when was this picture taken?" Dermott asked.

"That's him on O'Connell Street in Dublin two days ago," Mike continued, "we know you have some Russian connections and wondered if you, or they, have any knowledge of this guy's current intentions!"

"What?" Dermott seemed more annoyed.

"You know, just anything at all, any information would help."

"Don't be absurd,"

"I wasn'... ", Mike started.

Dermott cut him off. "Look, just because we have had a previous client who happened to be from Russia doesn't mean we know everything, about every Russian that has ever come here!" Dermott looked at the picture again, then turned it over to read the printed information on the back of it.

"Well, any help you, or your contacts can be ...." Dermott looked up at him again, "all the information is there on the back," Mike continued.

"We have had Englishmen at the farm as well, that doesn't mean we, or they will know anything about every single Englishman that sets foot anywhere in Ireland!" Dermott stated. This meeting was going wrong, and Mike could sense it.

"Okay, well it was just a thought," he paused, then thought about how he could recover it, "these are extremely dangerous guys, and they are certainly up to something," Dermott looked up at him, the intense look on his face dropped away as Mike kept talking, "finding the world's biggest international arms dealer and stopping whatever they are doing in Ireland is something we have to take a serious look at.".

Dermott looked back at the picture and nodded quietly "Aye, okay," he muttered.

"We really want to know, who he is meeting up with and what their intensions are," Mike tried not to smile, he had got it back. Dermott lifted the picture and again nodded once.

"Aye, no problems," Dermott looked up, "anything else?" he asked.

"No, that was it, anything for us?" Mike asked. Dermott's eyes looked over to one side then looked back at him.

"So, the SAS guys ... gone for good?" Dermott asked.

"Yes, it would appear so," Mike replied.

"Any idea where they went?" Dermott asked.

"We don't ask them questions like that, it tends to upset them. I understand you guys agreed it's best if government representatives are not seen coming and going from your farm."

"Aye," the scornful look was back over Dermott's face, "I need to be off then," Dermott turned and headed to the Land Rover, there was no farewell handshake. As he was doing up his seat belt, he watched in the rear-view mirror as the police officer got into the car with the empty brown envelope and slowly started to reverse the cheap car before turning in the layby space then heading towards the exit. Dermott tapped the communicator in his ear.

"Delta, November, that is him now mobile away from your location,"

"November, roger, Oscar did they have any cover out this time?" Dermott asked.

"Delta, Oscar, roger, two police on the hillside to your left, but they are now moving off, away from you back towards the car on the road behind them over,"

"Oscar, Delta, roger, what makes you think they are police, over?" Dermott asked.

"Well, they certainly weren't military, a stunned hare could have tracked them!" there was a collective laugh over the net. Dermott smiled.

"Roger, all stations, collapse down and I will see you back at the farm," Dermott glanced at the picture that he had dropped onto the passenger seat as voices echoed in his ear.

"November,"

"Oscar,"

"X-ray," The surveillance screen they had out, worked and worked well.

ooooo

Paul was walking from the farmhouse towards the barn as Dermott pulled up in the Land Rover. The transit van with the overwatch came up behind him, then it roared past him and headed off around the corner. Paul walked up to the drivers' window.

"Hey, how did it go?" he asked.

"Aye no problems," Dermott replied.

"What did they want this time?" Paul asked. Dermott reached over and picked up the picture on the passenger seat.

"Only if we knew anything about this guy," he said as he handed the picture over. Paul took the picture and looked at it, then turned it over and read from the back of it.

"Dominic ... Boat .... Can't say that I have,"

"Aye, me neither, but they seem keen to find out what he is up to," Dermott stated.

"I can see why," Paul raised his eyebrows as he read more information on the back.

"Where is Tyler?" Dermott asked, Paul nodded with his head towards the barn door.

"In there with her class," Paul looked up, "Why?"

"Well," he started, "he referred to the Russians and our connections to them."

"Okay, let's have a chat with her," Paul stepped back and nodded towards the parking area in front of the barn, "park up," Dermott gunned the engine and pulled away from him. As Dermott parked, Paul took slow steps towards the door of the barn, he kept reading the back of the photograph. The Land Rover fell silent as Paul kept slowly walking, studying what he was reading. Dermott walked around the Land Rover, they both got to the barn door at the same time. There was a burst of cheering from inside, the two men looked at each other.

"Sounds like someone is having fun!" Dermott grabbed the metal handle on the door.

"Yeah," Paul stepped back to allow him the space to open the large door, "I can see why they are keen about this guy!" Paul stated.

"Aye," Dermott replied as they stepped into the light of the barn. Dermott pulled the door closed behind them. They stopped by the wooden barrier and looked at the group in front of them. They were in a semi-circle, and everyone was dressed for training. Tyler was out at the front and had her training sword up in a defensive pose, one of the students was in front of her, also with sword uppermost. The sound of the door closing made them all turn and looked at the two of them. Paul waved with one hand, Tyler acknowledged, then looked back at the student in front of her. The two watched as the student stepped forward with his left foot, then brought his right foot up, maintaining the weight of his body central, this was about to be a duel.

"Twenty quid say she beats him in less than four moves!"

Dermott looked at the student then over at Paul. "Keep your money, she will beat him in less than three!" the two shared a short laugh as the student suddenly launched his attack. The woodened swords cracked together, then again, but as he was raising his sword for his third attack her sword struck the side of his head, flooring him. Another cheer echoed around the area. Tyler relaxed and beckoned the students around her. The student on the ground was helped up. Paul and Dermott watched, they could see her talking through the attack and how she defeated him There were nods and smiles, well for all except one who was still in pain from having his head struck by solid wood. The class broke up and headed towards their daysacks along the edge of the arena. Tyler turned and walked towards Paul and Dermott. The days training was over. Paul looked around and picked up the bathroom towel on the side of the arena. He threw it towards her as she approached. Tyler grabbed it mid-air.

"Thanks," she started to wipe her face down with it. She stopped directly opposite them, "so, how did it go?"

"Aye, Okay, all they were asking was if we knew anything about this guy," Dermott stated as Paul handed the photograph over. Tyler threw the towel over her shoulder and propped the sword up against the edge of the arena. She took the picture and studied it.

"Who is he?" she asked.

"Dominic Boat, international arms dealer, apparently spotted in Dublin a couple of days ago," Dermott explained.

"Any relation to Vincent Boat?" Tyler asked without looking up. Dermott and Paul looked at each other, then back at her.

"Err, yeah, this is his little brother," Dermott explained.

"How did you know that?" Paul asked, Tyler looked up and smiled.

"Oh, I read a book about how the Americans finally caught him last year," she looked at each of them in turn, "you two should read more books, they feed the brain!"

"Yeah, like I have the time!" Paul injected.

"They wanted to know if our 'Russian connections' knew anything about him," Dermott stated.

"Did they asked about Grishin or any of the others by name?" she asked.

"No,"

"Then it was probably nothing," Dermott and Paul looked at each other again, "but just in case," she continued as she handed the picture back to him, "do what checks you think necessary and pass it to the south they have something," Dermott took the picture and nodded.

"I will,"

"Say, while I have you," she started, "any news on that 'other' thing?" she asked, Paul looked at Dermott who straightened up.

"Yes, he 'is' who we think he is and what he is doing." Paul looked at the sternness that came over her face, she thought for a moment.

"Right, I want that stopped," she turned and walked over to her own day sack. She leaned forward and picked it up, then looked directly at Dermott. "Have him brought here, let's see what he has to say about a fair fight then!" Paul had a small smile, but the large grin spread over Dermott's face that made his face almost shine.

"It will be done!" he bowed his head once as he replied. Dermott was now an incredibly happy man.

Chapter 51 – Portballintrae, Northwest Coast

Sarah Wallace looked over the steering wheel of the old car, the engine coughed as she looked around, there was a row of houses on her right and a hedge row on her left, the far side of the hedgerow was a small grass field, the far side of which was a collection of houses. and a small, enclosed beach at Portballintrae. Behind the row of houses was a small housing estate, she had noticed nearly all the houses where painted white with dark roofing.

"I'm telling you; this is it!" She looked at Stephen Carter who was sitting in the passenger seat. Stephen kept his ginger hair short and always wore baggy clothes, he looked scruffy sitting there, in fact he always looked scruffy. When she first met him, he said she could 'dress me in the most expensive suit and I 'd still look scruffy', so she did, and he did, but that night out in Belfast had been their first date, almost two years ago now.

"This doesn't look like the entrance to a Neolithic site," she answered as she slowed down and pulled into the parking area. Stephen held up his phone to show her the screen. The red dot pulsed in the centre of the map on the screen. "Well, we are here!" he smiled. The other car pulled up along side them and the driver rolled the window down. Unlike the car she was in, the other car had four people in it. She nudged Stephen who looked out the passenger side window then started to lower his window. "Hey," Karen Richardson shouted over.

"Hey," Stephen replied.

"Are you sure this is it?" Adrian Campbell shouted over from the other car.

"Yeah, the map says we are here!" Stephen shouted back. There were two other girls in the back seat of the other car, Julie Allen and Ruby Meek were in discussion. Karen and Adrian looked at them and comments were passed between them.

"Are you going to start from here?" Karen asked. Her dark hair hung down the side of her face and her thick rimmed glasses sat on top of a permanent smile, Sarah had met her the day they all moved into the student accommodation at Queen's University in Belfast, she liked her instantly.

"Yeah, this must be it," Sarah shouted back. Karen turned and looked over her left shoulder at the two in the back of her old mini cooper. The 'in car conference' did not take long. Karen looked back at them and told them what they were going to do.

"Okay, we are just going to head down to the beach, and we will see you down there!"

"Okay," Sarah replied. There was a 'whoop' of excitement as the mini moved forward then reversed before turning and heading back down the way they had just come up.

"Right then," Stephen said as the screen on his new phone darkened, "let's get this done as they will eat all the food before we get there if given half the chance." Sarah smiled as she got out of the car, she felt the cold, it was not a bitter cold, but it was there. She looked up at the darkening sky.

"It will be dark soon," she commented as she pulled the duffle coat over her shoulders. Simon was zipping up the new puffer jacket that he kept telling people he bought but she knew that it was sent to him by his mum. She smiled every time she thought about the day the parcel had arrived, he had been so excited. Simon was standing at the front of the small car, and he was looking at her. He wasn't ogling her, far from it, she could see the 'starry' look he had, it melted her every time she saw it. She had other boyfriends before, of course she had, but her sister had labelled her 'a total dickhead magnet' as she seemed to be attracted to boys who treated her like dirt, and it was her sister who helped her through the court appearances and restraining orders to finally keep the worst of them away. That was before she had gotten into university, that was before she had moved to Belfast and that was before she had met the short, ginger haired guy who always seemed to be smiling, and he was always smiling at her.

"Yeah, sure, this should not take long," she smiled as she walked towards him. He tucked his hands into his pockets, he still was not keen on 'holding hands' in public and was quite shy when they were out and about, but he was getting better.

"Okay then," The two of them headed towards the road that led up to the two-storey white house at the end. The smell of the sea wafted over them, both turned and looked out over the darkening horizon. "I love being by the sea," he said out loud. Her eyes went from the horizon to looking at the side of his head, she felt herself smile at him again as they walked on. There was a small bungalow on the left and directly opposite on the grass verge was a break with a small worn-down path leading up and over it.

"This must be it!" she exclaimed, the two stopped and looked at the small, but steep climb, "The earth works must be the other side of this!" Sarah started up the bank first. She was wearing brown leather walking boots, but Simon was wearing training shoes that easily slipped in the mud. The bank was steep, and she had to grab on when going over the top, the far side was equally as steep, and she almost ran down it. Her feet sank in the wet ground at the other side. She looked down, her boots were up to the laces in the soft earth, but she could easily free herself as she stepped over to her left and onto a more solid patch of earth.

"Aww, shit," she turned and looked back at Stephen, his elbows were above his head as he tried to tip toe out of the mud, she could not help the short giggle that escaped from her mouth. "My feet are soaked!" he exclaimed.

"Should have worn boots then!" she smiled as she spoke. She walked forward then looked at what was in front of her, there was a slurping sound as Stephen tried to navigate his way back onto solid ground. Sarah pulled the small digital camera from her pocket and started to take pictures. Stephen stopped beside her and looked at the circular raised earthworks that was in front of them, the entire site was covered in grass, and it was wet and soggy. The inner circle was approximately the same height as what they had just climbed over,

"We could probably get a better view from those steps over there!" he pointed to the green painted, metal steps and short gangway ahead on them on the left. Sarah paused for a moment, "yeah, sure," and she set off towards the steps with Stephen choosing his footfalls carefully trying not to sink in the mud again. Sarah bounded up the steps, turned and looked back over the site from her vantage point, Stephen followed shortly afterwards. She stepped to the side to allow him to pass, she looked down at the mud caked around his ankles and the bottom of his jeans. She lifted the camera and snapped more of the large earthworks. The structure was huge, from where she was standing, she could see over the two circles.

"How come this one is smaller?" Stephen asked as he pointed towards the large white house. Sarah turned and looked around him. At the far side of the earth works were two smaller circles, both seemed to be attached to the side of a dark coloured stone outhouse that was separate from the main house.

"Because they were used for different things," she stated.

"Wow, how old is this place?" he asked.

"It is dated at 5,000 BC," she replied, he looked back at her.

"Someone build this 7,000 years ago?" he asked.

"Yeah," she nodded, "and all with handheld tools," she stepped closer to him. He looked into her face and smiled again, he lifted his right arm and placed it around her shoulders, he pulled her in closer and looked right into her eyes. She looked into his eyes. His mouth was open, but the words were not coming out, he was bad at this. She smiled and leaned forward and kissed his right cheek. "Come on, let's get this done." She walked towards the other side of the steps and started making her way down, "as soon as I am done, we can head to the beach with the others!" Stephen smiled and watched her as she looked around, took pictures, and looked intensely at the smaller of the earthworks. He looked around from where he was, from the houses on his right he could now make out several people on a nearby golf course, his eyes moved over the landscape down to the exposed beach, he knew it wasn't the one their friends were at. The wind was starting to pick up, he looked up at the clear sky, it was going to be a colder night tonight. When he looked at the white house, he spotted the sign on the high wood fence, *'keep out – no trespassing'* whoever owned the house was obviously tired of people climbing over the site. His looked to where she was walking in between the two smaller circles, heading towards another set of steps at the far side of the site. He bounded down the steps and landed on the ground. This time it was firmer and nowhere near as soggy as the other side.

"Hey, how come this side isn't soaked?" he asked.

"The centre of the large earth work had a water feature of some kind and is lower in the ground," she explained.

"Water feature? What? like a rockery or something?" She laughed at his question.

"No, like a large well or the like," she turned to head towards the other set of steps.

"Something similar? What? they cannot figure out what it was?"

"I have an idea!" she smirked.

"What?" he asked as he walked towards her.

"You build a time machine like what HG Wells did, go back 7,000 years and ask them!" she was giggling as he came close.

"Ha – ha," he tilted his head from side to side as he replied, "yeah I suppose I could, that would make a great conversation after all,"

"Yeah, it would be difficult, 7,000 years ago, they didn't speak English and you can't speak any other language!"

"I can speak a bit of German," he answered as she started up the steps.

"Don't think they spoke German either!"

A young couple were pushing a small baby buggy, there was a mass of blankets in the buggy, but he could not make out a baby in there. They did not notice him standing there, they where too engrossed in their own world to care about the scruffy looking teenager that was standing nearby, they laughed and headed off towards the long beach that was in the distance. Stephen looked down at the information board and started to read. Sarah arrived beside him.

"What have you got here?" she asked.

"The information board about the site," she took two pictures of it.

"Okay, I got all I need, let's find the others,"

"And get this party started!" he added, again the two shared a look and a giggle.

"Pretty sure they will have already started that one!" she playfully nudged him.

"Yeah, lets go," he went to walk back towards the steps, but Sarah pointed towards the small carpark at the bottom end of the tarmac path.

"I think, this is actually the way in, they are down there!" she stated.

"Thought so," it was his turn to smirk, "I knew the way we came in could not be it." She jumped a few steps to catch up with him, this time she reached out with her left hand and took his right hand, he stopped and looked at her, then looked around the empty car park.

"There is no one here, no one will see," she tightened her grip on his hand, she felt him relax, then they walked side by side, hand in hand towards the car park. There were only two cars there, one at each side, the far one they recognised as the one their friends had driven, the one that was close to the end of the pathway must have been driven by the young couple who had walked past them earlier. They walked across the centre of the car park, to their left was the single-story building complex that housed a fish and chip shop, a confectionary shop then beside it, according to the large sign on the wall, was the local town offices. All were shut. They headed towards the entrance to the car park, the road that led away from the car park, twisted out of sight as it bent around the block of flats and apartments that overlooked the small, enclosed beach, and it was a small beach. When they reached the edge of the car park, they could see how small the beach was, either side was enclosed by dark rock formations, the beach itself was a small crescent shape and was only about seventy metres long. The pathway this side of the carpark was a concrete one, that ran along the top of the slope leading down to the beach. The slope was steep, they walked along the pathway towards the concrete steps that went down the far side, at the bottom of the pathway was a small wall that enclosed the path. On the side of the beach, up against the wall was their friends, the party had already started. The music from a small set of speakers echoed up the slope. They had laid out two tartan patterned blankets on the ground with a small fire between the two. Adrian and Karen were on one side with Julie and Ruby on the other, laughter echoed up the slope.

"You were right," Stephen looked at her, she smiled at him, the fire in his eyes was back, she felt herself glow, "the party has already started!" the two laughed as they turned at the top of the path and headed down the large steps towards the small group.

"Look who finally decided to join us!" Adrian almost shouted, there was a cheer of approval as the two of them trotted though a small gap in the wall and arrived on the beach. Stephen looked at the small sign that stated, 'no dogs are allowed in this area, by order.'

"You all done?" Ruby asked.

"Yes, got everything I needed," Sarah smiled as she was handed a thin disposable white plastic mug that had wine in it. Stephen looked up at the towering apartment block. It was dark, not a single light was on. The music changed.

"What is this?" Stephen pointed at the small speakers as Julie handed him a mug.

"This?" she paused, "it's called 'possession' by Sarah McLachlan," Julie.

"Can't say I know her," he replied.

"My mum's a huge fan, we saw her in Belfast a couple of years ago, she is Canadian!"

"Great," Stephen looked at Sarah, he didn't know what to say next.

"Whose playlist is it?" Sarah asked.

"Mine," Karen replied, "here have a seat," she moved her daysack out of the way.

"Right, now we are all here, we can finally eat!" Adrian announced as he lifted up his day sack. The six friends sat around the small fire, paper plates were handed out, various Tupperware containers were opened, another box of cheap wine was also opened, and the friends enjoyed each other's company. They talked, laughed, ate, drank, and did not notice how quickly after the sun set how dark it was becoming. The flames lit up their faces, Julie had her arm around Ruby's shoulders, the two shared a long kiss.

"Hey, if you two need to 'find a room' then go for it," Stephen joked, "public displays of affection' are off limits tonight!" the two broke off, as Sarah kissed him on his cheek.

"Aww, getting jealous are we!" the group laughed.

"Hey, who the fuck are you looking at?" Ruby shouted towards the older man who was walking slowly past them. He had silver hair that was brushed back, he had a small beard the same colour as his hair. He looked 'distinguished' and was well dressed, he stepped back at the verbal assault. He looked at her with some surprise at first then disgust as he started to walk on. Julie lifted her phone and pointed it at the figure that was walking away from them.

"Yeah, that's right, keep going!" Julie laughed, she panned the phone around, "smile everybody," Adrian and Karen snuggled up to each other and smiled for the camera, she kept panning the phone around. "Smile for the camera Stevie!" she joked. Stephen blushed and looked down, Sarah put her head on his shoulder, the flames from the fire lighting up their faces. Ruby stood up and looked at the end of the walkway.

"Hey," she pointed towards the figure in the darkness, "he is taking his clothes off!" they all turned and looked at the back of the topless figure, he was tugging at his belt as he went down onto one knee behind the small wall, so he was out of sight. *"If you are looking at joining in, sorry old man, I do not do blokes!"* Ruby shouted at him. Julie panned the phone around to her, the light from the corner lit up Ruby's face.

"And I am very glad about that!" Julie joked, Ruby looked at her and winked at her. Adrian stood up and looked towards where the man had been standing.

"Hey," he shouted, "don't know what you are up to," the atmosphere changed among the group as a low growl echoed along the path.

"Did he have a dog with him?" Stephen asked. Julie lowered her phone as the rest of the group stood up and looked at the fur covered head that was slowly rising over the top of the wall. They could not see the eyes that stared at them.

"What kind of dog is that?" Ruby shouted as she pointed at it. There was another growl from the face that looked at them.

"Hey mister, you need to control your dog, they aren't allowed around here ..." his voice trailed off as the figure rose further over the wall.

"Sa-Sarah, what kind of dog has arms?" Stephen almost stuttered. Julie dropped her phone as the creature jumped up on the wall then leapt towards them. The phone bounced on the day sack then landed on the tartan blanket. The camera, still on, continued to look up at the clear starry sky. The phone listened to the screaming that followed. Some blood landed beside it on the blanket as the different screaming carried on. The pleading stopped as soon as it had started. The screaming echoed around the small beach, it echoed up over the dark, empty apartments, but the holiday homes had no one in them, all the phones could do now was to listen and look at the different constellations of the stars above it. The playlist continued, the different tunes continued to play, oblivious to what was going on with the group of friends at the small beach that was enclosed between the rocks, where no dogs were allowed in Portballintrae.

Chapter 52 - London

Alan Dukesby stepped out of the London Black taxi; he had paid for his journey before the driver had unlocked the doors. He was dressed in one of his smartest suits. He had his non-descript briefcase in his left hand and before he closed the door of the taxi, He gave the back seat a glance over to ensure he did not leave anything behind. With his right hand he closed the door and stepped towards tall building. The exterior was white sandstone, and the windows did not start until the first floor, something you would not notice if you were not looking for it. He walked towards the door, a face looked through the door, then with one movement the door opened, he glanced at the small sign on one side of the door, if you were not looking for it, you could easily walk past the entrance to the Cabinet Office Briefing Room (Alpha), or COBRA as it was commonly referred to. The door shut behind him and two members of the site security stepped forward, he walked through the electronic archway and stopped by the two uniforms. One held a plastic baton device that he started to wave over him.

"Major Alan Dukesby, Two Two SAS," he introduced himself.

"Are you carrying a personal protection weapon?" the one without the metal and vapor detector asked.

"Not today," he looked around, across the far side of the reception area a tall male figure who was also in a suit stood up, "I believe I am expected!" he added.

"Can you leave all electronic devices, such as phones, smart watches etc here please?" the security officer directed towards a drawer in the nearby wooden desk.

"I did not bring any, I have been here before," Alan replied with a smile.

"ALAN!" the figure shouted, waving with his right hand as he did so. The security looked over at the waiting Commanding Officer of the Special Air Service. He stepped back. Alan Dukesby headed towards the smiling face greeting him with a firm handshake.

"Good morning, Colonel," Alan smiled as he greeted his boss, he glanced around the reception area, there was no one nearby.

"Good to see you Alan, right I have had a look over your presentation and it is fine," he said as he handed him the USB flash drive.

"Thanks, who exactly is in there?" Alan asked. The Colonel turned and started to head down the ornate corridor towards the briefing room.

"This one is chaired by Home Secretary, but there is also the Foreign Secretary, Head of MI5, MI6, GCHQ, Met Police Commissioner, Head of the Association of Chief Police Officers, as well as all the usual military chiefs of staff," the Colonel looked at him, "there is quite a roomful in there,"

"Okay," Alan nodded, they walked on past the briefing room, Alan sawt the small sign on the door, they were heading towards the waiting room at the end of the corridor.

"But something I have just found out, when you are done here, you are to head over to the US Embassy and give the same presentation to a group of them," The Colonel stopped, Alan stopped and looked at him, this was something he didn't know. "It seems the Americans have been having similar 'situations' as well as us with our little furry friends!"

"Really?" Alan responded.

"Yeah, it sounds like quite a houseful,"

"Who is going to be there?" Alan asked.

"The US Ambassador to the UK, they have set up a multi-agency task force to co-ordinate what they have been doing, FBI, CIA, ATF, NSA, Justice department, homeland security etc,"

"Okay, that is no problem, when am I on?" Alan asked.

"One of the MI5 girls is on at the moment, and you are up next, the Americans have sent one of theirs over to bring us up to speed on what has been happening with them over the far side of the pond," the two reached the open entrance to the COBRA waiting room, there was one security personnel near the door. The inside of the small room had chairs along the sides with an area at the far end for making tea and coffee while you were waiting. On the right-hand side sat a young woman who looked up as the two men arrived at the door, opposite her sat a man with deep African features. He was well built and was wearing a suit that showed off his heavy frame. He looked at the two of them and a huge smile broke over his face.

"I believe you know Major Bowra from Delta," the Colonel extended his left hand towards the large man who propelled himself out of the seat, his arms opened as he did so.

"LUKE!" Alan shouted as he almost jumped through the doorway.

"AL," Luke shouted as the two friends collided in an embrace.

"I will leave you two, to it," the Colonel stated, but the two friends were not listening. They broke off the hug and the two sat down beside each other.

"How are you getting on?" Alan asked.

"Hey, I'm good, howz you doin'?"

"All good. What the hell happened after Scotland?" Alan asked.

"Well, when we got back to Bragg ..." Luke's American accent stood out when compared to the Englishness of Alan's, just by their body language showed they had been close. The Colonel turned and walked back down the corridor to leave the two friends and their catch up, the two did have a lot to talk about. He headed back down passed the door and paused near the security personnel. There were two seats at the side of the reception area, so he sat down on one and waited. He did not have to wait long when the door to the briefing room opened and one of the civil servants walked out. She looked over at the Colonel. He walked over to her.

"They will be ready for you in about five minutes," she stated without any form of introduction or greeting. Two others walked out behind her, the door was open and there was a lot of movement in the room.

"No problem, they are both in the waiting room now," he replied.

"Well, they can head in and set up if they want to," she answered, she turned and walked back inside without waiting for a reply. The Colonel was used to the type of person she was, the civil service seemed to attract them. He turned and walked away from her without giving it a second thought. He headed back down the corridor, as he approached the open entrance to the waiting room Luke's voice seemed to echo up the corridor.

"Then I said, 'well, I'm a US Ranger you son of a bitch," The Colonel stopped in the doorway. The woman had gone and there was only the two happy men in the room.

"And it all went south from there!" Alan was laughing as he spoke.

"And it all went south from there!" Luke replied, the two men burst into laughter, but quietened down as the Colonel walked into the room.

"I hate to break up this happy reunion, but it is time," he stated.

"Okay," Alan stated as they stood up. The Colonel walked out the door, closely followed by the two men. The Colonel led the way, but the conversation carried on behind him.

"Remember that assault in Afghan, outside the football stadium?" Alan commented.

"You mean the one where you brits came up against a chain fence and forgot your bolt cutters?" The Colonel glanced back at them, a small smile on his lips, he knew the tale.

"During the recce, all the gates were open!" Alan responded.

"Time spent on recon, is seldom wasted, I believe you Brits like to say!" The colonel walked on; he slowed as he got to the open door of the briefing room.

"Say, what was the fallout from the night in Jacksonville?" The Colonel had stopped by the doorway, before he looked over at the two smiling friends.

"There is only one rule about Jacksonville!" Luke commented.

"We don't talk about Jacksonville!" the two friends said in unison. They both laughed and shared the joke; the colonel got the film reference they were making.

"I have no idea what you two are on about," the Colonel injected, "pretty sure, I don't want to know!" he smiled at them, "Have you got that USB stick?" he asked.

"Yeah, sure," Alan reached into his pocket and handed back the flash drive, the Colonel walked into the room. Alan walked in after him, then Luke followed. Alan spotted the Colonel hand the flash drive over to another civil servant who was sitting just inside the door.

The room is smaller than what a lot of people would think. The walls were panel wood, and the main table in the middle of the room was a tick dark stained wood. The table was surrounded by chairs that were filled and there were several chairs at the side with various people sitting on them. Behind them on the wall were the screens the presentation would be shown on; the biggest one behind where they were standing. The civil servant reappeared and pointed to two empty chairs beside the door.

"You two can sit there," she directed to Alan and Luke. As they sat down Alan looked over at the blonde woman who was against the wall at the far side. He waved towards Lucy, who politely smiled and waved back.

"Wow, friend of yours?" Luke whispered; Alan looked at him.

"M-I-5" he whispered back.

"You still promised me dinner in the Dorchester!" Luke whispered.

"You still promised me dinner at the US consulate!" Alan whispered back. The two men looked at each other and laughed again. The civil servant attracted the attention of the occupied chair at the far end of the table. She was given a nod, then she spoke to the room.

"Ladies and gentlemen, thank you," the room fell silent, and all eyes turned toward her as the door closed. "We would like to carry on with the next presentation on the agenda," she looked at a small notebook in her hand, "and this presentation is by the military," she turned and looked at the Colonel who nodded then stepped forward, the civil servant took a seat on the same side as Lucy. Alan's eyes moved over to the main screen as the winged dagger emblem of his regiment appeared on the screen.

"Secretary, Ladies, Gentlemen, I am Nelson Royal, commanding officer of the Twenty Second Special Air Service Regiment," he looked over at Alan and Luke, "and I would like to introduce Major Luke Bowra, of the American Delta Force and Major Alan Dukesby, one of my squadron commanders in the SAS." All eyes looked at them, the Colonel carried on, "First of all, I want to thank Lucy, for the introduction to this situation, this part of the presentation is what happened with our first encounter during a special forces' exercise in Scotland when we hosted our friends from the US and Canada," he looked directly at Alan.

"Major Dukesby," the Colonel stepped back as Alan stood up and walked to where he was standing. The civil servant who the Colonel had handed the flash drive to reached out with the 'clicker' device so he could move his presentation forward. He nodded a 'thank you' toward him then turned and looked at the room.

"Good morning," he started, he pressed the button and a map appeared behind him, "our joint exercise was coming to a close and we were about to move into a 'live firing part of the exercise' when we first thought one of our soldiers had been involved with a gruesome accident," he turned and pointed toward the screen, a small red arrow appeared. "Here," he looked back at the room, "at first, we had no real idea what we were dealing with, then another joint UK/US call sign radioed in what they described as a 'live contact'," he paused again, apart from the military chiefs most in the room probably did not understand military 'jargon', "What that means is," he continued, "they had been engaged with real targets," he paused, "When we got there, what we found could only be described as 'horrific'."

"So, silver bullets all round then!" one of the politicians joked, there was a ripple of laughter around one half of the room, which was cut short when Lucy jumped to her feet.

"As I stated in my presentation, the myths and fantasy that surround these creatures are not myths and fantasy!" she death stared the face that made the comment, "they are real, as real as you and me, and we don't need strange 'spells, magic potions or silver bullets,' they are real, and they're here!" the room fell silent again. Lucy looked at Alan, "Sorry for jumping in,"

"No problem," Alan smiled.

"We can't have a pack of wild mindless creature's running around tearing people up," another of the politicians stated.

"They aren't" Alan stated.

"What?" the politician replied, "but you just said,"

"Yes, we were later to learn, that the group we encountered were in fact, 'on the run' from Eastern Europe and had nothing to do with those already here." There was another pause as the politicians looked at each other, some in disbelief. "The ones that already live here aren't a pack of wild mindless creatures running around tearing people up!" Alan looked at Lucy who then retook her seat, "quite the opposite in fact," he looked back over the room, "they live in a very ordered and structured society, and I do not believe they are any threat to us, but" he leaned forward and pointed towards Lucy, "we have heard they have strong connections inside Russia, and two members of the GRU have been visiting England and Ireland! What about that?"

"Former ... members, plus, you are talking about a connection that goes back farther than the last one hundred years of our history, in fact their history goes back past when we were still in mud huts and battering each other to death with clubs, they had established a worldwide feudal 'pack' system that predates any record we have of any recognised countries or established communities in the modern world." Alan stated.

"Well, I don't like the idea of packs of 'dogmen' running around just doing whatever they want!" another started.

"So, what do you think we should do?" the Home Secretary asked, "they aren't currently breaking any laws?"

"I want them all registered, I want to know exactly where each one is and what they are doing," the other politician commented.

"You mean, establish 'camps' to house them in, for example," Alan commented, the Colonel looked at him.

"Well, it is a start," the politician continued, "we need to keep them separate from normal society!"

"Yeah, and when we have them all rounded up in these 'camps' we could just tattoo a number on their arms so we can identify each of them!" Alan added, everyone suddenly got what he was referring to, Alan carried on, "well, if that is what you are proposing then count me out, I want no part of anything like that!"

"What happened to your grandparents by the Nazi's was a crime against humanity," the Colonel injected, everyone in the room got where Alan was coming from.

"No, we are not even suggesting that" the Home Secretary added.

"But how can we involve them and how can they even start to integrate with a modern society?" the other politician asked.

"They already do," Lucy stated, she stood up again and looked directly at the one who had spoken. "They have already integrated, they have been for centuries, they are teachers, doctors, police officers," she turned and looked at Alan, "even soldiers," she looked back at the Home secretary, "we, don't have to do anything, they already have done all this, and as you have stated, as a community, they are not breaking any laws, in fact they follow the law, the ones in Ireland have a pack motto of *'we defend these lands, not govern them!'* so no, I don't think we need do anything at all apart from monitor them, which I may add," she looked around again, "they are quite happy for us to do!" she paused, "they are not the real threat to us,"

"Then what is?" the Home Secretary asked, we were told this conference is to discuss a real threat to the United Kingdom," he looked directly at her, "what threat are you talking about if there is no threat from these ... wolves'" Lucy looked at the head of her service then at Alan then back over the room.

"The real threat is from the wolves' mortal enemies, the ones they call 'The Noctrailis.'"

"And who are these ..." the Home Secretary asked.

"The Noctrailis, or 'Nocs as the wolves refer to them," Alan added.

"And just who the hell are they?" the other politician demanded.

"Vampires," Alan stated. The room again fell silent in shock. Lucy stepped back and sat down again. The Home Secretary moved her hand in a commanding gesture.

"Major Dukesby, please continue."

Chapter 53

Tyler was sitting on the front of the Land Rover staring at the setting sun. Her eyes scanned the landscape, each detail. She could feel the warmth of the sun on her face. She was wearing her blue padded jacket, a patterned scarf around her neck and for a moment, she was at peace. Her eyes picked up the flow of the gliding swifts, she watched as they went around and around, her face smiled as she started to count the number of birds flying around as one.

"Hey," she looked over her right shoulder at Paul as he approached. He walked up and stopped beside the front of the Land Rover, "what are you looking at?" he asked. Tyler took a breath in then directed him towards the birds.

"You see those swifts gliding around just over there?" she directed with her head. Paul looked towards the setting sun; it took a couple of seconds before he spotted them.

"Now I do, yeah," he replied. Tyler fixed her view on the birds and started to narrate.

"They are swifts and what they are doing is called a 'Vesper Flight.'"

"A what?"

"A Vesper Flight, that is when swifts late in the evening fly high up, sometimes as much as 10,000 feet then glide down, they are actually sleeping as they do so," Paul looked at her, her face was calm and for a moment, she looked totally at peace.

"And how do you know that?" he asked, she smiled but kept looking at the sunset.

"I am an environmental engineer after all," she turned and looked at him, "you know, if you are going to protect nature, you should know about nature!" she smiled then looked back at the last rays of sunlight. Paul looked at what she was looking at. He let her enjoy the moment. He watched as the sun slowly disappeared behind the distant hills. She took a deep breath in, then jumped off the front of the Land Rover. "So, what's up?" she asked.

Paul looked at her, the peace was gone. "They will be here in about ten minutes," he stated, she looked down at first, but when she raised her head, she looked directly into his eyes.

"Is everyone in the arena?"

"Everyone onsite and what Dermott has out for site protection," he replied. She walked past him and headed for the driver's door of the Land Rover.

"Good, good," as she opened the door, she looked at him, "want a lift or you okay walking?" He headed towards the passenger door.

"A lift please!" As he jumped in, she was already seated, and the engine was on. They jumped forward as he slammed the passenger door. She spun the Land Rover around and headed back up towards the farm. She was driving 'angry' the peace of earlier was gone.

"They have been doing what we think they have been doing?" she asked.

"Yeah, Dermott did not say exactly what down the phone, but he sounded angry," Paul answered. The brake lights on the back of the Land Rover shone in the darkening night, it would not take long to get back to the farm.

Tyler drove into the courtyard and headed for the farmhouse. She braked and in one movement, turned the engine off, removed the keys and jumped out. Paul climbed out and as he was closing the passenger door, he acknowledged the group of people who were all gathered at the entrance to the barn, the lights inside were on. Tyler was already through the front door of the farmhouse; he could hear her voice from inside. Paul started to walk towards the waiting group of people, they were excited about what may be about to happen.

"But mum ...." Rhydian's voice came from the open door of the farmhouse.

"I said, NO!" Tyler shouted. Paul kept walking towards the collected group.

"So, what is going on?" one of the farm hands asked as he approached.

"Where has Dermott been? We heard they have grabbed someone!" asked another.

"You will all find out shortly, Tyler wants to..." he was cut off by the stomping that was coming from behind him, all the faces in front of him reacted and dressed back as an angry Tyler stormed past and headed into the noisy barn.

"Where is Dermott?" she demanded. Paul walked followed her into the main arena.

"Should be here any minute," one of the security team replied. She walked towards the platform as the pack fell silent. Paul stopped by the edge of the platform as she walked towards the centre of it. She looked out over the pack members as they shuffled forward to hear what she had to say. She watched as the main door was pulled shut. A hand was raised by one of farm hands who stayed by the door to signal it was shut. She had a serious look on her face.

"AN RUA!" she shouted, the pack shuffled forward, "An Rua, I have called you all here as we have to deal with a serious problem," Paul looked over the pack, there were no smiles, no happy faces, he looked back at his alpha. "We have discovered an individual, who, for the last few years has been holding dog fighting in one part of the farm that he owns," the pack burst into conversation, "we have also discovered that not only was this 'man' forcing dogs to fight to the death, but he has also been charging people an entrance fee to watch,"

"Bastard," one voice spat.

"Keep it down," Paul raised his voice, then looked back at Tyler.

"Once we confirmed what this shit has been doing, I tasked Dermott to take a team and bring him here," a small cheer went up, "as you know, dog fighting is not just illegal, but exceptionally barbaric," the pack shuffled, angry looks were exchanged, Tyler carried on. "So, this shitbag, when he gets here, instead of making two innocent dogs fight to the death, will be given a chance to fight a 'proper fighting dog' himself!" Paul felt his heart start to beat faster, the pack reacted.

"Let me fight him!" shouted one.

"No, me, I'll tear the fucker apart!" shouted another.

"He is here!" the shout came from one of the security team by the barn door. Everyone turned towards the sound of the heavy door being pushed open.

"Step back, make space," Paul shouted. The pack moved back, and a large space formed in front of the platform. Paul looked over as Dermott appeared escorting a large male figure with a small hessian sack over his head, his hands were bound behind his back, he had jeans and a light-coloured tee shirt on. Dermott marched him forward, the jeering started as soon as they entered the arena. Behind him two of the farm hands had another person, who also had their head covered and their hands bound behind their back, they too were marched into the arena. When Dermott got to the middle of the space, he pushed him over and there was a cheer as he fell on the ground, the second person was pushed onto the ground beside him. Tyler held her hands up and waited until the door of the barn was shut before she spoke.

"Dermott," she lowered her hands and Dermott looked up at her. "What did you find?" she asked. Dermott looked down with disgust at the twisting body on the ground.

"Well, this fucker has built his own little fighting pit inside one of the outside houses on his farm," the pack responded, Tyler again held up her hand and the pack went silent, Dermott continued, "he has a burning pit that he uses to dispose of the bodies afterwards," Dermott looked at the pack, "we did, however find ten bodies that he had not burnt yet," he turned and looked at Tyler, "he also has nearly twenty other dogs, from what we could see, mostly stolen family pets, Labradors and the like that he used for baiting the fighting dogs." Paul could feel the hatred flow from the pack towards the two on the ground.

"And who is this?" Tyler asked pointing towards the other one.

"This piece of shit ..." Dermott kicked him in his side, "is the one that videos all the fights, then sells copies of the DVD to all those who attend!" the emotion of the pack flowed over them, even Paul could feel himself getting angry. Tyler pointed towards them, then motioned to the space over to her right-hand side, away from the pack.

"Release them!" she commanded. Dermott stepped forward and grabbed the first one as two others grabbed at the second one. The sack was pulled off his head and the tape that was over his mouth was ripped off, as the small piece of tape that bound his hands was cut, Dermott pushed him forward, away from the pack. The second one followed suit. The bound man turned, his cubby face, red with anger, his hands ripped at the tape still around his wrists.

"Do you know who I am!" he shouted, "you're dead, you're all fukin dead!" he looked at his friend then towards Dermott, "when I get outta here, M' cumin back and M' gonna burn this fukin place to the fukin ground!"

"No, you're not!" Tyler stated as she jumped from the platform and walked towards him, the pack closed in behind her.

"Who, da fuk are youse?" he had a broad country accent, he almost spat as he spoke, his friend stepped closer to him.

"So, you like watching dogs fight to death for fun, do you?" Paul heard her tone of her voice, his wolf wanted to come forward, there was about to be a fight. The man in front of her was rubbing his wrists where the tape had been.

"So? They are just fukin dogs!" there was an instant reaction from the pack.

"Just fucking dogs?" Tyler repeated.

"Listen here, do youse know who I am? Cause, you're all fukin dead, understand!" this time he did spit at her. Tyler stepped to the side as his assault missed and landed on the floor of the arena.

"Oh, I know exactly who you are, Mr Colin Drum," Tyler was staring at him, recognition flared in his eyes as she carried on, "former Gaelic footballer who was kicked out of the GAA following convictions for the supply and intent to supply large amounts of cocaine and links with organised crime around Dublin," Tyler paused, "yes, we know who you are," the angry face bowed slightly from the waist as he lent towards her.

"Den, you will know when I say, 'you're fukin dead' that you know, 'you're fukin dead!'" he straightened up to address them all, "you hear dat, fukin dead! Der fukin lot of ya!"

"No Mister Drum, you are!" Tyler stated. Colin Drum looked at his friend who laughed with him.

"So, what da fuk do youse think you are ganna do? I will take down any wan of youse!" he laughed.

"Oh, want to fight, okay, we can arrange that," Tyler stated, "but since you like fighting dogs, how about you fight one of ours?" Claps and cheers rose from the pack, her statement had the approval of the gathered crowd. Colin Drum looked straight at Tyler.

"I can beat any one of youse, one at a time, or all together, and after I do," he looked around at the barn, "I'm gonna burn this place to the fukin ground!" he spat at her again and again, it missed. Tyler stared at him.

"Think you can take us all on, do you?" she baited him, Paul felt the emotion rising, the fight was imminent, the whole pack wanted to be at him.

"I gonna fukin bury you," Colin paused and looked Tyler in the eye, "Bitch." The smile was nefarious, as was the look in his eye. Tyler stepped back.

"Well, let's give them some room!" she shouted. The pack moved rearwards, "give him a sword!" she commanded. One of Dermott's security team stepped forwards and threw a Katana sword towards him, it landed on the ground in front of him. The pack moved further back so there was nearly fifty feet between them. Tyler stopped and turned around to face him. This time, she had a small smile on her face. Colin Drum, defiantly walked forward, picked up the sword and unsheathed it.

"I'm gonna fuk you up!" he pointed with the tip of the sword towards the pack, "I'm gonna fuk youse all up, *you hear me!*" he shouted, "no one, and I do mean, *no one,* lays a hand on me!"

"AN RUA!" Tyler shouted, she stared at him. "It's a dog-eat-dog world, fucknuts, and I have bigger teeth than you!" Colin Drum was confused, he was not sure what was going on. "No animal will ever die for your amusement ever again," she stated. Tyler looked at the two men, one was holding a sword in one hand and had anger over his face, the other had taken a step back, unsure of what was about to happen. Nothing in his whole life could have prepared him for what did happen next.

"Colin, what the hell is going on?" Tyler heard him ask, "who the hell *are* these people?" Tyler looked over at Paul and winked with one eye. She looked back at the two of them, then shouted.

"An Rua, show them who we are!" Tyler stood and stared, she did not move as there was an excited rush of clothes being pulled off, the tip of the sword dipped, and Colin Drum straightened up, he could not believe what he was seeing. Apart from the tall red-haired woman, the rest had all suddenly dropped to the ground, started growing hair, their faces started to change, but change into what? The anger that had flowed from him was suddenly replaced by fear. The arrogance was fast disappearing as some of the creatures in front of him, slowly started to pace towards him. Angry eyes stared at him, teeth were bore and menacing growls echoed towards him, he could not take his eyes off them, the creatures, they wanted him, and they were coming towards him.

"I ... I ... I..." he stammered.

"Now you know how each of those defenceless pets felt, just before you sentenced them to death!" Tyler's voice echoed around the arena, but Colin wasn't looking at her, his eyes darted between each of the whatever they were.

"Colin Drum!" Tyler shouted. He looked over at the stern face that looked back at him, unmoved by the creatures that were all around her, surrounding her, defending her, "I am Tyler Reynolds, of the clan, AN RUA of the Garou and I sentence you to die!"

"Wha ...." His mouth was open, his grip on the sword loosened, his head turned and looked at his friend, he spotted the dark patch on the inside of his jeans that was getting bigger. His friend screamed, turned, and ran towards the back of the arena, desperately looking for a door that wasn't there. Colin Drum looked back at the tall red-haired woman, who just looked back at him.

"An Rua" she shouted, ... "FETCH!"

Chapter 54

Nikki was sitting in the hire car given her for the next few weeks. The car park was quite busy, with a gym and a hotel beside it, and on the other side of the car park a Chinese restaurant and a drive through McDonalds. The drive to Coleraine that morning had not taken long, she looked at her watch, the person she was supposed to meet had not turned up and that annoyed her. Her phone beeped with a message, she looked at the name on the screen 'MIKE D-COP' it was Mike Dear, she had listened to the recording of the exchange in the layby with the one called Dermott, she was mostly happy with it, these 'wolves' did have a good grip on counter surveillance, they had been taught well in the past, but they did not have access to orbital imagery in the same way she had. She opened the message. 'HI HEARD BACK FROM THE FARM, THEY SAY PORTBALLINTRAE WASN'T THEM, AS THEY HAD A FUNCTION ON SO THEY WERE ALL AT THE FARM. THEY WENT ON TO SAY THEY WERE ALSO INVESTIGATING AS THERE MUST BE ANOTHER WOLF AROUND THEY DON'T KNOW ABOUT.' She read the message twice, then decided not to reply, she would speak to him face to face later on that day. She dropped the phone on the passenger seat and observed those around her. People were coming and going from the gym, the Chinese seemed to be doing ok and there were several cars lined up at the drive through. She noted people, what they were wearing, different cars, but she was glad she did not have to remember each detail anymore, the car she was in was rigged for surveillance, there were built in cameras that pointed out the front and back, every car and person that walked past would have their photograph taken. So far today, she had not seen anyone of interest. The phone started to ring, she looked at the screen, it was a withheld number, which meant it was probably work. She pressed the green button and held the phone to her ear.

"Hello," was all she said.

"Hi, it's me," she recognised Lucy's voice, Nikki perked up a little bit.

"Oh, hiya," she replied.

"So, what is happening there?" she asked. Nikki would not go into much detail as this was an unsecured phone, but she could say enough that Lucy would know what she was talking about. If the call was being intercepted, they would have a lot of guessing to do.

"The coffee meet hasn't shown, so this is a bit of a time waster," Nikki started.

"No real surprise there," Lucy added.

"No, not really, oh just heard from Mike, he said he spoke with the farm, and they know nothing; they were having their own function at the time," Nikki paused, there was silence down the phone so she carried on, "which is what I think they would say anyway!"

"No, that fits," Lucy answered.

"How so?" Nikki asked.

"Why would they lie about that? They are going to a lot of effort to hide themselves, things like that only attract attention, so yeah, must be someone else, plus, they do have their own functions, they are big things on their calendars."

Nikki thought for a moment before speaking again, "I would like to see one of them some time, I've read the description, sounds like a great night out!"

"Yeah, it does," Lucy answered.

"So, how did things go with you?" Nikki asked, shifting the conversation over to her. Lucy made an exasperated noise down the phone.

"Ugh, the presentations were great, just some of the idiots there were not listening to what was being said," Nikki could only imagine the briefings.

"Just remember, some people are like computers," Nikki's eyes moved over the people coming out of the gym.

"Computers?" Lucy asked.

"Yeah," Nikki looked around, "sometimes you have to 'punch' the information into them!" the two shared a short laugh.

"Yeah, that is good, I will remember that one," Lucy said.

"When are you back?" Nikki asked.

"Oh, a couple of days yet, say have you heard from that journalist?"

"McKenna?" Nikki replied.

"Yes," Lucy confirmed.

"No, but she has been throwing out stories about 'the furry and fang club' and her blog has been awash with comments and all sorts of nonsense the last couple of days."

"Anything of interest to us?" Lucy asked.

"Not really, she seems to have joined up with a journalist and broadcaster in the states, from Wisconsin," Nikki replied.

"Okay, well, we can keep an eye on that," Lucy became distracted with something around her, "sure no problem," she said to someone else, "okay, gotta go, see you in a couple of days," and the line went dead. Nikki looked at the blank screen then dropped the phone back on the passenger seat. She sat there for a few minutes, then looked at her watch, it was probably time to go, she looked up at the Chinese and the drive through, now, which one would she get lunch in. Suddenly, her shoulder bag that was in the footwell of the passenger seat started to ring. The phone in there was going off. The phone she had been using was just a 'burner' phone to use when she was over here, but the one in her bag was her normal work phone, she had forgotten she had it with her today. She lifted the bag up onto the seat and rummaged through until she found the phone, she looked at the screen, it was an international number. She pressed the green button and held the phone to her ear.

"Hello," again, it was a very brief greeting. The voice that responded was male and sounded Russian.

"Nikki? Hi, it's me," she recognised the voice, she felt herself react to the voice, she did not want to speak to him.

"Hi," her reply was almost a whisper.

"We are coming over; we *want* Foster for what he did to my brother!"

Nikki looked confused. "But he is dead? I have been to his grave!" she explained.

"*Non*," he raised his voice, "that is a lie, he lives,"

"No, he doesn't, he was killed last year by those knick-knacks people," the phone was quiet, "I can take you to his grave if you want, then you will see," the phone went quiet again, she could hear his breathing. There was a voice in the background, she could not understand what the voice was saying, the voice spoke in Russian, she could speak Farsi and Arabic but not Russian, suddenly she realised she must be on loudspeaker.

"We come," he stated, then the call was ended. Nikki took the phone away from her ear and looked at the screen, the number was still there, he did that deliberately; for him to leave a traceable number was no accident. Nikki thought for a moment, she had not been expecting that. She lifted her phone and scrolled through the few contacts that were there. She pressed one button and held the phone to her ear. The call started to ring, then the voice answered it.

"Exchange,"

"Extension 2823 please," she asked.

"One moment," the call paused, thankfully, they did not do hold music, then it rang once, then a recorded voice spoke.

"Leave your message at the beep," she recognised the voice as one of the other team members, she paused then the call 'beeped'.

"This is November India Kilo One One, Operation Harvest, I say again, Operation Harvest." She paused, then spoke again, "Contact trace, telecom received," she glanced at her watch, "today at twelve forty-two, subject, Vasyli Dusmanov. The subject has stated his intention to travel to Northern Ireland." Nikki looked around herself again, "my logstat, Coleraine, Northern Ireland, subject has left a traceable number," she looked over the top of the steering wheel, "out." Nikki ended the call. She sat there for a moment, that message would get a reaction in London, she would have to go back to Belfast so she could file the full report over the secure means later. She dropped the phone back into the bag. She started the engine and just before she moved off, she spotted the figure standing a few car lengths away from the back of her car in the rear-view mirror. He was staring at her car. He was scruffy, and was wearing an old green jacket, he looked like he had not washed in a few days, his dark ginger hair matched the thickness of his beard. She had never met Jason Apollyon before, but he was exactly what he looked like in all the photographs. She turned the engine off and looked back at him, she waved with her left hand, she waited for him to wave with his left hand as well, the agreed sign. He walked forward and she reached over and opened the door. He pulled the door open but didn't get in, he leaned inside and looked around.

"Where is Lucy?" he demanded. She looked at him, he looked scruffy and like he did not wash but he didn't smell that way, in fact, he had no smell at all.

"She isn't here, she's in London, she sent me instead." Nikki smiled and tried to make him relax. The face studied her, she looked directly into his eyes, there was a lot of anger there. "She said to say 'hi' and that you liked Canadian bacon for lunch!" He relaxed and climbed into the car, that was it, that was the arranged code word, she was who she said she was. He slammed the door in a way that made a thin, blonde-haired woman who had just walked out of the gym look over. Nikki looked at her then she looked away, she carried on towards her silver car. "So," she started, "I'm Susan. Lucy said you have a message for us?" Jason looked around, he looked down at the shoulder bag that was between his feet, he was not comfortable at all.

"I do," he spoke quietly. Nikki noticed his accent but could not quite place it.

"Okay, what is it?" she asked, Jason turned and looked straight at her.

"Tell Lucy, from me, 'You have done it; the war has begun!'"

∞∞∞∞

Cara-Marie was exhausted, she dropped her handbag on the floor. She hung her jacket, flicked off her shoes and slumbered into the kitchen. She returned with a large glass of wine then slumped back on her sofa. She clicked the tv remote, the TV came to life, it was still on the 24-hour news channel. The headlines scrolled along the bottom, she was reading them, but not really registering them. For a time, she just sat there, the last two days had been a roller coaster of emotions, highs, lows, and just long hours in the office. Her phone beeped with a message. She pulled the phone out from the pocket of her jeans. It was from Kevin. 'THE GROUP EDITOR HAS PICKED UP AND IS GOING TO RUN THREE OF YOUR STORIES FROM PORTBALLINTRAE, WELL DONE.' She read it a second time; she was too tired to care. She dropped the phone on the sofa and sat up so she could reach for the glass of wine. The phone bleeped again; this time it was from Mark. 'YEAH, GOT IT DONE AND FILED, SEE YOU ON MONDAY' Cara-Marie looked around for a second, she was confused, what did he mean he would see her on Monday? She looked over at the calendar on the wall, she counted over the days, it was Friday today, she had completely lost track of what day it was. Again, she was too tired to reply, Mark had sorted all the imagery for her stories. Yeah, that could wait until Monday. She took a large mouthful of the wine then lifted the TV remote, it was nearly teatime, so she flicked over to local news.

She had missed the headlines, but she didn't care, knew them already. they were still reporting from the scene at Portballintrae. The photographs Mark 'got from a friend' were horrific, but nothing they hadn't seen before. She had background bios on all six university students, living in student accommodation in Belfast and just out for the weekend. The police had found rolled up sleeping bags, and baby wipes in the cars, parents and families of the six. But the bit that had really pleased her was when Kevin had said yes to letting them print the very blurry picture that had come from the very old cctv camera on the edge of the nearby apartment block. She thought about what they had, the shape walking on two legs, was covered in some sort of 'fur' and had a head that in the darkness looked a bit like a dog. He had said 'no' to using the word 'werewolf' but they could run the picture. The response was amazing, her phone was nonstop, they were getting contacts from all over the world about the story. She had sent the picture over to her new friend in the US. They were running the story as well, but they were going to use the word 'werewolf'. They had done an interview over the internet; she had been sent the questions beforehand and it had gone down very well. She was exhausted, but she felt it would all be worth it. The news changed to a different story.

"And in another shocking event, this time on a farm near Dungannon, two men apparently fell into a pit and were savaged by dogs," Cara-Marie looked up, *"our reporter is on the scene,"* The footage then went to a young woman that Cara-Marie did not recognise, the light from the top of the camera lit her up, the background behind her was getting darker.

"Police responded to an anonymous 999 call which led them to the farm behind me, when they got there, they found the two bodies in a pit towards the rear of the complex," Cara-Marie was reaching for her phone, the reporter carried on, *"police discovered what they describe as a 'fighting pit' and several dogs in cages nearby, they also say that several dead animals were also at the scene, in a statement that was released only a short time ago they made the following public,"* the reporter lifted a sheet of paper and started to read from it, *"it is believed that this site is part of a large network of illegal sites used for dog fighting and dog baiting, a number of animals of a banned breed where discovered at the scene and had to be destroyed by police officers, video recording equipment and a large number of rewritable DVD's have also been seized,"* the news report went back to the studio and the main anchor.

"Have the identities of the deceased been released yet?" they asked, the footage went back to the young reporter.

"In the last hour yes," she read from the paper in her hand again, *"Mr Colin Drum, who owns the farm behind me and a Mr Aiden Loughlin who worked here at the farm, police say when they first arrived at the scene, other family members became violent, and a situation developed resulting in several arrests."* The tiredness has left Cara-Marie, she knew the name of 'Colin Drum' she jumped up tapped her and it started ringing. She paced around as it continued to ring. The call clicked into a pre-recorded answering message.

"Hi, this is Mark from Photos alive dot com, I can't come to the phone right now so please leave a message," there was a loud 'beep'. Cara-Marie almost shouted down the phone.

"Mark, when you get this, call, me, we have another one!" as she pressed the button to end the call, her phone started to ring almost immediately. She paused as she looked at her mothers' name on the screen. "Hi Mum, I am really busy at the moment, what is up?" she got the first words in before her mother could speak, she paced around the coffee table then headed into the kitchen. "What? tonight?" her face crunched up, "look Mum, I am not interested in 'whoever' is bringing their son to dinner ... I can find a boyfriend myself ...... no mum ..." Cara-Marie hung up the phone. She marched over to where her shoes were and started putting them on when her phone started ringing again. Her mother's name that filled the screen of her smart phone, and her mother was now angry that her daughter just hung up on her.

Chapter 55

Tyler walked through the open gate of the small cemetery on the Ballywillan road near Portrush. It was a clear day, but the wind from the sea kept the temperature down and the sun would be setting in less than an hour. She cradled the baby in her left arm and the small bunch of flowers she clutched in her right hand as she headed for the centre path, then turned right and started to make her way down towards where the Foster family of graves were. Rhydian had stayed in the Land Rover, the other Land Rover from the security detail that Paul and Dermott insisted go everywhere with her was parked. One of them walked down the road, to the corner staying on the outside of the old stone wall and another walked around the inside first, before she went in. If anything was to happen, she knew what they would do and how she was to react; being 'alpha' wasn't always getting your own way. She slowed, then stopped at Kyle's grave. She looked around, there was no one there. She slowly knelt down and dropped the flowers onto the middle of the grave. The baby did not make a sound. Tyler reached out with her right hand and let her fingertips touch the well-groomed grass that covered the grave.

"Look Kyle, this is where your daddy is!" she explained to the baby, who just smiled as his mother gently bounced him on her knee. She smiled at the baby and cuddled him closer. She read the name on the gravestone and felt herself welling up. Her body coughed as the first sob came out, she gently wept for a few seconds before she composed herself. Again, she looked around, there still was no one there, no one had seen her cry. She cuddled the baby again, then reached out to the grave again. "I miss you," she whispered towards the name on the headstone. Tyler glanced over at the graves beside him. She read the names and the dates, "well, at least you are in good company," she sobbed briefly again. The baby made a noise then tucked his head close into the arm of his mother. Tyler composed herself then stood up. She looked over to her right at the view from the graveyard, over Portrush and out to sea. "I see why you liked it here!" she stated. She wrapped both arms around the baby. "I'll see you again," she said as she turned to walk away. Tyler paced slowly past the other graves until she reached the end, then carried on to the gate. The passenger side door opened, and Rhydian jumped out.

"I'll take him," she said as she reached for the baby. Her brief smile wasn't a warm one, it was more one of compassion. Tyler nodded and handed little Kyle over to her. Rhydian nudged the passenger door closed and stepped towards the rear door, inside which was the baby car seat that little Kyle seemed to enjoy being in. Tyler walked around the front of the Land Rover; she did not acknowledge the security team as they closed in on their own Land Rover. Tyler moved slowly as she opened the drivers' door and climbed in. She sat there for a moment and looked down the road. Other cars and vans drove past, all ignored the two Land Rovers that were parked by the entrance to the small graveyard. Tyler looked over Portrush again, her eyes caught the small white shapes of two yachts out on the water, Tyler sat there and did not move until Rhydian climbed back into the front seat again. Rhydian looked at her as she clicked in her seat belt. Rhydian did not speak; Tyler was just having her moment. Tyler took a deep breath in, then turned and grabbed her seat belt. As it clicked into place, she started the engine of the Land Rover. Tyler had given Rhydian the communicator for her ear as she didn't want to listen to the constant updates the security team were sending to the communications building back at the farm, Rhydian was learning fast.

The Land Rover lurched forward, and Tyler pointed it at the far verge, in only a few seconds both were now heading away from Portrush. The inside of the front Land Rover remained quiet. This was only broken by the sound of an incoming call, which came through the audio system in the dashboard. Rhydian looked at the screen of Tyler's smart phone.

"It's Paul," she stated. Tyler nodded then pressed the button on the steering wheel.

"Hi Paul," Tyler kept driving, she looked around as the road rose and fell, the second Land Rover was not far behind.

"Oh hi, are you on your way back here yet?" Paul asked.

"Yes, just," Tyler replied.

"Great, just to give you a quick heads up, I had a call from Connor, thought it could not wait until you got back here, just in case he phones you directly," Paul explained.

"Sure, what is it?" she asked.

"A couple of things, they don't know anything about Portballintrae, and they are reviewing the footage we sent down to them, they seemed concerned that it wasn't one of us!"

"Okay, just what we expected, go on," she instructed.

"Well, he thinks it must have just been someone who is not from around here, they may have just been visiting," he replied.

"What? like on holiday or something?" Tyler crunched up her face as she spoke.

"He doesn't think we should rule that out."

Tyler was not impressed, "Okay, go on."

"He also said they have dealt with the Limerick problem and he's going to declare the whole island free of Nocs."

"That is brave of him!" Rhydian could hear the contempt in Tyler's voice.

"Yeah, I thought so as well, oh, also, I just heard from that 'Jason' fella, him and his brother are heading for a ferry as they are off to England. He said he has work to do over there," Tyler thought for a moment before she replied.

"Yeah, I bet he has, did he say where he was at the moment?" she asked.

"No, last we heard he had left the northwest and was heading back towards Enniskillen direction."

"There aren't any ferries to England down there," Tyler stated.

"No, but when we went through his genealogy, he does have some distant family near there, but I think we should keep a wee eye on him anyhow!" Paul added.

"I agree, anything else?" Tyler asked.

"No, nothing that can't wait," Paul responded, he would tell her about Alison Wallace's disappearance from the farm when she got back to the farm,

"Okay, see you then," Tyler replied glanced over at Rhydian. "What do you fancy for tea tonight?" Tyler asked. Rhydian let a large grin spread over her face.

"Fish and chips from that wee place on the promenade in Portstewart!" she exclaimed. Tyler smiled as she concentrated on her driving.

"Great, let that lot behind us know," Rhydian was grinning as she went to touch the communicator in her ear, "but tell them they can buy their own this time!" Tyler added, Rhydian laughed before she touched the device.

∞∞∞∞

Cara-Marie turned her car into the entrance of the small car park at Castleroe, she had not been here since the five teenagers were attacked and that was over two years ago now. There were only three other cars in the carpark, the sun was just setting so it was starting to get dark. Cara-Marie parked her car and grabbed her jacket as she got out. She closed the door and as she slipped the jacket on, she looked around. The tables were empty and there was an old couple walked an equally old spaniel dog at the end of a long lead. The old dog trotted along, with the old couple in tow behind him. The man lifted his hand in a wave, so she waved back. She recognised the two faces that smiled at her, she knew she knew them from somewhere, but she had no idea what their names were or how she knew them. 'The joys of being a local journalist' she thought to herself. She zipped up the jacket and pushed her phone into the pocket of her jeans, she decided against taking her shoulder bag. She headed for the path that led into the small wood. The old couple arrived at their car as she started on the path, this was where she was told to be. She started taking slow steps heading into the forest. Cara-Marie pushed her hands into the pockets of her jacket, it wasn't cold, or she would have gloves on, but...

"Cara-Marie McKenna?" the voice made her spin round. There standing in the middle of the path she had just been walking up was a tall woman with short blonde hair. *'Where the hell did she just come from?'* Cara-Marie thought to herself.

"Yes," Cara-Marie paused, she recognised the face, but couldn't recall where.

"I have been looking over your work and you are going in the right direction,"

"Erm, may I ask who you are?" Cara-Marie stepped closer to the tall woman.

"Of course, I am Alison Wallace," the name hit her like a brick, the memory of how she knew her came back with impact.

"Former police officer at Coleraine, you were with Kyle at Mountsandal!" Cara-Marie said the words before she even thought. Alison looked down then took a step forward.

"Yes, that is the one, I was there," she said as she looked up again.

"You left a very cryptic message," Cara-Marie stated, "what exactly is it you want?"

"Of course," Alison started, "you are on the right track, but things between the Garou and Noctrailis have exploded, there is to be a full-on worldwide war between the two!"

"And which are you?" Cara-Marie asked, 'Wolf or Vamp?".

"Neither ... my kind have managed to stay out of this whole thing so far!"

"Your kind?" Cara-Marie asked.

"Yes," Alison started, she went to say something then stopped herself. "Have you got your phone on you?" Alison asked.

"My phone?"

"Yes, your phone, have you got it on you?"

"Yes, of course," Cara-Marie replied. Alison slowly blinked then looked at her.

"Can you hold it in the palm of your hand please?" Alison asked.

"What?" Cara-Marie asked in reply. Alison stood and looked at her. There were sounds of birdsong nearby, then the passing of traffic on the nearby road. Cara-Marie relented. "Fine," she dug into her pocket and produced her phone.

"Can you hold it in the palm of your hand please?" she repeated. Cara-Marie extended her hand with the phone lying on it. She watched as Alison extended her own right hand, then extended her fingers. Cara-Marie eyes opened with surprise as the phone rose slightly then flew towards Alison hand, which she caught. Alison had a huge grin on her face as she walked towards Cara-Marie and handed her phone back. A shocked journalist took hold of her phone. "Right then, let's walk and talk, we have a lot of ground to cover," Alison stepped past her and started to walk into the forest. "Let me start by saying you are on the right track with the wolves," Cara-Marie jogged the short distance to catch her up as Alison kept talking, "also you probably are not going to believe much of what I am about to say but trust me," Alison looked at her, "it is all true."

"And what exactly do you want to tell me about?" Cara-Marie asked. Alison stopped at looked at her.

"What has been happening here for the last few years was just the start of a worldwide campaign by the vampires against the wolves," Alison looked at the face of the journalist, "would you like to prove that all your stories have been correct all along?" Alison turned and started walking again, "we have a lot to discuss, you and I," a smiling Alison said.

"And you can prove all this can you?" Cara-Marie asked.

"How about science-based evidence that you can collect then present in a court of law?" Alison responded. Cara-Marie McKenna's heart skipped a beat.

Down in the car park, Laura Patterson sat up in her car, the old couple had gotten into their car and were now driving towards the exit without noticing her. She looked at her phone and read the last message that she had sent.

'TEACHER: THE JOURNALIST HAS ARRIVED'

∞∞∞∞

The water broke by the end of the jetty as two hands grabbed the handles of the metal steps that went from the wooden jetty down into the water. Megan Due burst out of the water and pulled herself upwards, fighting for breath as she did so. Her arms and legs were weak, and she found it difficult to find her footing as she struggled to pull herself out of the water. Her whole body ached. Her hands and face were bruised, and her nose was still bleeding, as was the small cut above her left eyebrow. She collapsed on the jetty and rolled onto her back as she fought to regain her breath. Slowly, she lifted herself up and started to stagger along the T shaped jetty that stuck out of the water's edge into the lake. Megan fought to control the pain, but her whole body hurt, she limped down the jetty towards a signpost that was on the path that went along the water's edge, behind it was a small, but dense forest. To the right, the sign pointed towards the 'Lakeland walk' and to the left 'Castle Tully'. Megan staggered past it and headed towards the small castle ruins; she already knew where she needed to go. Her clothes were soaked, her body started to shiver as she staggered along the path. She followed the path as it went along the water's edge then rose up the side of a hill towards a single-story stone rectangular shaped building. It had once been an old farmhouse, but, if you looked through the windows it was now a coffee and gift shop. She struggled on towards the gate in the fence line in front of her. It was an effort to move her arms and her fingers, her knuckles had taken a battering. She limped forward and the gate closed behind her. She made her way up the short path to the rear of Castle Tully where she had put up the small domed tent. To see it was at least, a relief. The small padlock had a combination on it, she looked along the top of the zip and found the single hair that was across it, no one had been inside. It seemed to take ages for her to open the tent and slowly remove the sodden clothing. Her torso was covered in bruising, the fight with Apollyon had not gone the way she expected, in fact, she now knew she was lucky to get away from him. She rubbed herself down with the small towel before she pulled the dry hooded top over her body then slumped onto the ground. It was an intense effort to pull her trousers off, they seemed to be stuck to her, but every movement of pulling the dry jogging bottoms on caused even more pain. She wiped her legs down and pulled the baggy training bottoms over her cold legs. She stood up at the front of the tent and started to dry her long hair with a towel. She looked up at the night sky.

She liked this place, in the thirteenth century there had been a siege here, and the locals barricaded themselves inside, the Vikings on the outside made a pact with them that if they surrendered, they could all go free, so surrender they did. The Vikings then pushed them into the basement and slaughtered them all on Christmas day. No one had ever lived on the site since; the very thought made her smile. She looked up at the side of the Castle as the gate on the path that led to the main entrance opened. For a moment there was panic in her, 'had he found her?' was he coming to 'finish her off' the way he had shouted after her. The dark figure was than he had been, she relaxed and continued to rub her hair as the figure approached.

"It is about time you got here; I was starting to think I was the last of our kind on this island!"

Chapter 56 – English Bay, Vancouver, Canada, 2nd July 2015

Grishin was standing on the path separating the sand of the beach from the line of trees and the slow road. This area had been chosen deliberately for this meeting. He walked forward and placed his right foot on one of the shaped tree trunks laying along the beach side of the pathway, providing somewhere for people to sit and enjoy this view. English bay was in front of him, to his right were the mountains and hills along the north side of the City of Vancouver. Even in the growing darkness he could still make out the distant white sails of the yachts that were moored in a group, they were partly hidden from view from where he was standing by the piece of land that protruded out onto the water. This was covered in trees, and he now knew this to be 'Stanley Park' with all its -black squirrels, he arrived early waiting for the meeting that was about to happen.

"Hey," the female voice made him turn around. Approaching him was High Councillor Cindy of the Shen Tov pack. It wasn't a surprise; he had seen her at dinner in the hotel two hours earlier where the Shen tov had rented an entire floor for them and their security teams.

"Hello," he responded. The small group near her stopped and fanned out, her security team was trying not to get in the way of his. She was more formally dressed now in a pressed suit; at dinner she had been in a tracksuit and trainers. Grishin hadn't changed, he folded his arms as he looked back out over the water, the beach area was deserted, another reason why it had been chosen. She stopped beside him.

"So, they want a truce?" she cast him a glance then looked over the water as well.

"Well, we shall see," he grunted.

"This war has to end Grishin, we've lost over ten thousand of our kind worldwide,"

"And they have lost five times that," it was a statement from him, not a comment, he carried on, "we have gained much ground in Europe, Central Asia and central United States from them," he looked at her, "we currently, are winning." she glanced over at him.

"But we have lost South America and nearly all in Africa, and look what happened to the Silver eye, almost wiped out by the Noctrailis, only four of the entire pack survived the assault." He looked at her sternly before he spoke.

"We have gained so much ground and they have lost much more than us." He looked away, "at this meeting we need to convince them we can carry on, will carry on, we will not stop until they are totally defeated ... and we are prepared to do just that!" The evening was quiet, a car drove past on the road behind them, whispers passed between the security teams.

"Sir," the male voice made them both turn at look at Grishin's principal bodyguard, he had his hand at his right ear, he looked at both of them, "Sir, Ma'am, we have followed both the armoured cars through Gastown, they are heading towards the ferry port," he paused as he listened some more, "we think they may be arriving by seaplane!"

"Thank you," Grishin turned back towards the water and took a deep breath in. "How is Keria?" he looked at Cindy, "you have seen her, yes?" he asked.

"Yes, but she is still in intensive care, if she pulls through, she will be permanently disabled having lost the use of all four limbs," Cindy stared in front of her, Grishin could feel her anger rising, "her father died in the assault, her younger brother is taking over the Great Plains pack," she breathed deeply, "They lost over a third of their pack in the last six months."

"But they engaged a force nearly ten times their number, both Noc and Sapien, and, not only nearly wiped out the largest covens in all of Canada, scattered the survivors and won a great victory, ensuring security for generations of their children!"

Cindy looked at the ground, then lifted her eyes. "Yes, they did,"

"And your own pack," Grishin started, Cindy's eyes shot over towards him, "did the Shen Tov not have many successful operations around the middle east?"

"Yes, yes we did," her face broke in a small smile.

"They discovered a coven that had Noc's and sapiens to the north and west of you if I remember correctly!" he stated. Again, she smiled.

"Yes, from Beirut, to Damascus and all the way to Tunis," she looked over at him again, "but we didn't get them all!"

"They were about to launch an offensive against you all," he looked at her then looked away again, "Your alpha did exactly the right thing,"

"Yes, he did," Cindy had a confident smile on her face now.

"One thing," Grishin stated.

"What?" she responded.

"I have never asked before, but your pack name, Shen Tov, it is Hebrew is it not?" her crystal blue eyes looked at him.

"Yes, it is Hebrew," she guessed his next question so she answered it for him, "the literal translation into English would be 'Sharpened Tooth'" the two shared a glance and a grin.

"Sir," the voice behind them spoke again.

"Yes?" Grishin asked.

"They've landed by seaplane and are now getting into the cars," the bodyguard stated.

"How much security do they have?" Cindy asked. The bodyguard paused as he listened to his ear, he looked up.

"Twelve Noc's around two principals,"

"No Sapiens?" Cindy asked. The bodyguard shook his head then turned and retreated toward the tree he had been standing close to. Grishin and Cindy looked back over the darkening bay once more. "That isn't a surprise, their protection teams have really let them down," Cindy smiled.

"What do you expect when you use mercenaries!" Grishin grunted. Cindy looked at him, he glanced at her and carried on, "when you use 'hired guns' they have no loyalty to you." Grishin looked back over the bay, both spotted the small white seaplane descending through the darkness towards the surface of the water. Their eyes followed the brightly lit aircraft as it manoeuvred out of view behind the trees of Stanley Park. "Mercenaries do have their uses, but you need to remember they're only there for the paycheque." Grishin turned his shoulders towards her, "as we have seen, hit them hard once .... Then let them know they are going to be hit again .... And they run."

"We will need to reform the High Council, Keria will not be able to continue to serve," Cindy added.

"Yes, it's clear Gunnar's plane 'was' hit by an anti-aircraft missile."

"And what happened to Sundeep? His whole family was a targeted assassination." Cindy was getting angry again.

"But, once we identified and captured the two mercenaries who did it, after some 'pressure' we not only discovered several Noc locations, but also who was leading them, which helped us find and destroy nearly all of them in Southern Germany!" Grishin stated.

"Magna Germania certainly proved their fighting abilities," Cindy almost laughed.

"Once we head back to Russia, we can reform the council," Grishin explained,

"Yeah, we can," Cindy looked at him and smiled.

"Sir, three minutes," the voice behind called out.

"I doubt they will try anything tonight," Cindy stated as she pulled the Sig Pistol out from inside her jacket and pulled the top slide to the rear. She looked at the top bullet that was visible before she released the slide allowing it to slam forward. She replaced the pistol under her jacket out of view.

"Well, we have four overwatch teams in place, four cut off teams and nearly forty in our security details here," Grishin unfolded his arms and stepped past her, he gave a reassuring smile, "plus, it has been agreed this is neutral ground," he said as he started to walk along the pathway.

"It is," there was a mischievous look on her face. "Right, let's do this," Cindy stepped forward to walk beside him. The security detail all moved as one, the arranged meeting point was at the end of the path, this was either going to be a very short or a very long meeting. Cindy was confident of their position, but the war had to end, and it had to end tonight.

11 bodies found during rebuild of farmhouse along the North Coast – by Cara-Marie McKenna – 8th July 2015.

Eleven bodies have been discovered at the site of a rebuild of a farm that was gutted by fire just over five years ago. The bodies were discovered in a basement that had been built without planning permission some time ago, the owner of the farm complex stated the site had been rented 'for some time' and he had not been to the scene since the fire gutted the main building of the farm. Police stated the bodies have been identified as members of a close protection team that went missing in the middle east five years ago; a police spokesperson has stated they are keeping an 'open mind' in their investigation, and they are concentrating on possible links with organised crime.

Police have also stated they do not know how the bodies came to be there, but it is a major focus for their investigation and the company they were all employed by is co-operating with the investigation. When the fire occurred several military grade assault rifles were found at the scene by the Fire Service of Northern Ireland.

Police have requested anyone with information that can advance the investigation should contact Chief Inspector Wells at Major Investigations Belfast or anonymously at crime stoppers.